Tales

OF THE
TIME WARDEN

XANADAIR

authorHOUSE®

AuthorHouse™
1663 Liberty Drive
Bloomington, IN 47403
www.authorhouse.com
Phone: 1 (800) 839-8640

Published by AuthorHouse   09/08/2016

ISBN: 978-1-5246-3877-1 (sc)
ISBN: 978-1-5246-3876-4 (e)

Library of Congress Control Number: 2016914812

Print information available on the last page.

Chapter One

I t was a dreary night in Sevelan as the rain tapped gently on the thatch of the numerous rooftops, a gentle pitter-patter which disturbed very few, who had returned to their small cottages for the evening. Most of the oil lanterns which lit the humble village were doused, leaving an eerie darkness upon the saturated cobblestone streets.

Though there was one abode whose lanterns remained lit throughout the storm: those of a small Inn. An elaborate sign above the worn structure creaked lightly with the pace of the wind, the faded bold lettering on the sign reading "The Red Talon," A famed Tavern within the village. The tavern was run by a stern-looking woman weathered by time's ebb and flow.

Jessica the brew maiden was what they called her. She often stood out amongst the villagers, due to her long amber mane, which was oft kept neatly in a long braid which extended far beyond her knees, as she refused to cut even a lock of her hair for an unknown reason.

Jessica was well respected amongst the commoners; her fierce emerald gaze could make even the boldest of men quake in their waders.

"You best respect the lass; word has it she's got the strength of ten men," whispered one of the commoners, Gatsby, to his eldest son Samuel as he charged head long into her one cool spring day in the town's market. "You'd be well to apologize!" he barked. "Forgive the boy, lass; he don't mean no harm." He spoke quickly, ruffling the boy's matted, straw-colored hair.

"Daddy, is that the mean lady you told us about?" asked a little girl clinging tightly to the ageing man's leg; her messy blonde hair covered most of her face as she peeked out from behind her father's bony shins with one azure eye that matched her elder brother's.

Her father quickly silenced her with a wide-eyed look.

"It's really no problem," Jessica said unexpectedly. "Children will be children after all." She gave the girl a reassuring look.

"What's your name, little girl?" she asked, leaning toward her.

"OH! Um, Lucy—'tis Lucy, ma'am!" The girl smiled broadly as she spoke, showing the few budding teeth she had.

"Such a pretty name, Lucy!" Jessica said with a warm smile.

"You really think so?" The girl beamed.

"Absolutely!"

"Oh Daddy, I really like her!" Lucy said, beaming up at her father.

Gatsby seemed taken aback by Jessica's kindness. "Thank you, ma'am, 'tis her mother's name; she passed a fortnight ago, bless her soul."

"It grieves me to hear of such a thing. Please stop by the inn when you can," Jessica said, seeing Gatsby's solemn expression. "Your meals will be on me!"

"Why, it would be an honor, madam." Gatsby was in shock.

"Oh please, call me Jessica—no need for the silly formalities!" she said, with a small bow. "My husband himself passed in the winter two years prior, before the birth of my youngest, Gabriel."

"It pains me to hear of such," he replied, giving her a look of empathy.

Jessica nodded, looking at Samuel. "A quiet one I see, just like my eldest, Alec."

"Oh don't be fooled, he just knows he's in for it when he gets home!" Gatsby said, clapping Samuel on his back.

"Oh, don't be silly;
, he's done nothing wrong save for making new acquaintances," Jessica said, with a smile at Samuel.

"Suppose you're right," Gatsby said. "Well, it's been nice meeting you, but we best be off—much to do, so little time!"

"A pleasure!" Jessica called after them as they hurried off.

Nearly twelve years had passed since that day, leading to the present dreary eve within the small common room of the inn. Alec, a young boy of fourteen, sat idly by the large windowsill, staring blankly through a disheveled mat of dark hair, as the rain clouded his vision. All that was visible through the murk was the silhouette of a large statue within the town square, that of Sir Vinacent III, the founder of Sevelan.

Gabriel and Lucy sat nearby, huddling around the warmth of the large fireplace within the room. To the left was Sam, sitting at the bar, wooing Liz, one of the inn's buxom young waitresses, with tales of adventure that were, most of the time, highly exaggerated.

"You mean I haven't told you of my battle with the ogre?!" Sam said, lifting his mug of cider, as he was still not of age to drink. "Well, sit down, gorgeous; I'll tell you about it!" Sam spoke animatedly, taking a swig from his mug.

Lucy rolled her eyes. "Sam, would you quit badgering the waitress?" she scolded, giving him an annoyed look. "She's obviously busy!"

"Oh, it's no problem, dear; I love little Sam's stories, no matter how silly they seem!" Liz spoke up, playfully tapping Sam on the nose, being sure to give him a face full of her golden locks as she turned, hoisting her tray and disappearing into the kitchen when Jessica called for her.

Sam's face turned maroon as he glared angrily at his sister. "You really should butt out, you know," Sam said, taking another pull from his mug and slamming it down. "Can't you see how gorgeous she is? Who could resist?" Sam said, watching Liz, as she returned from the kitchen with a large order of cooked meat.

"Obviously, it isn't you," Lucy scoffed. "Always flirting with women—why can't you do something more useful with your time?"

Gabriel seemed oblivious to the rising argument between siblings, peering over his shoulder at his elder brother with one emerald eye.

"You all right, Alec?" he asked. "You've been staring out that window an awful long time."

Alec turned his head slowly toward his younger brother. "Not much else to do on a rainy night like this, really," he said, his eyes drifting lazily down to the palm of his right hand, where a peculiar mark was etched.

Alec had not known life without the strange mark on the palm of his hand, an hourglass with twelve runic symbols reflected in his hazel eyes. As he remained transfixed, a pensive look crossed his face.

He had always wondered what the mark was, but every time he had asked Jessica, she would quickly change the subject, suggesting he not dwell on it. He could have taken her advice, if it weren't for the dull pulsing sensation he experienced every so often in his right hand, due to the mark's presence. Once in a great while, he could even swear that the mark would glow a dull blue in color, though no one paid him any mind.

"Alec?"

Gabriel was now face to face with his brother, causing Alec to roll backwards off his seat, hitting the hard wooden floor.

"Ouch! What was that for?" Alec shot, rolling onto his side with a groan.

"What is with all the commotion?" Jessica had burst through the kitchen door to see Alec lying on the ground in front of Gabriel, and Sam and Lucy in each other's faces, drawing the attention of the commoners seated around the room.

"That is enough!" Jessica bellowed, causing Sam and Lucy to freeze. Jessica now had the two siblings by their ears. "Stop your bickering, you two! You're causing a scene in my inn!" she scolded. "Gabriel, Alec—to bed, the both of you!"

"But we didn't do anything!" Gabriel defended.

"And I suppose that's why your brother's on the floor!" Jessica snapped. "Don't argue with me, get to bed!"

Alec and Gabriel glanced at one another; unable to correct the misunderstanding, they decided not to fight it and slowly made their way up the long stretch of stairs to their shared bedroom.

"Now, as for the two of you!" Jessica pulled again on their ears, causing them to squirm. "I'm sure your father is expecting you home by now, so get going!"

One commoner chuckled as the two made their way to the door. "Kids these days," he said, taking a pull from a mug of bubbly ale.

"And just what do you have to say about "these kids"?" Jessica now turned on the man, furiously.

"Nothing ma'am, I didn't mean no harm by it!" The man spoke quickly, lowering his head.

"That's better," she cracked. "Finish your drinks everyone, it's getting late," she announced, much to the dismay of the commoners already seated, now hurriedly eating the remainder of their meals and quaffing their ale.

By that evening, the Inn was quiet. Jessica made her rounds, collecting the last of the plates with the help of Liz and putting out the inn's many lanterns.

"Something wrong, Madam?" Liz asked, seeing an agitated look on Jessica's face.

"It's nothing, something just doesn't feel right out there this night, you know?" Jessica said, turning toward the window by the door's entryway.

"You're right. It's felt this way all day, like something's gone terribly wrong."

"I'm going to investigate. You should get home to your family, girl." Jessica stated, retrieving a small traveler's cloak, perfectly fit for her short stature, from behind the bar.

Liz watched her for a moment as she quickly approached the doorway.

"Wait," Liz said. "I'm coming too."

"Do as you will, but know it's of your own choice," was all Jessica said, quickly leaving the inn, the door still ajar as the powerful gusts of wind billowed into the common room. A chill had quickly entered the domicile as Liz stood there a moment.

Liz took a deep breath before charging out the door in pursuit, quickly shutting the door behind her.

Chapter Two

"Have you retrieved the remains?" spoke a ghastly voice from the darkness. The howl of the storm lashed against the entrance of a large cave, located somewhere deep in the Surfire woods, a forest so vast it could rival the sea in its expanse.

"Yes master," spoke the shrill voice of a second man.

A towering figure sat cross-legged at the cave's mouth, facing the storm. The man took a deep breath. "Good."

Slowly the figure raised his head, revealing a scarred visage; a large white mask, stained with blood, covered the upper part of his face, ending at his upper jaw line, and a twisted grin formed on cracked and bleeding lips.

"Very good…"

"I have done well, master? May I ask for my reward?" The second man asked, kneeling before the much larger figure.

The large man's grin stretched, if possible, even wider as glowing eyes of ember narrowed behind the mask. "Yes… you may have…" the man raised one gnarled-looking claw towards the servant. "Your reward!"

The servant dropped to his knees in agony as his body decayed at a rapid rate, the remains he carried spilling from an oversized sack as his body crumpled to the damp stone floor.

"Now… rise, my servants, rise and claim the vengeance that is rightfully yours!" the man boomed, as a dim black aura enveloped the skeletal remains.

"Shelara Skyglaive..." the man hissed. "Lehion Skyglaive..." he cackled. "Garren Hydenforge... rise and do my bidding!" he roared, as three figures began to slowly reanimate before him.

The flesh from the expired servant began to slowly meld with the three before the man, as he laughed manically.

"The twin elf guards... children of the sky king... and the dwarf prince..." the man hissed. "You are now, my slaves... in death..."

Jessica halted in her tracks momentarily as a deathly chill shook her frame.

"Are you all right, Madam?" Liz asked, noticing Jessica's pale expression.

"I'm fine, nothing to worry about," she said, a feeling of foreboding still eating at her as she continued to walk.

The strength of the storm seemed to increase as Jessica made her way slowly along the darkened village streets, her cloak drawn close to her body for warmth, as Liz trailed quietly close behind.

"If you are going to follow me, I have one condition," Jessica called back to Liz over the howling wind.

"What is it, Madam?"

"You tell no one of where I went, understood?"

"My lips are sealed, Madam!"

"Good, quickly now!" Jessica turned on her heel, sprinting toward the forest at a fast pace. "Be aware of the trees! There are foul things afoot!"

Liz nodded without thinking.

"Yes Madam!"

"Would you cut the formalities already?"

"As you wish, Madam!"

Jessica groaned as she hurried along.

The path grew eerily darker as they pressed on; the storm seemed to increase steadily as they approached the vast sea of crimson oaks just ahead. Liz felt a creeping chill run up her spine, as if thousands of eyes were upon her at all times, as they continued.

"Madam?" Liz squeaked hesitantly, peering into the tree tops to see many dark eyeless sockets staring down upon them.

"Just don't look at them," Jessica said, increasing her pace.

"Madam, I can hardly see, let alone look at anything!" Liz called back.

"Best not to use light here, just stay close to me," Jessica replied. "And keep your voice down!" she hissed.

Liz shut her mouth immediately, closing the distance between herself and Jessica.

"Ouch! That's my heel!" Jessica grunted, sounding annoyed.

"Sorry Madam!" Liz quickly replied.

Jessica suddenly halted, causing Liz to collide with her. A low growling could be heard from all around them as the trees rustled in the howling wind.

"Do not move," Jessica whispered harshly, as the steady drone increased.

Jessica quickly withdrew a small vial from beneath her cloak, throwing it in the opposite direction.

"Now! Run!" Jessica shouted, breaking into a charge, as a sudden explosion of light filled the forest.

Liz glanced behind her as she tried to keep pace with Jessica, catching a glimpse of what pursued them.

A sea of swarming creatures threw themselves from the trees toward the light source; thousands of grotesque, pale beasts with razor sharp claws swarmed desperately to dampen the light.

"What are those things?" Liz squealed, continuing to run.

"Liz!" Jessica snapped.

Slowly one of the pale beasts lifted its mangled head, turning an eyeless face toward them, inhaling deeply. The others, however, seemed too preoccupied with destroying the source of their agony to even notice as one of their swarm quickly gave chase, sprinting towards the pair.

"Keep running!" Jessica hissed, as they continued through the now illuminated forest, while more of the creatures swarmed toward the light.

"It's gaining on us!" Liz squeaked, as they continued at break-neck speed through the towering forest.

"There!" Jessica muttered, throwing herself behind the base of a large oak, the roots having raised the timber high enough to create a hollow large enough for the two.

Liz quickly followed, hurling herself beneath the tree. The beast snarled, clawing at the oak. Its body proved too large to fit within the crawl space.

"That's enough, whelp…" a feminine voice echoed; a black chain now entangled the beast from out of nowhere, pulling it backwards. "The master has plans for you and your foul ilk…" the female voice cooed, and the beast seemed to suddenly relax, as if the chain were soothing to its large, twisted form.

"Who is that?" Liz breathed.

But Jessica quieted her with a firm hand.

"The geist tribe shall prove useful to the master's whim," the female voice spoke again; a small hand was visible from beneath the oak, seemingly caressing the beast's shoulder.

Jessica attempted to maneuver herself to get a look at the woman's face, but she was heavily cloaked.

"Gather your minions, shade geist, and follow me," the female commanded. The creature lowered its head in response before leaping out of sight, as the blinding light slowly died in the distance.

After the woman had departed, Jessica and Liz crawled from beneath the oak.

"Did you get a good look at her?" Liz asked, turning her head toward Jessica's silhouette.

"No," Jessica said. "But this bodes ill, for all of us," she breathed.

Jessica continued on, wordlessly. Liz followed close behind as they walked back toward the path.

Less than half an hour later, the pair had reached the end of the trail, a large stone wall barring their way.

"What are you looking for, Madam?" Liz piped, staring blankly at the large slab of stone.

Jessica quickly approached it, placing her finger within a hidden niche in the stone. She stood back, waiting.

"What are we here for, Ma-

Liz was interrupted as the stone gave way, revealing a secret passageway.

Liz stood there, agape.

"Are you going to follow? Or go home?" Jessica questioned impatiently. "I'm okay with either decision!"

Liz nodded mutely, walking toward the gaping entryway, Jessica taking the lead.

"Who are they, Makkari?" spoke the gentle voice of a young woman concealed behind a large red leaf oak.

The much larger figure of Makkari craned his neck, waiting for the two at the passage entryway to disappear into the darkness, before stepping out.

"Humans?" The big man spoke, his hand on one of the two large crescent moon shaped axes on his well-muscled back. "Perhaps they were the cause of the light from before?"

"Who knows?" The girl shrugged, stepping out from the shadows.

Both figures were adorned in traveler's cloaks; all that could be discerned was one was dwarfed by the height of the other.

"Should we follow?" the girl asked, looking up at her companion.

"There isn't time. We have to find the bearer," Makkari muttered.

The girl sighed. "I suppose you're right," she replied. "I feel the presence getting closer! This way, I think!" The girl pointed.

"This better not be another dead end," Makkari groaned; hoisting the girl onto his back, he sprinted into the trees.

"So you've come."

Liz froze upon hearing a deep voice, which echoed quietly through the hidden passage way. Jessica, however, was unfazed by the sudden disturbance in the silence of the dank cavern.

"Who's there?" Liz stuttered, feeling a chill creep up her legs.

"You've brought company, Jessica." The voice echoed again. "It's quite unlike you."

Jessica began to slowly walk farther into the cavern, Liz sticking close by, peering around nervously.

"I need to speak with you, Matthias." Jessica spoke, halting before yet another dead end. An hourglass symbol glowed dully upon a large stone slate, barring them passage.

Silence hung in the air momentarily. "Very well."

Slowly the stone slate shifted, revealing a small fire in the center of a small circular room. Sitting in the corner was a sickly looking man, a hood drawn low over his face. What caught Liz's attention the most was a long canine muzzle jutting from beneath the hood.

"Speak," the man commanded, stretching out one fur-covered claw in a gesture that they be seated.

Jessica seated herself before the fire; Liz did the same.

"The winds have turned foul, Matthias," Jessica spoke, her gaze unmoving from the man behind the flame.

Matthias nodded, taking a sip from a small water sack.

"Indeed they have, girl," Matthias stated. "Did you truly believe I of all others would be unaware?"

Matthias raised one clawed hand toward the hood of his cloak, withdrawing it.

Jessica gasped at the sight.

"Matthias…" she breathed.

Matthias' canine-like face appeared to be badly marred; blackened lines etched over the left half of his visage. But what stood out most were his peculiar hourglass pupils. One of the hourglasses had darkened to a pale crimson where the black marks traced; the other emanated a solid gold through the shag of his graying mane of tangled, matted hair. A pair of large, wolfish ears protruded from either side of his head.

"I am dying…" Matthias breathed. "And that can only mean one thing," he said, with a grim expression.

"Xen'trath is gaining strength…" was all Jessica said.

"Indeed…" Matthias's voice echoed. "The dawn strider is my sole link to this existence; if she should fall…"

"Then all hope is lost," Jessica finished.

Chapter Three

Alec opened his eyes to pitch darkness; the sound of a distant wellspring echoed through his mind. The young boy was no longer in his bed; instead he was met with a canopy of towering trees. The pale velvet light of Or'ganus, the red moon, penetrated the soft amber leaves of sturdy timber, serving as his only source of light. Cringing, Alec gazed down upon his form, which was vastly different from what he remembered.

Long dark hair hung loosely about his shoulders, framing a thin pale visage, veiling eyes the color of silver. His body was lithe, though much more toned than he last remembered. He was much taller than before, towering at six feet in height. A mud-caked traveler's cloak, a dull earthy shade, hung loosely from his body.

Alec peered through his dimly lit surroundings, the forest itself strikingly familiar to his addled mind. Emerald runes adorned the surrounding oaks, leading inward to the forest's epicenter.

Adjusting to his much larger form, Alec slowly waded through the thick muck toward a strange presence, which seemed to be calling to him. As he drew closer to his mysterious destination, a distant whisper within his mind grew steadily louder.

"Set us free…" it hissed. "We must… be free…"

The voice was like grating nails to his aching skull; as he pressed on, his body felt encumbered by a mysterious barrier, as if he were attempting swim through jelly.

"Come to us… Xanadair…" the voice beckoned again, this time calling him a name he was unfamiliar with.

The voice now multiplied into many, rising to a deafening level. Alec reached to cover his ears in an attempt to muffle the ear-piercing screeches grating at his psyche. He was shocked however, to find that his ears were now pointed, with a soft coating of fur, like that of a dog.

Alec set aside his thoughts of his present situation, continuing onward, slowly pressing against an invisible wall which suffocated him with every movement, a thick layer of brush barring his sight of what was beyond.

Gradually, Alec pushed his way through the last of the bramble inhibiting his view of a peculiar blinding light just beyond. A throbbing pain then encompassed him, causing him to cry out. He fell to his knees in agony, tightly grasping his throbbing skull in an attempt to shut the voices from his mind.

"Set us free!" The voices were now menacing. "You must obey!" they hissed.

Crawling now, Alec's body moved against his own will, his arms and legs dragging him toward the base of what appeared to be an ancient wellspring beneath the crest of a vast mountain.

"Hurry, time is short!" the discordant voices within his brain hissed venomously.

Alec pulled himself up to the rippling waters, peering within. His mind went numb at the chilling sight of his own reflection, a sight which shook him to his very core.

Eyes of solid gold gazed into his very soul, with pupils of twin hourglasses. A canine visage twisted into a menacing snarl. A large pair of curled horns crested his brow, where a long phantom-like mane billowed out from behind his grizzled appearance. Large black wings jutted from broad shoulders, dipping down to his lower back, where a lithe black tail hung low at his side.

But what befuddled Alec the most were the resonating blue lines snaking from a core within his chest, a vibrant hourglass symbol etched deep into taut blackened flesh.

The reflection gazed hungrily at Alec as the voices began to gain speed, making them impossible to discern.

The landscape itself began to spin violently all around him as massive clawed hands erupted from the dark waters, latching to his form and pulling him deep down into the well.

The voices, much to Alec's relief, were silenced upon his submergence. Slowly he drifted, deeper into the darkness.

"Xanadair!" spoke a muffled voice from above. "Do not heed their words!"

But the words fell upon deaf ears, as Alec slowly sank into the bliss of solitude within the unfathomable depths before him, closing his eyes, feeling at peace.

"Xanadair!" The voice steadily became less audible.

Alec slowly opened his eyes; his vision was met with familiar memories, as if they were being projected from his brain—pictures of familiar faces, individuals he had only ever seen while dreaming, swam through his fading vision.

"Fight it, Xanadair!" the voice called once more, causing a grating annoyance within Alec's peaceful world of silence. "Do not let him back into this world!"

A feeling of hatred boiled within Alec at that moment; an unquenchable rage shook his form as darkness enveloped him.

This man was disrupting his peace, he thought. He must be silenced.

"Go… Away!" Alec roared with a voice that was not his own.

The surface of the black waters began to churn violently, as Alec slowly rose to the surface, becoming the very monster he had seen in his own macabre reflection.

Alec glared darkly at the man before him.

"Have you lost yourself, Xanadair?" spoke the voice of the large wolfish man who stood before him, with hourglass eyes that matched his own, though dark with sorrow.

"Kill him!" a dark voice within commanded Alec.

"Xanadair, you don't have to listen to him!" the man shouted. "Remember who you were!"

Alec fought with all his might to disobey, but he could not hinder his arm, which slowly rose in the direction of the man.

Unexpectedly, the haggard stranger lowered his head, his eyes losing their light, as if knowing he stood no chance.

Alec could only watch as the man before him disintegrated into no more than a pile of cold sand.

Sadness panged deep in Alec's heart, as if he had known the man whose life he had just ended.

His grief was interrupted, however, by a deep, bone-chilling chortle.

"Excellent work, my little puppet," spoke a guttural voice directly behind Alec, a pale clawed hand gripping his blackened shoulder.

"The Kelondrekh binding…" the figure spoke, positioning himself in front of Alec. "To think it could overcome one of your limitless power… I am quite impressed!"

A ghastly being now stood before him, a hideous grin twisting his heavily scarred face. Sunken eyes, cloaked by a blood-stained mask, pierced Alec's very soul.

Alec's mind reeled in torment as the man laughed.

Slowly Alec's consciousness began to fade as the man placed one finger to his temple. "You will suit the master nicely…"

"Alec…"

Alec groaned, turning away as he was shaken roughly by a pudgy hand.

"Alec!" The familiar sound of Gabriel's voice echoed in his ears. "Wake up!"

Alec awoke with a start, sitting straight up with alarming speed; he slammed his head hard against the upper bed of the rickety cot in which he had slept fitfully. Falling backward against the ragged pillow of his own worn mattress he let out a low groan, his skull throbbing painfully.

"Gabriel?" Alec groggily asked, still in a daze.

"You were having a nightmare," Gabriel said, peering down at his elder brother, a concerned expression on his pudgy looking face. "What it looked like, anyway."

Alec peered around the dimly lit room; scarce rays of sunshine infiltrated the closed shutters, revealing the boys' untidiness. An unwashed pile of clothing lay in the room's center before a small wardrobe, which sat adjacent to the bunk beds the boys shared.

"I guess it was just a dream..." Alec replied with a yawn, attempting to roll out of bed.

Gabriel watched as his brother struggled to free himself from the thin sheets, which were tangled around his body, as he grumbled to himself.

"You gonna be all right?" Gabriel asked, as he helped to pull him free. "That bruise looks awful."

"I'll be fine, doesn't hurt a bit," Alec lied, as the fresh abrasion throbbed.

"Like hell!" Gabriel scoffed. "It's practically the size of a plum!"

Alec placed a forefinger to his temple, wincing. "Not like it's the first time this has happened..." he mumbled.

Gabriel sighed. "Well anyway, c'mon down and get some breakfast. Mum's cookin' already," he said, turning toward the door to their room.

"Just give me a minute to change," Alec muttered, stepping over the mound of clothing tossed haphazardly on the floor in an attempt to reach the wardrobe.

"All right, don't kill yerself," Gabriel said, swinging the door open with a loud creak. "I'll be downstairs with Sam and Lucy."

"They here already?" Alec asked, turning his head. "Bit earlier than usual, don't you think?"

Gabriel shrugged as he shut the door behind him.

Alec slowly pulled open the wardrobe, his mind now drifting back to the nightmare.

It was peculiar to him. He rarely had nightmares. In fact, he rarely dreamt of anything other than a single repetitive dream, which had haunted him since early childhood.

It was a fascinating dream, with wolf-like men and women. A girl with a strange crystal pendant and a large man with crescent moon axes were always key points of each and every dream he had.

"Xanadair..." Alec breathed. Who was this person Alec had played the role of in this particular nightmare?

Alec pondered a moment before realizing someone was at his door, knocking loudly.

"Alec?" spoke the high-pitched voice of Lucy. "Are you coming down for breakfast?"

"Give me a moment," Alec called, hurriedly pulling off his nightshirt and pulling a knit crimson tunic over his head, causing him to gasp from the swelling lump on his brow.

Alec hurried toward the door, pulling on a pair of breeches as he moved, stumbling over the laundry pile.

Alec swore to himself as he regained his footing, opening the door.

"There you are!" Lucy beamed. "C'mon, breakfast is getting cold. Wow, that bump on your head looks awful!" Lucy said, looking him over momentarily before grabbing Alec by the arm and pulling him down the long corridor of rooms which travelers rented for the night.

"We got a letter from Farenwehsk," Lucy said with a wide grin, practically skipping down the hall. "Our village is to host the festivities this year!"

This was news to Alec, as it was a very rare occasion Sevelan was chosen for anything of import, despite his mother's fame for her ability to brew the finest ale in all of East Belumron.

"Jessica the Brew Maiden," an older man, Tom Featherbrook, had once nicknamed her. "Best ale I ever had, I dare say!"

Jessica had kept the nickname, as it seemed to suit her perfectly.

"Rumor 'as it, she's got quite the brute strength, despite the looks of 'er," said Rebecca Farfield, a much older woman, to Tom, having taken a seat within the Red Talon for a cup of afternoon tea. "I 'erd she's a famed warrior!" Rebecca squawked. "Deadly she was, with massive hammers!"

"Pish posh," Tom croaked. "A mere pipedream, if you ask me."

Though Alec knew almost all of the people of Sevelan, not every day did he see the same old faces come through. This was mainly due to the village's location, being the center point between three other villages within the vastness of the Surfire wood, making it easily accessible for trade. The town market was always bustling with activity.

"Aren't you excited, Alec?" Lucy squealed. "Word has it, Najied the tome keeper will be here as well!"

That excited Alec more than anything else.

He had always enjoyed Najied and the tales of his travels. A whimsical elder who had been a dear friend to Jessica for countless years, despite his unquenchable thirst for ale and a warm bed in the linens, oft to the surprise of any unsuspecting waitress, he was a generous man filled with cheer and a vast wealth of knowledge.

Though what always befuddled Alec was his adept ability to sense one's presence, despite his total blindness.

"Alec?" Lucy spoke, bringing Alec back from his thoughts.

They had made it to the end of the corridor to the staircase and Lucy had proceeded ahead of him.

"You're drifting off again…" she teased. "Always with your head in the clouds!"

"Sorry!" Alec replied, hurrying down.

As Alec entered the common room, the familiar warmth of the place instilled peace within his mind. The faint scent of the nearby Surfire woods filled Alec's lungs as he took a deep breath.

"Over here, Alec!" Lucy called, waving to him and pushing out a chair next to Sam with her foot.

Alec groggily walked toward the table, seating himself in one of the hard wooden chairs at the well-worn table.

"Wha' 'appened to you?" Sam asked through a mouth full of food, gesturing at Alec.

"Hit my head," he muttered, not wanting to talk about it.

"Well, 'at's obvious, but 'ow?" Sam persisted, before swallowing.

"Sam, why don't you try swallowing your food before trying to talk to someone? You sound like a drunken Eldarian brute," Lucy scolded from the opposite end of the table.

Sam ignored her, however, shoveling the last of the eggs on his plate into his already full mouth.

Gabriel merely watched the two bicker as they always did, slowly nibbling on a sliver of pork as he rolled his eyes.

"Eldarian—really, sis?" Sam shot. "Bit of an over-exaggeration if you ask me; they can barely speak, as it is!" Sam defended with a hearty laugh. "Saw one jus' the other day, tryin' to make a purchase at the market. The owner thought he wanted to buy a goat!"

Lucy rolled her eyes as Sam grinned widely before finishing his plate.

Alec, however, paid no mind to the other three, having spotted Liz and Jessica whispering to one another behind the bar. Alec tried his hardest to eavesdrop.

All Alec could hear, though, was a name which sounded familiar to him—"Matthias"—and something about terrible danger.

Liz herself looked troubled by what Jessica was telling her.

Alec slowly moved his chair closer to the edge of the table, no longer caring about the plate of food that had been set out for him.

"Alec?" Sam gestured at him for the second time. "Was it another one of those weird dreams?"

But Alec ignored him.

"Don't think he wants to talk about it," Gabriel chimed in, finishing his plate and rising. "I'll have Mum get you a cool cloth for that bump of yours; it looks terrible!"

But Jessica had already noticed, coming up behind Alec unexpectedly and placing a cool linen cloth to his brow, which startled Alec, as she had stood behind the bar not a moment before.

Alec turned to Jessica. "Weren't you over there with Liz just a moment ago?"

"Where was I with Liz?" she asked, befuddled.

"You were standing right over there." Alec pointed toward the now vacant bar. Liz herself had vanished, returning from the kitchen with a large tray of eggs and pork.

Alec's mind was boggled, not understanding what had just happened; he turned to Jessica, who was giving him a strange look.

"I think you hit your head a little hard there, dear. I've been too busy cooking all morning to stop for idle chat!" Jessica said, retrieving the plates of the three who had finished their meals. "You should eat, Alec, your food's cold by now!"

Jessica turned, a grim expression marring her features, as if she knew exactly what had happened.

Walking back toward the kitchen, she met Liz, now standing at the bar waving her over.

Jessica sighed heavily, looking back toward Alec. *He's already showing signs of the pendulum, so soon?* she thought to herself, approaching Liz.

Alec merely sat there, astonished, as he watched the same scene repeat itself; this time, though, he gleaned more information. Yet another familiar name rang in his mind. Xen'trath the void beast.

Alec began to eat his meal, his gaze still fixated on the pair, watching Liz turn pale for a second time, as he chewed slowly on the now dried out pork and cold eggs.

"So did you hear what happened last night?" Lucy asked, as Alec reeled himself back in.

"No, I haven't heard anything other than what you've told me this morning," Alec replied, thankful that the subject of his dream had been changed.

"It was as we were heading here," she explained. "I overheard several commoners saying that there was a massive explosion of light in the forest last night, somewhere to the east."

"Load of rubbish if you ask me," Sam piped up. "Sounds like a tall tale to me."

"And you're one to talk, with your stories you tell to any beautiful girl to cross your path," Lucy shot, causing Sam to open his mouth momentarily, before shutting it, realizing reluctantly she was right.

"I had heard about that—restricting people from leaving the village, they are," Gabriel said, turning his head toward Lucy.

Alec felt a sudden chill run through him as a grotesque visage popped into his mind, that of the man from his nightmare.

"It's not just that though; there have also been mutterings of villages being burned to the ground in West Belumron; as of last night, countless acres of forest were destroyed!"

"You got the funny look again, Alec," Gabriel said. "You really sure you're all right?"

"Fine! Fine…" Alec quickly replied. "Was just thinking of something, is all."

Gabriel nodded slowly, still eyeing his elder brother with concern.

"What's the big deal about some trees anyway? They probably caught fire from the lightning in last night's storm," Sam said. "Yesterday was the first storm of the season; maybe the trees were still too dry? Could always go water 'em if you're that worried about it," he stated, with a note of sarcasm.

"It wasn't just *some* trees; it was nearly ten thousand acres!" Lucy retorted. "Could you be more careless?"

"This is me caring, can't you tell?" Sam said, giving Lucy a wide grin.

Lucy rolled her eyes.

"Maybe Sam is right? It does get pretty dry out there during the summer!" Gabriel defended Sam.

"Still, something just doesn't seem right about this," Lucy replied, glancing at Alec who had a pale look on his face.

Alec, having finished his plate, left the table without another word. He walked through the small doorway to the kitchen, where Jessica stood waiting for him.

Jessica's expression softened to worry upon seeing Alec's face.

"Alec, you don't look well, are you okay?" she asked, placing one hand on his brow.

"I'm okay, really. Just had a nightmare is all."

"Explain—it's not like you to have nightmares," Jessica stated, her gaze meeting his own.

"It's kind of strange, whatever it was, and there was a huge wellspring, voices echoing in my head." Alec explained. "The name they called me—I didn't know who it was—someone named Xanadair, and a monster with a white mask."

Jessica paled almost instantly.

"I'm sure everything will be okay; it was just a nightmare after all," she said hesitantly.

"Mum, that look on your face—you know who this man is, don't you?"

"I haven't the slightest clue," she replied, turning toward the counter. "Here, I have a list of things I need you to purchase from the market for tonight's festivities," she said, changing the subject.

She handed Alec the list, which was quite lengthy.

"If it's too much I can send Gabriel with you," Jessica said, regaining her composure.

"I should be okay; I can do it on my own," Alec said with a forced smile.

"If you insist, dear, just remember you can always come to me if something is bothering you!" she said. "And please, tell me if the nightmares get worse."

"I will, Mum, don't worry," he said, quickly turning to leave the kitchen.

Jessica stood stock-still momentarily, as she watched Alec leave.

"No… there isn't enough time!" she whispered exasperatedly.

Ten minutes later Alec had left the inn, stepping out into the sunlit village square, though something felt strange to him. The large statue in the square seemed to have altered. The head of the effigy, which Alec was most familiar with, now faced toward the east, as opposed to the west.

Putting it off as a trick of his mind, Alec walked past the statue, but before he could take another step Alec froze on the spot. The sudden feel of a gentle hand on his cheek caressed him momentarily, flooding his body with strange yet soothing warmth.

Alec shook off the peculiar feeling, continuing down the pathway toward the village market, befuddled by the unusual sensation which seemed to tingle within him.

Slowly a figure departed from the shadows of the statue—a tall, incorporeal woman with azure-colored hair looked after him, a gentle smile crossed her lips.

"The time approaches, my little black bird…" she gently whispered before fading back into the shadows.

Chapter Four

The town market was bustling with activity at this hour. A mad rush to prepare for the yearly rise of Organ'us, the red moon, was underway. Many elves—a foreign people to eastern Belumron, as the elves rarely involved themselves with the other races, most especially dwarves—flooded the village streets, preparing for the eve. The festival of Organ'us was a time of unity; grievances were set aside during this one day alone, where all races accepted each other despite their differences in culture.

Though not all were prone to be friendly, several dwarves could be seen huddled together around one of the many market stands, observing the weaponry the smithy had on hand. Glares of mistrust were directed often at elven passersby.

One dwarf seemed to have his eyes set on a taller elfish woman, who held herself resolute in what the dwarf believed to be arrogance. "There will be no purchase of elfish make from me; there be no finer forgery than that o' the dwarves, no matter wha' they claim," one dwarf said to the smithy, as he observed the many elven blades behind the stand.

"Nor would I be willing to take your filthy gold from your grubby palm, dwarf," the elf haughtily replied, with a sneer.

There was often bickering during this time, even though a peace treaty was signed between the elven and dwarfish kings. There remained much tension between the two races, since the battle over control of Feldresk Pass, the old kingdom, in which resided the world flame's rest. A long-fought war had bred much animosity.

Alec took his time within the market; the crafts of the elves and dwarves instilled curiosity in his young mind, as this was the only time of the year he was able to see the merchandise of each race.

Alec stopped at the stand of a large Eladarian man, who eyed Alec warily. "Wu u need runt?" The Eladarian spoke in broken English.

"Nothing! Just looking is all!" Alec spoke quickly, as the Eladarian race was not well known for their patience.

"Den beat it."

Alec quickly hurried along, not wanting to aggravate the brutish man.

Alec spent more than an hour visiting each stand. His curious mind had him asking questions of things from weaponry to armor from many an elfish or dwarfish smithy. Even some of the more arcane tomes intrigued him; as he opened a particularly dusty one full of old dark magic, one curse within the book got Alec's attention more than any other, as he leafed through *Melrog's book of dark magic*. The Kelondrekh curse, was a powerful spell which, as Alec read, took full control of its victim, as if they were a puppet, with many strings.

This particular spell shook Alec, as he remembered how he was almost entirely overwhelmed by it within his dream. He shut the tome quickly, handing it back to the shady looking Arcanieght behind the stand. The Arcanieght race itself was highly known for delving in all forms of Magic, ranging from Druidic to necromancy, and were often greatly mistrusted. In fact, the only one Alec knew of that he could trust completely was Najied the tome keeper.

"Hey, you..." a sudden female voice came from behind Alec.

Alec turned to see a tall cloaked figure before him; her hood was drawn low, revealing merely that she was of elven kind, due to her elongated ears, which two slits had been cut from the hood to accommodate.

"I have something that you might like," she said, with a small chuckle. She slowly withdrew something from her pocket. "Hold out your hand, youngling."

Alec did as he was told, and the woman dropped a small sphere into his palm, though taking a long moment to observe the hourglass mark on his hand. The woman smiled broadly.

"Thank you for the offer ma'am, but I haven't the money-

"Consider it a gift," she interrupted, before spinning and disappearing into the crowd.

Alec stood there a moment in confusion, observing the small sphere he now held in his palm. It was crystalline in nature, with a small familiar runic engraving upon it; the sun glinted off the black stone, which felt smooth in his hand.

Without thinking twice about it, Alec pocketed the sphere, trying to locate the elf to thank her, but she was nowhere to be found.

Befuddled by the strange encounter, Alec continued to walk through the town market, stopping at the stand of a much older woman, Molly, who had been a close family friend to Jessica since Alec could remember.

"Ello Alec, come to buy some supplies for yer mum's cookin, I'd wager?" she asked, with a toothless grin.

Molly was a woman of very abnormally short stature, a mere four feet in height, being a halfblooded dwarf—a rarity, as Dwarven females were scarce amongst their population. She eyed Alec through milky white cataracts, being nearly blind with age.

"You read my mind; here I have a list of what I need, if you have 'em," Alec replied with a smile.

Molly quickly scanned the list; though nearly blind, she still had one good eye which functioned as opposed to the other, which remained unmoving.

"Ah yes, I was expecting this from her!" Molly spoke animatedly. "Ah, I see she's pulling out her most famous brew for the occasion! You're in luck, I still have the dragon's breath hops she needs!"

Alec felt a wave of nostalgia wash over him upon hearing that, remembering the first time he had snuck a sip of his mother's famed brew, sweet yet powerful ale. He could almost anticipate how packed the inn would be this eve; as soon as word got out she was brewing her specialty.

"Such an herb is hard to come by, unfortunately," Molly said, bringing Alec back into focus. "It'll be twelve gold pieces, if that isn't asking too much."

"Not a problem at all, I've come prepared," Alec stated.

Haggling was Alec's specialty; he always had a way of getting prices at their best with little to no effort, due to the teachings of Najied one cold winter day, as they had sat before the fire with mugs of cider. They had spent hours enacting scenarios until Alec had it down pat.

Which was why Alec was often sent to the market by his mother, as he always came back with a near-full pocket of coin, with everything she needed.

"Nine gold pieces, fifty silver," Alec stated.

Molly chuckled. "Fraid I can't go that low dear, it is quite a rare thing to come by. How about eleven?"

"Nine seventy–five. These herbs grow very well during the fall, so you shouldn't have any issue with seeing more come through at a low rate," Alec said, with a grin.

Molly sighed. "Fine, fine, Nine seventy-five is as low as I'm going!"

"It's a deal," Alec said firmly, giving her a wink and handing her the gold.

"Don't know how you'll manage to carry all that back to the inn on your own, dear!" Molly said, with a chuckle.

"I'll manage, I'm sure!" Alec replied, hoisting the large sack of herbs over his shoulder.

"I put some potatoes in there too! Complimentary!" Molly said, with a smile.

"Ah, I was wondering why the sack felt heavier than usual. Thank you, Molly!"

"A pleasure—give your mother my regards!"

"Will do, Molly!" Alec said, waving at her as he walked away, disappearing into the crowded streets.

As Alec made his way casually through the market a sudden tingling began to reverberate through his hand, though this time it wasn't like before; it felt stronger and even more painful than he had last remembered.

Hoisting the sack over his left shoulder, he lifted his now free hand to inspect it as he continued to walk. To his surprise the engraving on his palm was glowing once more, and a dull throbbing pain trailed up his arm to the back of his skull as the resonating light from his palm steadily increased.

Alec's attention was entirely focused on the mark as he continued to walk, a whisper in his mind echoing throughout his brain—a faint, hardly audible sound he could not discern, as hard as he tried. Not paying attention to what was ahead of him, Alec walked headlong into a large figure directly in his path. As he fell backwards onto the street, the large sack of herbs broke his fall as a few potatoes rolled free.

"I'm so sorry!" came the voice of a young female. "Here, let me help you!" The girl extended her hand toward Alec, who slowly lifted his head toward her.

Alec froze at the sight of her. Blinking rapidly a few times, he could not believe who stood before him.

No, I must be imagining things, surely it's a trick of the sunlight, Alec thought, gazing up at her in awe.

Before Alec stood the girl that had haunted his dreams every night he slept, though she lacked the strange wolfish appearance which he recalled of her.

Gentle eyes the color of amber, with a bright warmth, gazed into his own, through a low-hanging trim of soft velvet hair that framed the girl's elegant features.

An apologetic smile crossed her face, a smile which Alec had always known deep within his heart and memory.

Before Alec realized he was gazing intently at her, the girl blushed.

Coming back to his senses he took her soft hand, which caused the mark to pulsate intensely for a moment, before the sensation vanished entirely as she helped him to his feet.

Thanking her, Alec stooped to gather the potatoes which had rolled from the sack with the help of the young woman, before rising to face the man he had so carelessly blundered into.

"Sorry for crashing into you!" Alec said, trying to get a glimpse of the man's face, which was masked by a low-drawn hood.

The much larger man remained silent, merely gazing at Alec.

"Don't mind Makkari here; he's always been a quiet one," she explained, with a light chuckle.

Makkari was possibly the largest man Alec had ever seen in his life, heavily muscled, with a stern looking face—that is, what could be seen of his face from beneath the black hood of his traveler's cloak. Burgundy leather straps crisscrossed the man's torso, supporting two very large axes, the heads of which were crescent moons—yet another figure, Alec had seen only while dreaming.

Noticing Alec's intimidation in the presence of the powerfully built man, the girl giggled.

"Oh don't worry, he won't hurt you!" she explained. "Many get that impression on first seeing him."

Alec eased up slightly, though his mind was still racing, his attention now directed on the sun which had begun its descent, signifying that it was later in the afternoon. He remembered he had to get back to the inn quickly to prepare for the festival.

"I'm very sorry, but I have to get these supplies back to the inn. It's the Red Talon in the village square—you can't miss it!"

"We may take you up on that offer!" she called after him, as he hurried away in the opposite direction. "We've traveled far and need to rest!"

But Alec was already out of earshot.

Makkari placed a firm hand on the girl's shoulder.

"Did you get a good look at him?" Makkari asked.

"I did; he has the mark…" she breathed. "He is the warden's new vessel."

"Remember to keep your distance; we cannot give away our location, my lady," Makkari warned. "In fact, if it truly was him, physical contact with him has put us all in jeopardy…"

"It was a close call, but I sensed the energy of the mark was redirected somewhere," she said, looking up at her companion. "What do you think it was?"

"Anything that can feed off the ward's energy can only be that of foul intentions," he replied. "We must keep an eye on the boy. I sense that he carries something dark in his possession."

The girl merely nodded as the two departed.

Alec walked at a quick pace now, unable to stop thinking of the sudden meeting, so enthralled in his own thoughts he failed to notice the same ghostly woman looking on after him from the shadows, a gentle smile upon her face. "The destined ones have met; your tale too will unfold soon, my little blackbird," she cooed before fading away.

Chapter Five

A n hour later Alec had returned to the Red Talon; his arms chock full of spices, which he barely managed to carry on his own.

Reaching for the inn's front door, he slowly tried to edge it open, a difficult task as his hands were clasped on two separate pouches containing the many assorted items on his mother's list. The dragon's breath hops, he was especially careful with; recalling the last time he had accidentally spilled the entirety onto the inn's floor, he made sure not to make the same mistake again.

Alec grunted as he struggled with the door, on the verge of dropping all he carried, when Liz spotted him and came to his aid.

"Thanks Liz!" Alec breathed under the weight of the sacks slung over his back. "Mum's list was quite more than I had expected this time."

"No surprise there," Liz replied. "She wants everything to run smoothly tonight. Word's already gotten out that she's preparing her dragon fire ale. I doubt we will have room to fit everyone tonight in the common room, let alone the bar!"

"Don't remind me," Alec huffed, smiling up at Liz, who seemed pale in comparison to her usual rosy features.

Alec slowly lowered the sacks to the floor, turning to face Liz.

"Liz, I was curious about what you and Mum were talking about before," Alec said, meeting her gaze. "You don't seem like your usual self; did something happen?"

"Oh! No dear, nothing at all!" she lied. "Just the news of the forest fires is all. It was probably due to the lightning."

"You're lying..." Alec stated, staring intently at her. "C'mon Liz, you always tell me everything!"

"Not this time Alec, I'm sorry," Liz replied quickly. "Your mother would have my head!"

Sighing, Alec hoisted the rucksacks back onto his shoulders, Liz carrying the remainder of the goods to the kitchen.

"I see you're back with everything I asked, and it appears nothing has been eaten this time!" Jessica piped. "How much did you get the hops for this time Alec?" she asked, hopefully.

"Got the hops for a little more than nine, for twenty-six pounds," Alec replied. "Wasn't able to get it much lower; the season for dragon's breath has been rather dry, and Molly knew it. She went easy on me, so tonight's profits will be thanks to her!"

"As I expected," she sighed. "I hope it'll be enough for tonight's masses."

Jessica approached Alec, hoisting the sacks he carried from him with ease and giving Liz a slight nod.

Liz smiled, still looking perturbed. Turning, she left the kitchen, leaving Alec and Jessica alone.

"Mother, what's the matter with Liz?" he asked. "She's not her usual self."

"She's caught a little of the flu, been wearing her down," Jessica quickly replied. "Now, don't mean to be a bother dear, but we have a couple of new guests. Could you please take these plates out to them?" she asked, completely avoiding the subject. "Can't miss them—large hooded man with a young girl."

Alec stared blankly at the contents of the plates, as they were loaded with an unusual amount of raw boar, with a small side of potato slices.

"Don't ask—was a special request," she added, noting Alec's expression. "Bigger one's a bit of an odd fellow; didn't say much save for renting a room and ordering a meal," she said.

"I know who you mean; I met them in the market earlier!" Alec replied, taking the plates.

"Don't bother asking if they would be more comfortable removing their cloaks. Neither of the two would," she added as Alec made for the exit.

Leaving the kitchen, Alec scanned the common room, spotting the table where the two travelers awaited him patiently. He approached them quickly, setting the plates down on the table.

"Hello again!" the girl piped, giving Alec a cheery smile.

"You two look exhausted; from whereabouts did you travel?" Alec asked, smiling back at her.

"Oh, Dun'valunh," she replied.

"That's quite a ways from here; name's Alec, by the way," he said, introducing himself.

"A-

She was interrupted by a grunt from Makkari, who was sternly gazing at her, shaking his head lightly in disapproval.

"Elizabeth!" she corrected. "My name's Elizabeth, and you already know Makkari here!" she said, giving the big man a sidelong glance before nibbling on a potato slice.

"I apologize for running off so quickly, before we could get acquainted!" Alec said, eyeing Makkari curiously.

"These potatoes are delicious!" Elizabeth said, popping another into her mouth. She smiled up at Alec. "Compliments to the chef!"

Makkari had begun to eat as well, shoveling the raw boar into his mouth, tearing through the meat with razor sharp canines, as though it were rice paper.

Elizabeth blushed as she watched him, embarrassed by his gluttony.

"Makkari... Slowly please, you're drawing attention to yourself!" she muttered.

The big man halted momentarily, giving her a slight nod.

"He gets carried away sometimes," Elizabeth said with a chuckle, turning to Alec.

"It's fine; I've seen worse of the sea dwarves that frequent the inn," he replied nonchalantly, watching Makkari.

Elizabeth laughed merrily. "Not so much as the Eladari brutes, though you rarely see one in a populated place!"

Alec chuckled before turning toward Makkari, extending his hand.

"Makkari, was it? It's nice to meet you both, truly!"

Makkari glanced down at Alec's hand and froze.

"The runes of this mark... No, it can't possibly be!" Makkari spoke for the first time, before grabbing Alec's wrist and turning his palm upward. "The seals are fading!" Makkari breathed, observing that one of the twelve markings surrounding the hourglass was now slowly ebbing away.

"Ouch! Let go, that hurts!" Alec grunted, but Makkari maintained his grip.

"Makkari, what is it?" Elizabeth asked, looking concerned.

"And this particular pattern..." Makkari placed one gloved finger on the six o'clock rune. "It's a veiling rune that only one has ever had the power to devise!" He seemed shaken. "No, it's not possible; he cannot possibly still live."

"What are you talking about?" Alec gasped, his wrist throbbing under Makkari's grip.

"Now I know how you've hidden yourself so long, in plain sight..." Makkari said, loosening his grip.

"Hidden? What do I have to hide from?" Alec asked, tugging his hand away.

"It's too late now; you've come in contact with a dark reanimation. I can smell the stench of necromancy upon you," Makkari breathed. "They will be on your tail within a few days' time."

Elizabeth paled noticeably.

"Wait, who are you talking about? What are they after?" Alec asked, nervously.

"You," was all Makkari said before rising, beckoning Elizabeth to follow him. "We will return by nightfall; in the meantime, I advise you to lay low."

Elizabeth rose from her seat, casting Alec a sidelong glance before following Makkari from the room.

"Wait! I still don't know what's going on!" he called after them.

Alec stood there for a moment, watching them leave. He massaged his sore wrist, still unsure of what was going to happen.

Deciding to put it out of his mind for now, Alec turned to retrieve the half empty plates. Returning to the kitchen, he cast a final glance over his shoulder, not realizing that Liz had overheard the entire conversation, as she now walked toward the bar.

"What can all this possibly mean?" Liz muttered.

By that evening the Red Talon was brimming, as expected. The dining hall barely contained half of the inn's occupants even with its substantial size. Men sat at the bar, quaffing the finely brewed ale Jessica had brewed throughout the evening and telling hearty tales to all who would sit and listen to them ramble on.

Najied had made his appearance within the inn with a bang, much to the excitement of the patrons, having merely popped in from thin air, the flame of a large phoenix signifying his entry in a spectacular display. As he took a seat on a low riding stool, the many children within the common room quickly congregated around Najied, as he prepared to tell the many tales of his travels—not before, of course, requesting a large mug of ale from Jessica to wet his beak.

"Najied! It's been far too long!" Alec called to him, waving at the elder.

The old Arcaneight chuckled. "Indeed it has, young Alec. Indeed it has…"

The tome keeper was a favored man amongst the townsfolk, a kind and generous elder, always with a tale to tell. Surprisingly to Alec, he looked no different than he ever had, as if he was untouched by time itself.

The elder always carried with him a walking stick. The head of a raven was carved at the hilt of the staff, and a small spherical gemstone was wedged in its wooden beak, which glinted a dull emerald in the firelight of the hearth he had his back to.

Setting the walking stick down in front of him, it transformed fully into a living raven. Its feathers were lavender in color. Turning its head, it dropped the gemstone into Najied's lap before nestling itself on the elder's shoulder.

"Oh! Oh! Tell the one about the Lanefrax again, Papa Naj!" a petite brunet sitting at the front of the crowd of children piped gleefully.

Najied chuckled at the nickname. "Oh, very well!"

The girl moved to sit herself on the old man's leg, giggling as she did.

"But first... Jessie dear, could I perhaps have a spot more ale?" he called to her, with a toothy grin.

"Heaven's sake, you old geezer, at this rate you'll be too faint to find your way out the door by the eve's end!" Jessica scoffed, topping off his mug.

"Oh, I'm sure I'll manage..." he replied cheerily, taking a long pull from the mug.

"I better not come down here the next morning to see you passed out on one of my tables again, old man; I mean it this time!" Jessica said heatedly.

"Was it the table last time?" he said, scratching his balding head. "My, my... I don't seem to recall it being that; I believe it was your linen closet the time before," Najied replied, with a hearty laugh. The raven cawed in response to the man's joyous laughter.

Jessica rolled her eyes as she walked back to the kitchen.

"Alec dear, could you please take these plates to the table in the far corner?" Jessica asked, seeing him try and failing to flee the kitchen unnoticed. "Oh, and keep an eye on the geezer for me, if you will," she said. "No telling where he'll end up sleeping next time," she finished, handing him the plates stacked with hot cakes.

"Oh, don't give me that look... he scared poor Liz half to death last time she found him snoozing in the linens."

The eve of the Red moon festival was the same as it was each year, no matter the location. But on this particular eve, the Red Talon was the favored place to hold the celebration, namely due to Jessica's ale, which even impressed those as stubborn as the Velenar sea dwarves.

Alec and Gabriel had their hands full that night aiding their mother in the kitchen, cooking food, or assisting the waitresses with serving the plethora of commoners and travelers which almost continuously flooded through the doors of the inn.

"Aren't those the two strange folk from earlier you were talkin' to?" Gabriel spoke from Alec's left. "They left quite hurriedly earlier, don't you think?"

Alec glanced in the direction Gabriel had gestured, to catch sight of Makkari and Elizabeth, sitting at a table close to where Najied was speaking and gesturing animatedly.

"Yeah, you're right. I just noticed them," Alec replied, his mind drifting back to what Makkari had told him.

"Oy lad, comin' through," barked a dwarf from behind Alec, who was standing in the stout man's path.

"Sorry," Alec said, moving to one side to let the dwarf pass.

"Hey Gabriel, take these plates from me, if you don't mind... I have something to talk to them about," Alec said, stacking the plates he was carrying onto his brothers already heavy load.

"Oh sure, I don't mind." Gabriel spoke with a note of reluctance, though Alec was already out of earshot.

Alec made his way to the table where Makkari and Elizabeth sat, nudging his way through the crowd, accidentally treading on the foot of a drunken elf.

"Ouch! Watch it, youngling!" the elf slurred, a disgruntled look etched on his otherwise elegant features.

"Sorry!" he apologized, picking up the pace, the elf leering at him.

Alec suddenly froze midway to the table, a shadowed figure catching his eye.

Slowly he turned to see a ghostly looking woman standing before him. A darkened aura seemed to engulf her form, encasing her in a cloak which resembled thick smoke.

Before Alec could even react, the woman withdrew her hood, revealing her ghostly visage—pale, yet beautiful.

Time itself seemed to have halted for that moment, as the woman gazed down at Alec. One of her eyes had the astonishing pupil of an hourglass, though dull and faded; the other was a bright azure. A long mane of Cerulean hair billowed out behind her, interconnecting stars tracing through.

The woman stooped to kiss Alec on the forehead, and a tingling sensation filled his frame as she pressed her cold lips against his flesh.

"The hourglass turns on the dais, Alec; you need to be able to see now..." she whispered in a musical tone. Taking his hand, she slowly rotated the three o' clock symbol on Alec's palm, seemingly heightening Alec's senses a hundred fold.

A split second later, the woman had vanished, leaving Alec staring blankly at a crowed of drunken dwarves laughing heartily as they spoke at the table in front of him.

"You all right, Alec?"

Alec jumped, turning his head to see Lucy standing behind him.

"Fine... why do you ask?" Alec replied, shakily.

"Alec... what happened to your eyes!" she exclaimed, a look of shock etched on her face.

"My eyes?" Alec asked. "What about them?"

"They're orange!" she squealed.

"Orange?" Alec seemed befuddled. As he gazed intently at her, he seemed to see an aura enveloping his young friend, a white hue which seemed unsteady, the sensation slowly faded, as the energy dissipated.

"Must have been a trick of the firelight; they look normal again," she said, eyeing Alec in a peculiar manner.

"Are you okay? You seemed to freeze almost solid for a good minute!" Lucy asked, concerned.

"It was nothing, don't worry about it." Alec said, smiling at her before turning to see Makkari gazing at him.

Alec approached their table.

"Give us a moment, if you would, Lucy," Alec said, turning toward Makkari.

"Oh sure Alec, I'll leave you alone for a bit." She replied, still looking perturbed.

Alec waited for Lucy to walk away, before he spoke.

"You saw her too, didn't you?" he asked.

Makkari simply nodded, his arms crossed in front of his chest, kicking out one of the chairs for Alec.

"Sit."

Alec sat himself down next to Elizabeth, who smiled at him shyly.

"Who-

Alec began to speak, but was interrupted by a raised hand from Makkari.

"Do not speak of her here," Makkari said. "This is of another matter."

"What, you mean the whole someone's after me thing?" Alec spoke, his eye color altering again to that of a pale red. "I would really like to know who exactly that would be!" His voice grew heated as he spoke. "Enough of this big mystery; I want to know who these people are, who this woman is."

Alec shifted uneasily in his chair, as the color of his eyes deepened in their reddish hue.

"Be careful boy, hold back your emotions," Makkari warned. "You'll give away quickly what she has done to you."

"She followed me through the town market all day long!" Alec's voice began to rise. "She thought I didn't notice her but I did!" His voice elevated in its volume. "These eyes—they see everything! I just pretend that I don't, pretend that it isn't there, but it is!"

"Keep your voice down, pup! You're bringing attention to yourself!" Makkari warned, eyeing the surrounding commoners who were now focused on the trio.

Not a moment later a resounding crash came from behind them, but Alec was the only one to hear it.

"Hourglasses…" Ashylanya breathed.

"Oh my goodness, I'm so sorry dear!" came the high-pitched voice of Liz in the background.

Alec turned, expecting to see Liz scrambling to retrieve the broken plates, only to watch the scene repeat itself before his very eyes not five seconds later.

Stunned, Alec gazed intently at the scene before him.

"What is wrong with you, pup? You look like you've seen a shade geist." Makkari spoke, his relaxed expression unchanged.

Alec turned slowly back toward them. "Did you see that?" he stuttered.

"The maiden who dropped all of her plates onto the dwarf's foot?" Makkari asked. "Who didn't see it?"

"No, I mean, that same exact thing just happened five seconds before!" Alec replied shakily.

Elizabeth merely gazed at Alec, open mouthed, as Makkari shifted in his chair, withdrawing a small glass shard from his coat pocket. He handed it to Alec.

"Look."

Alec was awestruck seeing that the pupils of his eyes had changed to the shape of twin hourglasses. A dull gold glowed within them, before they faded back to their normal shade of Hazel.

"Only five seconds?" Makkari scoffed, unimpressed. "Though I must say, it's quite unexpected for you to develop the strider's pendulum, at your age."

"Strider's... pendulum?" Alec asked.

"Now is not the time to explain. You are in danger," Makkari said, rising from his chair. "Your pursuers are drawing closer to you by the moment, especially giving yourself away like that."

"Please Alec, hear him," Elizabeth said, placing a gentle hand on his shoulder. "We have to get you out of here."

"Well, I'm not leaving," Alec said flatly, his eyes reverting to a dull orange. "Enjoy your meal," he added, as he turned to walk away.

Makkari's eyes narrowed as he watched Alec disappear into the crowd.

"What should we do, Makkari?" Ashylanya asked. "He's going to give himself away in no time, now that the strider's pendulum resides in his vision."

"We will keep our eyes on him..." he replied. "I was not expecting this... for the boy to possess the warden's mark, and the striders pendulum— it's inconceivable."

"You and I both know there is only one who ever possessed such a fabled power, Makkari," Ashylanya replied.

He chuckled heavily. "I know, and he's about as stubborn as she was," he said, taking a pull from an oversized mug. "Like mother, like pup."

Chapter Six

Alec's mind was overwhelmed now. He needed to know what was going on, and it was eating at his very core to be in the dark for such an extended period of time. Alec walked through the crowd to assist Liz in cleaning up the shattered plates, stooping to collect the remains of a large mug which had shattered on the hard wooden flooring. He looked up at her.

"Liz, I need to know what's going on," Alec said, in hopes of gleaning some kind of information out of her.

"Alec..." Liz sighed.

"Alec, there you are!" Jessica suddenly spoke from directly behind him. "You're supposed to be helping in the kitchen!" she scolded.

"Sorry, there was someone I needed to talk to," Alec replied, avoiding her penetrating gaze, still shaking as his nerves seemed to feel altered. No longer were they as they had previously been; it was if his whole form resonated energy now.

Jessica sighed. "Oh all right... I suppose things have died down enough to where we can handle things from here on." She said, "You go have fun dallying with that pretty girl you've had your eye on all evening; you're practically shaking with anticipation!"

Alec blushed deeply. "It's nothing like that!" he stuttered.

"Oh, I'm sure—off with you now, just stay out of our way!" Jessica said with a wink, before turning to see one of the waitresses struggling with an especially large order.

"Careful Emma! We don't want to lose anymore plates!" she called, before hurrying off to assist the overburdened waitress.

"There you are, Alec!" Lucy called. "Come on, you're missing all the fun!" she said, grabbing his arm and pulling him along.

"What was that all about earlier?" she asked as she led him through the crowded dining area. "Who were those two?"

"Just some weary travelers; they needed directions to the next town over," he lied.

"And I suppose you needed to shoo me away for that?" She glanced back at him with an annoyed look.

"Sorry."

"Oh, it's all right, I suppose. Now hurry, Najied is gonna tell another story! He said it's a good one!" she explained along the way, before coming to a halt before the elder man, sitting themselves down in the crowd of listeners. The floor felt oddly more comfortable than it usually was, hinting at traces of magic to make it seem so. Alec found it amusing.

"At least he's courteous enough to cushion the floor," Alec said to Lucy.

Lucy merely nodded with her gaze on Najied.

A moment passed before the room quieted considerably, then Najied began to speak.

"Tonight I will tell you a tale long forgotten," he said. "A tale in honor of a dear old friend I have not seen in far too long... truly an unexpected meeting," he said, glancing to his left at Makkari, which only Alec seemed to notice.

The tale of the Lycan began centuries ago... a race of formidable power. They were created by the gods themselves to hold together the balance of the fourteen worlds, seven dark and seven light. Each was ruled by a god of its own. One of the great fourteen, known as Verik, ruled with an iron will over the race of winged wolves known as the Anari.

During the times of darkness, a great war was waged, between Verik the balance keeper and the dark god Xek'roshule, ruling the vast expanses of the endless void in a time long forgotten. Xek'roshule, however, never showed his face upon the fields of battle... that duty he left to his lieutenant, Xen'trath the corrupted.

Makkari's jaw clenched upon hearing the lieutenant's name, his gloved fists tightening from growing anger.

Elizabeth placed a gentle hand on his shoulder in an attempt to sooth him.

A being known as a demorae, or one reanimated and corrupted after death to serve the dark ones, Xen'trath was feared by all who opposed him on the field of battle, a cold and ruthless monster who carved a path of blood. This led to an uproar amongst the gods. Having slain the son of Zaelbarath the god of the arcane, the war escalated to a cosmic battle so terrible, it was lost in history, with the end goal to forever seal the void away.

The gods themselves joined in the final battle, known as the siege of Laer, a terrible stronghold where Xen'trath had attempted to bring forth his dark master from beyond the void. The threat of oblivion hung over all creation.

All hope seemed lost, until a hero, a single Lycan by the name of Matthias stood before the mighty Xen'trath.

Makkari grew noticeably pale, seemingly restraining himself from uttering a word; Elizabeth's face was etched with concern for her companion.

Matthias felled the beast and thwarted Xen'trath's plan to summon his master by imprisoning the dark strider known by the name of Lucin, a mere half of a weapon created to annihilate all creation, and sealing the gate to the void permanently. Bringing justice to the gods, the war was drawn to a close, though the hero was lost to wounds most grievous.

Makkari jumped to his feet, casting an angry look at Najied, who met his gaze with a wink.

Turning swiftly, he left the room, ascending the flight of stairs to the rooms above, Elizabeth at his heel.

'What's wrong with him?' Lucy muttered, though Alec quieted her, as Najied continued.

Xen'trath is thought to still exist to this day, believed to have been resurrected by his dark master, though where he could be is a mystery.

After the fall of Xen'trath, the Lycan's seemed to fade from existence. Sightings of the renowned race grew sparse as long years passed and they alienated themselves from the thirteen other races and their gods.

It is prophesied that there are darker things coming in the future, that Xen'trath shall rise again. We can only hope such a day never comes.

Najied lifted his mug, taking a long pull as he ended his tale.

"Now, what do you say we continue our celebration, shall we?" he said, with a warm smile at his audience.

Several dwarves lifted their mugs to that, as the cacophony of chatter rose once again within the inn, and the celebration continued.

"What a strange tale…" Lucy said, turning to Alec.

Alec nodded in agreement. "That is definitely a new tale from Najied. I've never heard him tell it before…" Alec said, though the tale rang familiar in his mind.

"Let's go see what Sam and Gabriel are up to. They're sitting right over in the corner there!" Lucy said, gesturing toward the pair and hopping to her feet. Alec followed suit.

Following Lucy, he glanced over his shoulder at Najied, whose gaze was fixated on Alec, almost curiously.

"Wasn't that the hooded weirdo you were talkin' to earlier who left during the geezer's tale?" Sam asked, cramming potato slices into his mouth. "Saw you talkin' to 'im and that tha pretty girl earlier."

"Just some travelers I met earlier today," Alec replied, sitting down at the table and stealing a few potato slices himself. His mind drifted momentarily back to the dream, and the strange tidings this day had been loaded with.

"You listnen? Or you just gonna stand there gawkin' at me all night?" Sam chided, clapping Alec on the wrist. "I know I'm handsome and all, but c'mon," he said, bringing Alec out of his daze.

"Now as I was sayin', we should go!" Sam said, taking a large bite out of a thick drumstick.

"Go where?" Alec asked, befuddled.

"Wha', am I talkin to myself 'ere?" Sam scoffed. "I'm sayin' we should go to the forest!"

"Are you still going on about that?" Lucy chided. "Didn't you hear the others? It's dangerous out there lately!"

"And has that ever stopped us before?" Sam inquired, a wide grin etched on his features.

Lucy shut her mouth after that statement, knowing it was the truth.

"Oh, by the way Alec, you notice you've had someone keepin' a close eye on you all night?" Sam asked, giving him a knowing grin. "How was it?"

"I don't know what you're talking about," Alec defended, eyeing Sam.

"Oh, I think you do!" Sam remarked, winking slyly. "She kissed you, after all."

All eyes were now on Alec, who turned red in the face.

"Whoa, what the hell's with yer eyes, Alec?" Gabriel asked, noticing that they had shifted in color again, to a deep magenta. "You haven't been drinking Najied's elixirs again, have you?"

"Yes, he asked me to test it out for him, new mixture." Alex fabricated. "It's an eye color elixir, responds to your emotions!"

Lucy gave Alec a sidelong glance. "I didn't see you take anything from him since he's been here," she stated, eyeing him.

"Ah, he slipped it to me. You know me; I can be sly!" he continued to lie, trying with all his might to convince the trio.

"Should be careful with that stuff, could grow a third arm or somethin'," Sam chimed in, before sipping from his mug.

"But someone kissed you?" Gabriel asked. "Who was it?"

"No one, Sam's obviously snuck himself a few too many drinks," Alec quickly replied, with a laugh.

"Oh really? Someone's feelin' a bit modest, eh?" Sam teased. "All right, I'll leave it alone, but don't think I'll forget about it!"

"I'm with Alec on this one Sam; you really shouldn't sneak drinks," Lucy scolded. "And don't try to deny it, I've watched you!"

Sam chuckled, his face flushed red. "Suppose there's no getting past you, sis."

"Well anyway, let's go to the forest tomorrow then, shall we?" Alec said, with a yawn, hoping to change the subject.

"Atta boy, least someone's got stones 'ere." Sam laughed.

"Well, it's getting late; we should be heading home by now. Father's expected us hours ago!" Lucy said, rising from her seat.

Later that evening, most of the occupants of the inn had dispersed, leaving the common room mostly empty as travelers went on their way or rented a room for the night.

Lucy bid farewell to Alec and Gabriel, Sam having already gone on ahead.

Alec himself was on his way up the staircase when he was halted by a firm hand.

"Dear boy," came the voice of Najied from behind him. "Would you mind accompanying me on my way back to my cottage?" "It can be quite dangerous for an old blind man such as myself to be roaming the streets at this hour unaccompanied."

"Anything for you, my old friend," Alec said, turning toward the elder Arcaneight. "Getting some fresh air would be nice at the moment."

"Very well, let's be off then, shall we?" Najied quickly replied.

Not more than a few minutes later, Alec stepped outside the inn; the cool evening breeze swept through his hair, and dark windows of cottages flickered occasionally with candle light in the distance, as the few trees within the square rustled in the wind.

The full moon in the night sky cast a gentle amber light upon the pair as they set off toward Najied's cottage in the distance, a lengthy walk, as Najied lived on the borderline of the forest itself, having built the cottage at its location intentionally, not being prone to the hustle and bustle of the busy town during the daylight hours. He typically only inhabited this cabin during his stays in the winter, avoiding the harsh cold of the north.

After walking for what seemed like twenty minutes, Najied turned his head toward Alec.

"Dangerous game you were playing back there, boy," he said, eyeing Alec through milky white cataracts.

"What do you mean?" Alec asked, halting momentarily.

"Using the strider's pendulum in front of so many people. If any of them had noticed you..."

"How did you know that?" Alec asked, dumbstruck.

"There is quite a lot I know about you, Alec," Najied replied, continuing to walk. "There are many things that you yourself do not know."

"I managed to buy us some time by telling the tale and averting their watchful gaze," Najied continued. "There is something dark in your possession that I need you to give to me now so I may dispose of it, and having them breathing down your neck, though they mean well, is a nuisance."

"Something dark?" Alec asked, curiously.

"The sphere in your left pocket. I could feel its energy miles away," Najied said, stopping again. "I am quite surprised Makkari did not notice; he has quite the keen sense of smell for dark magic."

Alec briefly recalled his encounter with the elfish woman in the town market earlier that day, remembering that she had given him a black colored sphere. He reached into his pocket, withdrawing it.

Najied gazed down at the orb curiously. "It's fed off quite an abundance of your energy, Alec."

"My energy—you mean the mark on my hand?" Alec asked, extending it.

"Precisely," Najied replied, lifting the orb from Alec's palm.

Alec suddenly felt as if a weight had been lifted from him; a wave of relief filled his frame momentarily.

'An elfish woman gave it to me," Alec explained.

"I see, and did you get a good look at this elf?"

"Her hood was drawn too low to see much. All I could tell of her was that she was deathly pale, almost corpselike."

"It is good that I had come then; had you had this artifact in your possession any longer, the results would have been catastrophic. Though you still are not out of danger—I fear Makkari and the girl blundering into you so carelessly has given your pursuer your exact location."

"But who are they?" Alec asked curiously.

"Why don't you ask them yourself?" Najied said dryly. "I don't quite think myself to be a go-between for two parties. In short, they are very old friends, though I would rather have seen them under different circumstances."

"What do you mean?" Alec asked.

"Did you really believe the mark on your right hand was a mere birthmark?" Najied said as they drew closer to the old and rickety looking cottage.

"I always knew there was something strange about it, why?" Alec asked, curiosity eating at him.

"It is far more, which you will soon come to understand," Najied replied. "Time is short. These old bones are beginning to give way, but there is still one final task I must see to, and you Alec, must be ready."

Alec suddenly felt his eyesight shift; diving out of the way, he threw himself into the underbrush as a shadowy figure leapt at him, narrowly missing his throat.

The blood red moonlight illuminated a pale, skeletal creature; an eyeless face gazed hungrily at Alec as its elongated bladelike fingers grated together.

Jumping to his feet, Alec sprinted as fast as he could back through the forest trail.

"After him, you fool!" Najied's voice had suddenly changed, becoming hollow and deathlike. "Do not let him escape."

Another of the foul creatures leapt from the darkness in an attempt to lash at Alec, before halting mid-swing as its prey vanished suddenly.

Alec stopped running, noticing the creature was no longer pursuing him. He turned, eyeing it, as it jerked its twisted face to the sky, inhaling a deep rattling breath, as if trying to locate him.

"Imbecile! Do you know what the master will do to us if you let him escape?" Najied bellowed.

As Alec's vision shifted again, Najied's eyes became darkened pits; the flesh decaying from his bones as a shadowy aura enveloped his frame, that of pure and wretched darkness.

"Forgive...we...find..." the beast croaked with effort, obviously unfamiliar with speaking.

Najied threw his head back in an awful cackle before pointing the shaft of his walking stick at the creature. "No... you have failed me," he hissed. "You must be punished!" Najied shouted, as a white hot light struck the creature, causing it to violently explode before disintegrating into ashes.

Alec watched in horror as the shadows of the forest suddenly sprang to life and hundreds more of the creatures poured from the underbrush.

Turning, Alec continued to run as fast as his short legs could carry him; he had to warn the others, though he knew only Makkari and Elizabeth would believe the horror he had just experienced.

As Alec ran, his eyes caught sight of the same strange looking woman from the inn that evening. A gentle smile caressed her lips as she watched him. Alec knew that if it hadn't been for her, escape would have been impossible.

"Fly away, my little blackbird..." she cooed, before stepping back into the shadowy forest. "I will give you safe passage." The crimson moonlight contrasted brightly with her silky mane of azure, a color now formed purely of starlight.

Chapter Seven

Makkari breathed a disgruntled sigh as he paced the small room which he shared with Elizabeth.

"He must have known we would come. Curse him for making a fool out of me!" he spat.

"To think he would be here, of all places…" Elizabeth said, sitting at the end of her small cot. "It's baffling that he still lives, after all this time. And to be using an alias himself, he must have resigned himself to mere storytelling after what happened so long ago," she said, shifting on her cot to light a small candle within the room to provide some source of light.

"You know as well as I do that he bears the timeless mark, milady," Makkari interjected. "What is the old fool plotting? I watched him leave the inn with the boy almost an hour ago from the window," he said, his pace increasing. "He must have thought I would get angered enough I would leave so he could take the boy; we should have followed…"

Makkari had halted in front of the windowsill, the crimson light of the moon bathing his large frame.

"You know how he is; it's the same as when we were younger." Elizabeth chuckled. "He probably just needed a word alone with Alec. Being that it's Joden the tome keeper, he's in capable hands after all, though something about his energy felt strangely dark."

Makkari sighed heavily. "I suppose you're right, though the man's always been bothersome, even in his youth," Makkari remarked. "But not as bothersome as the boy's mark, and his contact with the dawn strider." Makkari lowered his voice. "A mere child has never been chosen to be the bearer of the Warden; his body should not be able to handle such energy."

"It may be the blood which courses through his veins, the strider's only true heir…" Elizabeth replied.

The pair was interrupted by the sound of heavy footfalls as someone quickly ascended the staircase.

"Someone's coming—your cloak milady, put it back on," Makkari directed, donning his own.

The distinct sound of frantic knocking reverberated in the small room, as someone attempted to gain entry. "Please let me in!" a muffled voice came from the other side.

"The boy's returned, but why do I sense panic radiating from him?" Makkari whispered, moving for the door and swinging it open as Alec charged inside, breathing heavily.

"Alec, what's wrong?" Ashylanya asked, rising from her cot. "Where is Najied?" She asked, avoiding using his true name.

"Pale beasts…" Alec breathed, panting heavily. "Najied—he took something from me and then tried to kill me!" Alec stuttered, through labored breathing.

Makkari quickly shut the door, approaching Alec. "Slow down, what is the meaning of this?" Makkari demanded, gazing down at him.

"Pale beasts…" Alec breathed, looking up at Makkari, with eyes a dark saffron shade. "They swarmed from the forest. I barely got away; the strange woman from before saved my life!" he gasped.

Alec froze as his eyesight shifted to that of a lime green, peering directly through the big man's cloak. Alec was in awe.

Sharp eyes, the color of sterling silver, gazed down at Alec through a long mane of tangled snowy hair. Various shapes and sizes of beads were braided in his long unkempt hair. Well-muscled arms were decorated with intricate tribal tattoos, which covered most of his taut chestnut skin.

But what astonished Alec most were the large wolf-like ears protruding from Makkari's mane, coupled with a long bushy tail, a hole cut in his black leather breaches to accommodate the appendage, coupled with a sleeveless matching tunic.

"Y-you…" Alec stuttered. "I've dreamt of people like you all my life, but they always had wings; where are yours?"

Makkari's expression darkened at those words. "Your eyesight has shifted to the left of the scale of the pendulum, allowing you to see through clothing. The fact that you aren't averting your eyes means you must still see me clothed, at least," Makkari said, shedding his cloak, which was now useless.

"As for the wings, though?" Alec began to ask.

"I thought there was something strange about Joden…" Elizabeth interjected, quickly changing the subject, noting the look of annoyance on her companion's face.

"Joden?' Alec inquired, casting Elizabeth a sidelong glance, his sight shifting back to normal, unable to see through Elizabeth's heavy cloak, though her hood was withdrawn, permitting her long silky mane of ebony hair, which fell to her mid–back, to hang limply. She gazed at Alec with eyes the shade of amber, through neatly combed fringe.

"Joden is the tome keeper's true name," Makkari interjected. "I told you to stay out of sight, you little fool," he said, with a grimace, approaching the windowsill.

"I didn't think anything of it. I've always trusted Na-Joden…" Alec corrected himself mid-sentence. "To think he would lie about his name—I wonder what else he's hidden-

Alec was interrupted by a raised hand from Makkari, silencing him.

"They're already here…" Makkari whispered, as he watched the shadows writhing just below. "Ashylanya, mask our scents if you would."

"A-Ashylanya?" Alec asked, turning to her, curiously.

"There is no longer a need to hide her true name," Makkari said. "Our cover's already been blown with your blundering, after all. Best learn to control the pendulum, boy, it will save your life one day. Had you seen the aura of this impostor, you would not have followed,"

Makkari said, taking a deep breath in. "You can practically catch his scent a mile away now that he's shed his disguise—a Skythe Litch."

"What's a Skythe?" Alec asked, befuddled.

"Dark and powerful beasts that usually permeate dreams to torture the dreamer from within, though a Litch is much worse," Makkari whispered. "A demorae Arcaneight, specializing in necromancy; it's why he could hide his presence so well…"

"But then, where is the real Joden?" Alec asked.

"Likely dead by now, or held captive, the Skythe having taken on his memories and traits—the perfect guise," Makkari said flatly.

"But why are they after me?" Alec asked, his sight shifting again, revealing the auras of energy spiraling just beyond the windowsill. "I can see a large amount of energy just beyond the window."

Makkari turned his head. "Slightly more to the pendulum's left, the energy sight, though why your vision is fluctuating so frequently is a mystery. As for why they are after you, they are not," Makkari stated. "They are after what is inside of you."

"And what exactly is that? What is this energy?" Alec asked, as questions flowed through his mind like a faucet.

"Jessica has her own means of protecting this inn, a favor Joden did for her long ago," Makkari replied, ignoring the previous question.

Twenty minutes had passed. Makkari sat idly by the windowsill, watching as the pale creatures below combed the entire village frantically.

Just below their room, Jessica sat with Liz, peering through the window cautiously.

"I should have known that monster had a trick or two up his sleeve," Jessica sighed. "Hiding in plain sight—even I was fooled."

"You couldn't have known, madam…" Liz replied, in a whisper.

"Enough with the formalities already; it's becoming quite annoying," Jessica chided.

"Sorry madam, it was just the way I was raised."

Jessica placed a hand on Liz's shoulder, silencing her as the Litch's presence seemed to amplify as he drew closer.

"Remember you fools, shed no blood as of this moment; this is merely to find our target!" Jessica heard the deathly voice of the Litch as he walked idly past the inn, as if it did not exist.

"Thank goodness for Joden's wardings," Jessica muttered.

Liz jumped as a shade geist suddenly walked in front of the windowsill, its ghastly visage haunting in the red moonlight, which highlighted its mangled features, making it look far more menacing.

"You have nothing to fear; they cannot see beyond the ley lines Joden placed," Jessica reassured her, with a firm hand on her back. "I'm just thankful Alec made it back to the inn before this occurred. I'm going to go check on him."

Less than a minute later, there came a quiet knocking on the bedroom door where Alec sat on edge, next to Ashylanya.

"Enter," Makkari stated.

Jessica opened the door, walking into the dimly lit room. "Somehow I knew you'd be in here Alec, poking your nose in where it shouldn't be. Tell me everything that happened."

Alec looked up at her, the same yellow tint in his eyes as anxiety enveloped him. "Najied isn't who he said he was, Mum," He replied. "He's something called-

"A Litch, yes, I am aware," Jessica interjected. "There are many things you need to know Alec, but now is not the time."

"He is already developing the strider's pendulum, Jessica," Makkari stated, moving away from the windowsill. "If it keeps fluctuating like this, he will give us away."

Jessica paled. "It's far too soon," she said.

"Mum, you know these two? AGH!" Alec cried out as the mark on his hand now flared a bright gold. His skull felt as if an immense pressure were bearing down upon it, as the scene around him faded out. His mind felt as though he was submerged under water, as the voices became muffled.

"Alec!" Jessica whispered exasperatedly.

But Alec had already lost consciousness, Makkari catching him before he could fall to the floor.

"The rune, are unraveling Jessica, and the strider altered one of them," Ashylanya stated, looking worriedly at Alec.

"I am aware," Jessica stated. 'You two seem very familiar to me; do I know you?' she inquired.

"Once upon a time, we were allies," Ashylanya replied in a whisper.

Jessica quickly approached Alec, checking his pulse. She sighed in relief to feel a beat.

"Something dark was in the boy's possession earlier today. I felt its energy..." Makkari said, looking up at Jessica and meeting her gaze.

"Did you get a look at what it was?" she asked.

"All I know is that there was a leeching rune upon it," Makkari explained. "Alec said the dark one took it from him before attempting to take his life."

The candle light flickered in the otherwise darkened room, as a draft of air billowed through the opened windows. Makkari quickly closed the shutters, turning back toward Jessica.

"It is rare to see an Anarian in town, let alone at all these days..." Jessica stated, eyeing Makkari. "From where about did you travel?"

"Western Belmuron..." Makkari replied. "Our numbers grow fewer as time passes. Since the times of the great war of the gods, we have remained hidden; as for where we come from, I cannot tell you that. I am forbidden."

"Wait..." Jessica breathed. "I remember you!" she whispered. "Makkari of the twin moons!"

"As I remember you. Jessica the-

"Shh..." Jessica interjected. "I prefer nobody know my past, in case of eavesdropping."

Makkari merely nodded.

"Dark times are upon us, so says Matthias..." Jessica said, eyeing the large Anari.

"Wait... Matthias!" Makkari exclaimed. "Matthias lives!?"

"I was as surprised as you were; the dawn strider is the only thing keeping him alive."

Ashylanya was in utter shock, frozen stock-still. "It can't be possible! We watched him die!"

"A long tale, for another time perhaps," Jessica replied.

"Take me to him," Makkari stated, heading for the doorway.

"Are you mad?" Jessica said, turning toward him. "Did you see how many of those foul things are out there, including a Litch?"

"I will deal with all who bar my path," Makkari said firmly. "Now, take me to him."

Jessica sighed. "If I must—knowing your fighting prowess, we should manage," she said, smiling up at Makkari.

"Ashylanya, would you be okay to stay here and keep watch over Alec? I don't want to leave him unprotected," Makkari inquired.

"Of course..." Ashylanya replied, sounding a tad let down. "Please give big brother my regards, okay? And stay safe!"

Makkari nodded as he departed the room with Jessica.

Ashylanya gazed down at Alec momentarily before lifting him onto the bed, resting his head on a pillow; she turned his right hand over, gazing down at his palm. One of the runes which had faced inward now faced outward, as opposed to the others which remained intact—all save for one, which was slowly fading.

Ashylanya sat on the bed next to him, gazing out the window, transfixed by the light of the blood red moon just beyond.

Chapter Eight

Alec regained consciousness what seemed to be hours later. A faint dripping could be heard through utter darkness. The repetitive sound echoed through his mind.

A thick scent of smoke penetrated his nostrils as the sound of a roaring inferno now permeated his surroundings.

Slowly he opened his eyes, finding himself lying on the cool damp earth within the center of a burning village; the blaze was consuming everything in its path.

Fresh corpses resembling Lycan lay strewn over the bloodstained soil. As Alec regained his composure, the scent of charred flesh stung his nostrils, making him gag.

Alec slowly got to his feet, gazing upon the devastation before him.

Before him was a young looking female on her knees; a ragged and charred looking dress was torn in several places, from what appeared to be a violent struggle. Her visage was masked, however, by the thick smoke which hung over the burning village, like a dark miasma. She appeared to be clinging tightly to a small child, who quivered in fear. She attempted to soothe the child by singing to him gently, as she rocked him in her scratched and bleeding arms.

As Alec watched them, the hair on the nape of his neck stood on end, as he heard the sudden heavy footfalls of someone behind him.

"Stay away, monster!" the woman suddenly cried, clutching even tighter to the child.

Alec turned to see the outline of a dark figure drawing closer to him. Attempting to move out of the way, he found his efforts fruitless, as his feet seemed to be rooted in place, as if each leg were weighed down by boulders.

He flinched, as the figure simply passed right through him, ignoring his existence. Turning back to where the woman knelt sobbing, he observed her struggling to stand.

Managing to do so, she turned on her heel in a desperate attempt to flee, clutching the child tightly, only to freeze in place as a narrow blade pierced her through her heart from behind, narrowly missing the child.

Time seemed to slow as Alec heard the thud of the woman's corpse slowly falling to the ground, a pool of blood forming around her as the light faded from her eyes, while she continued to whisper something inaudible to her child, before going silent.

The frightened child struggled free of his mother's death grasp.

What happened next chilled Alec to his very core.

The child knelt at his mother's side, shaking her with bloodstained hands.

"Mommy, you can't sleep now, please wake up!" the child cried, not understanding what had happened. "We have to go, before the bad man catches us!"

But she did not respond to the boy's plea.

"Mommy!" He shook her harder now, trying desperately to rouse her.

"She's dead, boy…" came a cruel, guttural voice.

The eyes of the child grew wide, filling with tears. "Mommy's not dead! Take it back!" he screamed, covering his ears as if he could simply make it all go away.

"Don't be afraid child, you will be joining her, all too soon…" the shrouded figure's laughter filled the vicinity of the burning village, with a cold that chilled Alec to the bone, unable to do anything but watch the gruesome display before him in horror.

The boy then turned, breaking into a run, only to crash headlong into the figure, who suddenly appeared before him, barring his path.

Lifting the boy by his arm, he removed the hood of his cloak, revealing the all too familiar hideously scarred face, a face that still haunted Alec's memories. Unchanged was the beast's expression of madness.

Deep burning eyes like embers gazed hungrily at the boy through a bloodstained mask which exposed only his lower jaw, twisted into a macabre grin, bordering the line of insanity. Alec noted one detail which had changed from his previous appearance. He too, bore the characteristics of a Lycan. Large tattered ears jutted from the man's skull, one ear resting behind a gnarled and twisted looking antler, like that of a stag on the left side of his head, protruding from a tangled matt of charcoal black hair.

"S-stop... you're hurting me!" the boy pleaded, struggling to break free of the monster's mangled claw. "Mommy!" the child cried out again.

The beast's grin grew even wider, a sight more grotesque than before, as he watched the boy squirm.

"Mommy, Mommy!" he mocked, in a shrill broken voice. "Is that all you ever say?"

"Leave him alone! He's just a child!" Alec's cry fell upon deaf ears.

The beast then withdrew a long blade from his cloak. The hilt was decorated in a grotesque display of gaping mouths, and a darkened aura engulfed the blade's edge, which seemed to bleed corruption.

Lifting the boy higher, he directed the blade toward the boy's heart.

Alec watched as he prepared to thrust the blade, only to be interrupted by a loud crack close by.

Another man had appeared, striking the beast in the ribs with a forceful blow, knocking him hard into the base of a large blazing oak.

The beast raised his head, gazing angrily at the one before him. "You... You're supposed to be dead!" the beast bellowed, leaping to his feet and charging at the boy's savior wildly, though the man had already vanished with the boy, his blade striking hard into the earth where his adversary had stood not a moment before.

Falling to his knees, the beast howled in rage as Alec's surroundings seemed to fade abruptly into another scene.

Alec found himself standing before the Red Talon inn. The boy's rescuer stood before the doorway, the boy unconscious in his arms.

Knocking on the door, he was greeted by Jessica, though she looked no different than she ever did, which befuddled Alec; it was as if Jessica was untouched by time.

She peered up at the tall man before her. "Matthias…!" she breathed. "I-It's been far too long! Please, please come in!"

As Matthias disappeared into the inn, the scene shifted yet again. This time, Alec found himself standing behind the bar of the Red Talon, watching Jessica and Matthias.

"You knew this day would come, Jessica," Matthias said, resting the boy on one of the older tables in the inn. Gazing down at him, he turned over the boy's palm.

Jessica gasped. "Matthias, why?" she said. "Why did you choose this boy to be the warden's next vessel?"

Matthias was quiet for a long moment.

"He bears the blood of the dawn strider… He is the key, to all of our futures." Matthias placed his own palm against the boy's. The marking upon Matthias' hand seemed to unravel, as a strange aura enveloped the boy's frame. The hourglass symbol was now imprinted, as if branded, into the boy's right hand.

Alec watched in awe for a long moment, wishing he was able to move closer, but finding that his feet were still rooted in place.

"I now deem this child Alecxandros, the new bearer of the ward."

Jessica watched in amazement, never having seen the process of the transferring spell. It intrigued her greatly.

"Watch over this one, Jessica," Matthias said, turning toward the door. "Treat him as if he were your own flesh and blood."

"But what will become of you, old friend?" Jessica questioned, her gaze fixed on the man's back.

Matthias turned his head. The gold aura in one of his hourglass-shaped pupils was now a deep shade of black. "I will watch over him from afar, as will his true mother, the dawn strider."

"And what became of the surrogate?" Jessica questioned.

"Dead…" Matthias said, a grim expression on his face. "Xen'trath butchered them all."

"How will you return to your own time period, Matthias?" Jessica asked. "You and I both know every era must have a warden."

"My time being the warden is done… I survived the war, despite the others believing me to be dead," Matthias explained. "And not every era requires a warden in a living vessel."

"What do you mean?" Jessica asked.

"The energies of the ward, though unstable, were stored within the abyssal seed, seeking a new bearer," he explained. "I am merely giving the ward a mortal vessel once more, due to the crystal's shattering. You yourself suffer from the results of that catastrophic event."

"Indeed, I have suffered," Jessica said with a solemn look, revealing a small black hourglass marking on the back of her neck, behind her long braid of hair.

"The fracturing of the seed created a paradox in time. Xen'trath and I were brought to this time period, thought to be dead, but still we breathe," Matthias continued. "Now there are four separate fragments, existing out of time and space. They meet in one time period only once every ten thousand years."

"Do you believe Xen'trath intends to gather the seeds?" Jessica asked.

"He very well might …" was all Matthias said, his hand on the door handle.

"Oh, I almost forgot…" Matthias said, walking back toward Alec's younger form. Taking hold of his palm, he adjusted the position of the symbols, causing a dim resonating glow to emanate from the marking momentarily.

"His true race shall be hidden now; when he comes of age, the symbols will be reversed, by the strider's hand," Matthias said, giving Jessica a sidelong glance. "Take good care of the boy. He is the only one of his kind that still breathes, as the striders long ago became Edelions."

Matthias swung open the door. "Though I may no longer contain the power of the warden, I will still watch over you from afar. Farewell for now, dear Jessica."

After Matthias departed, Jessica turned toward Alec's younger form on the table. Letting out a sigh, she gently lifted him, bringing him upstairs.

The scene then shifted to that of pure darkness, as if Alec faced a black canvas. "I will not be stopped," spoke a deafening voice in Alec's mind, as a large pair of blood red eyes opened before him, glaring deep into his soul.

Alec doubled over in agony as the voice resonated within his skull.

"The fourteen worlds... all of creation shall tremble before my might!" the voice boomed. "For I... am Xek'Roshule, lord of the void, harbinger of oblivion... heart of despair itself." The voice tore into Alec's mind like grating nails.

"All shall bend their knee... and worship me..." The voice was relentless against Alec's own mind, as it continued to speak, its volume increasing with every word.

"Not even you, little warden, can stem the flood of my endless legions... Not even by the blood of your mother, the fabled dawn strider, do you even hold a glimmer of hope!"

Chapter Nine

Alec awoke with a start to find himself in Ashylanya's bed. The warm cloth that was draped over his brow fell to his lap as he propped himself up, seeing Ashylanya sitting at the end of the bed at his feet, completely devoid of clothing.

Alec blushed, blinking twice, as his vision returned to normal.

Ashylanya seemed to be weeping softly; gentle sobs could be heard as she held her hands in front of her on her lap.

She had taken off her traveler's cloak, revealing her lithe form; she wore a knitted tailcoat blouse which mocked the colors of the night sky, deep cobalt, coupled with white breeches, which were patched in several areas.

One thing he had noticed, though, while his vision was altered, was the same peculiar hourglass symbol on her left shoulder blade, Jessica having had it on the back of her neck. The thought brought curiosity to his mind, but he decided not to reveal to her that he had seen her unclothed.

"Ashylanya?" Alec said, slowly getting up. "Where is Makkari?"

Ashylanya turned to face him, revealing her tear-stained cheeks. "H-he had to leave to see my big brother..." she replied. "Jessica went with him last night."

Alec leapt from the bed. "They went out while the shade geists were roaming about?" Alec asked, dumbfounded.

"Yes. But that's not what's truly wrong..." Ashylanya croaked. "Our village...I spotted it on the horizon—it was burning, Alec!" Ashylanya spoke through broken sobs.

"Ashylanya… I'm so sorry…" Alec replied softly; edging himself to sit next to her, he placed a gentle hand on her shoulder.

"H-he left me here, to watch over you; you passed out from the marking on your hand," she said, wiping the tears from her eyes with a handkerchief. "I'm just so worried about them, Alec!"

"I'm sure everyone will be okay…" Alec replied, attempting to reassure her. "Makkari likely went to their aid. He's a strong Anari; I'm sure everyone is okay!"

Ashylanya turned, gazing intently at him. "You're right, I shouldn't be worried, but I wish I could do something other than sit idly by while others die for my sake…"

"So many protect you, why is that, If you don't mind me asking."

Ashylanya shifted before reaching into her blouse and withdrawing a small crystal pendant.

Alec's palm began to glow softly as she showed him the gemstone within.

He flattened his palm for her to see, the stone itself having an effect on the marking.

Ashylanya nodded. "It's an abyssal seed fragment, that of the light, that is why your mark responds so," she explained.

"My name is Ashylanya Lightwish… I am the heir to the tribe seat of the Anari race…" She spoke somberly. "Daughter to Verik, our god and great leader… a burden I had wished to never bear."

"It must be hard to be so important…" Alec replied, still gazing at the crystal pendant.

Ashylanya gazed intently at him for a moment. "If only you knew," she said with a sigh.

"So why does that crystal make my palm glow this way?" Alec asked. "What is an abyssal seed, exactly?"

Ashylanya slowly rotated the crystal in her palm, momentarily in thought. "No one has ever been sure of what it is…" she said. "I've had this pendant since the day of my birth; still I am curious as to where it came from."

Alec nodded, his gaze shifting back to his palm.

"But never mind me... are you okay?" she asked. "You were sleeping rather fitfully last night."

"I'm okay, just another bad dream," Alec lied, though his mind churned upon the suspicion of his own upbringing.

"I have to go now though. I told the others I would meet up with them," Alec stated, before rising from the cot.

"If it's the forest you're talking about... I'm going with you!" Ashylanya caught him off guard with her response.

"But wouldn't Makkari be concerned?" he asked.

"Oh, that stubborn old prude wouldn't let a nymph out of his sight if he could help it," Ashylanya replied with a giggle. "I'd love to do something without him breathing down my neck for once, though I know he means well." She stood up, approaching Alec, as his vision shifted again without him realizing it. He watched the same scene occur again, before his very eyes, that had happened not a moment before.

Alec stood there speechless.

"Hourglasses again," Ashylanya said, eyeing him. "Mid-pendulum—don't worry you'll learn how to control it soon enough," Ashylanya reassured him. "I remember she had the same troubles." Ashylanya cut her sentence short, her hands shooting up to cover her mouth. "I fear I've said too much!" she said, brushing past him to leave the room. "I'll be waiting outside, when you are ready."

As Ashylanya left the room, Alec stood there momentarily, his mind drifting back to the dream. The face of the woman who died in the dream flashed again in his mind, bringing him chills.

Slowly, Alec left the room, making his way down the long corridor to the staircase, his mind wrapped around the idea that his life up till this point had been based on a blatant lie.

Making his way down, he saw Lucy at the foot of the stairs waiting for him.

"Your forehead sure healed fast!" she remarked, a look of surprise on her face, as she saw Alec walking down the stairs groggily.

Alec, however, completely ignored her as he walked past; walking toward the kitchen with a mind buzzing with questions that needed answering.

"Good morning Alec," Jessica said, turning her head as he entered, casting him a sidelong glance, noting the blank expression on his face.

Jessica had spent the majority of the morning cleaning the kitchen from the previous night's enormity of guests, as all the pots and pans were neatly stored beneath the small counters. Many ladles and wooden spoons hung upon the walls of the small kitchen, as well as a large assortment of knives, which glinted in the morning light through the sole small window within the kitchen, its shutters ajar.

Jessica stood at the sink, scrubbing the remaining dishes, when Alec approached her.

"Feeling okay, dear?" she asked, setting down the plate she had been scrubbing, which was caked with leftover black pudding. She approached him, placing a hand on his forehead, as she usually did when Alec looked pale.

Alec slowly looked up at her, meeting her gaze. "Jessica..." he said, his expression blank.

"Why, you haven't called me that in years, dear... what's-

"Are you really my mother?" he interjected, speaking softly, slowly brushing her hand away from his brow.

Jessica noticeably paled before she turned away, returning to the dishes.

Alec merely gazed at her back, unmoving.

"O-Of course, dear!" She stuttered. "You were born in this very inn!" She scrambled for words. "What brings up such a silly question?"

Alec approached her, placing a hand on her back. "Jessica..." Alec began.

"Please Alec, don't call me that, you're my firstborn son!" She said, desperation in her voice.

"Who is Matthias, and who is Xen'trath?"

Jessica suddenly tensed, dropping the plate she had been washing, causing it to shatter into a million pieces on the floor. She swiftly turned, kneeling down to Alec.

"Alec, please don't concern yourself with such." She placed her hands gently on his shoulders. "You're still far too young." Jessica's gaze was penetrating, her expression turning to one of fear as she saw the coloration in Alec's eyes had shifted, to a deep shade of blue.

So that day has finally come, she thought to herself, gazing down at the reversed symbol on Alec's palm. *She's unlocked the pendulum binding, that deep blue... sadness...*

"Now, I need you to clean some tables for me, dear," she said, changing the subject as she handed him a damp towel.

Alec sighed with a slow nod before he took the towel from her, leaving the kitchen.

Jessica breathed a tense sigh, still shaken by the revelation that time was running out. Alec was beginning to see the truth of things. The dawn strider would not undo the binding without good reason, after all, she thought to herself. Her mind drifted back to the previous evening, having had Makkari fight his way through the forest to Matthias's location, so determined to reach him, he must have slain a hundred giests with his bare hands; thankfully, the Litch did not make its appearance.

Their reuniting had been tedious, Makkari having been enraged that he was kept in the dark for so long; yet sorrow had filled the big man's eyes upon learning that his comrade was on the verge of death.

Jessica had avoided fighting, having vowed against bloodshed unless absolutely necessary ever since the Great War, so long ago.

"It's been a long time, brother," Matthias had said with labored breath.

"Do you know how long I've thought you dead?" Makkari boomed. "I severed my wings out of shame at having not joined you in the afterlife, to learn that you still lived!"

"Please understand, brother, it was a necessity that I remained hidden," Matthias had explained. "Xen'trath still lives, and he plots, even as we speak."

Makkari struck the stone wall hard with his fist, causing it to crack, as his knuckles bled from the impact. "That monster, still lives, still breathes and you just sit here?" Makkari scoffed.

"There is nothing more I can do, brother," Matthias answered, taking a sip from the water skin he had at his side. "I transferred the warden to the boy; he is the key to everything, the new master of the flows of time now."

"A mere pup—he is unable to control such power, such responsibility!" Makkari spoke heatedly.

"We have no time to argue, dear brother. Time runs short for me. The dawn strider is growing weak; if she should die, I would soon join her. My ties to this timeline are through her alone; even now, I suffer from time sickness. Two wardens can never exist in one time period, even if they no longer possess their power. Their bodies are forever altered by the warden's energy."

"I find you to have survived, and yet you are dying..." Makkari breathed.

"Irony at its finest," Matthias chuckled. "How is my sister, might I ask? She's usually with you at all times."

"Watching over the boy. The strider activated the rune for the pendulum. His body is adjusting to the newfound energies. He collapsed into a state of unconsciousness."

"I see. Please, give her my regards. It has been so long since I've seen little Ashylanya."

Makkari nodded, as Jessica remained silent through the entire conversation.

Two hours later, the sun had begun to rise, the geists having dispersed to the shadows, and the trip back was far smoother due to this.

Makkari and Jessica had remained silent the entire way back to the village. The leaves of the tall red-leaf oaks swayed in the gentle breeze, as the sun's light slowly bathed the forest in its ascent. The distant song of the mocking birds was the only other source of resonance within the otherwise quiet forest.

Jessica sighed, coming out of her daze. Returning to the sink, she continued to wash the soiled dishes, her mind troubled with what was to come, sooner than she had anticipated.

Chapter Ten

"You have disappointed me, Zel'nurath..." spoke the guttural voice of Xen'trath, as he paced before the kneeling Litch.

Sparse lighting illuminated the depths of the cavern through the canopy of towering oaks, casting shadows that resembled mangled and twisted arms within the cavern's depths, a faded rust color as the rising sun shone through, revealing little.

The echoing sound of Xen'trath's booted feet could be heard throughout the cavern as the large man paced, a grimace upon his gnarled visage.

"F-forgive me, master..." a familiar hollow voice echoed within. "There was someone else there, the wretched dawn strider—she cloaked him from us..." Zel'nurath explained quickly.

"You know very well what happens to those who speak out of turn." Xen'trath's hollow voice turned cruel as he casually tossed the severed head of a geist at the man's knees, spattering him with blood. The tongue had been violently removed.

"N-no!" Zel'nurath's deathly voice pled. "I have not completely failed you, master! Here, I bring you the dark sphere; the boy supplied it with ample energy for your use!" The Litch withdrew the stone from his robe quickly, showing it to Xen'trath.

"See master? I have done well!" Zel'nurath stuttered.

A wide grin now etched Xen'trath's face as he looked down upon his servant. "There is only one missing necessity..." he hissed.

"And what would that be, milord?" the Litch asked, looking Xen'trath in the eyes.

"The bones of a Litch…" Xen'trath sneered.

"No…" Zel'nurath now groveled before his master's feet. "Spare me master, I beg of you!"

Xen'trath chortled; his malformed grin was all that could be seen from the shadows.

Slowly Xen'trath raised one gnarled looking claw, and the Litch's skeletal frame began to crack as large black blisters formed where marrow seemed to be trying to escape from intense pressure.

The servant looked up a final time, desperately pleading for his life, before his body exploded, leaving behind not more than a long bone fragment, that of a narrow shin, as well as the dark crystal, on the otherwise charred stone floor where the Litch once knelt.

Xen'trath retrieved the stone and the shin bone from the floor, lifting the orb high above his head, his eyes narrowing. "Perfect—the child has served my purpose well, as have you, Shelara…" Xen'trath said, turning toward the cloaked figure of the elf, who now stood behind him.

Shelara knelt before her master as if forced to do so.

"Were you followed?" Xen'trath demanded. "Answer quickly, or be punished."

"No, milord," came the hurried reply of the cloaked female elf. "I did exactly as you asked; the boy suspected absolutely nothing."

"Excellent…" Xen'trath hissed. "And the boy's exact location?"

"Sevelan, milord; thanks to the energy signals he's given off, he might as well be a bonfire in a dark forest," she replied, her head lowered.

"This time, we are sure that we have found the correct bearer," Xen'trath sneered. "This energy locked within the prism is most definitely that of Xanadair, the fabled warden."

Shelara nodded.

"Did you get a good look at the marking on the boy's hand?" he demanded, eyeing his servant.

"Yes, though the pattern is different than its usual matrix. It seems designed to mislead us. Two of the symbols, the three and the nine symbols, face outward, while all the others face inward."

"Matthias intended to mislead us, it appears, by masking the boy's energies," Xen'trath said, pacing before his servant.

"Though as of last night, there has been a sudden spike in the energy the warden is releasing; something has changed," Shelara said, her head still lowered forcefully.

"The strider has released the pendulum," Xen'trath said with a grin. "I am aware."

"That could prove to be bothersome, really..." Shelara replied.

"Not quite; it is doubtful the boy has grasped how to use this ability as of yet, so this is to our advantage," Xen'trath interjected.

"Indeed, lord Xen'trath..." Shelara said, raising her head as the weight was lifted from it.

"Take the Litch's bone and the orb; you know what to do with them," Xen'trath ordered, eyeing his servant. "The only weakness in the strider is the warden's energy itself. Have Hydenforge craft an arrow from the Litch's bone. The orb must be forged into a point; it is malleable."

"An arrow, milord?" Shelara asked curiously.

"I resurrected the three of you for a reason...Garren will forge the arrow capable of permeating the Dawn Strider's protective field, and for that, I needed you, the finest archer of the entire sky kingdom, and your twin, the finest strategist within the kingdom to devise the plan of action," Xen'trath explained. "That, and you three, are the only ones who stand a chance to weaken the Reaper's toll for me, allowing me to slay her."

Silence hung in the air momentarily upon mention of the Reaper's toll. Shelara seemed to waver slightly, as if knowing just what she was resurrected to do.

"I will do as you wish, milord," Shelara said, forcefully, with a bow, before quickly vanishing.

Xen'trath turned slowly toward the depths of the cavern. "Soon master, the boy will be yours..." His voice became darker as he spoke. "We strike, at dusk!" Xen'trath 's shout was returned with a cacophony of roars of what appeared to be near a thousand cultists, mixed with corpse-like beasts, their claws grating eagerly with the anticipation of bloodshed.

"Soon…" Xen'trath spoke. "So very soon…" Xen'trath's harsh laughter echoed through the cavern, which seemed to reverberate through the now living walls.

"Xen'trath…" spoke a sudden voice in the beast's skull. "Be wary of the Reaper's toll."

Xen'trath grinned. "What purpose did I resurrect the three long dead heroes for, if not to deal with that nuisance?" Xen'trath spoke; a large pair of blood red eyes had appeared before him.

"She collaborates with Matthias… do not let your guard down," the demonic voice echoed.

"Matthias will no longer be a threat; all too soon… the dawn strider shall fall."

"You had better not fail me, Xen'trath." The voice hissed in his mind.

Xen'trath grinned, walking toward the mouth of the cave. One large Antler protruded from a hole in the hood of his cloak, the other merely a Lichen's ear, on the opposite side of his head. The light of the sun contrasted harshly with Xen'trath's marred face. His cracked lips stretched wide in a grin, revealing razor sharp teeth. His eyes narrowed as he gazed just beyond at the village of Sevelan in the distance.

"You will have the warden in your grasp soon enough, master…"

By mid-day Alec had finished the tasks his mother had given him, having decided to put the endless questions he had out of his mind for the moment. He set the damp cloth on the bar counter, turning toward the door.

"Alec…" said Jessica, who had quietly come up behind him as he had his hand on the doorknob.

Alec turned to face her as she embraced him in a lengthy hug. "I love you—you know that, right?" she said with a broken voice.

Alec smiled up at her. "Of course, Mum… regardless of anything, you were the one who raised me," Alec said, his voice quiet.

A single tear rolled down Jessica's cheek at those words. "Be careful out there, Alec. I'll tell you all you wish to know later," she said solemnly.

"Thank you," he replied, opening the door to the inn, letting in the warm breeze which wafted through the village, and shutting it behind him. The pungent scent of the bakery could be caught upon the wind even from afar, enticing to all those who caught the scent. The many cakes and pies the bakers made were always popular amongst the village. Alec himself would indulge in a sweet hotcake when Jessica sent him to the market, which was often.

"There you are!" said Lucy, who was sitting on a bench just outside the inn, looking annoyed. She cast him a sidelong glance, her expression softening upon seeing the look on Alec's face.

"Alec, are you okay?" she asked, standing. "You look awful!"

"I'm okay," Alec replied with a forced smile.

"Please Alec, you can talk to me," she persisted. "Even one as daft as an ogre can see that you're bluffing!" Lucy reached for Alec's arm, but he pulled away.

"It's just too much to explain right now; besides, aren't the others waiting on us?" Alec asked, casting a glance over his shoulder to see Ashylanya standing against the wall of the inn. She seemed to be reciting a prayer, her eyes tightly shut.

"I'm just worried about you, Alec," Lucy said, attempting to place a hand on his shoulder.

"Oh, will you just drop it?" he shouted, a disgruntled look upon his face.

That was a mistake; Lucy backed away, tears welling in her eyes. She turned quickly, before sprinting toward the forest.

"Lucy, wait!" Alec called after her. "I'm sorry!" His plea fell on deaf ears, as Lucy vanished beneath the underbrush.

A wave of dread now crept over him, knowing what was within those woods.

Panicked, Alec began to charge after her, but was halted by Gabriel and Sam, who had run up to him, leaving the path.

"Alec, what happened?" Sam asked. "I watched sis charge into the forest alone!"

"She said to meet her here, but why would she go in alone?" Gabriel asked. Seeing the look on Alec's face, Gabriel became worried.

Ashylanya, having finished her prayer, sprinted up behind them. "Alec, she didn't go into the forest, did she?" she asked, her expression one of fear.

Alec nodded.

"Then we have to follow her quickly!" Ashylanya exclaimed. "That forest is crawling with hostile shade geists!"

Alec froze, fear overwhelming him. "She charged into the forest. I just wanted her to stop asking me about what was bothering me was all!" Alec explained, before turning and breaking into a run. "We have to find her!" he shouted.

"Wait, what is a shade geist?" Gabriel called after him, but he had already disappeared into the forest, Ashylanya at his heels.

Sam let out a disgruntled sigh as he began to run after them.

"But are they dangerous?" Gabriel shouted after Sam, trying to keep up with him.

"Oh shut it, how bad can it really be?" Sam replied, breathing heavily. "The geists have always left people alone, after all."

Gabriel merely shook his head as they picked up speed, vanishing into the scarlet canopy.

Chapter Eleven

Lucy, having become too fatigued to run anymore, had taken seat beneath a large oak tree to rest. The forest around her was deathly quiet, as suspicious shadows flickered occasionally on the periphery of her vision within the plethora of red oaks.

"Hmph, who needs boys anyway..." she muttered to herself under her breath, her face tearstained. "I'll find out what's going on, on my own."

"Whoever needed men anyway...?" A sudden feminine voice spoke musically, permeating Lucy's surroundings, with a faint echo.

"W-who's there?" Lucy stuttered, slowly moving her hand over a moss-covered stone.

"Men—quite bothersome creatures, really..." the woman's voice cooed. "Oh, a rock of that size won't do dear; perhaps you stand a better chance with that branch, just over there?" Her voice seemed to ring with a note of humor as she spoke.

Lucy slowly turned her head. A tall and slender looking female who had not been there a moment before had suddenly appeared. Two others were with her, the hoods of their cloaks drawn low.

Lucy had only ever read about sky elves in old books; not ever having expected to encounter one in real life, she was awestruck.

The woman was well over six feet in height. A long mane of silky azure hair, which fell to her mid-back, hung limply about her arched shoulders, framing a pale yet stunningly attractive face. A runic symbol was tattooed upon her right cheek; a low-hanging trim partially covered her lifeless looking eyes, shrouded in darkness, a hollow amber glow within them, resembling dim lights at the nethermost recesses of an endless chasm.

The woman had long curved ears, which graced her features elegantly. Her arms were folded against her chest; visible cleavage could be seen through a tightly knit mahogany tunic. A black leather belt crested with symbols of elfish kind hung about her waist loosely, paired with black leather breeches.

The woman's pale lips parted in a mischievous grin as she watched Lucy tremble before her.

"W-who are you?" Lucy asked, hesitantly.

"My, my—isn't it proper courtesy to offer your own name first?" she replied, with a light chuckle.

"I'm not sure I'll oblige." Lucy's voice was now high-pitched, with a note of fear.

"Oh dear, then I'm afraid this won't be a proper introduction… Quite bothersome, really." Her eyes narrowed slightly as she spoke.

"Well, not that I don't wish to continue our little conversation," Lucy began, rising. "But I really think I should be off now!"

To Lucy's shock, her legs would not move. Feeling as though the world were now spinning around her, she fell back against the tree with a low whimper.

"Seems that we're at a bit of an impasse then…" The woman's voice darkened. "I cannot simply let you leave."

Lucy's gaze drifted sluggishly toward the woman, fear overwhelming her as her vision began to blur.

"You see that plant there, which you so carelessly sat upon?" The woman gestured, with her head. "Xeneth root takes effect rather quickly upon standing up, I'm sure you can agree to that," she cooed, as she slowly approached Lucy. The other two cloaked men followed suit.

"Don't worry, you won't be harmed." Her voice sounded faint to Lucy as she began to drift out of consciousness. "The master has plans for you, little Lucy…"

As Lucy lost consciousness, the woman turned away, as the other two kneeled down to lift her from the earth.

"Shelara, by the way…" the woman introduced herself. "Not that it matters, anyway."

As Lucy fell limp, the stoutest of the three hoisted the sleeping girl over his shoulder.

"Be careful with her, Garren," Shelara said, turning her head toward the dwarfish man. "The master specifically stated that she be unharmed."

"Aye, I 'erd 'im." The man spoke in a thick tone.

"Lehion, I leave the rest to you," Shelara stated, walking off into the forest.

The taller man sighed. "Always being left to do the dirty work," he complained. Lifting the collar of Lucy's shirt, he etched a symbol on the nape of her neck with the tip of his finger. "Bring her," he said, turning to follow Shelara.

Garren merely nodded, following the taller elfish man, halting momentarily at the sound of heavy footfalls.

Garren turned his head to see two figures charging past without notice, yet another trait of being dead yet alive again at the same time: one may choose to be seen. Garren did not seem inclined to follow the pair as they charged off in the opposite direction; not feeling the need to reveal himself to them, he merely shrugged, following Lehion, who beckoned the dwarf.

"Don't ye treat me like some pup," Garren scoffed, crinkling what was visible of his bearded face.

"Shelara's captured another, you fool," Lehion retorted.

"Already?" Garren seemed surprised. "That lass, always so damned proficient," the dwarf muttered, as he followed Lehion.

"She's close!" Ashylanya called from behind Alec. "I can catch her scent on the wind!"

Alec had stopped to catch his breath; having run through the forest without pause for thirty minutes, he breathed heavily.

Ashylanya, however, seemed unaffected as she stopped next to him, taking a moment to examine her surroundings.

"She came through here," Ashylanya said, stooping to retrieve a snapped twig nestled into the lush earth beneath them. "Though there is also the scent of three others; the stench of death hovers in this area," Ashylanya observed. "She was taken from here by someone."

"Lucy?" Alec called, only to hear the distant chirping of the mockingbirds in the distance.

Alec turned his head toward Ashylanya. He froze as he observed her being impaled by razor sharp claws, the blade-like hands protruding through her abdomen, a pale beast standing directly behind her.

"Ashylanya!" Alec cried.

"What is it, Alec?" she asked, eyeing him with unease, seeing that his eyes had taken the shape of hourglasses once more. The beast, which had been unmistakably been a shade geist, faded away.

Alec suddenly tackled Ashylanya into a damp thicket as the same geist narrowly missed recreating the macabre scene for a second time.

Ashylanya's eyes met his own briefly, her cheeks turning a rosy pink as Alec realized he was lying directly on top of her. Quickly he rolled aside with her as the geist pounced, catching its claws in the trunk of the sturdy looking oak.

"C'mon!" Alec blurted, springing to his feet and pulling Ashylanya with him as they fled deeper into the forest, the geist struggling to free itself from the timber.

As they ran, the shadows within the forest sprang to life, as more shade geists joined the pursuit. Countless trees flitted by as they ran at top speed through the ever-darkening forest, as deep black clouds rolled in like smoke in the skies above. Howling wind had begun to billow through the timber as a violent storm encroached upon them, as they ran.

"We have to get back to your village and warn them before it's too late!" Ashylanya shouted over the now deafening wind.

"But what about the others?" Alec called back, as he slammed head-first into Sam not a moment later, who had darted from behind a tree, causing them both to fall backwards.

Alec was momentarily dazed as he tried to get to his feet. Sam seemed to be shouting something, but he could not hear him over the earsplitting ringing that now filled his head.

Sam grabbed Alec by the arm and hoisted him up with Ashylanya's help, as they began to move at a fast pace.

As Alec regained his composure, he noticed Sam's left arm, which was bleeding freely from a deep gash.

"Sam, your arm!" Alec muttered, barely audible.

"Geist got me," Sam quickly replied. "Took me by surprise; I hadn't expected them to attack!" he panted. "I'll explain on the way, but for now, can you walk?"

Alec nodded as Sam lowered him to the ground.

"We have to get back to the village!" Sam blurted as they charged through the forest. "But first, we have to lose them!" Sam gestured at the writhing mass now behind them, in fast pursuit.

"How!?" Alec shouted over the wind.

"I've got an idea—well, an idea was given to me by someone I encountered in the woods along the way!" Sam explained. "An angelic woman with blue hair!"

Alec and Ashylanya glanced at each other as they continued.

A geist leapt toward Sam, only to be caught in midair, Sam having braced his good arm, knocking the wind out of the beast, sending him flying backward with a loud crack against a large boulder.

"What are you two staring at?" Sam blurted, seeing the look on their faces. "I told you, I'll explain on the way! We have to move!"

The three broke into a run as a deep fog seemed to slowly creep through the forest. Heavy rain had begun to pelt the trio; wild veins of lightning streaked the skies, followed by low rolls of deep thunder. The geists had now flooded the forest entirely, seeming to pour from every direction.

"Just a bit farther!" Sam called back over the now roaring storm which assailed them. "The clearing! We have to make it there!"

"Are you mad, Sam?" Alec spat. "We'll be totally surrounded!"

"Just trust me, the star-lit woman has a plan!" he called back, narrowly missing colliding with a tree, having not paid attention.

The geists had now become a mass of endless proportions, surrounding them on all sides as they entered the clearing. The three youth panted heavily as heavy rain drenched them to the bone.

"We're surrounded, Sam!" Ashylanya huffed. "What plan do you have that can get us out of this one?"

Sam suddenly looked frightened. "Where is she?" he exclaimed, scanning the perimeter.

The geists now had formed a wall on all sides of the trio, closing in slowly, their blade-like claws grating together with anticipation of bloodshed. A million eyeless faces seemed to gaze deep into the souls of the three, a sight which chilled Alec to the very marrow of his bones.

"She said she would be here!" Sam shouted exasperatedly.

"Well, they want me, don't they?" Alec said, stepping in front of the two. "Leave the others alone, and I'll go with you."

"Are you mad!?" Sam scoffed. "You're trying to reason with bloodthirsty monsters!"

Sam, however, was quieted by Alec's stiff hand.

"Alec, don't do this…" Ashylanya said, placing a firm hand on his shoulder. "You have no idea who it is you deal with."

"Then who is it then?" Alec barked, his eye color shifting to a deep orange, bordering on a dull crimson. "Who the hell is after me, exactly?"

"Alec…" Ashylanya began.

"No, I am tired of being kept in the dark; I want to know right now!" Alec shouted, his anger rising as his eyes slowly took on a full crimson color.

Alec had failed to notice the wall of geists was drawing closer to them, ignoring his offer of self-sacrifice; their grating claws generated an eerie harmony as they grew more eager for their prey.

"So this is it then…" Alec muttered. "We're going to die here."

"Alec…" Sam began, his eyes fixated on the skies above.

"What, what is it?" Alec said heatedly. "What could possibly be-"

Alec stopped talking as he too now gazed into the sky, where a bright light now radiated directly above, illuminating their surroundings in a ghostly light.

"Get down!" Ashylanya cried, withdrawing her pendant as she threw herself against the two, bringing them down against the earth.

Ashylanya's pendant shone a pure white light, as Alec's mark did the same. An agonizing pain split his skull as his palm throbbed heavily.

Opening one eye, Alec watched in awe as the creatures before them turned to dust, one by one, as time seemed to slow.

A great white inferno billowed down from the sky, passing over three harmlessly, merely cascading down the walls of what appeared to be a large spherical dome, which protected them from the flames' wake.

The inferno died down moments later, leaving only a large ring of char behind as it dissipated, having disintegrated all in its path; even the once proud trees, which had stood a moment before in the clearing, were burnt to no more than piles of ash.

"What in god's name was that?" Sam asked, slowly getting to his feet, dusting himself off. He received no response, however, as Alec and Ashylanya were fixated upon who was before them.

"No..." Ashylanya gasped, seeing that the woman of starlight stood before them. A single arrow had penetrated her chest, as azure-colored blood oozed from the fresh wound.

Alec fell silent, slowly walking toward the woman before him, who wore a saddened smile, her breathing now labored, as the arrow had punctured her lung.

Tripping over his own feet, Alec fell into the woman's arms.

"W-who are you...?" he asked, gazing up into her large eyes of pure turquoise, the color having shifted, just as Alec's had.

Alec's eyes were a deep blue now as he gazed into her eyes, tears rolling down his cheeks.

The woman merely smiled, a sad expression upon her face, as a single tear rolled down her soft, pale cheek. She embraced him gently before abruptly dispersing into an array of miniature stars, which slowly ascended to the heavens above. All that was left behind was the blackened arrow that had slain her.

Ashylanya drew near to Alec, who stood gazing down at the arrow, before his eyes shifted to the stars, which slowly drifted away, dispersing one after another. "You know now who she was, don't you?" Ashylanya asked coming to his side.

Alec nodded wordlessly as his gaze returned to the arrow lying in the charred earth before him. Alec felt rage build inside him as he scanned the perimeter for the culprit in the death of his own true mother.

"She gave the last of her energy to protect you... entrusting me to use my pendant to shield you from the flame of her dying light."

Alec slowly turned his head toward Ashylanya. "She's not coming back again, is she?"

"I'm sorry, Alec..." Ashylanya replied. "She was taken off guard; whoever crafted this arrow is a fine smith, and the head of the arrow—I recognize the energy; it was in your possession at our first meeting." Ashylanya said, observing the arrow. "Litch bone shaft... I know who did this; there is only one with the expertise to fashion such an arrow, and what's most troubling is, he died long ago."

"Well then, we find him!" Alec blurted. Still trying to pinpoint where the arrow had been fired from, his vision shifted again; as he caught sight of an energy signature in the distance momentarily, Gabriel's own energy was close by, along with that of a something reanimated by necromancy. "There!" Alec shouted, pointing in the direction of the energy source.

But before Alec could take another step, the energy signature simply vanished, leaving Alec blind to the killer of his mother.

"Whoever it was, they have Gabriel!" Alec exclaimed.

"We cannot follow them," Ashylanya said, placing her hand on Alec's arm. "If they are who I think they are, we stand no chance against them. We have to get back to the village and warn the others."

Sam glanced at Alec with a confused expression. "How did you know where they were, Alec?" he asked curiously.

"No time to explain," Alec said flatly. "Let's get moving then."

Sam nodded absentmindedly, eyeing Alec. "If you say so," he huffed.

The storm had let up momentarily, leaving the clearing deathly quiet. The heavy clouds loomed above as if at any moment they could hail upon the trio once more.

Alec stood there for a moment, gazing down at the palm of his hand. Hot tears rolled freely down his cheeks, and he failed to notice that one of the twelve runic markings on his palm was nearly faded away entirely.

"The runes are fading..." Ashylanya gasped. "That should not be possible..."

Alec did not reply as he brushed past her, heading toward the untouched canopy of trees. Ashylanya stood there momentarily before following Alec back into the forest.

Somewhere in the distance, a cloaked figure watched Alec from behind a badly scorched oak as he left the clearing.

A saddened expression graced the shadowed features of Shelara before she harnessed her bow, lifting Gabriel with ease. Having masked their energies with a simple rune, she disappeared into the shadows.

"What's the matter with you now?" Sam asked, seeing Alec's tearstained cheeks as he approached.

But Alec ignored the question as he continued to walk. "We have to get back to the village and get help," Alec said, casting Sam a sidelong glance. "It's our only chance of saving Gabriel, and since they have him, I would wager they also have Lucy."

Sam paled at those words. "Little sis..." he breathed. "What the hell are we waiting for?" Sam said, charging off into the forest.

Ashylanya seemed perturbed by the aura she sensed earlier during the strider's display of her power; the familiarity of those energy signals chilled her.

"If we don't hurry, I don't know how long they will last," Ashylanya said, glancing at Alec as they began to increase their pace.

"Then we have to go back for them! There's no time to get help!" Alec exclaimed, turning on his heel.

But Ashylanya grasped his wrist, halting him. "And we will go back for them," she said reassuringly. "But we need to get help first, more than ever now, knowing just who we are dealing with. There is only one who stands a chance against them."

Alec lowered his head in defeat. "Well then, what are we waiting on?" he said, before breaking into a run, close at Sam's heels.

Ashylanya stood there for a moment, watching them.

"I don't think anything will be enough to stop him now... with the three heroes of legend as his puppets..." she breathed before following them.

As Alec walked through the forest, a sudden voice echoed through his mind. "It's all your fault, you know..." Alec was suddenly overwhelmed by a crushing presence as a mocking voice filled his mind; he glanced through his surroundings, meeting Sam's gaze, his eyes having become hollow pits in his skull, as his facial features became obscure.

Alec suddenly felt hot, as if he were going to burst into flames at that moment, his vision shifting rapidly, overwhelming his senses.

"Your fault they are in danger..." the voice continued coolly. "Your fault that they are in my hands already..."

"Shut up!" Alec cried, falling to his knees, his eye color changing rapidly to pale amber, his pupils forming into the shape of hourglasses as he witnessed Lucy being tortured by a large man in a dark cave. Alec cried out.

The voice chuckled darkly. "Your suffering will soon end, once you are mine!" the voice boomed. Suddenly the presence disappeared, leaving Alec gasping on the forest floor.

"Alec, are you all right?" Sam asked, kneeling at his side.

Alec looked up at Sam momentarily, his face having reverted to normal. "I-I'm fine... let's just get the hell out of here!"

Ashylanya had caught up with them, her gaze fixed on Alec. "Your pupils are starting to take on the permanent effects of the pendulum," she breathed, gazing at the small twin hourglasses in Alec's eyes.

"The episodes are getting worse," Sam said, eyeing her. "What the hell is going on with him?"

"The seal on his palm is unraveling…" she replied with a grim expression.

"And what does that mean?" he persisted.

Alec's legs suddenly gave way, and he fell to his knees. Ashylanya hurried to his side to catch him before he fell unconscious in her arms.

"The strider is gone now; there is no longer anyone holding the balance in check," she replied hurriedly. "Grab his other arm, Sam, was it?"

Sam nodded, moving to Alec's left and hoisting him over his shoulders. "I have him, don't worry."

"But your arm…" Ashylanya gestured at Sam's still bleeding arm, walking toward him.

"Don't mention it; I'll be fine," he replied, wincing from the obvious pain he was trying to hold back.

"At least let me wrap it, so it doesn't get infected!" Ashylanya offered, tearing off the hem of her blouse.

Sam nodded reluctantly as he held out his arm. Taking his arm carefully, she wrapped it tightly to stem the bleeding. "This should help, for now at least."

"Who are you, anyway?" Sam interjected. "None of this was happening before you and your friend showed up," he said in an accusing tone. "Everything was peaceful…"

Ashylanya gave Sam a hurt look before letting out a broken sigh. "You're right…" she said quietly.

After she had finished wrapping his arm, Sam stood up with Alec and began to walk, wordlessly.

"I'm so sorry…" Ashylanya breathed.

But Sam ignored her.

Chapter Twelve

Lucy began to stir, slowly opening her eyes; she was greeted by total darkness, lying on a cold stony surface with her hands tied behind her back. She groaned, sitting upright as she tried to identify her surroundings.

"Ah… Finally awake, my dear?" spoke a guttural voice in her vicinity, echoing throughout the cavernous location she found herself in.

Lucy saw someone appear before her, as she slowly lifted her head toward the towering figure. She screamed at the sight of the man's face.

"Now that's not very polite of you…quite hurtful, actually." The twisted face of Xen'trath loomed before her with a feigned expression of sadness mixed with humor.

"W-who are you…?" Lucy squeaked, averting her eyes.

Xen'trath grabbed hold of her face with one gnarled claw, turning her head. "You will show me proper respect, worm," he leered. "After all, a fisherman never introduced himself to his bait before, now did he?" Xen'trath bore an all too familiar twisted grin upon his scarred face as he spoke.

"B-bait?" Lucy asked, hesitantly.

"Indeed, you shall be perfect to draw out the bearer…" Xen'trath sneered, his gaze penetrating Lucy's very core.

"I-I don't know what you're talking about…" Lucy said, carefully working at the bonds which held her hands firmly in place.

"Though it wouldn't be fun to miss out on the opportunity to shed blood… I merely told you a plan I've cast aside… though I still have use for you, my little human," Xen'trath hissed, "you and the other little one they are currently bringing to me."

"W-wait, you have more than just me?" Lucy's voice was filled with terror.

"Indeed..." Xen'trath's grin widened again. "Pudgy little boy..."

"Gabriel..." she gasped.

Xen'trath seemed to be lost in his own fantasizing now, muttering to himself. "No... I think I'll destroy your pathetic little village, regardless..." Xen'trath spoke as though he were a madman, cackling to himself at the very thought, a look of glee etched on his macabre features.

Lucy froze at what he had just told her. "N-no! Leave them alone, you monster!" she screamed, trembling with fear.

"Ah... such familiar words—I believe that's what his surrogate mother said, right before my blade rent her flesh..." Xen'trath seemed to be lost in his own fantasy of murder and chaos.

"W-whose surrogate?" Lucy stuttered.

"Why, the bearer, of course..." Xen'trath hissed.

"Alec...?" Lucy breathed, without thinking. "You're insane!"

Xen'trath cackled at that statement. "An understatement, I assure you," he replied, his eyes narrowing. "I really must thank you though—wasn't sure what name they had called it this time."

"I'm such an idiot..." Lucy muttered under her breath.

"That should make it slightly easier to catch, now that you've narrowed it down for me." Xen'trath was lost in thought again, his eyes closed. "Ah, Sevelan, such a small and defenseless little village." He spoke in a hollow tone. "A pity, it won't be as fun to burn it to the ground." Xen'trath seemed disturbingly disappointed by this fact. "Only one in that village is even a threat to me, and I've already got cards to play to put her in check..."

"It? Alec isn't a thing; he's a human being, just like me!" Lucy shot.

Xen'trath laughed manically at those words, his fiery gaze returning to Lucy. "I don't believe you know just how wrong you are, little girl," he spat. "He is far from you and your little friends; in fact, he's far from being human at all..."

"You're lying!" she barked, before turning her head in time to see Gabriel tossed carelessly onto the floor beside her.

A trio of figures now stood at the cavern's mouth.

Lucy gasped, attempting to inch her way to Gabriel's side.

"You've returned..." Xen'trath said, turning toward the three.

"Yes, my lord." Shelara, the head of the three, spoke.

"YOU!" Lucy shrieked.

Xen'trath raised his clawed hand with lightning speed, snapping his fingers.

Lucy tried to speak, but found her jaw was now immobile.

"What have you discovered?" Xen'trath demanded.

"The lad was in the forest with this one." Garren spoke, kicking Gabriel with a booted foot.

Lucy squealed at this, tears running down her cheeks, as she rubbed her wrists raw against her bonds.

"We let the others go, just as ye commanded, lord Xen'trath," he finished, ignoring Lucy's interruption.

"All goes according to plan then?" Xen'trath hissed, his grin broadening.

"Yes milord, though we lost a very large portion of our geists to the dawn strider." Lehion spoke now.

Xen'trath's grin widened even further at these words. "Which means..."

"The dawn strider took the bait, milord; I felled her personally," Shelara replied, though the expression she wore was one of sadness, as opposed to glee.

Xen'trath appeared to be ecstatic at this news; his face contorted to that of a madman. "Then the geists have served their purpose."

"Sorry milord?" Lehion replied, in shock. "Half of our forces have been obliterated; how can this be good news?"

"Hold your tongue, whelp; you will speak when spoken to." Xen'trath scowled before beckoning Shelara closer, to have her whisper in his ear.

"Forgive me, milord," the man quickly replied, wavering.

"You are forgiven, solely because you did not disappoint me," Xen'trath said, seemingly filled with joy at the news he had received.

Slowly Xen'trath lifted his claw toward the taller man. "But you will not go unpunished."

The man let out an agonizing cry as he fell to his knees.

"Let this be a warning to you," he said, lowering his arm not a moment later.

"Y-yes...milord," Lehion gasped in relief.

"The boy lives, for now..." Xen'trath said, pacing before the three. "I will make him watch as his precious village crumbles before him."

Lucy whimpered as Xen'trath turned his attention to her, approaching her.

"As for you, my dear..." Xen'trath's voice grated her ears as he spoke. "I have a very special part for you to play in this little drama..."

Lucy looked up at him in terror before her eyelids began to feel heavy, her body falling limp as she lost consciousness.

"Prepare the others..." Xen'trath ordered, turning his head toward the trio. "The hour is upon us... the dawn strider... IS DEAD!" he shouted in triumph.

The sun had begun to set, though hardly visible through the gloomy skies above. Scarce shafts of sunlight escaped through the breaches in the clouds, illuminating the small village in the distance. The vast expanse of trees swayed ominously in the rising tempest, giving the appearance of a vast sea of glimmering rubies upon an ever-darkening horizon.

Somewhere in the distance, Matthias cried out in agony as his limbs slowly began to blacken before his eyes, the corruption he had fought so hard to hold back now eating away at his form. The final glimmering light of his left eye's hourglass began to fade away into a deep crimson as he coughed, blood spattering the walls of the cavern. Slowly, Matthias rose; walking toward the hidden passageway, he opened it, walking out.

Matthias grasped at the walls of the cavern as he walked, to keep himself steady.

"The strider has fallen… there is still one more thing I must do…" Matthias wheezed, coughing again.

The weakened warden slowly approached the mouth of the cavern, inserting his hand into the center of a dais on the entryway. Upon his touch a vast array of lines slowly lit up, glowing blue as they snaked along the aged stone, a large hourglass symbol within the center illuminating brightly at his touch.

Slowly the walls of the cavern gave way, opening the doorway to the hidden location within the woods.

Matthias took a shallow breath as he exited his place of hiding, for the first time in what felt like centuries. His pace was labored, as he slowly made his way through the forest, gripping the sturdy oaks for support. His gaze caught the charred remains of a large patch of forest in the distance.

"There…" Matthias huffed, almost stumbling in the direction of the strider's final resting place.

"Ceri… You will have vengeance…" Matthias spoke the strider's name for the first time in generations, as if speaking her name would summon her to his location. It would no longer do so; he knew deep down that the infamous Dawn Strider had fallen, and all hope for this era was lost.

After what seemed to be hours, Matthias entered the charred clearing where Ceri had fallen, his vision catching a singular arrow in the epicenter of the ashen landscape.

"The Dawn slayer's shaft…" Matthias breathed. "So it's true, the infamous three have been resurrected."

Matthias retrieved the arrow, holding it with two hands. He gazed a long moment at the very weapon that had slain a dear friend of his, and the only link Matthias still had to exist within this timeframe.

"Do you appreciate it…?" spoke the guttural voice of Xen'trath suddenly. "Such fine craftsmanship…"

Matthias slowly turned his head toward the very man who had devised the undoing of Ceri.

"You will not succeed, Xen'trath; you underestimate the boy," Matthias replied, coughing again, blood spattering the earth before him.

"Oh dear Matthias, feeling unwell, are we?" Xen'trath's mocking voice cooed.

"You will pay… for your transgressions. You no longer even retain even the slightest hint of your old self, so fallen to corruption you are," Matthias wheezed. "The boy will be your undoing."

Xen'trath laughed harshly before appearing before Matthias, kicking him hard in the ribs.

Matthias gasped in pain as Xen'trath stood over the weakened warden.

"How does it feel, Matthias?" Xen'trath hissed. "To be the weak one for a change!" He boomed, kicking Matthias again in the stomach.

Matthias crawled along the charred earth now, trying to reach the location where a small budding flower sprouted through the ashes. The final resting place of Ceri, the dawn strider, was only a few feet from him.

"How does it feel to be useless, to be pathetic, to be powerless?" Xen'trath shouted, kicking him with each phrase.

Blood now dripped from Matthias' mouth, as he continued to crawl toward the flower's location.

Just a few more feet… he thought as Xen'trath assailed him.

As Matthias reached the destination of the budding flower, he placed one finger to the earth, etching a small runic marking into the soil. *It is done…* he thought to himself, falling limp as Xen'trath's shadowy blade pierced his heart.

Matthias let out one final breath before dispersing into naught but a pile of ashes, joining the earth.

"And so ends the tale of the mighty Matthias, greatest warden of his era," Xen'trath mocked, a wide grin upon his face. "And now there is only one nuisance remaining…" Xen'trath said, looking up toward the village of Sevelan. "I'm coming for you, Reaper's toll."

Xen'trath turned, departing the scene, failing to notice the engraving Matthias had etched into the soil before the sole budding flower in the otherwise barren clearing.

A small rune pulsated, the same rune etched into Alec's palm at the eight symbol's location, which was now inverted, completing the pattern upon Alec's hand in its fullest.

"What's happening to him?" Sam asked as Alec's hand began to glow a bright gold, the symbol upon his hand changing positions.

"Matthias…" Ashylanya breathed.

Sam and Ashylanya watched in amazement at Alec's sudden transformation: a long bushy tail formed, poking a hole through his breeches, as his ears elongated to those of a wolf.

"What the hell's happening?" Sam gasped, setting him down against a large oak tree.

Ashylanya stood there in amazement as she watched Alec take on the immature Lichen form, the mature form being the full wolfish appearance of her elder brother.

"The final alteration to the seal has been undone, which means big brother…" Ashylanya fell silent, realizing what it meant—that Matthias would only undo the seal if there was no other choice.

Ashylanya closed her eyes, a single tear rolling down her cheek, realizing that her elder brother had fallen.

Chapter Thirteen

Night had fallen by the time the trio had reached Sevelan; Sam had begun to look pale due to the deep wound on his arm, which had taken on an ugly purple hue visible through the tattered cut of Ashylanya's blouse.

Ashylanya kept a close eye on him, concerned he might succumb to his wounds at any moment.

"You should let me let me carry him, for a little at least..." Ashylanya offered.

Sam, however, stubbornly refused as he continued to walk, his pace becoming labored as they slowly walked toward the village square, which was nearly empty, most having returned to their homes or sought the comforts of the town's many pubs and inns for the evening.

The occupants of the village were unsuspecting that any moment, they could be frantically defending their own lives.

By the time they had reached the inn, Ashylanya had to support Sam's weight on her shoulder as he began to weaken.

Alec grunted as Sam collapsed into the door, putting his full weight onto him before slowly turning the handle and swinging the door open. Alec's new appendage hung limp at his side. Sam dropped Alec on the hearth before collapsing midway through the doorway with a low groan.

"I see you're all back—safe and sound, I hope!" Jessica called from behind the kitchen doors.

Jessica's voice trailed off as she entered the bar through the double doors of the kitchen.

"There's no time to explain!" Ashylanya blurted. "We have to help him!"

Jessica hurried to Sam's side. Casting a quick glance at Alec, she went pale. "Matthias..." she whispered. "So that feeling from before—I was right..."

Deciding helping Sam was a priority at the present moment, Jessica turned her full attention to him, deeming that Alec was in better condition than Sam. "Hot towels, in the kitchen, dear, if you would, please!" Jessica said, turning Sam over. "Quickly, dear!"

Ashylanya nodded before disappearing through the kitchen doors.

Alec had begun to stir letting out a low groan as he rolled himself over.

"Seems like you two lost your hearing when I told you to be careful!" Jessica snapped at him as she tended to Sam.

Moments later, Ashylanya reappeared with a small wooden bucket as Jessica lifted Sam with astonishing ease, carrying him to a sturdy table within the center of the common room.

"Where are the others?" Jessica asked, casting a glance back at the door as she tended to Sam, pulling a small bottle from a leather belt hidden beneath her blouse.

Ashylanya looked to Alec, who was still in a daze as he attempted to rise from the floor. His new tail flitted in annoyance as pain wracked his body, his ears folded back.

"These wounds..." Jessica breathed as she gently removed the torn blood-soaked blouse from Sam's arm. "Only a shade geist could cause these wounds..." she said, turning her head toward Ashylanya. "You're both going to explain everything that happened; do not spare even the slightest detail!"

Ashylanya spent the next hour reliving what had occurred in the Surfire woods with Alec, Ashylanya doing most of the talking, as Alec had been fixated on what his sudden transformation had brought.

Jessica carefully cleaned Sam's arm as she listened, having already carefully spoon-fed him the contents of the small bottle.

By the end of the tale, the color had run from Jessica's face; her visage could be mistaken for an Edelion's as pale as she was. Her eyes held a note of fear within them as she began to tremble.

"No... I-It's too soon..." she breathed, clenching her fists.

Without another word, Jessica lifted Sam from the table before turning abruptly and kicking it onto its side.

"Mum, what are you-"

"There's a handle under the rug, Ashylanya dear, if you would please..." Jessica interjected.

Ashylanya nodded, moving aside the rug to reveal a hidden doorway leading downward. Slowly she pulled the handle. A low creaking groan emerged from the long unused hatch, a thick cloud of dust escaping as she lifted the heavy door, swinging it open fully.

Jessica disappeared down into the passage way of the cellar, each step she took in her descent followed by a low creaking upon the aging stairway.

Returning a moment later, she stood before the two. "Both of you," Jessica said, eyeing the two, "get inside now. I've rested Sam down there. I want you two to stay down there, and no matter what you hear, do not dare come out!"

"But-"

"No buts, you will stay down there, no matter what," Jessica said, eyeing Alec. "Understand?" Jessica's voice had a note of urgency as she spoke.

The quiet outside the inn was broken by piercing screams, and a series of explosions suddenly rocked the inn on its foundation, sending mugs and plates crashing to the floor as the thick scent of smoke now permeated the air.

"It's begun..." Jessica breathed. "Quickly, get inside now!" she shouted, grabbing hold of the two, pulling them toward the entrance.

"No," Alec said, firmly as he gazed into Jessica's eyes, his eye color shifting to pale amber.

"Alec, listen to me!" Jessica pleaded. "We are all in terrible danger-"

"I will not lose my mother twice," Alec interjected, lowering his head.

Jessica froze, tears now welling in her eyes, as Ashylanya placed her hand on Alec's own, her gaze fixed on him.

The three stood there silently for a moment as the clashing of steel echoed through the walls around them, the scent of blood and fire intermingling to create a sickening odor. Screams and frantic shouts continued within the village square.

Turning, Jessica stooped in front of Alec. Getting down onto one knee, she placed a firm hand on his arm, gripping tightly. "Alec please, I'll be okay, I promise you!" she said, her voice wavering. "You weren't supposed to know about any of this; you aren't ready for this burden!" Her tear-streaked face was now illuminated by the firelight just beyond the heavy paned windows of the inn, as cottages were set ablaze, one after another.

"I had hoped you would live a happy and carefree life here, but that is no longer possible," Jessica breathed.

Jessica embraced Alec tightly, now sobbing into his shoulder. "I love you, Alec. Don't you ever forget that: no matter what happens, I will always love you!"

They were interrupted by Liz quickly entering the inn, her dress tattered and cut, as if she had narrowly escaped an encounter with a vicious attacker.

"Jessica!" Liz wheezed. "They are everywhere!"

Jessica's attention was then turned to Liz, quickly approaching her, noting that she was grasping her side in an attempt to stem the flow of blood from her abdomen. "Liz, come with me quickly," Jessica said hurriedly. "Ashylanya, do you know how to tend to wounds?" Jessica asked, casting her a sidelong glance.

Ashylanya nodded.

"Good, now all of you, into the cellar," Jessica said firmly.

"Madam, are you unwell?" Liz asked. "Your face is tear-stained!"

"I'm fine, now please, no more talking; we have to get you all down to the cellar." Jessica spoke with urgency.

As the group made their way down to the cellar, Jessica halted Ashylanya. "You may not remember me, it was so long ago," Jessica whispered, "but please, keep them safe!"

Ashylanya nodded. "Of course, Lady of the Reaper's Toll."

"Don't call me that, please," she quickly replied. "I discarded that name long ago."

Ashylanya nodded before turning to enter the cellar, the inn shaking violently as another blast reverberated through the now fully blazing square just beyond. The smoke had become so thick it was becoming hard to breathe.

Together the four entered the cellar, Liz lagging behind due to her wounds, as they descended the staircase.

The cellar itself was long unused. Cobwebs blanketed the walls of the small windowless room, and a single table sat in its corner, where Sam rested unconscious.

After lighting the small dust-caked torches along the wall one by one, Jessica turned her head one final time toward the four, tears still in her eyes, before quickly ascending the staircase, slowly shutting the door behind her.

She quickly stooped to replace the rug to conceal the entryway, making sure that it was inconspicuous; she replaced the table over the entrance.

Jessica let out a low sigh before approaching yet another table within the room and overturning it. She quickly knelt to the floor, running two fingers along the boards before halting at a small crease in the wooden lath. Carefully she lifted open a secret compartment, revealing two very large hammers below.

The mallets were ornately designed. Runic symbols of dwarfish kind were etched into the steel, the truncheons themselves having been gifted to her by a dear old friend who had long passed on. The hilts were wrapped neatly in aged and sturdy leather which was dyed a pale maroon.

Jessica scrutinized the maces. A look of nostalgia dawned upon her aged face as she slowly reached downward to retrieve them, hoisting the mallets with ease, despite their size, from their long undisturbed hiding place.

She swung the heavy looking maces before turning toward the doorway, waiting for the barrier Matthias had created to be breached and the heavy door to give way. She waited in deathly silence as the battle cries drew closer to her.

Chapter Fourteen

"Gabriel."

A voice which sounded distant to the young man's addled mind echoed softly as he slowly began to stir, his skull throbbing from the forceful blow which had rendered him unconscious a few hours before.

"Gabriel, wake up!" The voice, which was now distinguishable as Lucy's, sounded desperate to him as he slowly opened his eyes to be greeted by near total darkness, the scattered rays of crimson from the chasms vast opening being the only source of light within.

"Lucy?" Gabriel croaked. "Is that you?" Slowly sitting upright, he turned his head toward her darkened silhouette, hardly visible before him.

"C'mon Gabriel!" Lucy muttered exasperatedly. "We have to get out of here!"

Gabriel groaned, as he slowly eyed his dim surroundings.

"Where is here exactly?" he muttered, still in a daze.

"No time to explain!" Lucy replied quickly. "I managed to free myself from my bonds, now hold still while I get yours!"

Lucy hastily cut at the rope which bound Gabriel's hands tightly together with a jagged stone she had found, successfully severing the bindings. She helped him to his feet.

Gabriel wobbled unsteadily for a moment, regaining his composure.

"You wouldn't mind freeing me as well, would you, girl?" spoke a low rasping voice from directly behind the pair.

Both Lucy and Gabriel turned toward where the voice had come from to see a haggard looking man sitting against the cold stone wall of the cavern.

"I dare say it has been rather taxing on these old bones to sit on such a hard surface!" the old man said, with a hearty chuckle.

Gabriel gave Lucy a sidelong glance, seeing her befuddled expression. "I don't recall seeing you here before…" Lucy said, her attention turning back to the old man.

"That's because I was being harnessed of my energy to create more of those foul beasts when they brought you in…" the old one replied. "Fear not, you will not come to harm, should you free me," he added, as if reading the minds of the two.

Gabriel nodded at Lucy, seeming to feel at ease in the old one's presence as she turned to approach him. The man, having maneuvered his hands as far as he could to expose the bonds, waited patiently for Lucy to cut him free.

Lucy cut at the bonds, which were engraved with a peculiar runic marking, unlike the ones that had tightly bound her own wrists. "You…" Lucy breathed, catching a glimpse of the old man's face as he edged himself forward.

"Najied, the tome keeper… how is it possible that you of all people were captured?" Lucy asked, befuddled. "Being an Arcaneight, could you not just teleport yourself away from here?"

"Ah, that would be why my bindings are engraved as such…" Najied replied, as Lucy cut away the last of the bonds on the elder's hands.

Najied let out a sigh of relief, feeling his energy returning to him as the leeching bindings were severed. "Ah, much better, thank you, dear!" Najied croaked, slowly rising with the assistance of Lucy.

He then slowly turned toward the entrance to the cavern, walking toward the gaping exit, which now resembled a large maw in the harsh contrast of the moonlight just beyond.

Halting, Najied turned his head toward the duo. "Let us be off then, shall we?"

Gabriel gave Lucy one final glance before hurriedly following the old one toward the cavern's exit.

Upon leaving the cave, the trio was met with thick smoke, which wafted through the darkened forest before them. The light of the blood-dyed moon above generated an eerie contrast to the smog now drifting through the towering trees, as a blazing light flared brightly in the distance.

Lucy gaped at the terrible sight before them, as Gabriel let out a terrible cry.

"That's in the direction of the village!" Lucy screamed, before the pair broke into a run, quickly disappearing into the underbrush.

Najied merely gazed after them. The firelight in the distance reflected in his large milky eyes as he stood there a moment more before suddenly disappearing with a small pop.

After the three had departed, a darkened shadow detached itself from the cavern, gazing after the pair, his sight focused on the runic markings he had Lehion place upon them.

The all too familiar twisted grin formed upon his darkened face, as Xen'trath raised the shaft of the arrow which was used to slay the dawn strider, plunging it into the cavern's stony surface.

An immediate reaction occurred, as the cavern seemed to suddenly come to life. "Just enough energy left..." Xen'trath hissed. "Galakrond the molten shall live once more," he said before vanishing as well, leaving behind the darkened clearing where the cavern's opening now loomed through the smoke.

A deep breath sucked in long-deprived air as the mouth of the cave began to shift, and loose stones rolled away from above its entryway, revealing a colossal snout. What looked to be searing smoke began to billow from what now appeared to be a colossal reptilian mouth, as Xen'trath's laughter echoed in the distance.

A sudden quake rocked the Red Talon as Jessica fought with poise which belied her fragile appearance. The quake caused her to lose her balance momentarily as a cultist wildly charged at her with a twisted looking dagger.

Leaping to her feet, she swung with ease the massive hammers she wielded, crushing the man's skull, the skull of the twenty-fifth cultist who proved bold enough to charge blindly into the now shambled Red Talon, where Jessica made her final stand.

Nearly every table within the inn's common room was turned on its side; shards of glass from shattered plates and mugs littered the floor of the once proud domicile.

Swinging her left truncheon low, she shattered the shins of another, drawing out a shrill cry of agony that was quickly silenced by the weight of her heavy mace, which was brought down, caving his chest.

The numbers of the cultists seemed endless as they flooded through the now shattered doorway before her.

"Twenty-eight, twenty-nine..." she muttered to herself as the onslaught continued, crushing the pelvis of yet another cultist before swinging her mace back to counter the blow of a second, larger man who had evaded her, crushing his ribs.

Her maces now shone with a dull crimson hue in contrast with the firelight as the blood of her foes trickled from them; the stench of charred flesh stung her nostrils from the burning corpses littering the village walkways.

She gracefully sidestepped another who had leapt at her from behind, attempting to impale her.

Spinning around smoothly, sweeping her attacker off his feet, she brought her mallets down upon his spine with a sickening crack.

"Thirty," she spat, as she continued her struggle.

Jessica suddenly froze, feeling the shaft of an arrow graze her left shoulder. A searing pain shot through her arm as she let out a gasp, blood flowing freely from the fresh wound.

Slowly she turned her head toward where the arrow had come from.

"Jessica the Reaper's Toll..." spoke the voice of a woman before her. "I never imagined I'd see you, of all people, in a place like this... A public servant, how unlike you..." The woman stepped from the shadows, revealing herself. "Quite bothersome, really..."

Jessica froze at the sight of the woman before her.

"I-Impossible…" Jessica breathed. "Shelara, you died… So long ago…"

"Ah, so you do remember!" Shelara replied, her voice hollow and lifeless. "It was such a cold night, eons ago."

"Shelara, what have they done to you!?" Jessica shouted, her voice wavering, as she gazed in horror at the long dead elf before her, who had an arrow aimed directly for her heart.

"You already know what—and who—is responsible. There is no more need to feign ignorance, dear sister," Shelara said, a smirk crossing her lips. "A pity, one I so valued as my closest friend is now my most powerful adversary…" Shelara finished, her lifeless features forming an expression of sorrow as she spoke.

"Shelara, you can fight this!" Jessica cried. "Remember who you were! You never would let yourself be controlled by such a cowardly spell!"

"I am truly sorry, sister, but this specific spell gives me no choice. Xen'trath has mastered the art of the Kelondrekh curse," she said dryly. "I have no more control of my own fate; I cannot disobey."

"The Kelondrekh curse—the spell that is the heart of creating Demorae! Such a spell has been forgotten for eons!" Jessica exclaimed. "Only one was ever able to use such a powerful spell, and you and I both know it was not Xen'trath!"

"I know, sister… and you know who it was, but that matters little now; you must end my torment. Please sister, do not hold back."

"You leave me no choice, Shelara; forgive me," Jessica said, slowly raising her mallets.

"I would like nothing more than this pain to end," Shelara said. A sad smile crossed her cold lips as she fired off an arrow, Jessica narrowly evading it, as she rolled behind one of the overturned tables.

"Still as skilled as ever, sister; the past hundred years hasn't dulled your prowess in the slightest, it would seem!"

Jessica was silent momentarily, shaken by Shelara's words. "H-how did you know the exact number of years?" She stuttered.

"Xen'trath has kept a close eye on you, dear sister," Shelara replied, firing off several more arrows at unimaginable speed.

Jessica leapt, strafing to avoid the arrows as she drew close to Shelara, cleaving upward with her left mace, though Shelara skillfully dodged, countering with yet another arrow as she fired it off in midair, using the doorframe as a foothold to leap toward Jessica.

"Xen'trath knew all along where the boy was held; he thought I was fooled by his lies," Shelara continued as they fought. "He's been waiting patiently till the time to strike was right."

Jessica was shocked by this information as she leapt, rolling away from yet another series of arrows fired in her direction, using the tables for cover.

"Xek'roshule knows all, and sees all," Shelara said, leaping into the air, though she was taken off guard when Jessica came up from behind, having maneuvered silently though the darkened room.

Jessica swung at Shelara, who parried the attack with her bow, breaking it in half.

Shelara sighed. "You really shouldn't have done that, sister," she said, as the two halves of the bow transformed into an elegant set of twin blades, as if being forged by the air itself, the metal steaming from the heat radiating from the twin elven blades.

Jessica was awestruck at the sudden transformation.

"The works of the skyforge never cease to amaze me!" Jessica shouted, readying herself, for she knew that Shelara's true expertise was in swordplay.

This fact always came as a shock to the elf's quickly defeated foes, though few ever had the fighting prowess to force Shelara to have to use her blades.

"Are you sure you can stand before me with my blades, dear sister?" Shelara asked, charging at Jessica, who parried each blow with ease.

"You forget who you're talking to here!" Jessica barked.

Shelara cracked a smile. "It truly has been a long time…"

Chapter Fifteen

Alec sat on the cellar floor, in awe, watching his mother fight. His vision having shifted to that of an x-ray, he watched every move she made.

Alec wasn't sure if he had heard Shelara correctly though; their voices were muffled by the chaos just beyond the inn, but he could have sworn she mentioned something regarding not having fought for one hundred years.

Ashylanya sat with Liz, tending to the deep wound in her side. Having stemmed the blood flow, she had cleaned the area, wrapping the wound in fresh linens Jessica had given her to use for triage.

"I may not know who you are, but thank you," Liz said, with a small bow.

"Oh! Um, Ashylanya!" she replied with a smile. "It's nice to meet you. I've seen you with Jessica quite often; are you close?"

They were interrupted, however, by a sudden quake which rocked the earth beneath them. Sam tumbled off of the table, letting out a low groan, as Alec lost his balance, falling to the floor.

"Are we having an earthquake?" Sam grumbled, slowly rising from the dusty floor. "Where the hell are we?"

"The cellar in the Red Talon," Liz answered, smiling at Sam.

"Didn't know the inn had a cellar," he replied, still in a daze.

"Madam Jessica kept it hidden all these years, for just such an occasion," Liz explained. "Only the waitresses know about it."

Sam nodded absent mindedly.

"Any idea what's going on up there?" Sam asked, seeing dust fall to the floor as heavy footfalls pounded the floor above.

"Jessica's fighting the one who captured Lucy and Gabriel…" Alec replied, somehow knowing this to be true, yet another mystery of the dawn strider's pendulum.

"Can you see it?" Sam asked.

"Every detail," Alec replied. "She's fighting someone called Shelara…"

Ashylanya's expression darkened. "It's as I feared then; he is on his way…"

"Who is he?" Sam asked, giving her a sidelong glance.

"Xen'trath, the mind breaker. Lieutenant of the endless void," she replied, a grim expression on her face.

"And who is that?" Alec asked, turning his head toward Ashylanya.

"The one who's after you," Ashylanya replied, meeting his gaze. "Or rather, he's after what's inside you."

"You mean, whatever is inside me that gives me these strange powers, Xen'trath wants?" Alec asked, turning to face her.

"Not him, but his master."

Alec's vision shifted again, causing him to cry out in agony. He watched as Jessica fought the woman above. Two others were on their way to join the fight, as Alec's eyes burned a bright gold, his hourglass pupils shining in the darkness, though narrowed in pain.

"The dawn strider is no longer here to keep you balanced, Alec; you are becoming unstable," Ashylanya said, a worried look etched on her face.

"I heard about her," Liz interjected. "So it's true then, she was killed? Which means-"

Liz shut her mouth, seeing the expression on Ashylanya's face.

"Which means my brother is also gone…" she breathed.

"I am so sorry, milady," Liz said, bowing her head low.

But Ashylanya did not reply.

"Enough of this waiting around nonsense; we have to get out of here and help!" Sam blurted. "I'm not keen on hiding like some sort of rat."

"Calm yourself Sam, and keep quiet," Liz hissed. "If they find us, we will all be killed. Jessica can handle herself."

Sam seemed irritated at the idea of remaining in one spot. Wincing at the pain in his arm, he looked down at the bandages.

"Damned geist—didn't see him coming. If it weren't for the star-lit woman, I'd have been a goner for sure."

"You had direct contact with the Dawn Strider, so that explains how you were able to exert such strength against that shade geist in the woods," Ashylanya said, enlightened.

Sam seemed to pause momentarily. "I guess you're right. I may be strong, but I'm not that strong," he gloated, flexing his muscles for Liz, who chuckled at his display.

Alec's eyes shifted again, snapping out of his vision. "We have to get out of here! Mum's in danger!"

"What did you see, Alec?" Ashylanya asked, approaching him.

But Alec was shaking now, his composure shattered by what he had foreseen. "A dragon..." Alec breathed. "An enormous skeletal dragon!"

The color in Ashylanya's face drained at those words. "So that's what he plans..."

"What is it, Milady Ashylanya?" Liz asked, curiously.

"Galakrond the molten..."

"Galakrond?" Liz said, rising from the floor, wincing from the pain in her side. "I've only read tales of him in old dusty tomes, is he really that dangerous?"

"He's the reason that there is a vast expanse of desert just north of the Surfire woods," Ashylanya replied grimly.

"And this monster is alive again?" Liz persisted.

"I'm so stupid!" Ashylanya breathed. "I should not have left that arrow behind!"

"What the hell are you two talking about? I've never heard of any dragon that could cause that much destruction," Sam interjected.

"Xen'trath has used the energy he took from Alec to reanimate a dragon the size of half of this continent."

Sam began to laugh.

Everyone turned their heads toward him as he did so, eyeing him uneasily.

"You really expect me to believe-"

He was then interrupted as he was knocked off his feet, as another earthquake shook the inn's foundations.

"He's trying to free himself from the earth," Ashylanya breathed.

Just above the four, Jessica continued her fight, holding back Shelara's blades, barring them with her truncheons as she was knocked from her feet during the last quake.

Kneeing Shelara in the gut, she threw the elf off her, rolling to the side, evading both of Shelara's blades, which pierced the floor. Quickly, Shelara spun to parry Jessica, who swung her maces at the elf's side.

"This is no place for a proper fight," Shelara mused before leaping backwards through the hearth of the inn. Jessica rushed after her, readying herself for any attack.

Shelara took Jessica by surprise, cleaving at her shins with both her blades, as Jessica leapt to avoid amputation. Shelara disappeared into the smoke which now permeated the air of the burning village square. The silhouette of the now shattered statue of Vinacent III looming in the thick fog was all Jessica was able to see.

All around her, chaos reigned. Almost every cottage that had once stood in the village square was now set ablaze; bodies of men, women, and even children littered the paths as those few who had survived fled for their lives with what they could carry.

Jessica readied her weapons, suddenly seeing another silhouette approaching her from the suffocating miasma. The figure walked with a limp; labored breathing could be heard as it drew closer, coming into view.

"Molly!" Jessica shouted, reaching out to catch the elder woman as she fell. "Gods, what have they done to you!"

Molly held tightly to where her left arm had once been, trying to stem the flow of heavy bleeding from the devastating wound.

"Jessie dear, is that you?" Molly wheezed as she spoke, her breathing heavy as she gazed blankly up at Jessica.

"Hold still, Molly, I'm going to try to help you, okay?" Jessica said, as she lifted the frail woman, carrying her toward the shattered statue.

Setting her down, Jessica removed her belt from around her waist to wrap it tightly around the remaining stump of Molly's arm.

"There is no saving this old gal, Jessie..." Molly croaked as she brought her remaining hand up toward Jessica's face. "I've lived quite long enough now, please," Molly said, with a smile. "I can see him now, my husband... his hands reach for my own," she wheezed.

Jessica had a pained expression on her face, realizing that Molly was right; she had already lost too much blood to be saved.

"You have other people to help; you and I both know... you are the only one who can..." Molly breathed once more before her hand fell limp, her eyes staring off blankly into the distance as the elder woman breathed her last.

Jessica sat motionless for a moment, gripping her dear old friend's hand tightly.

Slowly Jessica looked upward at the ruined statue, glaring menacingly at Shelara, who was now perched atop it, gazing back at her with a hollow sadness in her eyes.

Jessica then heard heavy footfalls to her left, giving her warning to roll to the side, just in time to evade a large axe aimed to cleave her skull.

Jessica quickly turned, parrying the blade of another before leaping backwards. She turned to face her new foes, hammers at the ready.

She froze on the spot, in shock.

"Garren Hydenforge... Lehion Skyglaive..." She identified the two cloaked figures which stood before her by their weapons. "Not you too!"

Before her stood two more old friends, and for the first time, Jessica knew that her life was in jeopardy.

Chapter Sixteen

Alec began to feel panic creep up on him as he sat against the tightly shut door within the dimly lit cellar. His vision having shifted back, he was no longer able to see what was happening above. His tail flitted nervously as he pressed one elongated ear to the door, trying to hear anything he could of what was happening above, to no avail.

"We have to get out of here!" Alec said, trying to force his way out, gaining little ground as something heavy rested against the door.

"Alec, we're safer down here, by the look of things," Sam said, resting his back against a wall, ignoring the searing pain in his arm. "We should just wait it out."

Alec looked twice at Sam, as if he couldn't believe what he was hearing.

"He's right Alec, leave this one to your mother; she can hold her own," Liz added.

"That doesn't sound like the Sam I know," Alec said, eyeing Sam and ignoring Liz, before continuing to press hard against the door. "The Sam I know," he grunted, "would leap at the opportunity to join the fray."

Ashylanya merely watched as Alec struggled with all his might to move the door.

Sam let out a sigh, hoisting himself to his feet and approaching Alec.

Alec cast Sam a sidelong glance. "Now we're talking."

"You two really shouldn't go up there!" Liz interjected, but was ignored as Ashylanya herself joined in the effort to move the door.

Liz sighed. "I guess there is no stopping them…" she muttered.

Alec smiled, turning his full attention to the door. The ground beneath them began to shake again heavily as the three pushed with all their might. The quake having moved what was blocking the doorway, it swung open with one final push.

The four were immediately blinded by the soot which engulfed them upon exiting the cellar.

Coughing, they stumbled as they made their way toward the sound of a furious battle just beyond. Alec's sight shifted again, giving him clear vision through the smog. "This way," he muttered. "Stay close to me."

Alec's tail flicked nervously as the sound of battle drew nearer. His hearing enhanced by his new canine ears, he felt as if he were mere inches from the fray.

Alec peered cautiously out one of the now shattered windows; what he saw shocked him beyond belief.

Just beyond, Jessica fought valiantly against not one, but three opponents. The grace with which his mother moved left Alec awestruck; even seeing it with his vision before did not compare to what he saw now.

Jessica's battle prowess was that of elegance; in Alec's changed eyes, her energy sparked a fiery red, filling the clearing in Alec's view, far overpowering the three she faced.

"Mother…" Alec breathed. "Why did you hide this for so long?"

Ashylanya was now at Alec's side, observing the battle. Liz and Sam joined them at the window, merely watching as Jessica swung her truncheons with ease, parrying every swing from the three opponents she faced.

"Ye haven't dulled a bit, lass!" Garren shouted as his axe was blocked from behind, as Jessica swung her mace back to parry his strike. "Glad to see the years haven't dulled ye in the slightest!"

"Behind you!" Lehion shouted, as he swung his blade.

The trio, astonishingly enough, warned Jessica of every swing beforehand, which befuddled her audience just behind the doors of the inn.

"It's as though they want her to succeed," Liz gasped.

"It's because they do," Ashylanya replied, casting Liz a sidelong glance. "They are Demorae, but they retained their feelings. They are essentially puppets, the victims of a curse of necromancy known as the Kelondrekh curse."

"The Kelondrekh curse?" Alec asked. "I read it in a tome somewhere in the market the other day—strange Arcaneight fellow who was selling tomes; it was a dusty tome of black magic."

"Impossible, such a curse has been banned for generations," Ashylanya interjected. "Are you sure it wasn't something similar?"

"No, it clearly was; it was even used on me in a dream I had not two nights ago."

This information disturbed Ashylanya, as she shifted uneasily.

"It seems like the void is rising up once more, preparing an army..." Ashylanya spoke, her voice wavering. "The Arcaneight in the market—did you get a good look at him?"

"Yes, seemed a bit odd; his eyes were as black as charcoal, his skin was deathly pale, he kept rather to the shade, and refused to even raise a hand toward the sunlight."

Ashylanya's expression darkened. "I know of the one you speak of..." she breathed.

They were then interrupted by a large crash, as the final barrier holding the inn together shattered.

"Move!" Liz shouted, pushing the three out of the way as the walls collapsed around them.

"Liz!" Alec cried.

But the young woman did not respond.

Alec frantically dug through the rubble in an attempt to free her, with the aid of Sam and Ashylanya.

But she was nowhere to be found. "Liz!" Alec shouted again, but again, there was no reply.

"She's gone, Alec..." Ashylanya breathed. "I can't sense her energy anymore..."

Alec sat there for a moment, in shock at Liz's bold sacrifice.

Jessica was distracted by the sudden collapse of the inn; seeing the three standing before the rubble, panic arose within her.

"You three, run away!" Jessica shouted.

Her distraction cost her, as Lehion's blade bit deep into her thigh, causing her to let out an exasperated gasp.

Falling to one knee, Lehion tried with all his might to halt his blade from impaling Jessica.

"Move Jess, I can't hold back!"

Lehion plunged, his blade stopping right at Jessica's chest, as he seemingly froze in place.

"Seems like I've arrived, just in time..." croaked a voice just behind Jessica.

Lehion breathed a sigh of relief.

Slowly Jessica turned her head toward the man behind her. "Joden!" she gasped.

"You know very well that I discarded that name long ago, dear Reaper's Toll," Joden chuckled, emphasizing her own title.

"Thank goodness you're here," she breathed.

"Took you long enough, old man." Shelara drawled, giving him a look of annoyance. "You've always been so bothersome..."

"Not as bothersome as it would have been if I had arrived even a second later, dear Shelara," Joden replied, with a smile.

"So th'coun'er curse worked; I 'ave control of me body again," Garren interjected, clasping and unclasping his hand with freedom.

"I wasn't aware the Kelondrekh had a counter curse..." Jessica stated, eyeing Joden.

"It was quite hard to come by. I journeyed far to receive the tome in which it was contained," he replied. "Quite taxing on these old bones."

The party was then rocked again by yet another vast quake, as a large patch of forest was torn away; the head of a leviathan slowly began to rise, stirring from its long undisturbed slumber. The ground beneath them began to crack as the monstrous beast struggled to free itself. A skeletal snout jutted from the forest, huffing as it struggled with the earth binding it.

Lucy and Gabriel had reached the forest's edge when the quake reached its highest point, the ground beneath them splitting in twain as Gabriel leapt across before the gap had grown too wide.

The exhausted pair breathed heavily as they passed through the underbrush. Having run at breakneck speed toward the village with no rest, the youth were on the verge of collapsing.

The heavy cloud of smoke had begun to dissipate, revealing the ghastly sight before them. The two froze in horror at what they saw.

"N-no!" Lucy cried, in shock, falling to her knees before the burning village just beyond. "T-this can't be real!" she cried in a broken voice.

Gabriel was beside himself, joining Lucy on his knees. "It's all gone!" Gabriel's pained voice cracked.

The earth shook again beneath them, as a terrible roar could be heard in the distance.

"Lucy, Gabriel!" cried the voice of an older man. "Thank the gods you're safe!"

Lucy turned to be embraced by her father tightly; Gatsby had tears in his eyes, joyous that his daughter was safe. "Where is your brother?" Gatsby asked, scanning the surrounding landscape, expecting to see Sam appear through the smoke at any moment.

"I dunno, we were separated hours ago!" Lucy replied quickly.

"And Alec?" He asked, eyeing Gabriel.

"Same, Lucy and I were held captive together by a madman, according to what she told me..."

"We have to move, though; we can't just stand here idly," Lucy said. "The others could still be alive!"

Gatsby seemed frightened by the idea of walking the corpse-littered streets of the once proud village, but held back his rising fear. "You're right, we should at least make sure the others are safe."

Nodding, Lucy turned and began to walk into the village, Gabriel and Gatsby behind her, picking up their pace as they went with urgency.

The entirety of the village was in chaos; almost every building had been razed to the ground.

All around, cries could be heard from the few survivors. The trio stopped before a woman kneeling before the bodies of her husband and child. Her eyes were wide as she held the body of her lifeless child in her arms, slowly rocking, as if she had lost her sanity.

The three began to walk again, disappearing into the thick fog of smoke; the stench of mutilated and burning bodies of the dead which were now strewn over the paths of Sevelan caused Lucy to stop abruptly to vomit. Gatsby stood over her, gently caressing her shoulder as she heaved.

Various scavengers had already made their appearance all around, as vultures fought over the remains of the brutally slaughtered villagers.

"Why...?" Gabriel breathed. "For what reason could we have possibly deserved such carnage!" Gabriel said, observing his surroundings, which chilled him to the core.

The screams and the pleas of the dying filled their ears. Mothers could be seen frantically searching for their children amongst the wreckage as the trio slowly continued, stopping momentarily at Lucy and Sam's childhood home.

Soft tears streaked Lucy's cheeks as she sobbed; Gatsby grasped his daughter tightly in his arms as he cried too.

Gabriel stood there absentmindedly, the sounds all around him dulled to his senses as he watched the couple cry.

They continued to walk, casting one final glance at their ruined home, Lucy's face etched with a pained expression.

As the trio approached the crossroads in the village they froze, ducking behind the rubble of a stone wall, which was left partially standing.

A low growl could be heard just beyond, as the distinct sound of flesh being torn from bone reverberated through the wreckage.

Slowly Lucy peered behind the wall, to see a large pale beast feasting upon the remains of a dead man, hungrily tearing through the remains. The creature looked similar to that of a shade geist, though much larger and more animalistic. Its snout was bloodstained, as its razor sharp teeth tore away at the flesh of its victim. The beast's vertebrae jutted out from the flesh of its hunched back, trailing all the way down to a reptilian tail, which ended in a distinct barb soaked in blood, indicating that this was not its first victim.

"What do we do?" Lucy whispered to Gabriel.

"It looks distracted; maybe if we move carefully enough, it won't see us," Gabriel replied, catching a glimpse of the beast himself before quickly ducking back behind the wall as the beast turned its head toward them.

"Get ready to run…" Gabriel warned, as the creature's growling deepened. Its soulless black eyes were now fixated on their hiding place, as if it could see through the stone itself.

"Go!" Gabriel shouted, charging out from behind the wall, Lucy and Gatsby close behind.

The beast howled as it launched itself toward them in wild pursuit.

The three ran as fast as their legs could carry them, but the beast was quickly gaining on them.

"There!" Gabriel shouted, pointing toward a cellar which stood ajar, but Gatsby did not hear him, as he charged in another direction, separating from the pair.

"Dad, no!" Lucy's call fell on deaf ears, as Gatsby disappeared into the smoke.

The youth threw themselves inside, Gabriel reaching for the door and swinging it shut.

The beast hurled itself at the doorway, its sharp claws tearing away at the door piece by piece.

"C'mon!" Gabriel shouted to Lucy, who watched in horror as the beast tore away their only line of defense.

Lucy was riddled with worry for her father, who had gotten himself lost within the chaos, unwilling to leave without him.

Gabriel turned to meet a dead end, the staircase leading into the upper cottage having collapsed during the village's decimation.

"There's no way out!" Gabriel cried, hopelessly.

The two stood there, watching as the monster just beyond carved its way toward them in furious bloodlust.

"I'm sorry, Lucy…" Gabriel whispered, now holding tightly to her as the beast shattered the doorway, barreling toward them.

Lucy shut her eyes tightly, feeling the creature's putrid breath upon her face as it halted momentarily before letting out a deafening roar, opening its jaws wide.

The creature was silenced, however, as its eyes rolled back into its head before collapsing onto the cellar floor, mere inches from the two.

Slowly they opened their eyes. A large axe, fashioned in the shape of a crescent moon, was lodged between the beast's shoulder blades, severing its spinal cord, as the wielder of the weapon stood over his slain foe triumphantly, one large booted foot planted on the small of the beast's back.

"Are you wounded?" the low voice of Makkari spoke, as his stern looking face came into view, eyeing the frightened youth.

Both of them shook their heads furiously, speechless at being saved just in the nick of time.

"Good, come with me," Makkari said, turning to leave the cellar.

"T-thank you!" Lucy called after him, but Makkari did not acknowledge her, as her thanks were deafened by the same earsplitting roar from before, as the ground rumbled again.

"Time is running out; follow me or be left behind," Makkari said, as he began to walk.

The pair did not argue, quickly following their rescuer and disappearing into the smog.

Chapter Seventeen

Jessica had lost her footing, stumbling back into Lehion's arms, as the earth below shook violently, the mammoth dragon struggling now with all its might to free itself from its tomb of earth.

Thanking him, she turned, feeling a cold chill run down her spine.

"Xen'trath…" Jessica breathed. "Alec, take the others and run!"

"No! I refuse to run anymore!" Alec shouted, his eyes shifting to a deep amber in irritation, meeting her firm gaze.

"It isn't safe here Alec, please!" she pleaded.

"Your false mother is right, boy…" spoke a harsh voice from the cold darkness, which echoed all around them. "But know it matters not where you flee, I will always find you."

The hideous figure of Xen'trath slowly departed from the shadows, from atop the rubble of a decimated cottage, still supported by weakened beams; a broad grin etched his macabre features.

"Alec please, take them and run!" Jessica's voice was now panic-stricken as she struggled to rise, her leg searing with pain.

"Xen'trath… I thought you had died long ago." Joden spoke, eyeing the twisted man before him. "Though now I know why the energy I felt imprisoned within the dragon's maw felt familiar."

"I never die, old fool…" Xen'trath sneered. "I still must repay you, however, for what you did to my beautiful face…"

Najied chuckled. "Your face lost its beauty long before that particular battle, upon your fall into corruption."

"Silence!" Xen'trath roared, causing all but the tome keeper to quake. "Enough talk, give the boy to me, or I shall take him from you by force..." he demanded, as a set of twin blades seemed to extend from the flesh of his forearms, extending far beyond his mangled claws.

"Not while I still draw breath!" Jessica bellowed.

Xen'trath laughed long and hard, echoing through the ruined village. "Do you think that you are powerful enough to stop me, now that I possess the strider's arrowhead?" Xen'trath chuckled darkly, withdrawing the head of the arrow from his pocket and holding it high.

Moaning and screams could be heard as Xen'trath's subordinates collapsed to the ground, quickly decaying into dust as their souls were drawn into the shard.

The only ones left standing were the three Demorae who stood protectively before Jessica, as all of the demons and cultists who followed Xen'trath had been absorbed into the crystal itself.

Ripping open his cloak, Xen'trath lodged the gemstone into his own chest. Black blood oozed from the location, as he underwent a grotesque transformation right before their very eyes.

"A fragment of the abyssal seed... I should have known!" Ashylanya breathed, as her own pendant lit up, shining brightly through her blouse.

Xen'trath now took on an even more hideous form: his limbs twisted as his legs melded into a serpentine appearance, twisting around each other as two large clawed feet dug firmly into the ground. Shedding his cloak, an extra set of arms sprouted from his torso, as black lines etched from where the stone was embedded; the pits in his eyes now flared a deep fiery red.

"Now, do you see?" Xen'trath's voice had taken on a deep rumble with each word, shaking the earth around him. "I am invincible...!"

"You're a corrupt traitor to the Anari kind..." Ashylanya corrected, eyeing the monstrosity before her.

Xen'trath chuckled darkly.

"Within me, I bear the powers of a god!" Xen'trath roared. " take the boy from you then, by force..."

Jessica leapt toward Xen'trath, though her attack was parried ease, as he cleaved downward with his left arm, narrowly m her jugular.

"Jessica the Reaper's Toll..." Xen'trath rumbled. "It never sur me that Matthias would leave the boy to you..." He sneered.

"How many of my subordinates have you slain?" he sai mocking tone. "Hmm... was it one hundred million, perha hundred million?" He gazed into her eyes, chuckling.

"Two hundred thirty million nine hundred and two!" she hastily parrying another strike from one of Xen'trath's ne' having grown blades of their own.

"Such a bold statement..." Xen'trath hissed. "Are you sure I will make the nine hundred and two?" he said, laughir

Jessica's eyes widened. "How did you-"

"I've always known, Jessica. I've kept my eye on you s' days of counting began!" he barked, pushing her back.

"But in the inn..." She breathed.

"Do you really think I'd come here if I did not have a pl had eyes and ears everywhere!" he scoffed, sweeping at l she jumped to evade. She landed on the edge of Xen'tra kicking him square in the jaw, causing him to double b; landed gracefully.

"I'm surprised you can still fight so well..." Xen'trath i been over a hundred years since you last lifted your ma even broken your oath of peace, it seems." he said, lau; revealed more information only she would have known.

"Just how long have you been watching us!?" she sho

Xen'trath cackled, which was drowned out by a dee the earth beneath them, as the wyrm roared again.

"Do you really believe Matthias had me fooled?" Xen' "That I was unaware of where he had hidden the boy reasons for waiting, for biding my time, and it was for t' he bellowed, jabbing one elongated finger into his ch

himself with his blade, only to watch as the wound closed completely seconds later.

An arrow flew at Xen'trath, though he caught it expertly between two fingers, snapping it in two.

Xen'trath turned toward Shelara.

"I knew you three would betray me all along; I knew the old fool Arcaneight would free you of the Kelondrekh curse…" Xen'trath spat.

"But how long can you fight my will…" Xen'trath cackled. "You are still bound to me in death!" he bellowed, pointing an elongated claw at Shelara, causing her to double over in agony as she grasped at her temples.

Garren roared, charging toward Xen'trath, only to feign and cut through the last sturdy beam of the cottage, causing it to collapse.

Jessica jumped, landing hard on the earth next to him.

"Do you really think you can defeat me so easily?" Xen'trath said, stepping from the rubble, the last of his tattered cloak burning away, revealing taut blackened flesh, which was heavily scarred from severe burns from a battle long ago.

Jessica was sickened by the beast's foul appearance.

Lehion and Shelara stepped up to Jessica's side.

"Shelara, didn't I shatter your bow?" she asked, still gazing at Xen'trath.

"You know me well enough, sister; the works of the sky forge are eloquent in ways one can never imagine," she mused.

Jessica nodded with a smile at her dear friend.

"Done with the chatter yet?" Xen'trath called from the roaring flame, his voice darker and more terrible than ever before.

Jessica was suddenly distracted by hurried footfalls. Makkari approached the group quickly, Gabriel and Lucy in tow.

"Alec! Sam!" Lucy cried, hurrying toward them, on the verge of tears.

"What the hell's going on here!?" Gabriel shouted over the roar of the flames.

"Makkari!" Ashylanya squealed, running toward him and flinging herself into the big man's arms. "Makkari… It's him!"

They both froze at what they saw emerging from the flames. Aghast, Lucy gripped tightly to Sam's arm. Gabriel merely stood there, agape.

Makkari let out a deep growl, as he watched Xen'trath emerge. "So the story proves true... Xen'trath lives..."

"I-it's him...!" Lucy breathed.

"You know this monster?" Alec asked, looking back at her.

"He's the one who held us captive..." was all Lucy said, still gazing at the monstrosity before her.

Xen'trath towered over the four directly in front of him, gazing down on them in contempt. Seeing Makkari, his eyes narrowed behind his mask. "I would have expected you to be whimpering, little Makkari... After what I did to-"

"You dare to taunt me!" Makkari boomed, charging toward Xen'trath. He did not make it far, however, before his feet were suddenly melded with the earth below.

Makkari glared at the demon before him with hate-filled eyes.

"Now Makkari... I'm sure if Matthias could see you now..." Xen'trath emphasized the name, with a low hiss.

"You bastard..." Venom dripped from each word Makkari spoke, as he gazed furiously at the monstrosity before him.

"Now... I give you one last chance: hand the boy over to me, and I may allow you to live!"

Lehion scoffed. "Do you really expect us to believe those words?" he demanded, readying his blade.

Xen'trath chuckled again, a cold demonic sound, which emanated through the now eerily quiet streets of the ruined village.

"You know me too well, Lehion..." Xen'trath hissed. "Very well, I will kill all of you, and take what my master so desires!" he mused, as he drew forth his final blade, the very one from Alec's nightmare, which shook him as he watched it slowly meld with Xen'trath's hand. The gaping mouths seemed to come to life; the wailing of the dead echoed throughout Alec's mind.

Garren charged, swinging his axe, as Shelara let fly several arrows, Jessica and Lehion having strafed in an attempt at a flanking maneuver.

Xen'trath parried every blow, dodging the arrow aimed for his skull. He roared, knocking back the three closest with a mighty push, sending them soaring into the rubble in opposite directions.

"Mum!" Gabriel cried, still in shock at his mother's fighting prowess.

"Fear not boy, your mother is a skilled fighter," Joden said, placing a firm hand on Gabriel's shoulder.

Gabriel looked behind him, having just realized Joden's presence.

"The tome keeper?" Why are you here?" he asked, turning his head toward him.

"Are you asking why I'm still alive? Or perhaps, why I'm at this particular place? Many seem to ask the former," the old man said, furrowing his brow.

"Erm, the latter," Gabriel said, giving him a strange look.

"Ah, yes... As for that, I don't really believe I recall! My, my..." Joden seemed to be thinking, a confused looked on his wrinkled face.

"Is this old man serious?" Gabriel whispered to Alec, glancing back at Joden, who seemed to be muttering to himself.

Alec, however, was still fixated on the battle, paying no mind to anything else.

Xen'trath had not even a scratch upon him, as he fought against the four. Jessica was the only one who seemed to be suffering from exhaustion. She ignored the seething pain from her thigh as she charged again with Garren.

Xen'trath parried her swing. Catching Garren by the throat and impaling him, he crushed the dwarf's windpipe. Garren glared menacingly into Xen'trath's eyes as he slowly began to crumble into ashes.

"Pathetic..." Xen'trath scoffed, before casting Garren's limp form aside.

"Sorry, lass..." he mouthed at Jessica, unable to speak. His body disintegrated before them, leaving no more than a smoking pile of dust.

Jessica roared, taking the chance to strike hard into Xen'trath's side, cracking his pelvis in two.

Xen'trath glared at her unfazed, using his free hand to backhand her, sending her flying back into the five youth, who were huddled close together around Joden.

Alec caught her, falling backward himself onto the hard cobblestone.

Xen'trath swung violently, beheading Lehion mid-charge, his body crumpling to the earth, joining Garren in a similar fate.

Shelara looked on with sorrow as her two closest companions fell; gazing upward at Xen'trath, cold malice filled her eyes.

"Do you see now… you have no hope!" Xen'trath boomed, as his pelvis seemed to right itself, healing completely. He pointed a claw at Shelara, causing her to double over in agony as her flesh began to burn. Her body slowly disintegrating, she gazed back at Jessica.

"Forgive me, sister…" she breathed. "I failed you…"

Those were Shelara's final words, as her body collapsed, leaving behind naught but her traveler's cloak.

A single tear rolled down Jessica's cheek as she watched her friends die one after another. Alec gripped her shoulder tightly.

Rising, Jessica stood alone before the much larger figure; the firelight gave a terrible contrast to the demon's twisted visage.

The five youth looked on in horror as Xen'trath slowly approached.

"If you lay one hand on them, I will enjoy every second of tearing the flesh from your bones!" Makkari boomed, attempting to free himself with all his might. But Xen'trath ignored Makkari's idle threat, as he continued to walk toward them.

"Step aside, woman, before you join them in the afterlife," Xen'trath hissed.

Jessica gazed back at the six behind her, an apologetic look in her eyes. "Joden, take care of them for me," she said, turning toward Xen'trath.

"Mother, no!" Alec cried out, gripping her arm. Gabriel joined him in a feeble attempt to hold her back.

Jessica pushed them both back at the feet of Joden.

"I will never let you hurt MY CHILDREN!" she cried, charging at Xen'trath full force, knowing her end was imminent.

Xen'trath caught Jessica with one arm, knocking the wind out of her and sending her sailing backward, where she lay limp on the rubble-littered walkway.

Xen'trath then turned his attention to Ashylanya.

"I really must thank you, girl," Xen'trath hissed. "That pendant of yours has ripened the boy's power quite nicely. I can feel it radiating from within me…" Xen'trath chuckled, his face contorted into a wide, toothy grin.

Ashylanya glanced at Alec, who was gazing at his palm, which had begun to glow a bright blue, his tail coiled around his lap, as he sat upon the cobblestone, gazing up at Xen'trath.

"Let's see how he handles his power under raw emotion, shall we?" Xen'trath gazed at Alec, directing his blade toward Jessica.

"Mother!" Alec cried, before doubling over in agony, the hourglass symbol pulsating hard.

Gabriel looked at his brother with concern.

"What's happening?" Lucy asked, nervously gazing at the pulsing mark, as Sam tightened his grip on her.

"Oh, nothing yet… But you shall see, all too soon!" Xen'trath yelled, leaping toward Jessica, who opened her eyes just in time to roll, evading Xen'trath's blades as the walkway shattered from the impact of his blades.

Jessica struggled to her feet, raising her truncheons with effort, her strength waning. The pain in her thigh continued to seethe as she defended herself desperately, knowing what would happen to Alec should she fall.

Joden seemed to be whispering something under his breath in a tongue Alec couldn't identify, his walking stick placed in front of him.

Xen'trath arced his blade back, drawing Jessica's attention as he struck her with a side sweep with the shadowy blade, biting deep into her abdomen. The flesh where it struck quickly decayed.

Jessica gasped in pain; as blood flowed from the wound, Xen'trath knelt before her with a low chuckle.

"Why do you care so much about this 'thing'? He's not even your offspring, and yet you treat him as such, why?" He spoke, his head now resting over Jessica's shoulder.

"You will never understand, you son of a-"

She froze as Xen'trath's shadowy blade pierced her rib cage, slowly sliding deeper as it punctured her lung, sliding clean through her.

"Sorry, I didn't quite hear you..." Xen'trath mused. "I'm a what?" he taunted, taking sweet pleasure in her agony.

Xen'trath stood, peering down at the dying woman before him, as she gazed up at him with empty eyes. Coughing up blood, she collapsed onto her side.

"Mum!" Gabriel cried, running toward where she lay. Alec seemed frozen in place, a look of horror etched upon his face, as the mark pulsated even harder, slowly turning from blue to bright gold, his eye color turning a deep purple as time seemed to slow.

Xen'trath retreated into the shadows with a low chortle.

Alec crawled toward her, pain wracking his body, as hot tears stung at his cheeks. Reaching her side, he gently turned her over, holding her in his arms.

The firelight danced around them, casting dark shadows upon the group, flickering along Jessica's pale face. She slowly opened her eyes.

"I'm sorry... Alec..." she wheezed, gazing up at him as the earth rumbled once more, the wyrm drawing closer to freedom. "I'm sorry I can't keep that promise..." she said, fighting to stay conscious.

Alec broke into tears, sobbing hard. Teardrops fell onto his mother's cheek as he held her tight.

"Mother, please don't leave us here all alone!" Gabriel cried through harsh sobs.

Jessica caressed both their cheeks softly, giving Alec a sad smile. "You two won't be alone, dear... you all have each other..." She coughed, blood leaking from her lips as she spoke.

She turned her head toward Gabriel.

"Be strong, Gabriel, for me… please… take good care of yourself and Alec…" she whispered, fading fast. "I love you all very much…" she wheezed. "I know, Alec, that you were not my son by blood, but know that you will always be… in my heart."

Jessica beckoned him closer to her lips, whispering something to him as she lowered her hand to her pocket. Withdrawing something unseen, she placed it in Alec's hand, closing his fingers around it. "You will know… when the time is… right…" She struggled to speak now, as her breathing became labored.

The warm loving light in Jessica's eyes began to fade as she breathed her last breath. Alec gently kissed her on her cold brow, closing her eyes with two gentle fingers.

Gabriel sobbed with Alec, as Sam and Lucy cried as well, kneeling next to her. As the gentle light of the sunrise graced Jessica's pale yet still beautiful features, Alec rested her body on the cold cobblestone.

Slowly, Alec raised his head, staring blankly as if seeing something in the shadows, his eyesight shifting to a bright red in color, as rage he had never felt before boiled within his frame, as the mark on his palm continued to resonate a solid gold.

"Touching…" rattled the voice of Xen'trath. "Tell me, how does it feel?" he hissed. "To lose your mother not once, but twice…" he mused coldly. He gazed intently at Alec as he reemerged from the shadows.

"You monster!" Ashylanya cried, anger etched on her tear-stained features. "How much pain and destruction can you bring before it's enough for you!?"

Alec slowly got to his feet, his head lowered. "You…" Alec trembled. "I'LL FUCKING KILL YOU!" he screamed, running at Xen'trath.

Xen'trath backhanded Alec hard across the face, causing him to fall backwards, hitting the shattered stone.

"Big words, for someone as pathetic as you…" Xen'trath sneered.

Xen'trath was then forcefully knocked off his feet with a heavy blow from Makkari, sending him soaring into a still blazing cottage, causing it to collapse on top of him.

Giving a nod of thanks to Najied, he turned toward where Xen'trath now slowly rose, shaking off the rubble.

"Now that hurt... I have to say, little Makkari, your strength has always been quite formidable."

Xen'trath's voice permeated even the dragon's roars at this point, deep and hollow, his voice emotionless. He slowly emerged from the flames; his head had been violently twisted backwards on his shoulders. Reaching upward, he placed a hand on his stag's horn, snapping his neck back into place, with a sickening crack.

Makkari's eyes narrowed.

Ashylanya rushed to Alec's side, tears of empathy streaking her soft cheeks. "Alec..." she breathed, gazing at him with sorrow-filled eyes.

But Alec did not hear her. Slowly, Alec opened his palm, gazing down at what Jessica had given him.

A small coin rested there; engraved within the worn metal was a single word: "Hope."

Alec clasped the coin tightly before sliding it into his trouser pocket, his gaze shifting back to Xen'trath, the dancing flames contrasting hideously with the beast's cold, expressionless visage.

"What's the matter, little Makkari?" Xen'trath spoke condescendingly. "Still mourning the death of your old friend? Or is it that you didn't die honorably at his side, as you so thought at the time?" Xen'trath's grin returned, as he observed Makkari.

"Enough of your words, demon..." Makkari spoke, trembling once more with rage. "I will sever your tongue from your treacherous mouth!" he bellowed, charging at Xen'trath.

Quickly sidestepping, Xen'trath caught Makkari in the gut with a powerful fist having withdrawn the blade, to prologue the suffering, causing him to gasp as the wind was knocked out of his lungs. "You still let your rage blind you, little Makkari," Xen'trath mused, throwing him backward with one arm.

Alec let out a gasp, falling to one knee as the hourglass symbol began to resonate even brighter, almost searing his palm. Gazing down at his palm, he watched as one of the twelve symbols surrounding the hourglass completely faded away.

Joden was now behind Alec; having finished his incantation, a firm hand was placed upon Alec's shoulder. "You must fight it, boy; do not let this rage consume you!" Joden turned Alec toward him, his gaze meeting his own.

"It's already begun..." Joden breathed.

Alec's eyes had now become full hourglasses, the pupils having completed their transformation, as a bright gold began to replace the red within his eyes.

"You mustn't set it free, Alec; its power will endanger us all!" he pleaded.

"The old fool is right..." Xen'trath said with a low chortle, his gaze drifting behind Alec.

Alec slowly turned his head, to see Lucy and Gabriel were now emanating a faint light.

"What did you do to them?!" Alec demanded, glaring fiercely at Xen'trath.

"Just a simple precaution..." Xen'trath leered. "I cannot have you slipping through my fingers again, now can I?"

Makkari lifted himself from the ground, turning toward Joden.

"What is he talking about?" Makkari demanded.

"The Warden's veil... our only chance of escape..." Najied replied, though his voice was drowned out now by the sudden quake of the leviathan, which had managed to free itself from the earth.

A vast skeletal wyrm now blotted out the sky above them, taking in a deep breath.

"Quickly now children, give me your hands!" Joden said hurriedly. "Ashylanya, you know what to do!"

Ashylanya nodded, withdrawing the pendant from her blouse and holding it skyward, as the dragon exhaled a bright blue flame, which drifted harmlessly over the group, leaving a barren wasteland in its path as the Surfire woods themselves now were set ablaze.

Lucy and Gabriel gave their hands to Joden as the dragon took in another deep breath. Xen'trath stood unfazed as he watched the dragon prepare to breathe in again, soaring overhead, carving a charred path in its wake as it exhaled once more, obliterating the forest in one fell swoop.

"You will not interfere with me, old fool!" Xen'trath boomed before leaping toward them, only to be repelled by the barrier Ashylanya kept resolute with her pendant. "Please hurry, I can only hold out for so long!" she cried.

Joden began to mutter yet another incantation, causing Lucy and Gabriel to fall to their knees as the Arcaneight extracted the runes Xen'trath had placed.

A dark aura began to rise skyward from the two youth before slowly dissipating to join the surrounding smoke left in the dragon's wake.

Letting go of their hands, Joden opened his eyes, falling to one knee.

"You'll be all right now, children," he gasped; his flesh had begun to blacken, trailing upwards to his forearms as he spoke.

"But what about you?!" Lucy said, gazing at the man's quickly decaying flesh.

"I have lived quite long enough…" he stated, turning toward Alec, as the wyrm circled in the sky, taking in yet another deep breath.

"Your hand please, Alec," he said, holding out his own, which had begun to rot away.

Alec held out his hand, as Joden reached to touch the hourglass within the center of his palm.

The dragon exhaled once more, only to have the azure flame pass harmlessly over them once more. Ashylanya fell to one knee, trying her hardest to keep the barrier up.

"I should have killed you when I had the chance!" Xen'trath boomed, clawing desperately in an attempt to pass the barrier before him, his face contorted with rage. Xen'trath attempted to lunge toward them, but his legs were now rooted in place.

Ashylanya gasped as ley lines suddenly began to pan out from Alec, forming a large hourglass, intertwining lines etched around the group as a bright light engulfed Alec's form.

Sam and Lucy were in shock, gazing at Alec in his truest form, if only for a moment. Gabriel reached out slowly.

"Best not to do that now, boy," Joden croaked.

Gabriel withdrew his hand quickly, transfixed by his elder brother's transformation.

Before them stood a towering white Anari, with eyes of solid gold. Long braided hair hung loosely about his shoulders, which emanated pure starlight. Vast emerald wings arched on his back as the ley-lines completed their revolution, creating a circular perimeter around the companions.

"It can't be..." Makkari breathed.

"But it is..." Joden gasped. "Xanadair, the keeper of time..."

"Everyone, hold on tightly to one another, do not let go, no matter the cost," Joden instructed.

Makkari caught Ashylanya as she fainted from overexertion of her pendant's protective shield.

He held her close, as Sam and Gabriel huddled close to Makkari. Lucy, however, stood there momentarily, a single tear rolling down her eye, knowing the fate her father had met. Slowly, she too huddled close to Makkari, holding tightly to him.

The wyrm took in one final deep breath; as time seemed to slow, Joden touched the hourglass on the center of Alec's palm as the wyrm breathed out before the elder faded away into dust.

Suddenly, the group was engulfed in a golden aura.

"NO!" Xen'trath bellowed. "I WILL NOT FAIL AGAIN! NO!" His voice was grating as he shrieked as his form unraveled, along with everything else beyond the circular matrix.

The party then vanished in the blink of an eye.

Xen'trath stood there a moment, as the drake's flames passed harmlessly over him. His macabre visage twisted once more into a wide grin as his eyes narrowed behind his mask. The light of the rising sun gave harsh contrast to the burned remains of the now barren lands in every direction.

Slowly Xen'trath righted himself, brushing the dust off his black leather breeches.

"Well done, Xen'trath..." spoke the sudden deep rumble of a demonic voice.

"All goes as planned..." said Xen'trath, turning toward the vast pair of blood red eyes suspended in the emptiness before him.

"Well done indeed...!" the voice boomed.

"The old one bought your act, as you promised," the voice hissed.

Silence hung in the air momentarily.

"Now go, my loyal servant... there is much work to be done."

"Much indeed..." Xen'trath said. Turning, he walked off into the sunrise, along with the dragon, who seemed to fade from existence.

Chapter Eighteen

Alec awoke in a daze. Slowly opening his eyes, he found himself in a towering forest. The lush earth below was thick with azure-tinted grass, which had broken his fall, from what he could remember of his journey.

Slowly, he got to his feet; his body ached from the forceful power he had exerted which had brought him to his present location, remembering little of what occurred previously.

Alec took a moment to observe his surroundings. Tall trees towered as far as the eye could see. The dark violet shade of the leaves cast a dark yet peaceful light through the forest. Scarce shafts of sunlight penetrated the vast canopy, where unfamiliar birds nested, peering down at him from the safety of their posts.

A sense of peace washed over Alec momentarily before realizing he was alone, having been separated from the others when a mishap had occurred during the blurry memory of another being taking full control of him.

"Anyone here?" he called, listening carefully, but the only sound that echoed through the forest was that of gentle birdsong.

Alec jumped at a sudden rustling not too far away, Hurrying to the location, he spotted Ashylanya slowly emerging from a patch of amber-colored bushes.

"Ash, are you okay?" Alec asked, kneeling at her side.

Ashylanya stared blankly at him momentarily before slowly rising, her body feeling heavy from fatigue. "I'm okay..." she breathed, exhausted from keeping the barrier up for so long, which had saved them from the dragon's breath. "Are you okay?" she asked, blushing slightly, unfamiliar with the shortened version of her name.

"I'm okay…" Alec replied, turning. "We should look for the others; maybe they're close by."

Ashylanya gently grabbed his arm. "We won't find them here," she said, eyeing Alec. "You don't remember what happened, do you?"

Alec's tail brushed her hand as she spoke, causing Alec to quickly pull it to the side, his face turning red.

"Sorry! Almost forgot you had one of those," she said with a giggle.

"Seems so natural to me now, I forget it's there…" Alec replied, trying to move his tail with sheer willpower.

"Takes practice," she giggled, as it brushed against her again on its own.

Alec grabbed hold of it again, pulling it back in embarrassment.

"Well, I don't see you with one!" he teased, seeing the look of embarrassment on her face.

"Oh?" she replied, leaning forward. "That's because I can hide it at will!" she said, as a long bushy tail emerged from her breeches. Her ears also took on their natural form, gently resting nestled in her silky mane of dark hair.

"There!" she said, waving her tail at will, her ears perking slightly.

"How do you do that?" Alec asked in amazement.

"Do what? Oh, only a few of our kind can—useful at times!" she replied, smiling broadly.

"So the Anari… is that what we are? I mean, I've heard the term before but they are what humans call Lycans?" Alec asked, his ears perking in curiosity.

"We resemble Lycan in appearance only," Ashylanya explained, her tail waving gently by her feet. "Lycan themselves are boorish, with low intelligence; the Anari are quite the opposite."

Ashylanya glanced around the forest momentarily, her ears perking up at a nearby reverberating sound, only to see a large groundhog emerge from one of the bushes, its young clinging tightly to its back as it moved through the thick grass.

"Lycan lose themselves upon full transformation, unlike Anari, whose traits become enhanced during full transformation, keeping their minds."

"Full transformation?" Alec asked, endless questions brimming in his mind.

"Full transformation takes many long years to master. It is a process of vigorous training and concentration, and you took on the full form of an Anari when we entered the time veil, which is unheard of," she continued, now playing idly with her tail. "The form we currently take is that of an immature Anari; very few have achieved full transformation without losing themselves, becoming Lycan."

"I see…" Alec said, his mind drifting back to the cloudy memory of what had occurred not two hours ago. "I can hardly remember anything at all—what happened?"

Ashylanya paused for a long moment. "We entered a matrix, known as the Time Warden's veil, sending us back in time, though how far, I have yet to interpret. Your mother never explained any of this to you-"

Ashylanya quickly shut her mouth, seeing the look on Alec's face. "I'm sorry, I didn't mean-"

"It's fine," Alec interjected flatly.

Alec suddenly turned his head, hearing soft footsteps in the distance. Ashylanya, hearing it as well, turned her head toward the location of the sound.

"This some kind o' corchip I'm inturruptin?" spoke the thickly accented voice of a dwarf, who now stood several yards from them.

Alec and Ashylanya glanced at each other before turning their heads away, blushing madly.

"If it is, don't mind leavin," said the dwarf.

The stout frame of the dwarf appeared from behind a tall oak tree, glaring at the two with a smirk.

The dwarf seemed familiar to Alec's mind. A long bushy beard covered his rounded, squashed-looking face. He continued to gaze at the two with lime-colored eyes. The dwarf was adorned in thick leather; a steel chest plate covered his upper torso, which was engraved with a symbol resembling a six-headed hydra. Plated shin guards covered his short, stubby legs, but what struck Alec as peculiar was that his beard appeared to have the texture of sea weed, with a faded mossy tint.

"Who are you, sea dwarf?" Ashylanya asked, immediately recognizing the telltale signs of his race.

The dwarf turned his head, spitting on the forest floor. "And what should I tell ye' my name for, Anari?" the dwarf asked, eyeing her.

Alec suddenly recognized the dwarf, as a flash of a memory coursed through his mind. "You're Garren!" Alec blurted.

The dwarf seemed befuddled. "And how exactly did ye' know that, Anari whelp?"

Ashylanya turned toward Alec, whispering in his ear. "Be careful of what you say; I still don't know what era we are in. It could disturb the balance."

Alec nodded.

"What are ye' whisperin to him abou'?" Garren demanded. "It better not be bout my beard, lest I draw me axes on the spot!"

"No, not at all!" Alec blurted. "You have a very fine beard, sea dwarf!"

The dwarf seemed put off by the compliment.

"I'll ask ye again, how is it you know me name?" Garren demanded.

"I am Jessica, the Reapers Toll's son," Alec blurted, receiving a wide eyed look from Ashylanya.

The dwarf froze before breaking out in a fit of hysterical laughter.

"You seem to find that quite amusing, dwarf," Alec said, eyeing the stout man.

"The Reaper's Toll has no offspring, an' to think for a momen' she would 'ave any business with an Anari is simply un'eard of; she despises the Anari!" the dwarf spat.

Ashylanya seemed to shift uneasily on the spot, her tail hanging low at her heels.

"Tha' woman, settle down an 'ave kids—the idea is laughable, especially with an Anari!" He continued to laugh, heartily.

"I watched you die-"

Alec was silenced by a pinch from Ashylanya.

"Me? Die?" Garren seemed to be amused by the thought, looking down at himself. "Don't appear to be an Edelion quite yet, lad. I still 'ave many years in these ol' bones!" He scoffed, his grin widening through his thick shaggy beard.

"Jessie don't associate 'erself with Anari folk, so you sayin you seen 'er then?" Garren asked, cocking one bushy brow. "If ye 'ave, she owes me quite a handsome sum o' gold with 'er luck gamblin with me," he went on, scratching his beard.

The idea was ludicrous to Alec, but now he knew she was somehow still alive, the idea brought a vast wave of relief to him. As his tension relaxed, his tail, once raised high at his back, lowered to his heels, the tip flicking gently.

"Where are the other two?" Alec asked, eyeing the dwarf.

The dwarf stopped chuckling, a look of suspicion crossing his face. "An 'ou do you mean?"

"Shelara and the other elf, Lehion," Alec replied

"An 'ow does one such as yerself know of 'em?" Garren asked, suspicion etched on his features.

"Jessica told me to tell you something to win your favor..."

"And what would that be, lad?" the dwarf asked.

"The hydra greets the toll; the dawn creeps the horizon."

Garren paled noticeably through the shag of his beard. Turning abruptly, he began to walk into the forest.

"You commin, er wha?" he called to them over his shoulder.

Ashylanya cast Alec a sidelong glance, a confused look etched on her features, before the pair began to follow the dwarf deeper into the unfamiliar woods.

Not far from Alec and Ashylanya's location, Makkari found himself alone, walking through the forest he knew like the back of his gloved hand, though what shocked him most was the fact that this forest had been utterly destroyed, nearly ten thousand years prior.

He gazed up at the violet-colored leaves in the tall, proud oaks, trees which were also extinct, due to the aftermath of the great war of the gods. Makkari beheld his surroundings, befuddled.

"This isn't possible," Makkari muttered, as he trod upon the all too familiar grounds of his homeland, walking through the forest of the Anari origin with ease.

"Vanarette, the forest of origin…" Makkari breathed. "This can't be real." Makkari felt a wave of peace wash over him momentarily as he stopped, taking a deep breath. "Lady Ashylanya was here," he muttered, trying to locate the trail of her scent.

Makkari knew every detail, from the smallest river to the largest tree, within this forest, so long had he inhabited the vast sea of violet. A sense of nostalgia upon the sight of the forest tingled in his brain.

"Why in such a rush, Makkari…?" spoke a sudden calm voice from a nearby towering elm.

"That voice…" Makkari breathed. "Nadrek?"

A lithe figure landed at Makkari's feet with gentle ease, as if he weighed no more than a feather. An elder Anari male stood before Makkari, though he was ghostly in appearance.

"It's been a long time, my boy," Nadrek said. "My how you've grown." The elder Edelion beamed at Makkari down his elongated snout, through a phantom-like mane, with eyes the color of a dully glowing azure.

"So it was true… You truly have joined our ancestors as an Edelion…" Makkari breathed.

Nadrek nodded; a solemn look crossed his appearance momentarily.

"Where is my little niece?" Nadrek asked, seeming to look around for her with a sweeping gaze. "I find it shocking that she's not with you."

"Long story, but we were separated. I caught her scent a few moments before you arrived. I intend to continue my search." Makkari spoke; a look of worry etched on his visage.

"Oh dear, that is troublesome," Nadrek replied, showing concern.

"I'd love to stay and ask you many different questions, but I'm afraid finding the princess is a priority at the present moment," Makkari stated.

Nadrek sighed. "You know I would help if I could, but I am bound to these acres of woods. I am unable to stray very far…"

"Understood," Makkari said with a nod, before turning.

"Do come back soon; the festival of Organ'us begins in three days' time!" Nadrek called after him.

The elder Edelion watched as Makkari disappeared into the forest, breathing a sigh. "Always in such a hurry, that one…" he mumbled. "Each time we meet—my, my…"

Nadrek seemed to fade away after those words, dissipating completely.

Chapter Nineteen

Lucy opened her eyes, to be greeted by a large cat, nose to nose with her.

Letting out a scream, Lucy backed away from the large feline; the cat cringed slightly from the shrill cry before approaching her and licking her nose with its coarse blue tongue.

"Fear not, girl," spoke a man she suddenly saw sitting before a campfire. "Alavanda will not harm you." The voice of the man was familiar to Lucy, as she regained her composure.

Lucy glanced at the man, a much younger version of the tome keeper Joden, who sat hands outstretched before the bonfire he had created.

The panther-sized cat was now lying directly on top of Lucy, as it began to groom her hair with its tongue.

"Please tell it to stop…" Lucy groaned through the sound of the feline lapping at her.

"Alavanda is not an 'it'. She is a leophan." Joden seemed to have an amused look on his face, as he watched his companion lap away at Lucy.

The leophan purred in her ear before rising to slink back to her master.

Lucy looked to her right to see Gabriel and Sam sprawled out on the lush earth, tattered blankets having been laid over them. Looking up at the trees, the leaves were saffron, as opposed to the ruby-colored trees she was accustomed to from her homeland.

Lucy turned back to the older man. "Najied?" she asked, still hazy.

"Don't quite know who that is, I'm afraid," the man replied. "My name is Joden, keeper of the tomes of light."

Joden was still quite old, despite his younger appearance, though not nearly as aged and broken as she recalled him from before. His tangle of silver hair was shoulder length, framing a thin face with a long crooked nose. The familiar large golden eyes gazed at Lucy with a note of confusion.

The only other difference Lucy noticed was that the raven head within the man's walking stick now no longer clasped the small gemstone in its wooden beak.

"Joden..." she breathed. "I remember you were with us when we left in that time veil thing!"

Joden cocked one bushy brow. "I do not recall such an event... in fact, I don't believe we have met," he replied, eyeing Lucy. "What is your name, girl?" he asked, a look of disbelief on his lined face.

"Lucinda, Lucinda Leynaras!" The syllables rolled awkwardly from her tongue, unaccustomed to using her full name.

"Leynaras... I've heard the name before." Joden seemed pensive as he spoke. "Though I don't recall them having any children..." he said. "Where are you from?"

"The village of Sevelan," she replied, confused by what he had said previously.

Joden placed one nimble finger to his lips, pondering. "Ah..." he said. "Never heard of it!" he concluded. "In fact, knowing these lands so well, such a place has never existed; are you sure you didn't hit your head when you landed, Lucinda?"

"Just Lucy, please... and no, I'm sure I didn't," she said, stunned by this information.

How far back have we come? she wondered, her gaze drifting back to the two sleeping boys.

Sam groaned, rolling onto his side.

"Please ladies, I can only handle so much at once!" he muttered in his sleep.

Lucy rolled her eyes, bringing her hand down on the side of Sam's head, causing him to fly into a sitting position, his eyes half closed.

"Lucy, that hurt!" Sam groaned, opening his eyes fully. "Where the hell are we?" he asked groggily, looking around at the quiet forest.

"Balgavian, within the forest of Dawn…" Joden replied, eyeing him with one large golden eye, as he stroked Alavanda's mane.

"The hell is that?" he groaned.

"I'm now very certain he, at least, has hit his head," Joden muttered to himself, watching Sam take in his surroundings.

Gabriel was next to awaken, slowly sitting up, gazing at where he was just in time to see a large unfamiliar bird fly overhead.

Slowly he laid back down, pulling the woolly blanket Joden had given him back over his head.

"Gabriel, you all right?" Lucy eyed the curled-up form of Gabriel beneath the blanket.

"Oh fine, fine—just a dream anyway, no big deal!" he groaned. "Any minute now I'm gonna wake up and everything will be back to normal."

"But you're not-" she tried to say, but Gabriel interrupted her with a quickly raised hand from beneath the cover to silence her.

"Nope… I'm pretty sure!" His muffled voice sounded shaky and high pitched.

Lucy sighed, pulling the blanket off him.

Gabriel opened one of his eyes, seeing the same odd looking bird staring down at him from its nest in the large elm tree above.

Slowly he curled back into a ball. Bringing the blanket back over his face, he began to shake violently.

"A dream!" he yelled, his voice muffled by the covers. "I'm dreaming! The village was never destroyed, and Mum never died!" his muffled voice yelled.

Lucy's expression changed to one of sadness, looking down at Gabriel.

"We all lost someone, Gabriel; you're not alone," she said, her memory drifting back to her father disappearing into the fog, the dragon's breath having most likely consumed him whole.

Sam had a solemn expression on his face, as if knowing what Lucy was thinking; he placed a gentle hand on her shoulder.

Joden merely observed the trio. "Now I'm certain they are just crazed..." he muttered, seeing Lucy turn back to him.

"I know this sounds absurd, but please hear me..." she said, a tear rolling down her cheek.

Sam gazed at Lucy, sadness clouding his sapphire eyes.

"I'm listening," Joden replied, still stroking Alavanda, who purred deeply.

Lucy spent the next few hours explaining everything that had occurred up till this point, stopping occasionally when Joden raised his hand to stop her a moment, to ask a question.

"Jessica the Reaper's Toll... And Xen'trath of the void..." he breathed, a drawn expression on his face.

"Please, continue..." he stated, tense from the information he was hearing.

When Lucy had finished the tale, all the color in Joden's face had drained, his head lowered.

"Xanadair, the Time Warden..." Joden breathed. "No..." Joden looked up at them.

Suddenly the aged man sprang to his feet, belying his age, Alavanda following suit. "We must seek out Matthias; we are all in terrible danger! Prepare yourselves, children; we depart within the hour!"

A short while passed, when the three were mounted behind Joden on the back of the leophan.

"This cat is huge..." Sam stated from behind Lucy.

Gabriel, however, remained deathly silent, as Lucy gazed back at him with concern.

"Hold on tightly, children!" Joden bellowed, digging his heel into the big cat's side.

The leophan sprang forward, nearly toppling Gabriel as he clung tightly to Lucy, trying to stay on the leophan's back.

As Alavanda gained speed, Gabriel secured himself, a frightened look on his weary face, having been drained physically and emotionally within the span of a mere day.

The group disappeared into the underbrush, as a shadow slowly departed from the trees, gazing after them.

"Sister, dear sister… where are you, Ceri?" The voice of a tall woman mused. Cold black eyes, watched the group as they vanished into the distance. "Lucin needs her little sister now…" The woman spoke in third person, as if crazed by some unknown entity.

All that was visible of the woman was a black mane of hair; fiery stars panned out through the long strands, which framed an angular yet angelic-looking pale face.

"Make us whole again, dear sister, please…" she breathed, as yet another shadow departed from the woods.

A large man held the woman by a chain, which connected to his chest. The all too familiar mask distinguished Xen'trath in all his menacing horror, though he had not been transformed yet; he retained the appearance of a fully matured Lichen, though a darkened aura enveloped his well-muscled frame.

"We shall find Ceri, my love, fear not," Xen'trath said, with a wide grin. "It's only a matter of time before the master's plan unfolds!" he said, with a harsh laugh.

Chapter Twenty

Alec and Ashylanya followed the dwarf for what seemed like hours, until finally he held up one stubby finger.

Taking a small rune-etched stone from his pocket, he placed it on the forest floor. A moment passed, and the pair glanced at each other, a look of confusion upon their faces, when suddenly the patch of forest before then melted away, replaced by a shabby log cabin.

Garren approached, knocking in a pattern on the heavy oaken doorway, causing it to open with a low creak. Garren beckoned them with a wave of one pudgy hand.

"Garren, you're back…" spoke the cool voice of a female within the cabin's shadows. "What are you bringing Anari here for?" she asked. "You're always returning with something useless, bothersome… really."

The woman was tall and lithe, a traveler's cloak draped over her frame; she leaned casually against one of the walls of the abode, eyeing the dwarf and the two who followed.

"Shut it, Shelara," Garren cracked, entering the cabin.

Shelara chuckled, folding her arms. A hateful glare was given to Ashylanya and Alec from beneath her long azure-colored hair; one piercing teal colored eye was visible from beneath her trim.

"Why do you bring these two, Garren?" spoke a man's voice from a wooden chair, facing a small fireplace. He turned the chair, causing it to creak and groan against the sturdy wood, grating to the ears of Alec. He faced them, arms folded in front of his chest.

"This boy 'ere," Garren jabbed a meaty thumb at Alec, "spoke the words only we and Jessie know, Lehion."

Lehion was much different than Alec had expected without his cloak.

A mane of dark black hair hung loosely about the elf's shoulders, framing a long thin face. Deep violet colored eyes gazed at them seeming to analyze every detail of them.

The elf wore a grimace upon his otherwise elegant features; one feature that he shared with Shelara was the tattoo symbol upon his right cheek.

"How can that be, Garren?" Lehion drawled. "You know as well as I, she does not favor the Anari." Lehion's eyes narrowed slightly as he spoke.

"This lad claims the lass to be 'is mother." Garren couldn't keep a straight face at these words.

Lehion's eyebrow twitched, as Shelara snorted.

"Well, not technically by birth…" Alec defended. "But she raised me!" Alec interjected, eyeing the three before him.

Ashylanya gripped Alec's hand, squeezing it.

"Oh come off it, the woman's a killing machine!" Shelara spat. "You really expect us to believe she would have a soft spot for you!? After what your kind did to her mother!? Shelara shouted, closing the distance between herself and Alec. They were nose to nose.

"No… that's… It can't be true," Alec stuttered, looking to Ashylanya for support, but her head was lowered.

"Well, it is!" Shelara barked. "They showed the poor ol' gal no mercy…" she hissed.

"You're lying!" Alec shouted to her face.

"S-she told me her mother died of old age, passing the inn down to her," Alec breathed.

"Alec!" Ashylanya breathed.

"I don't care if it alters time, I want answers!"

Ashylanya put her hand on Alec's arm, a sad expression in her amber eyes.

"What made-up world do you live in, boy!?" Shelara chided. "She has an inn?" she scoffed.

Alec took a gamble, praying it would work; he lifted his hand, showing his palm over Shelara's shoulder.

All but Shelara grew deathly quiet.

"What are you doing, boy?" she demanded.

"Shelara… Back away…" Lehion breathed as his eyes widened.

She slowly stepped back; glimpsing Alec's palm, she paled.

"Inconceivable…" Lehion gasped. "Upon a mere child?"

Garren gazed at Alec, his mouth half open.

"Alec…" Ashylanya breathed.

Another of the symbols on Alec's palm had faded more than halfway, as all attention was fixated on the young Anari.

Lehion rose from his chair, approaching Alec.

"This can't be—the Time Breaker Seal!" he breathed, touching Alec's palm. "And it's unraveling… that should never happen." Lehion's voice wavered as he spoke.

"Who gave you this seal, boy?" Lehion demanded.

"I was told a man named Matthias…" Alec replied. "He passed it on to me, saying that I was to be the new bearer of the curse, of endless time, in a dream I had once."

Lehion was dumbstruck when he heard the name.

"There is no way; it isn't impossible!" Shelara cracked.

But she was silenced quickly, with a firm hand from Lehion.

"Tell me everything you know; do not leave out even the slightest detail." Lehion spoke quickly now. "And you—don't fear altering time; you've already done so, simply by being here," he directed at Ashylanya.

"Both of you, tell me all you know." Lehion was firm with his words.

Ashylanya nodded, her hand still on Alec's arm.

Alec and Ashylanya spent well over three hours reliving what had happened prior to and since their arrival. The two elves were fixated upon them, as Garren listened, smoking from a small pipe, facing the windowsill of the small cabin.

Disbelief was etched upon Shelara's face; Lehion, however, seemed to be as still as if carved from stone.

As they finished speaking, the room was completely silent. A dull ring filled Alec's mind through the undisturbed silence as the elves merely gazed at the pair, when suddenly Lehion broke the silence, rising with a low creak from the floorboard.

"Xen'trath..." He breathed. "Just what do you intend?"

"You really expect me to believe that crock of-"

"Shelara, they speak truthfully," Lehion interjected flatly.

"On wha groun's?" Garren said, eyeing the elf.

"What else? The boy's marking..." Lehion replied, slowly turning his head toward the two.

"You don't belong here; you are not in your own era," he breathed, gazing at the two.

"What do you mean?" Alec asked, baffled.

"Ask the girl; I dare say she knows exactly what I mean..."

Alec slowly turned his head toward Ashylanya, eyeing her with a look of confusion.

Ashylanya's head was lowered, her hands clenched tightly in her lap.Slowly she reached up, unbuttoning her blouse.

Alec turned bright red, his eyes shifting to a light rose color, but when he was about to turn away, she turned her back, lowering the upper half of her garment.

There, on her left shoulder blade, was a small black hourglass marking.

———————————————————

Somewhere within the forest, Makkari sat against a tall oak within a familiar clearing, one he knew very well, as he had spent much of his childhood here, sparring with his dearest comrade.

His muscles ached from fatigue, his efforts to find Ashylanya having been fruitless; he resigned to rest for the evening.

Slowly, Makkari pulled off the glove on his right hand. The moon cast a gentle light upon a small black hourglass marking on the back of his hand. He gazed intently at the mark for a moment, and he then looked toward the moon, unblinking.

"To think I'd end up here again..." he muttered to himself, with a deep sigh.

Makkari suddenly rolled out of the way, sensing something barreling toward him; narrowly he evaded his skull being crushed by a large truncheon. The weapon left the tree splintered and cracked.

Makkari glanced over his shoulder, evading yet another potentially fatal blow. The big man withdrew his axes, facing his attacker.

He froze, his eyes widening.

Before him stood a young woman with flame-colored hair braided all the way down to her heels; she readied her mallets, eyeing Makkari furiously.

"Jessica?" Makkari breathed, parrying a heavy blow as she leapt toward him.

"How is it you know my name, you wretch?" the younger version of Jessica bellowed, attempting to overpower the much larger Anari.

"I am not your enemy, girl!" Makkari shouted, knocking her back.

Jessica scoffed. "As if I'd believe the words of the foul Anari race that killed my mother!" she bellowed, swinging at him again.

That's right… it hasn't happened yet, he thought to himself, parrying yet another blow from Jessica's furious swings.

Makkari halted before the woman, as if feigning defeat, kneeling to the ground.

"I see you give in, but I must still take your life; justice shall be mine!" Jessica boomed, bringing down her mallet, only to be struck hard in the gut by Makkari, knocking the wind out of her, before he backhanded her across the face, rendering her unconscious.

Makkari spat, rising from the ground with a low grunt. He looked down at her. Breathing a heavy sigh, he lifted her limp form over his shoulder; he carried her to a large rock, resting her gently against it.

"Always so hotheaded, Jessica…" he muttered under his breath. "Just like me."

Looking down at her once more, he hoisted his axes, replacing them into their harness, having dropped them to carry Jessica. He gave her a final glance as he departed.

Chapter Twenty-One

Alec, even though he had seen the mark on her previously, was baffled by it, as he gazed at her rounded shoulder.

Slowly, he placed his hand on the marking as Ashylanya whimpered from a warm touch over the ice cold image.

"Ashylanya..." Alec breathed. "I've seen this mark before, but what does it mean?"

"The Timeless Touch..." she breathed with a wavering voice.

"I don't understand—how does that answer my question?" Alec asked, befuddled.

"It means, ever since the curse was placed upon me, I have not aged even a single day in over ten thousand years..." Her head was lowered as she spoke, hot tears landing on her hands as she held them clasped in front of her.

"Ten thousand years...?" Alec breathed, astonished.

"I'm so sorry Alec, I've hidden so much from you! I've known where we are, all along," she said softly.

"What do you mean?" Alec asked, gently caressing the mark, as if trying to wipe it away.

Ashylanya pulled her blouse back over her shoulders; fastening the buttons, she turned toward Alec.

"I was born in this time, exactly nineteen years earlier..." she said through harsh sobs, bringing her hands to her face.

"Ash..." Alec breathed with an empathetic look upon his face.

Ashylanya threw herself into Alec's arms, sobbing in despair.

"No... for tha curse to 'ave been placed, th'abyssal seed would 'ave to be..." Garren breathed, having stopped huffing on his pipe.

"But that's impossible!" Shelara blurted. "He's too strong to let the seed fall to another's hands!"

"The seed itself was fractured around this time. It now exists out of time and space, and therefore, Matthias IS the embodiment of time currently..." Ashylanya added.

"What exactly do you mean, girl?" Lehion asked, eyeing her.

Slowly Ashylanya withdrew the pendant she carried around her neck, causing an immediate reaction to Alec's palm, which resonated a dull blue once more, pulsating.

"No, that can't be..." Lehion gasped. "A fragment of the abyssal seed...?"

Ashylanya nodded.

"Once every ten thousand years, the seeds meet in one time frame; should they be reassembled, it could spell doom for us all." Ashylanya's voice faded out.

"So Matthias took on the Warden's energy upon the seeds fracturing?" Shelara asked, still not believing what she was hearing.

"It is quite befuddling, I know, but the event of the seeds fracturing can only ever happen one time, no matter if one goes back to try and stop it. What's done is done, and therefore, a living vessel is necessary," Ashylanya continued.

"But why then does this boy have the warden's mark?" Lehion inquired.

"That's because the mark's matrix has been altered to accommodate the warden's unlimited power," Ashylanya replied. "As opposed to the past, where the mark merely kept the seed from swallowing you whole, its purpose has been altered."

"So that would mean that Matthias is the time warden's living vessel now?" Shelara asked, still trying to understand.

"Yes, and he died, in the time we came from... Perhaps this time the outcome will be different. A war is coming, of cosmic proportions..." Ashylanya breathed.

"But if there is no seed to fracture, how is it that you retain the Timeless Touch?"

"The curse can never be removed, not unless the seed is reassembled by the right hands and used to do so," Ashylanya said, eyeing the three.

Ashylanya rose from the floor, approaching Garren at the windowsill, looking out.

The moon was full that night, casting a gentle light upon the sea of violet, her homeland of Venarette.

"We've already altered time greatly, just by being here; you are right, Lehion... and now, new paths of history will be carved." Ashylanya sighed. "Forgive us Alec, but the home you used to know is gone, forever..."

Alec was in utter shock at this news.

"It appears Xen'trath has fooled us once more, into coming back to this time. We have weakened Matthias..." Ashylanya said.

"And how is that?" Alec asked.

"Two wardens cannot exist in the same time period for an extended period of time... both wardens will be weakened greatly by an illness known as Time Fever, if I am correct," Lehion answered for her.

Ashylanya nodded.

"But then why does he show no signs of illness?" Shelara asked, eyeing Ashylanya. "Time sickness takes its toll rather quickly from what I've read in old dusty tomes in Valaresk, my homeland. It is said, that should the warden ever require a mortal vessel that two cannot exist at once. In fact, from what I've read, the energies of the warden would be too powerful for a mere child to handle."

"Alec is no mere child; within him he carries the blood of the Dawn Strider," Ashylanya answered.

"Impossible," Lehion scoffed. "The strider conceived a child?"

"Yes, only one... and he stands before you." Ashylanya spoke in a low voice. "I witnessed it firsthand, when we were enveloped in the Time Veil."

Alec's vision shifted to a pale plum color, as he suddenly was able to see the magic which surrounded the cabin—a large reinforced wall of energy hovered before the abode on all sides, and he could see, for miles, other blips of magical energy drifting through the atmosphere.

Alec shifted his gaze momentarily to the right, seeing a deep black energy slinking through the forest; a chain linked the two who walked in the shadows.

"There's someone out there," Alec blurted, interrupting Ashylanya. "Someone chained to another; I saw their energy from afar."

"How far off?" Lehion asked, withdrawing small, elegant dagger from his holster.

"About two hundred yards," Alec replied, watching as the dark energies continued to move.

"So it is true, you bare th'blood of th'strider in yer veins..." Garren breathed. "A legend was all I thought she ever was... a mere tall tale at that."

Alec suddenly doubled over in agony, as his sight shifted once more to pure silver.

"Please, please help me!" a voice cried in Alec's mind. "I can't take this pain anymore!"

Alec felt his presence suddenly shift into a dark clearing, where a pale woman wept. Dark tears stained her cheeks as she cried. "Sister, please help me, Ceri!!!" the woman cried, revealing her eyes, which were hollow and cold. Black pits gazed into Alec's own as Alec gazed at the Edelion before him. A long chain rattled from behind her, linking her through her chest to another.

"Please... Make this pain end..." she pleaded, eyeing Alec, who was in spirit form.

"Silence Lucin..." came a dark and cruel voice. "We shall find her, and you will become one with her once more. The master has a plan to awaken her!"

The voice was very familiar to Alec, sensing the energy of Xen'trath close by, but before he came into view, Alec was being shaken roughly.

"Alec, are you okay?" spoke the voice of Ashylanya. "What did you see?"

"A woman with dark starlit hair; the stars were like embers of fire!" Alec wheezed. "She was chained to someone—she was chained to Xen'trath!"

Lehion and Shelara went pale. Garren dropped his pipe.

"Xen'trath has the Dusk Strider in his possession?" Ashylanya breathed.

"Yet another figure of ol' folk tales…" Garren muttered. "Th'hell's going on here…"

"She keeps muttering for someone called Ceri…" Alec breathed, as he clasped his skull, flashing images of the two entered his brain, searing his mind with each image. A large weapon of mass destruction, odd steel constructs filled his brain, obliteration of the fourteen worlds, he witnessed, all at once.

Alec keeled over, losing consciousness, falling limp into Ashylanya, who caught him as he fell.

"He still doesn't quite have control of the pendulum yet…" she muttered.

"It's getting quite late, anyway…" Shelara stated. "We should rest for the evening; whatever's out there should not be able to sense the barrier disguising us…"

"Unfortunately, we are short on blankets. You will have to use these to keep warm," Shelara said, throwing a pair of traveler's cloaks onto Ashylanya's lap, over Alec's face.

"I'm sorry Alec…" Ashylanya breathed. "I'm sorry to drag you into all of this…"

As she spoke, Alec's tail gently wrapped itself around her arm, as she cradled him in her arms, gazing down at him with a gentle smile.

Chapter Twenty-Two

" "Think I'm gonna be sick," Sam groaned, having ridden on the leophan's back for hours. The three youth were sore from clinging tightly to the large cat.

Lucy glanced back at Gabriel, who still had his head lowered as he clung tightly to her. His tear-stained cheeks shined in the moonlight as the leophan made one final bound, exiting the large golden forest, which glowed an eerie light in the evening, as if the trees themselves were light sources on their own.

Joden brought the leophan to a halt simply by caressing the beast's fur.

"We've arrived, just in time it seems."

The four now faced a large open plane, filled with lush azure grass which waved gently in the moonlight through a soft refreshing breeze. The scent of many varieties of flowers penetrated the nostrils of the three youth, bringing a sense of peace.

Not a hundred yards away was a small village, fortified with large walls made of timber in the distance. The gates were tightly shut for the eve, as the guards stood at their posts; seeming to catch sight of the four from a distance, they whispered amongst themselves.

"He should be here at this hour," Joden said as the leophan slowly walked toward the distant village.

"Joden?" Lucy asked. "Why is this man so important?"

"Why?" he said. "Because there can only ever be one of his like."

"But what is he?" she asked, curiosity eating at her.

"He is the vessel of a being known as Xanadair, the Time Warden," Joden replied. "As is, as you claim, this friend of yours," he replied, looking troubled.

"But you said there can only be one, right?" she said. "Then how-

"That's what troubles me," Joden interjected. "If there really is a second Warden, it will create a paradox," he said gravely.

"A paradox?" she inquired, cocking one of her eyebrows.

"All that you once knew will be unwritten; the time you knew will be gone forever..." Joden said, eyeing her over his shoulder.

"This is why we must see Matthias; only he can confirm the truth of your tale." Joden finished, as they approached the much larger than anticipated gated entrance to the village.

"State your business!" a croaking voice came from atop the post behind the gate.

"I am here to meet an old friend; we have an urgent matter to discuss," Joden called back to the man atop the gate.

"Joden? Is that you?!" the man called from beyond. "Open the gate; hurry, you fools!" the man barked.

The gate to the village creaked open, allowing the four to enter.

Alavanda seemed relieved to unload the four from her back; having carried them a long distance, she was heavily fatigued.

They were greeted by a shorter man, beaming up at the elder Arcaneight.

"Joden, my old friend!" His croaking voice sounded overjoyed at seeing him.

"Galfrie! It has been far too long!" Joden stooped to clasp the man's short, stubby hand.

Galfrie was an older looking dwarf, a mere four feet in height. He was adorned with plated armor that was much too large for his stature, and long graying hair framed a rounded face. An eye patch covered the man's left eye, as the other, a lime green, gazed at the taller man before him.

"I must say, Galfrie, you look in much better shape than when we last met!" Joden said, clasping the dwarf's shoulder.

"Ah yes, the pox have left me—not before doing their damage, gods be damned, but I am faring much better than before!" said Galfrie, pulling back the sleeve of his tunic, revealing a heavily scarred arm.

"Well now, at least you're in one piece! It could have been worse!" Joden rambled. "I remember-"

"Don't we have 'urgent' business to attend to here?" Sam interjected, cutting Joden off.

"Ah, I believe I let myself get carried away; forgive me, Galfrie!" Joden bowed before the short man.

"Very well, old friend, perhaps another time!" Galfrie replied, returning to his post.

"You didn't have to be so rude," Lucy chided, eyeing Sam.

"Well, don't you want to know more as well?" Sam retorted.

"Let's just go…" Gabriel chimed in, still in a state of depression.

Both glanced back at Gabriel, feeling helpless to lighten his mood.

Joden's brow furrowed as he watched Galfrie return to his post. A faint scent of dark magic caught the wind; Joden could sense it all too well.

"Let's be off then, shall we?" Joden said, as he had begun to walk the narrow cobblestone streets of the dark village.

"Where exactly are we, Joden?" Lucy asked.

"Ah, the village of Getherbhen, the halfway point between two vast forests: the forest of dawn, the one we just left, and to the west is Venarrette, the forest of origin."

"I see…" Lucy said, eyeing the cramped village.

Every building was tightly packed close together, with narrow pathways that snaked through the village. A certain air of darkness seemed to permeate their surroundings, as not a single lamp was lit at any hearth within the town.

Every so often Lucy heard a cry in the darkness, that of a female; harsh sobs could be heard through the streets, as a depressed air seemed to engulf the party.

"Something does not feel right here…" Lucy stated, eyeing Joden.

"I know, just do not make eye contact with any of the commoners. I have a feeling I know exactly what's going on here…" Joden said, eyeing his surroundings. A dark presence hid within the shadows nearby.

The cloaked figure had its hood drawn low as it watched the four pass by. A wide fleshless grin formed on what could be seen of its face as it maneuvered its fingers; threads seemed to be linking the skeletal being to several of the commoners around.

"Is this the one, worm?" the dark, deathly voice of the figure echoed quietly to a short and stout figure before him.

"Do you think he suspects?" came the gruff voice of Galfrie.

"The warden expects all…" the dark presence whispered. "No, the young warden is not among them…" it hissed.

"How can that be, master?" the puppet that was Galfrie asked in a broken tone. "The master told us they would all be arriving together…"

"It seems things did not go as intended…" the deathly voice whispered. "No matter, we still have the warden of this era surrounded…" it hissed. A deep rattling sound swept through the darkened alleyway as the figure finished speaking.

"They are in our grasp… at least… they will lead us to the boy," the figure said, with one final deep rattling breath, before departing into the shadows.

The three youth followed closely. Joden seemed to grow tense, as the darkness seemed to deepen as they walked, eventually coming to a halt at the front of a small pub.

An old wooden sign, creaking in the wind, read 'The Lycan's Fang'.

"Fitting place for him to take shelter for the evening…" Joden muttered, slowly opening the wooden door and entering with the trio close behind him, not wanting to be left out in the darkness.

"You didn't know that he'd be here, did you?" Lucy accused, eyeing the elder.

"Hadn't a clue, to be honest, but I can track his energy. I know where he is, generally, at all times," Joden said, glancing at Lucy.

"But then, why can't you pin point Alec?"

"That's either because the tale is false, or his sealing is of a different nature, and his power has yet to come forth," Joden explained. "Speaking to Matthias should prove if your tale is indeed the truth."

The pub itself was dimly lit, with few tables. Patrons sat huddled together talking in whispers. Joden himself only paid mind to the sole figure sitting at the bar, his back turned.

A worn traveler's cloak draped the figure, making him indistinguishable amongst the other patrons. All that could be discerned was that he had a long canine snout and two silver fangs pressed firmly against his fur coated face. He held out his hand, gazing at the marking on his palm, which resembled the one Alec had, as Lucy had seen it, though the runes of this mark were connected with small lines, making a tetrahedron-like pattern.

Joden approached the figure; three behind him eyed the patrons warily.

"Good evening, Matthias."

The wolfish man turned his head, nodding in greeting. "It's been a long time, Tome keeper, and I know what brings you here..." Matthias spoke in a low tone. "I do not sense him though; he is not with you." This seemed to concern the Anari greatly.

"We were separated upon our arrival..." Lucy said, eyeing Matthias, who silenced her with a steady hand.

"Careful, we are not among friends here; something dark lurks in the shadows..."

"A reaver?" Joden muttered.

Matthias grinned. "You can sense just about anything a mile away old friend."

"Age and experience are all I can really give myself credit for," Joden replied.

"Its strings litter the walkways everywhere. This whole town has been subdued by a single reaver," Joden whispered.

"A powerful one, if he can control so many..." Matthias chuckled. "And by the looks of things, we're no longer safe here..." he continued, eyeing the patrons. Every head in the inn had been turned toward them, eyeing them with bloodlust.

"It looks like we have a fight on our hands, my dear old friend," Joden said, placing his staff in front of him.

"That we do..." Matthias replied, a lithe blade slowly sliding down his arm as he took a final pull from a mug of red wine.

Chapter Twenty-Three

Later that evening, Alec stirred. Ashylanya sat by the windowsill, staring off blankly at the moon, her face tear-stained.

"Ashylanya…" he breathed. "Are you okay?"

"I'm so sorry I hid all of this from you, Alec…" she whispered, as Alec approached her at the windowsill, gazing out at the moon with her. "I just didn't want anyone to know about it. I've lived far too long, and I've grown weary of this existence…"

"It's okay… I understand, Ash…" Alec cooed, giving her a gentle smile. "You are my friend, even if we only recently met; I'd have done the same," Alec reassured her.

"Thank you, Alec…" she whispered, hugging him tightly.

The marking on Alec's palm began to glow dimly once more in their embrace.

"That pendant of yours," Alec said, eyeing her, "every time I come into contact with it visually or physically, my mark glows… why is that?"

"It's because it's a fragment of the warden's original prison. Long ago, the gods created him to bear the weight of time on his shoulders," she explained. "But he was deemed a danger to the gods, as everything he touched turned to dust."

"I see…" Alec said, still gazing at Ashylanya.

"The eternal seed, before it was corrupted, becoming the abyssal seed, was what the gods contained him in, and each era had a designated bearer," she continued.

"But why did they choose me? Why is this strider so important?"

"You are the first who has had to physically bear the time warden at your age," Ashylanya said with her gaze still upon the moon.

"The strider was created by the gods as a precaution; if the worlds of the fourteen were ever to fall to corruption, she would be used to purge the worlds entirely," Ashylanya explained. "She too was imprisoned, deemed a danger to all, as she was created by all fourteen gods; she has a dark and a light half: the dawn strider and the dusk strider."

"If the striders were ever to become whole once more, all existence would be in grave danger..."

Ashylanya idly wrapped her tail around two fingers as she spoke. Alec himself gripped his own tail, which felt soft between his fingers.

"We really should get some rest, Alec, I can see a long day ahead of us tomorrow..." Ashylanya said, smiling at Alec.

Not thirty minutes later, Ashylanya lay asleep on the floor, her tail casually rested between her legs, as her ears twitched slightly every so often.

Alec merely watched her as she slept; something deep within him made him feel comfortable and safe around her.

Garren had awoken, sitting at the windowsill, keeping watch; every so often he took a puff from his small carved pipe.

Shelara and Lehion both slept on the floor next to each other, the back of Shelara's hand resting on Lehion's chest.

Alec's gaze shifted to the ceiling of the small cabin, beginning to doze off, trying to fight the sensation. His efforts were in vain, however, as he drifted to sleep.

"Alec..." a soft voice hissed.

Alec slowly opened his eyes.

"Alec..." the voice seemed to draw closer, as Alec slowly regained his composure.

Alec slowly rose, gazing down; he saw his own sleeping form before him.

Glancing around the room he saw the others, who now resembled mere paintings on a dark canvas. The smoke from Garren's pipe seemed to be caught unmoving, as the dwarf was mid-blink, his eyes half closed.

"I know where you are, Alec..." the voice hissed menacingly.

Alec was petrified; slowly he turned, coming face to face with an all too familiar pair of blood red eyes.

"You will be all of their undoing!" the demonic voice boomed.

"L-leave me alone..." Alec stuttered.

Alec's mind was suddenly filled with horrific images of death and blight. He fell to his knees in pain as the familiar shine of the twin hourglass pupils overwhelmed him.

"They do not care about you, boy..." the voice croaked. "You are a mere tool for them to continue their meager little existence...!" The demon's voice echoed in his mind, with cold and cruel laughter. "You and the girl will both serve my purpose in the end," the demon hissed.

"What the hell do you want with us?" Alec asked, his voice broken.

"I exist out of time and space. You are in my hands now, guided by my hand, whether you like it or not..." the voice mocked.

"Shut up!" Alec shouted.

Alec awoke with a start; slowly turning his head, he noticed Ashylanya wasn't lying next to him anymore.

Carefully, as not to wake the others, he got to his feet. Slowly Alec walked toward the door of the cabin, edging it open.

His new ears perked up at the sound of gentle singing in the distance.

Closing the door behind him carefully, he began to walk toward the source of the beautiful singing.

Passing through a small patch of trees, concealing himself, he saw Ashylanya, sitting by a small creek, her bare feet dipped in the gently flowing waters.

In her hand was her small gemstone pendant. She twirled it idly, watching the sunrise as she sang.

Alec's breath was taken by the sweet and smooth melody. Ashylanya's voice was so perfect and beautiful, it astounded Alec.

He slowly approached her, ignoring the pulsations his palm was giving off. As it glowed brightly once more, he sat down next to her.

"You sing so well, Ash..." he breathed with a smile; his eyes had shifted to a light violet, matching the leaves within the forest.

Ashylanya blushed, having not noticed his presence until he spoke. Slowly she opened her eyes, gazing at him.

"Alec, I thought you'd still be sleeping." She giggled, a shy look on her face.

"Oh? Is someone a bit shy to sing in front of others?" he teased, with a grin.

Ashylanya's blush deepened. "Maybe a little..." she said, softly.

"You look pale, Alec... is something wrong?" she asked, eyeing him with a concerned expression.

"Just another bad dream..." he replied with a half-smile.

"What was it about?" she asked. "Tell me everything you can about it."

Alec tried to explain, but all he could truly recall were a vast set of blood red eyes, which pierced him to his core; any other details he tried to relay were stalled, as his tongue felt swollen.

"I can't really recall any more than that. I forgot most of it after awakening," he replied, seeing the pale expression on her face.

"Blood red eyes..." she breathed. "He's placed a tongue curse on you; you won't be able to tell me about this dream," she said, still gazing at him.

"But how did you-"

"Because I had a similar dream, and I myself cannot speak of its details," she interjected.

"Lady Ashylanya!" a familiar voice shouted, from just beyond the forest's perimeter.

Both turned, seeing the large form of Makkari running toward them.

"Makkari!" Ashylanya shouted back. Rising from Alec's side, she hugged him. "I thought we had lost you in the rifts of time!" Ashylanya said.

"I am relieved that you are unharmed," Makkari spoke, before eyeing Alec. "Better not have tried anything funny, pup," he said, with a low growl.

Alec's tail suddenly fled between his legs, his ears folding back.

"No, Makkari, he was very polite," Ashylanya defended, backing up to face the big man.

He gazed at Alec a moment more before turning his head toward her.

"Where are the other pups?" he asked, glancing around his perimeter.

"Only Alec and I managed to find each other," she explained.

"I see-"

Makkari was then cut off by a blade pressing lightly to his throat.

"State your business with the lady, quickly, lest I sever your head from your body." The stern voice of Lehion spoke from behind him.

"Makkari Ashencrest… bodyguard to Lady Ashylanya," Makkari stated, his eyes directed toward the blade at his throat.

"That blade…" Makkari breathed.

"This true, Lady Ashylanya?" Lehion asked, pressing in a little more with the edge of his blade.

"It is, please don't hurt him!" she shouted.

Lehion eased, lowering his blade.

Makkari turned his head, glaring at the elf.

"Apologies, never know who to trust these days, what with the Sulmothian shifters lurking about."

"Sulmothian shifters?" Alec asked.

"Draconic beings with the ability to take on any form… I have been fooled one time too many by those foul creatures, the ones who have fallen to become Demorae," Lehion explained.

Alec nodded in understanding.

"Sulmothians?" Makkari glanced at the elf. "So we truly are in that time period…" he muttered to himself, a grave expression upon his visage.

Makkari caught sight of the elf's marking on his right cheek, his eyes narrowing slightly. "An Amari sky elf, royal guard… what is one of your kind doing on the surface world?" Makkari asked, looking puzzled.

"I am no longer a guard, I abandoned that post long ago, but you need not know more," the elf said, eyeing him with a frown.

"Lehion!" shouted Shelara, sprinting to his side, Garren in tow.

"Who is this Anari?" Shelara asked, glaring at Makkari.

"Two royal guards and a Velenar sea dwarf..." Makkari seemed to be even more puzzled by this. "Ah... I remember you now!" Makkari shouted.

"What are you talking about, you lumbering oaf? We have never met before," Shelara hissed.

"Be more respectful Shelara, he remembers us as we were in the tale they told us the previous night." A grim look crossed Lehion's face in his explanation.

Makkari immediately looked toward Alec and Ashylanya. "What exactly have you told them? Do you not understand that-

"I will say it again; you have already altered time simply by being here..." Lehion interjected, eyeing the big man.

"I was always under the impression that the Velenar and the Amari did not get along..." Makkari stated, eyeing the three.

"As I've said, that is none of your concern," Lehion said, firmly. "We have no time to stand here idly; we must find Matthias before it's too late."

Makkari froze, his eyes widening. "Matthias... still exists in this time frame?"

"Indeed, Anari, he does... which means-"

"The war of the gods approaches us..." Makkari finished Lehion's sentence.

"Indeed..." Lehion said, turning toward the cabin. "We won't be needing this anymore; we will hide it for now..." Lehion stated, removing the carefully placed stone, causing the hovel to dissipate, the patch of forest from before replacing the humble abode.

"A disguising ward—you are quite adept with rune crafting, elf," Makkari praised, eyeing the stone in Lehion's hand.

"Only th'finest o' the sky kingdom!" Garren chimed in. "If you could see 'is 'andywork!"

"Enough Garren, remember, we are still among strangers after all, regardless of who they are."

"Aye lad," Garren said, before turning toward the patch of forest. Shoving a handful of tobacco into his small pipe, he lit it, taking a long draw from it.

"How is it that you know of Matthias, Anari?" Shelara asked, eyeing Makkari. "The man doesn't even associate with his own kind, let alone anyone else…"

"He is like a brother to me; together we fought many battles. I remember sparring with him in our youth, before he was chosen to become the next warden, and we slowly drifted apart from that point forward…" Makkari said with a pained expression on his face.

"It would seem, if that's the case, that the time we all feared would come is fast approaching," Shelara stated. "Bothersome, really…"

Makkari nodded, grimly.

"It would seem that time hasn't been altered by just us, if he is the physical bearer now, as opposed to merely carrying the eternal seed with him," Makkari said, before turning. Placing two fingers between his lips, he whistled.

"What is it that you are doing?" Lehion asked. "You'll draw all of the geists to our location!"

He was cut off, however, by the loud rumble of padded feet, as five leophan bounded from the forest. The leader of the pack was a sturdy female with a long white mane. Several braids decorated the fur of the large feline; its large sky blue eyes gazed into Makkari's own.

Garren seemed awestruck by the sudden appearance. Recognizing the leader of the pack he turned to Makkari.

"I've only 'erd tales of you… and yer battle prowess… you mus' be Makkari of the crescent moons!" Garren beamed.

"That I am…" Makkari said proudly, mounting the large leophan before him, hoisting Ashylanya up behind him.

Alec merely stood there, awestruck. "What are these things?" he gasped.

The creatures before him were a mix of a panther and a lion. The leader of the pack yawned before eyeing Alec.

"They are called leophans and this here is Lady Sholuun, leader of the pack."

"Now that would make this journey a lot less of a bother," Shelara mused, approaching a leophan and reaching to touch its mane, causing it to back away momentarily, before nuzzling her hand and allowing her to mount.

The six companions had mounted the leophans now, and the party was off not a moment later, as Makkari dug his heel into Sholuun's side, causing her to bound off into the forest, the other four leophan following suit, as the party vanished into the woodlands at intense speed.

Chapter Twenty-Four

J oden and Matthias had backed into the bar, the children standing behind them, as the commoners slowly twitched and jittered like puppets, slowly closing in on them, they could hear Alavanda growling ferociously just beyond the door clawing to enter.

"Alavanda, flee!" Joden commanded, with no further sound from the big cat, only heavy footsteps could be heard as the leophan did exactly what it was told.

"The day I feared has come it appears, they are not here for us, and we are merely in their way." Matthias spoke quickly.

"What do you mean, old friend?" Joden said, eyeing the macabre display before him of twitching and jolting commoners, as they stiffly moved closer to the group.

"The coming of the second warden of course..." Matthias breathed. "Curse Xen'trath, he just couldn't leave it be!"

"So they are here for Alec?" Lucy asked, from behind Matthias.

"Indeed, and I can sense the anger of the reaver just beyond, that he is not among you, which means their plan was flawed, at least slightly," Matthias answered, quickly beheading a patron that had drawn too close, its head bounced along the floor, rolling under one of the tables within the pub, its mouth still moving in a gruesome display.

"This village is infested with drones," Matthias muttered.

"Drones?" Lucy asked, befuddled as she eyed the twisted men and women, frightened.

"Victims of a reaver, their souls consumed, they are naught but empty shells of who they once were..." Joden explained.

"Hand me a sword I'll help fight them off!" Sam shouted.

"Now's not the time boy, we have to get out of this village, we are all in danger as long as the reaver lives."

One of the twisted looking commoners opened its jaw wide as it let out a hollow roar, leaping at Joden, only to quickly turn to dust from a blast of flame from the head of the elder's staff.

"This way, Children!" Joden shouted, as they maneuvered around the bar toward the back exit.

"But what about Matthias?" Lucy asked gazing back at him.

"He can handle himself!" Joden shouted, now go!"

The drones took on a darker appearance as the seconds past, long claws had formed on their hands, grating together in eagerness to shed blood, their eyes becoming hollow and soulless as their flesh began to decay rapidly from their bones.

"Go!" Joden shouted, as the three hurried toward the exit, Matthias sending yet another head flying in their direction, its fleshless face still moving as if trying to bite at Lucy's ankles.

Lucy shrieked, stomping on the head of it until it stopped moving, her left ankle soaked in blood from her hurried action to spare her leg.

The four of them bolted for the back door, as Joden burned yet another to Ashes who tried to bar their way, they swung the door wide open, to be greeted by a thick fog which had not been present on their arrival.

"The reaver's making its move." Joden said, grimly.

Despite the rising sun, the village itself was filled with a dark miasma, clouding the light from entering, more ghastly figures could be seen fidgeting as they jolted toward the four, Joden casting spell after spell to burn away at the seemingly endless numbers.

"How long do you think you can resist, Arcaneight..." Spoke a low rattling voice which echoed through the village. "Even one such as you, with your endless power, cannot hope to stop them all!" The deathly voice roared, as a slashing blade sliced through the fog, cutting the sleeve of Joden's cloak.

"This way children!" Joden shouted, as they ran through the now crowded village. "Even if he is a powerful reaver, he cannot control every puppet at once!" He said, as they pushed their way through the soulless crowd, which eyed them seemingly envious of their living forms.

"Is that a fact…?" The deathly voice rattled, as the drones now barred their passage, the reaver let out a cold laugh.

"So… where is the other little warden the master told us to capture?" The voice hissed.

"As if we'd tell you!" Sam barked.

Gabriel seemed too frightened to speak, quivering, Lucy gripped his hand tightly, to try and settle his nerves, to no avail.

"Why are these things after my brother?" Gabriel croaked. "Why can't we just go home?!"

Lucy looked at Gabriel sadly, as the wall of puppets slowly jolted and slid their feet toward the group, closing in all around.

Joden, began to mutter an incantation, as the drones closed in, the staff even though lacking its crystal burned brightly as a ring of blue fire suddenly flared up around them, keeping the puppets at bay.

The reaver simply chuckled, as it threw one drone after another to their deaths as the flames licked at them and burnt them to Ashes in seconds.

"Poor old fool…" The reaver taunted. "You think losing a few of my thousands of slaves is going to alter the outcome in any way?"

Joden's appearance darkened, as he lowered his head; the reaver slowly coming into view.

Lucy and Gabriel were aghast at what they saw; Sam curled his hand into a fist, withdrawing a small dagger from his breaches.

"Sam let Joden handle this, they obviously don't die easily!" Lucy said, exasperatedly.

"You really expect me to just stand around doing nothing?" Sam blurted, driving the dagger deep into one of the drones skulls who managed to crawl through the flame unhindered, though badly chard.

"Your efforts are in vain, boy… my army, is endless!" The reaver boomed, as he continued to throw one after another into the flames. "How long can you keep up with me, Tome Keeper?" the skeletal figure taunted.

The fog lifted now, revealing the Reaver's full and terrible form, thousands of long strands of what looked as if they were ghostly strings panned out all along the endless crowd of dead villagers.

Lucy turned her head away, unable to stand the sight of the monstrosity before her.

The figure was well over seven feet in height, lacking flesh, it's deathly maw appeared in the shape of a constant grin, as soulless black eyes gazed at Joden, a dark veil of flame like shadow engulfed the reaver, its long bony fingers moved his pawns into play one after another.

A large scythe the figure carried in a third hand beneath the cloak jutted out from the shadowed flames, the faces of the dead carved into the hilt in a macabre display.

"A wielder of a Soul eater's blade…" Joden was aghast. "It is no wonder he can control so many."

"What is that?" Sam asked, looking up to Joden.

"A soul eaters blade, can only be carried by a figure able to deal with its diminishing properties, it eats at ones soul the longer its used," Joden explained. "There is only one other who I know of that wields such a blade."

Joden was interrupted however, when the figure drew in a deep breath, inhaling the flames that protected the four, slowly the flames began to dissipate as Joden tried with all his might to keep the flames burning brightly.

"It's useless, old fool…" The voice of the reaver echoed in his mind, as he continued to consume the flames around them, allowing his macabre puppets to step forth closing further in on them.

The reaver quickly moved, lashing at Joden, and cutting deep into his arm, severing it.

"Agh!" Joden cried out, as the flames dissipated entirely, the reaver standing above him, raising its scythe to deal a final blow.

The reaver was interrupted however, when Matthias suddenly appeared before it, lashing deep into the reaver's side, cutting deeply; causing it to retreat into the shadows.

"Timely appearances as usual, my old friend." Joden gasped. "Now if you would please…"

Joden held out the bloody stump of his arm to Matthias, who looked downward at it from beneath his hood, a bright flash filled the clearing, as Joden's arm seemed to regrow.

The three youths were awestruck, as they watched Joden regain his hand as if it were never touched.

"What did you just do?" Lucy gasped.

"A time reversal spell…" Matthias replied, only one of my expertise can perform such a spell, you're lucky I came as soon as I did, I can only reverse something that happened moments beforehand…"

"I am grateful dear old friend." Joden said, raising his head toward Matthias.

"I'm not through with you yet…!" The mocking voice of the reaver echoed, appearing from the shadows and cleaving downward, Matthias however did not waiver, he did not even appear to move a muscle, and the reaver screamed out in agony, as it was torn in two, by Matthias's speed in which he cleaved upward with his blade, causing the creature to burn to Ashes before him with one final echoing cry.

"Ah, but I am through with you…" Matthias mocked, his gaze fixated on the blade the reaver left behind, as all the macabre puppets collapsed into dust all around them, the fog lifting entirely revealing the rising sun, which contrasted eerily with the dark and quiet streets of the now vacant town.

Matthias quickly approached the blade. Lifting it, he poured his energy into it, causing it to rust and crumble in his grasp.

This however, caused Matthias to gasp, coughing up blood as he fell to one knee.

"Matthias!?" Joden called to him, exasperatedly.

But Matthias held up one hand, indicating that he step no further toward him.

Slowly Matthias withdrew his hood, turning to face Joden.

"The Time Fever has already set in…" Joden breathed, observing Matthias's haggard looking features.

The eyes that should have been a solid gold, were a dull red in hue, blood leaked from the Warden's lips as he gazed up at Joden, his braided mane of hair was in tatters, as if he had not groomed himself in weeks.

"So their tale was true…" Joden breathed.

"Indeed, old friend… The prophesied second warden has come, the one of the striders blood, just as I foresaw…"

"What game is Xen'trath playing at?" Joden asked Matthias, eyeing him uneasily.

Matthias chuckled. "You can never tell with that one, old friend…" Matthias wheezed. My brother grows stronger by the moment; I must find the boy…" Matthias said, before suddenly vanishing, leaving the four staring blankly at where he stood not a moment before.

Chapter Twenty-Five

It was mid-afternoon before the six companions decided to stop and rest for a short while. The leophans had slumped to the soft earth, happy to have a break from a constant pace. They gnawed eagerly on the remains of a freshly slain buck Shelara had taken down with a skilled arrow to its skull.

Garren sat quietly on a large moss-covered boulder with Lehion, casually puffing on his pipe as he blew smoke rings. Shelara sat at the base of one of the large elm trees within the forest, eating a fresh apple as she gazed at a large map.

Makkari was the only one not at ease, pacing before Shelara, eager to continue their search.

"Calm down, Anari... You're making me dizzy just watching you," Shelara chided. "It's quite bothersome really..." she said, taking another bite from the apple.

"We don't have time to waste just sitting here!" he retorted, his tail flicking impatiently.

"We are not as full of energy as you seem to be, and neither are the leophans," she replied, sounding annoyed.

Ashylanya sat behind an elm opposite Shelara, idly twirling the small pendant she wore between her thumb and forefinger.

Alec had approached her, sitting down beside her. "That necklace..." Alec began. "You've had it since birth, you said, right?"

"Yes, ever since I can remember, this necklace has been with me," Ashylanya replied, glancing at Alec. "It's always felt quite strange, cold to the touch, though it is constructed of pure light energy, from what I've gleaned from it."

"Do you think it could have anything to do with my mark unraveling?" Alec asked, eyeing the gem, which made his palm glow.

"It shouldn't; it would require more crystal shards completing its full form to have that kind of effect."

Alec felt uneasy in the pendant's presence, as if it were draining him of his energy.

"All my father told me of it was that it was special in its own way, and that I should protect it with my life," she said, still twirling it.

"Break's over!" Garren called over his shoulder, before climbing down from the rock. The leophans seemed too content to budge, but with effort they were on their feet again, though reluctantly.

"Guess we have to go now." Alec said, rising. He held out his hand to help Ashylanya to her feet.

She thanked him, lightly taking his hand.

Alec froze as his body suddenly pulsated.

"Alec? Are you all right?" Ashylanya asked, standing up and looking at him with concern.

But Alec did not hear her; his entire body pulsed violently, his head now pounding.

"You... cannot escape my wrath!" a booming voice filled Alec's mind. He looked up to see a dozen armored men riding large wolves approaching them fast through the trees.

"Look out!" he cried, his eyes shifting to golden hourglasses once more. "An ambush!"

Ashylanya looked behind her just in time to see the small platoon charging toward them.

"Defend yourselves!" Lehion cried, as Shelara leapt to her feet, drawing her bow and felling one of the riders.

Makkari withdrew his axes, beheading one rider, before bringing his axe down upon his mounts skull, causing it to yelp before lying motionless.

Ashylanya knelt by Alec as the others clashed with their attackers.

Garren swung his axe low, dismembering one of the wolves' legs, sending its rider tumbling to the earth, as the leophan joined in the fray, fighting the wolves as their riders were dismounted one by one.

Makkari roared, striking another in the head, the man's steel helm flying off.

"No... it can't be!" he breathed as he finished his opponent with a strike to the chest.

Lying on the cold earth was another Anarian male, though twisted and corrupt looking, its eyes sunken into its skull as its flesh had decayed.

"Demorae Anarians?" Makkari spoke, baffled. "What is the meaning of this!" he roared, cleaving another's shoulder, as Garren leapt behind Makkari, parrying the blow aimed for the big man's skull and cutting into the attacker's torso.

"Don' let yer guard down just yet, lad," he bellowed, cleaving through the shoulder of another attacker.

Lehion had drawn his own bow, firing off arrows at intense speed and prowess, felling one man after another.

"Ashylanya!?" Makkari looked around, panic-stricken. But the girl was nowhere in sight.

The attackers retreated, leaving their dead behind. The attack stopped nearly as soon as it started, one of the riders having captured Ashylanya as she tended to Alec.

"Ashylanya!" Makkari roared, sprinting after them.

Shelara knelt by Alec's side, hoisting him onto her back.

"We're going after them, hurry!" Lehion called, as they quickly mounted. Sholuun, having followed her master, was nowhere in sight; only the four remaining leophans stood at the ready.

Lehion gazed back at the corpse of the Anari. What *can this possibly mean?* he thought to himself as they followed the retreating attackers.

As the party vanished from sight a towering figure departed from the shadows, a wide grin upon his face, as he tugged along his prisoner, who was chained to him.

"The fools fell right into my plot..." Xen'trath chortled. "Soon my dear Lucin, you shall see your sister again!"

"S-soon?" Lucin stuttered. "Yes... take me to her, take me to Ceri, please!"

"All in good time, my dear, all in good time..." Xen'trath chuckled, fading back into the shadows.

Somewhere in a distant valley Matthias doubled over in agony, a sense of urgency overwhelming his form as blood leaked from his lips, the fever worsening as his body pulsated.

"The boy's experiencing something; I can feel it in my very core!" Matthias breathed. "Fear, agony... regret... helplessness..." He trembled as he knelt on the valley's stone path.

Matthias regained his composure, slowly continuing onward through the dark canyon. Birds of prey eyed the man warily, as if he were about to become a meal.

"Not today..." Matthias mocked, his red hourglass eyes turned toward the birds with a smile. He continued to walk; stumbling, he fell to his knees again. "Curse this illness... curse you, Xen'trath, for doing this to me!"

A breeze swept through the canyon, refreshing the Anarian, as he remained on his knees. His blade felt heavy in its sheath; his muscles felt tense.

"Something has happened; my little sister, has been captured," he breathed. "I must find this boy; I must equalize the balance..."

"You won't find him before me..." spoke a harsh voice through the canyon.

"Xen'trath!" Matthias yelled, only to hear his own echo reverberate in his ears.

Slowly Xen'trath's shadowy form stepped from the shadows of the canyon.

"How can this be? You were near the boy not a moment ago..." Matthias breathed.

"Thanks to her..." Xen'trath yanked the chain, as the dusk strider fell to her knees. "I can be anywhere I want to be... though be it in spiritual form; my true body rests somewhere hidden…" Xen'trath said, with a broad grin upon his wolfish features, which were steadily showing more corruption as time passed by.

"There will be no killing me today, I'm afraid… I merely came bearing a message…" Xen'trath sneered. "In two days' time, I shall use the enhanced power of Organ'us the blood moon to channel the opening of the darkened portal. I will bring my master back, using the girl…"

"And why is it that you tell me this?" Matthias scoffed.

"Merely to taunt you, as I so love to do… knowing how helpless, how weak you are… there is nothing you can do…" Xen'trath sneered.

"He will stop you…" Matthias breathed.

"Who will stop me?" Xen'trath seemed to lose the bemused look. "The boy? Don't make me laugh; he can hardly control his newfound power, let alone bring my plan to a halt!" he hissed.

"Please Matthias, free me, from… him…" Lucin breathed.

"Quiet, you bitch…" Xen'trath slapped her across the face, causing her to double back.

"Alec will find a way to stop you…" Lucin whispered. "I feel it in my soul…"

"I said be quiet!" Xen'trath bellowed, kicking her in the gut, causing her to cry out in pain, her dark hair draped over her pale face, the burning stars illuminated brighter than ever in her flowing phantom like hair.

"Now brother, I shall leave you here… you will most likely die, before reaching the precipice of the strider's run…" Xen'trath mocked, as he slowly faded away into the shadows.

"Curse you, Xen'trath, for all you've done…" Matthias breathed before losing consciousness.

Chapter Twenty-Six

J oden and the three youth continued on through the now completely desolate village. The darkness had dissipated with the reaver's demise, but not before decimating the entire population of Getherben, rendering it a ghost town.

Upon leaving through the now ruined gate, they were met with Alavanda, who seemed overjoyed to see her master unharmed. A gentle breeze caressed the group as they stepped foot outside the village, leaving it behind.

Upon the vast plane, a forest of violet could be seen in the distance; a distant mountain could be seen, within the forest's center.

"Joden, that mountain there, what is that? I don't remember there being a mountain from my time," Gabriel asked, to the surprise of Lucy and Sam.

"Ah that would be the Strider's Tear. It is said that long ago, that is where the infamous Dawn and Dusk striders collided with Balgavian, leaving a permanent scar upon the face of this world, in their creation," Joden explained. "It is now a vast lake, with many streams that run through it. A path leads to the top, known as strider's run."

"I see; so that's my brother's true mother's birth place then?" Gabriel inquired.

Sam and Lucy glanced back at Gabriel with that question.

"Yes, that is indeed where his mother was born," Joden replied, without skipping a beat.

"It's so beautiful," Lucy breathed, taking in the scene from the far distance, still shaken from the recent struggle for their lives.

Joden smiled, looking down at her.

"The echoing planes are indeed a sight to behold," Joden said, his tense expression lightening upon the cool breeze which caressed them. Alavanda nuzzled her master for attention, as he scratched behind her ears.

Sam turned toward Joden now. "About before—what was that fire you used? How did you do that?" he asked, looking up at the Arcaneight.

"Ah yes, it's an ancient spell, known as a soul flame curse. I am an Arcaneight; only those of my race can use magic to such a degree..." Joden then demonstrated by lifting his staff.

The three gasped at the deep blue radiance the simple wooden rod gave off. He placed the tip of the staff to the earth, causing a wide variety of flowers to sprout up around them.

"Oh c'mon, are flowers the best you've got?" Sam blurted.

Joden chuckled, touching Sam's arm, causing it to blossom as well.

"You were saying, boy?" Joden said, with a chuckle.

"All right, all right. Just get this stuff off me!" Sam said, attempting to brush the foliage from his arm.

"Shame, it would be a good look for you! You could be an ent!" Joden teased; as he touched the staff to Sam's arm, the foliage dissipated.

"I'll pass, thanks," Sam chided.

"So where to next?" Gabriel asked Joden.

"The forest of origin, Vanarette—it's about a day's travel from here," Joden said. "It would seem Matthias went off to find your friend, and he has headed in that direction."

"And how can we be so sure that he's in that forest?" Sam asked.

"That forest covers more than half of this continent; it's a safe bet he's within," Joden replied.

"Is it really that big a forest?" Lucy asked, in awe.

"Indeed, many have lost their ways within this forest," he said. "But fear not, I know it very well," he added, seeing the looks on their faces.

"All three of you must be exhausted. We will rest soon, but I'd like to put some distance between us and this village first, if you don't mind."

The four walked for nearly an hour, not riding on the back of Alavanda to give her much-needed rest. Lucy continued to eye the leophan warily, expecting at any moment she could be groomed again by the big cat.

They halted when they came to a sloping expanse of land, a dark looking canyon in the distance, which had not been visible up till this point, having been blocked from view on the plains they walked.

Joden placed the tip of his raven head staff to the earth, muttering an incantation as a dim light began to snake around their perimeter.

"I have placed a barrier, to cloak us from unwanted eyes, it will only last a few hours, though; we move when the barrier dissipates," Joden explained, eyeing the three youth.

Gabriel had already lain himself down upon the lush grass; Lucy and Sam huddled together for warmth beneath one of the blankets Joden had lent them.

Joden smiled to himself.

"Ah, to be young and full of life again," he muttered as he rose to make a small fire, much to the relief of the siblings.

Gabriel remained oblivious; silent tears rolled down his cheeks as he lay on his right side, facing away from the others.

Lucy placed a comforting hand on the young boy, as he drifted into an uneasy sleep.

"I can only imagine how different things here are for you three." Joden smiled gently as he lit a small oaken pipe he withdrew from one of the many pockets in his robe, after packing it with dry tobacco. He took a puff, his eyes fixed on the large canyon as the sun sank low on the horizon.

A sense of foreboding shook the old Arcaneight for a moment, before the feeling passed, as he continued to gaze into the canyon.

"Matthias, what are you up to?"

Matthias seemed to know that someone was speaking of him, as he regained consciousness. He had laid himself upon the canyon's surface, unable to continue, though the crushing presence had fled, indicating that Alec had been relieved of whatever burdened him. His thoughts drifted to his sister, who was now awakening in the distance.

"I'm on my way, Ashylanya, just outlast him..." he breathed, as he continued to walk, his pace labored.

As Ashylanya stirred, regaining consciousness, she only recalled being attacked and struck on the back of her head.

She opened her eyes to see that she was tied to a gnarled looking oak.

"Where... am I..." she breathed. A throbbing pain in her skull caused her to wince upon turning her neck to observe her surroundings.

Ashylanya faced a vast lake, on the precipice of the strider's run, recalling this area as sacred Edelion land.

"Exactly where you are needed, my dear..." spoke a cold, guttural voice.

A figure approached from behind another oak; glowing ember eyes gazed at her.

"You...!" Ashylanya gasped.

Before Ashylanya stood the shadowed figure of Xen'trath, though this time, his body lacked the scarred appearance, nor did he possess the looks of a demon; all that was familiar was the stark white mask the man wore, which was stained with blood.

But what chilled Ashylanya the most was that he was an Anarian.

A long black tail hung low at his feet, the tip flicking gently, and large wolfish ears rested back into a dark and tangled mane of hair.

Xen'trath grinned; though not as grotesque as his future form, the sight still chilled her to the bone.

"The time approaches, girl. Soon I shall use you to enhance Lucin's power to open the gateway, and free my master!"

"W-what do you mean?" she breathed.

Xen'trath laughed. "I suppose revealing this phase of my plan won't hurt... You're going to die anyway..." Xen'trath sneered.

"I used you, and that boy so well, no one suspected that sending you back in time, to this precise era, would benefit my master in the end," he hissed. "I planted two runes upon the children I captured, to send you back to this exact time frame, when all four shards should meet in one era!"

Ashylanya paled, unable to turn from Xen'trath's gaze.

"That necklace you wear—you knew exactly what it was, didn't you girl?"

Ashylanya's eyes widened as her pendant slowly lifted, revealing the crystal.

"I waited ten years for you two to finally meet. Ten years of careful planning..." His voice grew steadily more menacing.

"But how did you-"

"How did I know? Being part of the past?" Xen'trath scoffed. "My master exists out of time and space, naive girl." Xen'trath's grin broadened even more as he spoke.

"That crystal you bear is one of four. Combined, they will recreate the abyssal seed, the legendary artifact that can control the warden itself." Xen'trath's rattling voice was filled with glee now, as everything seemed to run so smoothly in his plotting.

Ashylanya was speechless as she gazed down at the now pulsating crystal.

"When you met the boy, the seed fragment fed off the Warden's energies, empowering it enough to bring back one of the seven dark gods," he hissed.

"You monster..." Ashylanya breathed.

Xen'trath laughed a hideous laugh, which echoed across the surface of the vast lake before them.

"Tomorrow's eve, the night of Organ'us, is the only window to use the seed's power to enhance the dusk strider's... abilities."

"No... it can't be..." she breathed.

"I really must thank you! I had hoped you would become attached to the boy," Xen'trath hissed. "The seed fragment has absorbed a magnificent supply of energy from the Warden himself!" Xen'trath boomed, his voice sounding as if it were many as he spoke.

"No... you won't succeed, you monster!" Ashylanya cried.

"Oh, and who, child, will stop me?" he scoffed, glaring darkly at her.

Ashylanya felt her consciousness fading again, as the demon's laugh echoed through her mind.

"Alec... please hurry," she breathed, losing consciousness.

Chapter Twenty-Seven

Alec had regained consciousness, having searched with the others for hours, trying to find Ashylanya and Makkari, but their efforts proved to be fruitless.

"We have no choice; we must stop and rest, the leophans grow tired," Lehion said, bringing his fatigued cat to a halt. "We will set up camp in this clearing tonight," he instructed, dismounting.

"But Ashylanya-"

Alec was interrupted by a firm hand on his shoulder.

"We will find 'er lad, going on righ' now would be dangerous, I mean look at ye, yer practically quaking in your boots," Garren said, patting Alec on the back.

Alec looked down at himself to find that he indeed was shaking; his tail flitted around nervously; his ears were folded back in concern.

Alec's eyes had also shifted to pale apricot, indicating that he was under severe anxiety.

"I suppose you're right," Alec sighed, joining the others by the small camp fire Shelara had prepared.

"What happened to you earlier, Alec?" You were fine before you sat down next to Ash," Shelara asked.

"I really don't know… She had her necklace out, and for some reason, when I touched her hand, everything went black," he explained, gazing down at his palm.

"Necklace? You mean the one she always wears?" Lehion asked.

"Yes."

"It would seem that the fragment of the abyssal seed is draining your energy upon contact," Shelara interjected.

"Then it truly is a fragment of the abyssal seed... I doubted that it was at first, with the energy of light it gave off; it had not one ounce of darkness in its matrix..." Lehion said, seeming pensive.

"Every time she takes it out, I feel as if my energy is draining, and the marking on my hand pulsates a bright blue," he finished, seeing a look of shock on the elf's face.

"Xen'trath has had us fooled all along," Lehion breathed. "He used Ashylanya to get to you."

"Strange to think that Ashylanya would have something like that in her possession," Shelara added, stoking the fire with a long stick.

"The abyssal seed..." Alec said. "But it's only a fragment, as you said, so why does it have such a terrible effect on me?"

"It is a dark artifact, which was destroyed long ago," Lehion explained. "Its fragments were lost in the flows of time and space, existing outside of those boundaries," he continued, taking a moment to throw another log into the fire. "The seed was once called the eternal seed, before its corruption; it was used as a prism to contain Xanadair, the time warden..."

"Xanadair... I've had a dream involving him before," Alec replied.

"He is your very soul, your very being," Lehion said, gazing at Alec. "Living vessels were only used as a last resort to retain the Warden's power."

"But why does the Warden require a vessel?" Alec asked.

"That's because if the Warden is free for even a moment, he will age all of creation into dust so vast is his power."

Alec was stunned by this, gazing back down at his palm, noticing that only ten of the twelve markings remained surrounding the central hourglass.

"So that means... Xen'trath-"

"Intends to gather the shards of the abyssal seed, in order to gain control of the Warden's infinite power," Lehion interjected.

"He won' ever get all the pieces, not with me kingdom in possession o' one of 'em." Garren joined the conversation, plopping himself down by the fire, outstretching his hands, to feel the warmth.

"That bodes ill either way, further proving the theory that all four fragments have merged into one single era," Lehion stated, with a grimace. "The eve of the blood moon is tomorrow. I believe I know exactly where they have taken Ashylanya."

"And where is that?" Shelara asked, casting Lehion a sidelong glance.

"The Strider's tear..." Lehion said, still gazing into the flames.

"An' 'ow can we be so sure o' that?" Garren asked.

"I have a feeling, with what Alec experienced the previous night, that Xen'trath intends to use the dusk strider in combination with Ashylanya's pendant to bring back one of the seven dark gods..."

Garren paled noticeably.

"It is the closest gateway to his location, and being that it's the birth place of the dawn and dusk striders, her energies will be amplified enough that he might just be able to pull it off, but the blood moon is his only window. He must be stopped there."

"So we journey into the heart of an Edelion village in pursuit?" Shelara asked with her gaze still on Lehion as she spoke.

"Precisely..." Lehion said.

"But what exactly are Edelion?" Alec asked. "I've always heard the term when referring to the dead, but what are they?"

"Spirit beings, the village we set off to is an Anarian ancestral ground. Many spirits reside there," Lehion explained. "How is it that you didn't know this?"

"I was raised by Jessica; I never learned anything about any of this, nor anything about what exactly I am," Alec whispered with his head lowered.

Lehion nodded, still reluctant to believe that he was raised by Jessica, even though proof had been unearthed.

Alec's eyes shifted to a pale fuchsia, his ears folding back with slight embarrassment.

"So wha' now, Lehion?" Garren asked, staring into the fire.

"We won't have enough time if we rest here too long; we must reach the Edelion village before the dusk of Organ'us's rising," Lehion said, before standing.

Shelara sighed. "Came all this way, in the wrong direction... how bothersome... really..."

Half an hour later, the party had set out again at a steady pace toward a large looking mountain in the distance; a trail could be seen from afar, leading around the mountain itself.

"Is that where we are headed?" Alec asked, feeling a strange sensation creeping over him the closer they came to the mountain.

"Tha' it is, lad, tis where Lehion said they keep the lass," Garren called from his leophan.

"I feel so strange the closer we get to it!" Alec called out.

"Not surprising, being that you bear the blood of the very beings that created this mountain!" Shelara called out from behind them.

Alec looked onward to the mountain pass that drew ever closer as they increased their pace.

The birthplace of my mother... Alec thought to himself. *Such a strange thought that here is where she was created...*

Alec's sight shifted suddenly as he clung to the back of his leophan; as a mass of energy enveloped his vision, he could see many eyes upon them from the tree tops, those resembling Anari.

Looking onward, he felt Ashylanya's energy from afar, seeing her with a dark presence close by, at the precipice of the mountain itself.

"Ashylanya really is up there!" Alec called to them. "I can see her energy!"

Alec's eyes had shifted to a pale azure, with a ring of maize surrounding his retina, allowing him to see both spirits and the immense energies which permeated the air all around them. The lake within a large looking crater atop the mountain glowed brightly in Alec's vision, bringing awe to his youthful mind.

"You sure, lad?" Garren called.

"Positive, and there's another with her; his energy is very dark and heavy!" Alec called back to him.

"Xen'trath... I knew he'd have a hand in this..."

"But that's not all! I see another one with him, the same girl as before, with the fiery stars in her hair!"

"So I was right…" Lehion muttered. "Hurry now, it will be a day's travel to reach the precipice and we cannot be even a minute too late!"

Alec nodded as he dug his heel into the leophan's side, increasing speed, as he surpassed the other three.

A smirk crossed Lehion's face as he watched the boy go on ahead. "Seems he really has feelings for this girl, to be so eager to run ahead into almost certain doom… Ah, the blissful ignorance of youth…" he muttered, with a grin, as he too increased the speed at which his leophan bounded, the others following suit.

"We'll make it there in half the time at this rate," Lehion muttered.

Chapter Twenty-Eight

As evening fell, the three youth had rested plenty. As the barrier dissipated, Joden prepared for departure, dousing the fire they had set. A cool breeze wafted over the vast rolling hills of the plains as they mounted, setting off toward the large nearby canyon.

"Why are we going through there, Joden?" Lucy asked, as the leophan bounded toward the mouth of the canyon.

"This is the only way into Vennarrette, through the canyon of Urshek." Joden called behind him.

"But isn't it dangerous in the night?" Lucy asked, feeling nervous.

"Fear not, Lucy, you have one of the finest Arcaneights with you; the three of you shall come to no harm!"

That did not help Lucy's nerves as they sped toward the gaping chasm before them.

"But can't we enter through the forest itself?" Sam blurted. "There's clearly another way, just over there!"

"I'm afraid that's not possible!" Joden replied, over the sound of the leophan's bounding.

"And why is that?" Sam asked.

"There is a powerful barrier, placed by the Anarian Edelions, intended to ward off intruders; through the canyon is the only passage we can take," he shouted.

Sam himself felt uneasy about the moonlit canyon before him, as they drew ever closer to the mouth of the desert-like valley.

Upon reaching the entrance, the party came to a halt.

"What are Anarian, some kind of bird?" Sam asked, looking puzzled. "Didn't think birds were this smart."

The elder broke out into a fit of laughter at this, chuckling as he turned to Sam. "No no, the Anari race is that of Lycan, such as Matthias and your friend."

Sam stared blankly at the Arcaneight.

"Oh..." Sam said, turning to Lucy. "I still don't get it..."

Lucy rolled her eyes.

"He means that Alec and Matthias are a race of werewolves, called the Anari," she said, looking to Joden for confirmation.

"Exactly..." Joden said, turning toward the mouth of the canyon. "Now stay close, children; this canyon is famed for its attraction for bandits, among other dangers," Joden instructed, as the three nodded uneasily.

"The canyon itself only appears large from a distance. I know a shorter route that will lead us straight into the heart of the forest," Joden said, casting a glance at the youth in hopes of reassuring them.

They dismounted Alavanda before entering the ominous-looking valley.

Somewhere in the distance, Makkari caught the scent of powerful magic as he walked through the darkened forest, his mind drifting back to the Demorae Anarian he had slain.

Having lost all scent of the attackers, Makkari found himself in yet another familiar clearing through the trees, following the scent of the strong darkness he sensed with a keen nose.

"Xen'trath..." Makkari hissed, before turning on his heel, sprinting toward the vast mountain in the distance. Sholuun ran alongside him as Makkari leapt onto the big cat's back, sprinting off into the distance.

Recalling what Nadrek had told him, he knew time was short before the rise of Organ'us was to occur.

"So they have brought her to the Lake of the Strider's tear, but for what purpose?" Makkari muttered, holding tightly to Sholuun's mane. "What could Xen'trath possibly-"

Remembering what exactly resided in the lake, Makkari dug his heel hard into Sholuun's side, causing her to increase speed as they bounded through the forest, trees flitting by at lightning speed.

"I have to reach her before it's too late!" Makkari breathed. "Stay strong Ashylanya… I am on my way!"

Alec had thought he had caught the scent of Makkari on the wind as they charged through the forest, for a fleeting moment, his new sense of smell was powerful in comparison to his human form.

"I think Makkari is headed in the same direction we are!" Alec called. "I caught his scent on the wind!"

"If so, we will meet up with him at the strider's run!" Lehion called over the heavy footfalls of the leophans.

The sun had begun to rise again in the distance as the companions charged through the woods, the mountain drawing ever closer, causing the tingling sensation within Alec to further increase as they edged closer to the village of his own ancestors.

Alec himself had begun to alter in appearance as they quickly approached the mountain, Lehion noticed; his hair was growing in length, its color changing to that of a ghostly azure.

"Alec, what's happening to you?"

The party came to a halt as Alec glanced back at the others, his eyes now glowing dimly.

"What do you mean?" Alec asked.

"Your hair and your eyes—they changed…"

"They have?" Alec didn't seem to have noticed the alteration until this present moment, as his bangs now hung low over his eyes; a pale azure color clouded his vision.

"So th' legend is true…" Garren breathed.

Alec had now gained the appearance of his birthright; his black fur-coated ears now jutted through a long mane of silky, almost phantom like hair; the gleaming of star light could be seen within, panning out along the length of his hair, which now fell to the nape of his neck. His eyes glowed a dull azure as his sight seemed to enhance even further. He saw every aspect of the four he now gazed at, from their internal organs, to every flaw in their bodies.

Alec turned his head to see the very essence of the Edelion village just beyond, seeing clearly the spirits which hovered in the trees out of reach, merely observing the group as they gawked in amazement at Alec.

"Alec, I don't think it's safe for you to go any further," Lehion stated, eyeing the boy. "Your form may become unstable, just as it did with your mother, so long ago."

"Nonsense…" spoke a sudden voice from the trees, as a tall figure leapt down, standing before them.

"So the child of prophecy finally arrives…" Nadrek now beamed at Alec; his phantom mane hung loosely about his broad shoulders.

"Who are you?" Lehion asked, his hand on the hilt of his blade.

The Edelion chuckled. "Be at ease, friend, I have not come to harm you."

Lehion removed his hand from his blade.

"It isn't like you can harm an already dead one, such as me anyway…" The Edelion chuckled heartily.

"So you have brought the boy with you, and Matthias is on his way… at the top of this mountain, a demon works to reopen the gateway. He must be stopped, and only this boy can do it," Nadrek quickly explained. "So you must let him pass…"

"And who are you to decide?" Shelara demanded, glaring at the Edelion.

"Nadrek, leader of this tribe, ancestor to the princess Ashylanya Lightwish," the Edelion introduced himself with a bow. "You need not introduce yourselves; I already know you, all too well."

"And how is that?" Shelara asked, befuddled.

Nadrek chuckled again. "Did you think that these trees were merely timber?" he asked, eyeing the elf. "I have eyes everywhere in this forest. I even know where you keep your cabin—rather nice place for it, I might say," Nadrek said, with a hearty chuckle.

"But time is short; there is no time for idle chatter." Nadrek regained a look of seriousness. "You must reach the top of this mountain before nightfall; even as we speak, Xen'trath prepares the ritual that will reopen the gateway, allowing Xek'roshule back into this world."

"Unfortunately, you may go no farther on the backs of your leophans. They have grown weary, and you cannot depend on them to climb such a steep cliff," Nadrek informed them.

"You must set off on foot..." Nadrek said, as the leophans leaned over to allow their riders to dismount. "We will keep watch over them; go on ahead now—be swift!"

Leaving the leophans and the Edelion behind, the group swiftly began to move through the forest, though Garren seemed to be falling behind.

"Me legs can only go so fas'!" he called after them, as he tried to keep up.

Alec moved with determination, thinking of Ashylanya, wondering if she was okay.

"Seems we've lost Garren... bothersome, really... always getting left behin-"

Shelara was interrupted as Garren slammed into her side, having lowered his head, charging after them.

"Dammit Garren, watch where you're going!" Shelara winced at the fresh bruise now forming on her hip.

Garren found himself slung over the bruised elf's shoulder, grumbling to himself, humiliation etched on his bearded face as they continued on.

Alec suppressed a chuckle.

"Somthin' funny, lad?" Garren chided, glaring at Alec as they continued.

"No, not at all!" he said, trying with all his might to keep a straight face.

"It's what you get for not watching where you're going," Shelara scolded. "This isn't the first time I've been battered by you blundering about."

Several hours later, the companions reached a clearing on the edge of the cliff of the strider's run, deciding to stop and rest momentarily.

Alec was relieved to rest, though a part of him wanted to continue on; his legs ached almost as much as his stomach, as he realized he hadn't eaten in days.

The group was now approaching the Edelion village, which was the midway point to the precipice of the Strider's Tear, surprisingly lush with trees; the path itself was far from narrow.

"Be prepared to move at sunset," Lehion said, turning to the others. "We rest for now."

Shelara withdrew a small bit of dried meat from a pouch on her belt, handing it to Alec. "Keep up your strength, Alec; you're going to need it…"

Sighing, Alec slumped down against a tall oak, grateful for the meal Shelara had provided him. He ate with intense hunger, his stomach feeling satisfaction to have sustenance for the first time in days. Reaching for a small water skin, he drank deeply from it, letting out a sigh of relief, feeling refreshed.

Alec's mind drifted back to Ashylanya. Even though he had just met her, it felt to him as if he had known her his entire life. Anxiety built within the young man, as he thought about her safety, not wanting to sit idly by while she was in Xen'trath's hands.

"You sure the girl was taken here, lad?" Alec overheard Garren speaking to Lehion.

Lehion looked toward the dwarf.

"She possesses a fragment of the abyssal seed," he whispered. "I know Xen'trath well enough to know he plots to use her when Organ'us is at its peak."

"But 'ow, lad? The fragments themselves are useless without the other three." Garren said, taking a puff from his pipe.

"Being that the crystal is fused with the Warden's own energy, it has likely gained enough power sapping it from Alec," Lehion said, taking a bite of dried meat. "It's the only explanation as to why his seal is unraveling," he said, after swallowing.

Shelara joined them, having listened in. "We are limited on time then." Shelara sighed. "If that seal fully unravels…"

"I know very well what will happen," Lehion interjected. "We must find a way to stop it." A grave look was etched Lehion's face as he spoke. "If the seal unravels the time warden will age this world into oblivion upon his release," Lehion finished solemnly.

Alec was shocked at what he had heard; raising his hand, he gazed at the mark. The third of the twelve symbols had already begun to fade.

Chapter Twenty-Nine

"Just how big is this place, Joden?" Lucy asked, her legs aching with fatigue as they trekked through the winding, narrow canyon.

"We are halfway through now," he replied, as they continued to walk.

"Could we possibly get a break, old man?" Sam asked, breathing heavily.

Gabriel had already seated himself, unable to walk any further.

"I suppose we could rest here for a while," Joden sighed, turning.

Lucy sat next to Sam beneath the shadow of a large plateau, drinking from a small water skin before handing it to Sam.

"I wonder if the others are all right…" Lucy said with a note of concern etching her features.

"Sure, they're fine," Sam replied, taking a long pull from the water skin. "Alec can handle himself, though maybe not with a sword…" he said, handing Lucy back the water skin.

"Well, neither are you, Sam," Lucy chided.

Sam merely grinned at Lucy.

"There're many things Dad taught me that you aren't aware of," Sam said, casting his sister a sidelong glance. "Ever wonder where I'd disappear to for so long in our youth?" Sam said, his grin broadening.

"What do you mean?" Lucy asked, puzzled.

"Dad taught me to use a sword; he said he would teach me, so I could protect you," Sam said with a smile.

"Dad?" Lucy now gazed at Sam. "Really now, you're joking! I didn't know he knew how to wield a pen let alone a blade!"

"Dad hid it for a long while. Ever wonder why our path was fairly clear of cultists as we walked through the village as it was burning around us?" Sam said, solemnly. "He protected us, to his last dying breath... he always said, he would never forgive himself if he had let either of us come to harm."

Tears welled in Lucy's eyes at these words. "Thank you, Dad... wherever you may be..." Lucy whispered, with a smile.

"You know, he wanted to teach you archery as well, before... you know..." Sam's expression was morose.

"I never knew..." Lucy breathed.

Joden suddenly leapt to his feet at the sound of a stampede of heavy footfalls heading their way.

"Hide, children!" he directed, in a harsh whisper.

The three flung themselves behind a large boulder, Joden joining them quickly with Alavanda.

A large militia charged past them, at least two hundred strong.

"Demorae soldiers, here?" Joden breathed, as the stampede of horseshoes pounded against the cracked earth.

"W-who are they?" Gabriel breathed, watching them go by.

"Servants of the corrupted one, Xen'trath..." Joden whispered.

"Are they demons?" Lucy breathed.

"No, they are reanimated spirits of the dead, known as Demorae, their revival for the sole purpose of serving the one who brought them back from the grave..." Joden explained. "But why here, of all places?"

Joden suddenly froze, knowing exactly where they were headed. "Quickly, we have to follow them!"

After the entire platoon had passed them by, Joden quickly stood.

"We must make haste, quickly children!" Joden shouted.

The four were immediately mounted on Alavanda's back, racing through the remaining trek of the eerily dark canyon.

Makkari had caught the scent of demorae upon the wind as he walked through the forest, increasing his pace now, reaching the ancient ancestral village through a path only he knew.

Sholuun panted heavily, having run for hours without pause. He was greeted by an all too familiar archway leading into the village, intricately decorated with ancient symbols, all illuminated in a light blue haze.

Upon entering, Makkari felt peace wash over him momentarily, as he gazed upon the vast structures within the tree tops of the ancient oaks within the village.

The same type of symbols as on the archway decorated each tree, indicating the home of an ancestor. With each new ancestor to pass on, yet another rune would be added to the archway, indicating the new inhabitant of the ancient village in the trees.

Small wicker lanterns, filled with lightning bugs, hung all around the village giving a calming lighting to the path, which was carved of pure amethyst.

The movement of the lightning bugs created specks of shadow all around the path, belying dancing shadows in the night.

"You made it just in time, Makkari…" spoke the sudden voice of Nadrek, from behind the big Anari. "Hope you had no difficulties reaching us."

Nadrek suddenly materialized in front of Makkari, a wide toothy smile on his transparent face.

"Nadrek, have you seen any sign of Lady Ashylanya?" he asked hurriedly. "I can sense her somewhere nearby!"

"My little niece? I have… she is at the precipice of the village before the Strider's tear. Xen'trath has her held captive. We would assist, but he has placed warding barriers in his perimeter keeping us out."

"The men who took her were headed this way!" Makkari shouted.

"Indeed, and they made quite a fuss bringing her through; unfortunately, we were powerless to touch them."

"But that's not all, Nadrek… these men were Anari demorae!"

A grim look etched the face of Nadrek upon hearing this news. "No… it's not possible… Xen'trath, what have you done?" The Edelion, if possible got even paler than he was before.

"If it really is him, and he has Ashylanya… No, this is not good at all," the elder said, pacing before Makkari. "Ashylanya bears one fragment of the abyssal seed, as does Xen'trath…"

Makkari froze. "Wait, what do you mean?" Makkari asked.

"Ashylanya's pendant—Matthias sent it to another time, in order to prevent this very incident from ever occurring," Nadrek said gravely.

Makkari seemed speechless at what he was hearing.

"Matthias gifted it to his father, in the far-off future, to keep it out of the dark one's hands," Nadrek spoke gravely.

"SoluVerik…" Makkari breathed.

"Indeed… SoluVerik raised three pups, Matthias, Ashylanya, and Mateuse… though Mateuse chose a much darker path…"

Chapter Thirty

"'Ave any o' you seen th' lad?" Garren called from his post, which was a large stump of a tree which had been felled sometime long ago.

"Now that you mention it, he has been rather quiet..." Shelara replied.

Lehion's brow furrowed as he inspected his surroundings.

"You don' think-"

"Let's go!" Shelara barked, knowing exactly where Alec had gone.

The three hurried along the winding path to the Edelion village, at breakneck speed.

———————————————

"Have you forgotten me, Ashylanya?" the cold voice of Xen'trath hissed.

"W-what do you mean?" Ashylanya asked, trying subtly to loosen her bonds.

"No... I suppose you were too young to remember," Xen'trath said, gazing at her. "But really... How could someone forget... their dear elder brother...?" Xen'trath hissed, a large grin on his ever twisting visage.

Ashylanya froze in shock. "You're lying!" she breathed.

"That hurts me, little sister," Xen'trath said, with venom in his voice. "It truly does..." Xen'trath frowned.

"You and Matthias... were always father's favored..." Xen'trath spoke through clenched teeth.

"No... It can't be true!" Ashylanya cried.

"Oh, but it is, sister... Though it matters not; I killed all emotion long ago," Xen'trath hissed.

"The time is near. Ready to die, sister dear?" Xen'trath spat the last two words.

———————————————

"Mateuse is now the one you know as Xen'trath..." Nadrek spoke, gazing at Makkari.

Makkari felt like he was struck by those words.

"No... it cannot be..." Makkari breathed.

"It does not surprise me that you were unaware... It was kept a closely guarded secret by SoluVerik for centuries." Nadrek said, turning to see an armada rushing toward the archway to the village.

Nadrek made a sweeping motion with his hand, causing the entire village to come to life. The Edelions seemed to step from the base of every tree.

"Brothers and sisters... Defend yourselves!" Nadrek shouted, as dark riders trampled through the village archway.

"Makkari!"

Makkari turned to see Alec running toward him.

"Get away from here, boy!" Makkari shouted, drawing his axes just in time to parry a rider's blade, cutting into his chest with his axe's sharp edge.

Alec had snuck into the village before the attack, hoping to find Ashylanya; he could sense her very near.

"I refuse to run like a coward!" Alec shouted, drawing an elfish blade Lehion had given him to use as a last resort.

Makkari found he had a new level of respect for the boy, as battle cries were shouted from every direction.

The clash of steel on steel reflected a bright crimson light, the blood moon having risen. A dark energy enveloped the village.

One dismounted foe charged at Alec, impaling himself on Alec's blade as he ducked under his foe's attack.

Makkari dismounted and felled one rider after another with his axes, parrying a rider from behind and ripping him from his steed.

Alec was barreled over by a strange looking creature that resembled a corrupted ape.

Long ragged hair covered glowing yellow eyes; its maw was open wide, trying to sink its teeth into Alec, when it was suddenly blasted away by a blinding light, disintegrating the beast entirely.

Dazed, Alec sat up to have Ashylanya fling herself into his arms.

"Please get away from here, Alec; I don't want to lose you like I've lost everyone else!" she cried, holding onto him tightly.

Alec, startled at first, held her back as she sobbed into his shoulder.

Poor Ash, she's lost so much in only a few days... Alec thought to himself, letting her tears roll down his back.

Alec's vision then suddenly shifted to reveal a Sulmothian atop him, but it was already too late, as a blade penetrated his gut, followed by a hollow chuckle.

Alec froze, as the hair on the back of his neck stood on end, his ears twitching. A deep cold penetrated his very being as the blade bit deep.

"Fooled you, love." The mocking voice that was not Ashylanya's filled his ear.

The impostor had transformed; cold scales suddenly pressed against him. As the demorae's hair turned a dark red, she sat up on him, exposing her half naked form. A cruel yet seductive smile crossed her full lips. The demorae gazed at him through eyes that were darkened pits with no light, carved into an otherwise elegant face.

"You will die... Just like everyone else, love." She twisted the dagger in his gut, bringing a gasp of agony from Alec.

"What have you done with Ashylanya, you monster..." Alec gasped, fading slowly out of consciousness.

"That," she touched his bottom lip, "is none of your concern, darling; your death, however, will be quite an exquisite treat for the master." The Sulmothian succubus cooed.

Before losing consciousness, Alec saw movement behind the demorae. A bow thrust forth from behind a thick patch of bushes, letting loose an arrow directly into the demorae's back.

The Sulmothian howled before falling limp against Alec.

Shelara let fly another arrow, striking her target in its chest, causing it to fall to the ground in a heap.

Makkari charged, severing another's head from its shoulders in one smooth motion; as Sholuun bit clean through another's arm, severing it from its body, black blood spurted from the wound which quickly cauterized with dark magic.

Sholuun turned, finishing her prey with a clean bite through its throat.

"Sholuun! Leave this place; I will not see you come to harm in this battle!" Makkari shouted.

The big cat acknowledged Makkari, bounding off into the trees.

Garren barreled wildly into the fray, crushing the skull of one demorae unfortunate enough to cross his path with the brunt of his battle axe.

"The hell were you!?" Garren shouted, carving into another's chest with his axe, an arrow whizzing past the dwarf's head felling another demorae.

"Ye almost took me bloody ear, elf!" Garren turned, shouting at Lehion as Makkari sliced through the torso of another figure charging at Garren.

"Less talking and more fighting, dwarf!" Makkari barked, bringing his axe down and cleaving another in half.

Suddenly the surrounding area grew cold as a heavy energy pressed down on them.

The demorae riders stopped in their tracks as they looked toward the source of the energy, suddenly vanishing from existence.

"Wha' the hell is goin on 'ere!" Garren shouted.

"The energy is coming from the well! We must hurry!" spoke a tense voice from behind Garren.

Makkari turned to see Nadrek's battered form limping toward them.

"An Edelion...?" said Lehion, approaching with Shelara. "How can a spiritual body be injured, let alone die?"

"Their blades are imbued with black magic capable of slicing through even our flesh..." Nadrek breathed, gazing around at the blue crystalline dust that signified the remains of the Edelion who fell during the battle.

"You know this one, Makkari?" Shelara asked.

Makkari nodded.

"An ancestor to Lady Ashylanya, brother to SoluVerik," Makkari said, eyeing Shelara.

"There is no time for proper introductions; we must make haste! Even now, Xen'trath attempts to unleash one of the seven back unto this world!" Nadrek shouted.

"Then we must hurry!" Makkari shouted, sprinting in the direction of the lake. A dark aura continued to emanate heavily from the body of water just beyond the forest's perimeter.

As Shelara turned to follow, she heard a pained groan from nearby, almost forgetting about Alec in all the commotion. She quickly approached the corpse of the succubus, kicking it to the side, kneeling down beside him.

"These wounds... we must get him somewhere safe!" she called to Lehion who was still close by.

Lehion lifted the boy from the ground. "He will survive; we must hurry to the lake, before it's too late!"

Nodding, Shelara quickly followed him from the now stained crystal path, Garren and Makkari already having run ahead.

Moments later Lehion and Shelara entered the clearing before the lake.

Lehion set Alec down gently against a fallen tree, before running ahead to join the others, casting a final glance back at the much changed form of the boy.

Lehion and Shelara came to a halt behind Makkari and Garren, who appeared to be petrified by what they saw.

A colossal wellspring was before them, in the lake's epicenter, a stone path having been raised recently as moss covered the slick stones. Xen'trath had reconstructed an ancient gateway through dark magic, which billowed forth from the churning waters as if it were smog.

Before the well, just at the end of the mossy path, was Ashylanya, who hung suspended upon a pedestal within a large arcane sphere. Intricate runes were painted into the earth in blood, surrounding the perimeter of the darkly emanating construct of Xen'trath's creation.

Makkari gazed angrily at the back of the man who stood in front of her, his arms raised high, muttering an incantation as Ashylanya's pendant glowed brightly.

Next to Xen'trath was the weeping form of Lucin, her energy being syphoned from her to keep the sphere balanced.

Xen'trath grinned broadly. "I see you've all arrived," he hissed. "Just in time…"

Chapter Thirty-One

"Alec..." A distant, unfamiliar voice called his name. "Do not die this way, Alec..." The voice drifted closer. "Fight it..."

Alec opened his eyes to utter darkness.

"Who are you?" Alec breathed, though he felt strangely at ease.

Alec suddenly found himself in a dimly lit room. Endless shelves filled with clocks and hourglasses stretched as far as the eye could see. The dim candlelight reflected off the face of one very large clock overhead, slowly ticking away.

"Where am I?" Alec asked, staring in awe at the endless array of time pieces.

"Enoria... The realm of lost time..." the voice spoke softly.

Suddenly, a tall figure appeared before him. A long white cloak adorned with an hourglass engraved on each shoulder draped the unbelievably tall man, except he was not a man, but an Anarian.

The figure's visage was snow white, fully transformed, resembling a Lycan.

But what amazed Alec the most were his eyes.

The same hourglass pupils he had seen himself with, though these eyes were brighter, the hourglasses more complete, these eyes gazed at Alec gently.

"I am Xanadair... The warden of time..." the Anarian spoke, his gaze unmoving from Alec's own. "I have observed you from the time you were born, till now..." he said, pulling a small clock from one of the shelves.

Alec merely gazed back at the prominent figure, speechless.

"You are the first of my vessels I have brought into my domain…" Xanadair seemed to speak directly into Alec's mind, as his mouth remained unmoving.

"But why…?" Alec asked, awestruck.

"You are the sole heir to the Strider, and therefore you are the only one who can share this link with me…" Xanadair explained. Turning the minutes of the clock back with one finger, he placed it against Alec's wound.

Alec gasped, as the wound seemed to heal completely.

"I don't understand…" Alec breathed.

"You and I are the same… for the dawn and dusk strider were created using my energies, eons ago," Xanadair said, replacing the clock back onto the shelf.

"But how is that possible?" Alec asked, befuddled.

Xanadair chuckled. "Your soul was created by a fragment of your mother's and my own soul… unlike my previous vessels." Xanadair seemed to gaze into the boy's very mind.

"But why me?" Alec asked.

"It was of most inconceivable chance that you even exist… I was able to send my daughter, the dawn strider, back in time to birth you," Xanadair explained. "You were born to serve a sole purpose…"

"And what is that?" Alec asked.

"To stop the end, of course…" Xanadair beamed. "You were born of the strider, the reason… for you feeling as if you have known all those you do for your entire life…" Xanadair seemed to read Alec's mind as he spoke. "For you feeling as if you've known Ashylanya throughout your entire existence, was the result of my energy, which touched all those around Matthias, the day I was set loose for a moment, placing the Timeless Touch, upon all those in my vicinity during the seeds fracturing."

"So all the dreams I've had…"

"All memories, some being memories of what is to come and some of the far past…" Xanadair answered. "Are you afraid, child?"

Xanadair asked, seeing Alec's mind flash back to the corrupted version of his own body.

"You fear hurting all those you love…" Xanadair said with his gaze still unhindered. "But fear not, I have a solution," Xanadair stated.

"A solution…? Alec asked.

"You, being born of the strider, will be the first to ever wield my blade," Xanadair said. "Not even Xen'trath knows of this. That fool believes he is the only one who can alter what is to come." Xanadair grinned.

"A blade?" Alec asked.

"My blade, the Time Render, has not seen use since time itself was young," Xanadair explained. "You are the only one who can wield it, for all others who have tried have aged to dust in moments."

"Is it really that powerful?" Alec asked, in awe.

"Be warned, the blade has drawbacks," Xanadair said, his eyes narrowing slightly. "Each time you call the blade forth, it will age you one hundred and eighty-two days every five minutes, as well as those around you who do not bear my curse." He explained.

Alec seemed to don a look of intimidation at these words. "But I do not know how to use a sword…" Alec breathed.

Xanadair chuckled.

"Do not fear, each time the blade is called, I myself will take control over you temporarily, until you can wield it properly on your own…" he reassured.

"This is all so much…" Alec sighed.

"Give it time; you will understand." Xanadair said, touching Alec's chest with one hand. A warm energy coursed through him as his consciousness faded away.

"You bastard…!" Makkari boomed. "You would use one of your own blood as sacrifice!?" Makkari readied his axes, eyeing the beast menacingly.

"It matters little to me; she is a mere tool to bring forth a grand design," Xen'trath hissed, still facing Ashylanya and the steadily rising wellspring.

Makkari leapt at Xen'trath, only to be blasted back by a simple raise of one of Xen'trath's hands.

"Still you let your rage consume you, Makkari," Xen'trath sneered. "It is for this reason that you are no match for me."

Makkari roared, charging across the path, bringing his axes down upon Xen'trath, only to be parried by the corrupted Anarian without even a glance from Xen'trath, a dark blade materializing, holding back the axes.

Shelara and Lehion took the opportunity to fire off their arrows, but Xen'trath caught each one with ease, unblinking.

"I suppose I must do away with you all, to sustain proper concentration..." Xen'trath turned to face them. The lake itself seemed to freeze as he stepped off the path. His footsteps panned out an icy path which expanded across the surface of the lake where he trod.

Garren charged in from behind, nearly skidding on the ice, sweeping at Xen'trath's legs, but Xen'trath leapt, skillfully avoiding the blade.

Landing on his feet, he turned as Makkari swung both axes. He parried, before punching Makkari square in the jaw with all of his might.

"Every last one of you..." Xen'trath sneered, evading yet another arrow, "are mere pathetic worms..." He hissed, as Makkari fell to the now fully frozen lake. Xen'trath pressed against his skull with one large booted foot.

Xen'trath then disappeared, reappearing directly in front of Lehion. Grabbing him by the throat with one hand, he brought him down to the ground.

"You elves were always a pitiful and weak race... It isn't a wonder I was so easily able to defeat your king!" he bellowed, a grin twisted upon his face as he blocked Garren, before slicing into his abdomen with his blade's edge.

Shelara was livid. "You dare to insult my people!?" she bellowed as she fired off another arrow. Skidding on the ice, she slid, readying another arrow and letting it fly. Xen'trath chuckled as he held up one hand, the arrow fading away into dust, Shelara's bow following suit.

She cried out in fury, drawing a blade from her cloak, launching herself at him.

Xen'trath evaded the blow, catching her by her throat.

"Pitiful…" he hissed, before crushing her throat and casting her limp form to one side.

Nadrek was seen nearby focusing on an incantation, as Xen'trath appeared before him, striking him hard in the skull with the hilt of his shadowy blade, causing him to fall limp to the earth.

Xen'trath gazed at his defeated foes. "Is this really all you could muster?" Xen'trath bellowed, before freezing suddenly.

"Do you really think I didn't know you were there, boy?" Xen'trath shouted, throwing what appeared to be a vast ball of green fire at the small row of oaks, causing them to burn to ash within seconds.

Xen'trath glared darkly at Alec, who stood before him.

"I knew you would come, boy…" Xen'trath hissed.

Alec stood silently, his head lowered.

"Come to give yourself to me? Did you finally realize you have no hope of defeating me?" Xen'trath's cold voice fell upon deaf ears, as Alec slowly began to walk forward.

"Your friends are dead, boy… Just like your precious mother!" Xen'trath taunted, as Alec drew closer.

Xen'trath glared at Alec as he simply walked past him.

"What can you possibly do alone?" Xen'trath continued to taunt.

Alec, however, paid no attention to the corrupt Anarian, as he walked toward Ashylanya.

Xen'trath laughed.

"It's futile; that barrier is impenetrable! The master shall claim her soon!" Xen'trath shouted after him, as he took a step onto the moss covered walkway. A large rift had begun to slowly open above the well, as a vast pair of claws slowly emerged through the tear in reality.

Alec approached the large sphere containing her.

"It's useless! Simply touching the barrier will kill you-" Xen'trath's eyes widened as Alec placed his right hand on the barrier.

"Impossible…" Xen'trath breathed.

The prism which held Ashylanya slowly unraveled, and Alec caught Ashylanya in his arms as she fell.

A loud cry of bitter rage echoed from the rift above the wellspring, as the gateway shut itself. Losing all source of energy, Xen'trath's spell had been undone.

Xen'trath merely gaped at Alec, who had turned, walking back the way he came.

"Fool!" Xen'trath shrieked. "You will suffer for this!" he boomed, bringing his blade down on Alec's head.

Alec lifted his right arm, parrying the blade. Slowly, he raised his head, only one closed eye visible through his azure mane. Alec opened his eyes, drawing a gasp from Xen'trath at what he saw.

"No... How could you wield such power?!" Xen'trath seemed to quake now. "There is no way that you have grasped it to this level!" He cried.

The one eye visible to Xen'trath was a solid hourglass, though a bright azure replaced the gold within his eyes as he gazed menacingly at the beast.

Slowly something began to materialize against Xen'trath's blade.

"What... are you...!" Xen'trath hissed, as he watched a large golden chain slowly emerge from the center of the hourglass in his palm, snaking around his arm. The chain ended at the hilt of a blade, which formed over Alec's arm like a gauntlet.

At the tip of the gauntlet formed two blade edges, which joined together in a sharp point; a large plate formed over the hilt, like that of a shield.

Within the plate rested a large rotating hourglass. A white-hot light filled the empty space where the blade tips joined.

"What... is this!" Xen'trath's voice was filled with shock as he spoke.

Alec simply stared at the demorae Anarian, his eyes narrowing.

"So... this is the true power of the one born of the strider's blood..." Xen'trath hissed. "No matter, I will still kill you!" Xen'trath shrieked, bringing his blade around only to freeze in place midswing.

Alec vanished, appearing behind Xen'trath.

Several gashes formed on Xen'trath's chest as blood spurted from the fresh wounds; the chain connecting him to Lucin shattered.

"This speed can only be one..." Xen'trath glanced over his shoulder in time to see Alec's leg swing, kicking Xen'trath hard, causing him to lose his footing. He fell hard against a large oak.

Lucin merely stood by, watching the scene play out. "So this is my nephew... he's almost exactly like his mother..." Lucin's sanity seemed to have returned to her as the chain binding her to Xen'trath had been severed by the blade Alec wielded.

"This... is not over!" Xen'trath hissed, as he suddenly dissipated into a black mist, fading away in retreat.

Alec stood there for a moment, as an emerald light washed harmlessly over him, a final spell cast by Xen'trath in his flight. He gazed at the spot Xen'trath had been not a moment before.

The blade on his arm slowly vanished, his eyes returning to their normal hazel coloration, though the hourglass shape remained in his pupils.

Alec looked down at Ashylanya's unconscious form, noticing her pendant glowed a bright azure. The light continued to glow brighter, enveloping them as well as the others within the area.

Alec turned, as he watched the gentle light heal the defeated companions, their wounds closing. Alec was awestruck by the display.

"Thank you, my little nephew..." Lucin breathed, as she dissipated, fading from reality.

The voice of the Dusk Strider echoed in Alec's mind; it faded away moments later as the light had begun to fade and the others began to stir.

"Wha' the hell appened?" Garren groaned as he slowly got to his feet, nearly losing his footing on the still icy lake.

Shelara and Lehion both stood as well, curious as to what had brought them back.

Makkari jumped to his feet, immediately flocking to Ashylanya and Alec.

"How did you...?" Makkari asked, gently touching Ashylanya's face with his large gloved hand.

"I'm as curious as you are," Alec said. "I blacked out, and when I woke up, I was standing here with Ash in my arms…" Alec explained.

Makkari stared blankly at Alec.

"Alec!" familiar voice called; the sound of heavy footsteps came from behind him.

Alec turned to see Lucy, Sam, and Gabriel before him.

In his surprise Alec almost dropped Ashylanya.

"Thank goodness you're all okay!" Lucy cried, hugging him tightly, despite Ashylanya being between them.

"Can't breathe…" Ashylanya gasped, as she had begun to stir.

Lucy backed away, gazing at the two. "Alec… Your hair—it's… blue!"

"Real ladies' man, Alec," Sam said, clapping Alec on the shoulder.

Ashylanya blushed as she gazed up at him.

Alec felt his own face grow warm, as the familiar pink in his eye color returned in embarrassment.

"Glad you're all right!" Gabriel said, hugging his brother. "Did you get taller?" he asked, eyeing Alec.

Alec recalled what the warden had told him, realizing he had used the blade for more than five minutes, aging him almost a full year.

"Really?" Alec asked. "I guess I do feel a bit different, now that you mention it," he said, looking down at his own frame, after setting Ashylanya back on her feet.

"Alec…" Ashylanya breathed, hugging him tight. "Thank you…"

Alec gazed back at her with a shy smile.

Lucy suddenly gasped, seeing the two elves before her, along with the dwarf.

"You three!" she shouted, gazing at the three she had seen before their arrival in this time period.

"Do I know you?" Shelara asked, turning toward her.

"I met you three, in my own time," Lucy explained. "You were servants to that monster!" she breathed.

Lehion stepped forward.

"Servants? Of Xen'trath?" Lehion asked. "So the tale is proving truer by the hour..."

"It would seem we got here a bit too late..." Joden stepped into the clearing, having lagged behind with Alavanda to rest, insisting that the three go on ahead.

Lehion turned, seeing the old Arcaneight.

"Joden the tome keeper..." Lehion said, gazing at the elder. "Who else are we going to be reacquainted within the next few days?" he questioned with a half-smile on his face.

"It indeed has been a while, old friend." Joden replied, turning toward Alec.

"So that's the boy I've heard so much about," Joden spoke under his breath.

"This is all so confusing," Sam muttered to Lucy.

Lucy nodded, still transfixed on the elves.

"So if they are here..." Gabriel said. "Maybe Mum in this time period too?" Gabriel's mood seemed to lighten at the idea.

"So yer the lad's wee brother he told us abou'." Garren eyed Gabriel. "So tha means you too are Jessie's boy?"

"Yes, Jessica was my mother; she died though..." Gabriel's eyes were filled with sadness.

"She still breathes lad, rest assured." Garren patted him on the back. "Though I highly dou' she'll recognize you," Garren said, still eyeing him.

"She's alive?" Where is she?" Gabriel asked, feeling a wave of relief wash over him.

"No one knows, she's a bit o' a wanderer."

Gabriel lowered his head.

"I encountered her, boy," Makkari said, facing him. "She tried to take my head though..."

"You did?" Garren asked, raising a bushy eyebrow.

"Yes, within this very forest. I had no choice but to knock her out cold, to stop her from swinging at me," Makkari replied.

"Then we have to find her!" Gabriel said excitedly.

Sam and Lucy overheard them speak, eyeing each other. "How is it possible that Jessica is alive in this era?" Lucy asked, looking puzzled.

"Wouldn't that make her centuries old?" Sam added. "She sure didn't look it!"

"I can explain why…" Ashylanya said, lowering her head.

Alec looked at Ashylanya, a hint of empathy in his eyes.

"When the time warden's crystal, the abyssal seed, was shattered in this era, all those within the crystal's vicinity were cursed with immortality, frozen in time…"

"But how do you know that?" Lucy asked.

"Because Makkari and I," Ashylanya began, looking toward the big Anarian, "are victims of that very curse…" she finished, looking to Alec, who placed a gentle hand on her shoulder.

"Exactly when…" Lehion said, looking to Ashylanya. "When is this event due to unfold?"

Ashylanya raised her head. "Exactly three years from this day."

Chapter Thirty-Two

The party that had become ten companions had left the lake behind, returning to the Edelion village. Exhausted from the long struggle, Ashylanya seemed drained of energy as she walked close to Alec and Makkari.

"Anyone know where tha' other fellow Nadrek wen'?" Garren asked, as they walked.

"Now that you mention it, I don't remember seeing him when we awoke…" Shelara replied.

Their question was answered as they entered the village through the forest outskirts.

Nadrek stood waiting for their arrival, and the whole of the village stood at his side.

"Welcome friends," he spoke. "This night we celebrate in honor of our fallen kin. We will show the demorae that they cannot daunt us with their attacks." Nadrek's voice echoed. "We owe a great debt to these champions, for it was they who saved this village from total destruction." Nadrek's words seemed to instill a great rise in morale to his kin, as they cheered.

"Let the festivities begin!" Nadrek shouted.

The small village suddenly came to life as the Edelion began to celebrate. A large banquet appeared before them; the large table was packed with every food you could imagine, with fresh cooked meats and vegetables for all to indulge.

A large bonfire was started in the village's center; casks full of ale appeared outside one of the large huts at ground level, with welcoming warmth wafting from its entryway, as the village began its celebration of the rise of Organ'us.

Lucy merely stood agape. "But we didn't do anything really!" she said, looking to Sam, who seemed distracted by the large table of food.

"Just relax; a break can be good at times…" Shelara spoke to Lucy from behind.

Gabriel had joined Sam at the table, piling their plates high with all they could get their hands on.

"I could use a drink any'ow," Garren said with a grin as he headed toward the makeshift bar.

Lehion followed after the dwarf.

"Lehion, you too?" Shelara scoffed. "You're so bothersome when drunk…"

"Like you said, a break is always good every now and again!" Lehion repeated the same words Shelara had said out of context.

"Doubt he'd beat me at drinkin anyhow," Garren said, eyeing Lehion.

"Is that a challenge?" Lehion scoffed.

"Sure is, lad." Garren replied, as they walked toward the bar.

Shelara sighed. "Those two…"

Makkari simply stood there, eyeing the others as they went their separate ways.

"C'mon Makkari, lighten up a bit! You're always so tense!" Ashylanya teased.

"You too!" Ashylanya grabbed hold of Alec's arm.

Alec chuckled following after her.

"I guess I could use some rest," Makkari muttered with a smirk.

"Just us girls now, darling…" Shelara said, turning to Lucy. "There's much I wanted to ask you," Shelara said, smiling.

"Likewise," Lucy replied, as she followed Shelara into the bar, finding a seat away from the two knocking back ale as if it were water.

Joden had joined Nadrek in a small hut at the pinnacle of the village in the tree tops, sipping brandy as they played a game of chess.

"What's on your mind, Joden? I've known you long enough to know that look on your face," Nadrek asked, with a smile.

Joden took another sip of brandy.

"The boy—I am curious to know how he managed against such a powerful foe..." Joden answered, moving his knight on the chess board.

"All I can say is," Nadrek moved his queen in front of his king, "the queen will always protect her king."

"And what exactly do you mean by that?" Joden asked, a puzzled look on his face.

"I've known my little niece for as long as she's lived," Nadrek said as he took Joden's knight with his queen. "Ashylanya protects the boy, little does he know," Nadrek said, taking a sip from his mug.

"Before losing consciousness earlier, I witnessed what she protected him from an attack the boy himself did not see."

Joden seemed uneasy as he listened.

"As Xen'trath retreated, he cast a dark curse at the boy; Ashylanya activated the pendant to shield him, in turn healing the others," Nadrek said, moving his rook.

"The time warden seems to favor the boy, though I do not know why; perhaps it is the blood which runs through the boy's veins," Nadrek said.

"How do you figure?" Joden asked, taking the rook with his own queen.

"The ancient blade of legend, the time reaver..." Nadrek said.

Joden froze, fixated on Nadrek.

"The boy is able to wield it without dying..." Nadrek said, eyeing Joden.

"That blade has only ever been heard of within one of my dusty old tomes... it has not shown itself since the beginning of time itself!" Joden breathed. "Are you sure it was that very blade?"

"As sure as I've ever been, in my lengthy existence," Nadrek replied. "I am as puzzled as you, old friend... Checkmate."

Joden glanced down at the board.

"My, my, I seem to have gathered rust in my stratagy..." Joden muttered.

Nadrek chuckled. "Clear your mind, let us enjoy this night," Nadrek said, eyeing Joden. "For I fear we have much hardship just upon the horizon."

"Much indeed..."

"There is much I wanted to ask you... so much it's almost bothersome, but I'll keep it to only a few questions," Shelara said, sipping from a small glass of red wine.

"I'll do my best to answer, but I only encountered you a few times," Lucy explained, her face tinged pink, as Shelara had given her a glass of her own.

"First, you said that we served that demorae, Xen'trath; why?"

"I only know a little from what I overheard Joden say to Jessica. Something about a curse called the Kelondrekh, and not having your own will..." Lucy spoke with a light slur in her speech.

"The Kelondrekh curse... the only way he could have done that is if he had killed us with that nightmarish blade of his..." Shelara said, taking another sip.

"You are quite the lightweight," She said, noticing Lucy slumped in her seat. "Only gave her two glasses," Shelara sighed, as she eyed the sleeping girl, her head still full of unanswered questions.

Shelara heard a loud shattering of glass from behind her; turning, she saw Garren and Lehion in a heated argument, having knocked one of the glasses to the floor.

"This is why Lehion shouldn't drink..." she muttered.

"Now you said you 'ad the nex' roun'!" Garren slurred.

"No, it was you!" Lehion had the same slur in his voice as he spoke, ignoring the broken glass on the bar floor.

"Fine, 'ows fifty-fifty soun' to ye?" Garren's speech was hardly understandable.

"Sounds good to me, half-pint," Lehion taunted.

Garren's face turned bright red. "I'll give you half-pint, elf!" Garren drunkenly shouted, as he tried to leap at the elf, only to end up flat on the floor.

Shelara stepped in, holding the dwarf back by his arms.

"Let me at 'im; no one calls me half-pint 'n gets away with it!"

"Fine, next round's on me!"

The three turned, seeing Sam in the doorway.

"You all do realize the ale is free, right?" Shelara said.

"Now that's me kind o' ale!" Garren said, righting himself.

"You've been drinking it for free for the last hour!" Shelara scoffed.

Garren and Lehion gave Shelara a blank look.

"Idiots..." Shelara muttered, walking back to Lucy as Sam joined the other two at the bar.

Just outside the bar, Gabriel wandered the village in search of Alec, with no luck.

"You lost, pup?" spoke a voice from behind him.

Gabriel turned to see a towering Edelion standing before him, looking down at him over an elongated snout.

"Was just lookin for my brother; he's with a girl named Ashylanya," Gabriel said, gazing up at the much taller figure.

"Ah, the Lady Ashylanya... I do believe I saw them at the bonfire," the Edelion directed, with the point of a long clawed finger.

"What's your name, pup?" the Edelion asked.

"Erm... Gabriel," he replied nervously.

"I see... My name is Renekai..." the Edelion stated.

Slowly backing away, Gabriel turned. "Well, I must be off, gotta catch up to my brother! Was nice to meet you, er, sir."

Gabriel walked away from the Edelion at a fast pace in the direction of the bonfire.

As Gabriel disappeared, the tall figure grinned widely as his appearance transformed entirely.

A young seductive looking woman stood in his place. Dark violet hair spilled down her scaled shoulders to her mid-back. Velvet colored eyes followed the now distant Gabriel. Her scantily clothed flesh was azure. A scaled tale drifted lazily at her heels behind her.

"It was very nice to meet you indeed."

Makkari stood by, watching Ashylanya dance with the Edelions around the bonfire. Alec was with her, as she had dragged him in, and it was strange seeing such a broad smile upon her face. He had not seen her with such a smile since she was very young.

"Come join us, Makkari!" Ashylanya called, but he politely declined.

Ashylanya seemed happier around Alec, Makkari noticed.

"Hey er, Makkari, right?" Gabriel asked, coming up from behind.

Makkari nodded, still gazing at Ashylanya, who danced with Alec.

Gabriel followed his gaze.

"I didn't think my brother was the type to dance, with a girl no less," Gabriel stated. "He's always been shy around girls," he said, his gaze fixed on the two.

"Gabriel, come and dance with us!" Alec called, pulling him into the circle by his arm.

Makkari sighed.

"They act as if nothing ever happened..." he muttered to himself.

Later that evening Nadrek provided a few small huts within the tree tops for the companions to stay the night. Garren and Lehion had already passed out on their small makeshift beds, having drunk too much.

Shelara sat on the end of her bed, having laid Lucy down on her own bed.

Gabriel and Sam had fallen asleep almost immediately.

Makkari and Joden stood on the small connecting bridge between the huts. Both seemed to be in deep thought as they gazed at the large crimson moon in the night sky.

Alec and Ashylanya, however, had not gone up to their rooms yet, though everyone was too exhausted to notice.

The two young Anari sat upon the grassy cliff edge that overlooked the village, gazing at the moon.

"Such a beautiful night..." Ashylanya said, with a gentle smile.

"It really is; I've never seen the moon at this angle during the rise of Organ'us…" Alec replied, smiling at her.

Ashylanya giggled as her tail brushed against Alec's own.

"Thank you, Alec. For saving me before…" Ashylanya whispered, now gazing at him.

"I would not have been able to bear losing you; I feel as if I have known you my entire life, Ash." Alec spoke softly, as his own tail gently wrapped around hers.

Ashylanya blushed deeply. "I feel the same way…" she breathed.

Ashylanya seemed to be edging closer to him now, her hand now gently over his own.

"Ashylanya…" Alec breathed as the color in his eyes shifted to deep lavender, as he slowly closed the distance, his eyes now half closed as Ashylanya's face drew nearer to his own.

"I feel like I can never leave your side…" Her voice was soft, with a light tremble.

As Alec and Ashylanya drew close, their lips nearly meeting, they were interrupted.

"Hope I'm not intruding…" spoke a firm voice from behind the trees behind the pair.

Ashylanya and Alec turned away from each other quickly, both blushing madly.

A tall cloaked man stepped from the shadows.

"W-who are you?" Alec asked, staring at the man.

"Matthias… and my how you've grown, Alec…"

Makkari seemed to be the only one to notice the two had not gone to bed. Knowing this, he set out to search for them, an easy task as he was able to catch their scent on the light wind blowing through the towering trees.

Though what misled him was the distinct yet familiar scent of another.

"Matthias?!" he breathed, as he sprinted in their direction.

"Matthias!" Ashylanya breathed. "I haven't seen you in so long!"

"You know him, Ash?" Alec asked, puzzled.

Matthias chuckled. "I would hope she does; I am her elder brother, after all."

Alec looked from one to the other, awestruck.

Matthias then drew back the hood of his cloak.

A long mane of pure white hair hung low at his back, sharp jagged ears jutted from his mane, which overshadowed his eyes, which resembled Alec's though they had a pale crimson hue.

Alec simply gazed at the fully matured Anarian state of Matthias. But what confused him was the dull coloration of his eyes that should have been gold; a sickly look filled the appearance of the Anarian before them.

"I had hoped this day would never come," Matthias gasped, coughing into his hand, hiding the blood from the sight of his sister. "I seem to have underestimated Xen'trath's determination," Matthias said, gazing at the two. "I must send all of you back to your own time, else we face grave danger..."

Alec merely nodded, his gaze fixed on Matthias' own.

Ashylanya gripped Alec's hand, concern etched on her face.

"Your pendant, Ashylanya," Matthias wheezed. "You know what it is, do you not?"

Ashylanya pulled the small crystal into view. Matthias' eyes narrowed.

"Xen'trath told me..." She breathed. "B-but is it true, Matthias, are we really kin to that monster?"

Matthias sighed.

"So he told that to you did he...?" A grave look crossed Matthias's face. "Yes... it is true. I meant to keep that a secret from you, sister." Matthias lowered his eyes, a sorrowful look on his canine visage.

"I-I understand," Ashylanya said softly.

"You are as forgiving as always, sister. Thank you," Matthias said with a weak smile.

"That pendant—I brought it to the time you came from, to keep it out of Xen'trath's clutches." Matthias said. "I did not expect that he would wait patiently for ten thousand years to pass to bring it here." Matthias continued. "You may have recalled, sister, that you did not feel the stones presence for quite some time, I replaced it in your sleep, to take it to the time you came from. When the time was right, I gave it back..."

"I was not aware of this... I had thought that the stone had felt different." Ashylanya said, gazing at him.

"forgive me, sister. I had no other choice."

"But why is it so important to him?" Alec asked.

"It's one of the four fragments of the Time Warden's previous prison; with all four assembled, he can control the warden, hence controlling time itself," Matthias explained. "Its power alone has the ability to re-write history itself."

Alec gazed down at Ashylanya's pendant.

"What I still don't know is what Xen'trath's plans are that require two wardens..." Matthias said, glancing at Alec.

Matthias's ears perked as he heard footsteps quickly approaching, turning his head, he saw Makkari barreling toward them.

"So it really is you..." Makkari breathed, gazing at his former comrade.

"Makkari, you were brought to this time as well, I see... That mark on your hand is proof." Matthias eyed Makkari.

"How did you...?" Makkari said with a look of confusion.

"All who possess the Time Breaker's Touch—I can feel the marking upon them as if it were on my own flesh." Matthias said, seemingly able to see through Makkari's glove where the mark was located.

"It has been too long, Matthias. I still cannot overcome that day I thought you had fallen..." Makkari breathed.

"The day that everyone thought me dead, you mean? I have known it, but it appears to be different this time... blurred to my all seeing eyes..."

Matthias broke out into a fit of coughing, falling to his knees.

"Brother!" Ashylanya cried.

But Matthias held up his hand as blood dripped from his lips.

"The fever is overcoming him..." Makkari breathed.

"Which is precisely why I need to send you all back to your own era, as soon as possible!" he wheezed. "Please, take me to the others who are with you..."

Makkari sighed.

"I fear the future has already sustained much damage," Makkari said, eyeing Matthias. "But I will do as you wish... Alec, grab his other arm..."

Alec quickly approached Matthias' right side. "That won't be a good idea," Matthias breathed. "To touch me with the warden in you as well would create a paradox itself."

Makkari nodded, as Alec backed away.

Makkari then hoisted Matthias onto his back, beginning to walk back down toward the village.

"What causes this illness?" Alec asked, eyeing Matthias.

"The presence of two wardens in one era will instill Time Fever, due to a paradox in the natural flows of time..." Makkari explained over his shoulder.

"Then why am I not in the same state?" Alec asked.

"That's because you bear the blood of the dawn strider," Makkari said as they walked down the sloping hill toward the Edelion village. "You are the warden's ultimate vessel; you can bear his energy better than any warden has ever been able to."

The four had reached the village as the sun had begun to rise, Organ'us dissipating in the distance, causing an eerie glow in contrast with the light of the sun, which cast long shadows over the forest below, but Alec and Ashylanya had yet to feel fatigue as they walked at a quick pace.

"Please, bring the others to me," Matthias directed as Makkari set him down in the village center. Matthias stooped over, coughing yet again, spattering blood onto the amethyst path.

Ashylanya observed her brother with deep concern.

"That won't be necessary," spoke a voice from behind Matthias.

Matthias slowly turned his head.

"Matthias... you look unwell..." Shelara had approached from behind, gazing at the crippled Anarian.

"Why exactly, is it unnecessary, Shelara?" Matthias wheezed.

"Because I've already gathered everyone; they await you in the village's exit, to the east," Shelara replied.

Matthias' eyes narrowed. "And how is it that you knew I was here?"

"Matthias, dear, you are very easy for me to sense, especially with your current inability to mask your aura," Shelara said with a shy smile crossing her lips.

Matthias nodded, still gazing at Shelara, suspicion still etched his features.

"Follow me; I will take you to them," Shelara directed, turning.

Alec and Ashylanya glanced at each other. Something about Shelara felt different to the two.

Makkari seemed to notice as well; as her scent did not match the elf's own.

The four followed the elf to the village's eastern gate, where the others awaited them.

"Right on time; we almost left without you!" Lucy called, waving to them.

"And where is it you think you are going?" Matthias breathed, stepping forward.

Immediately all eyes were fixed on him.

"Matthias…" Lehion breathed. "You look like the reaper could claim you any minute!"

"Never mind that, I must send these five back to their own time to make things right. Please step aside," Matthias interjected.

"W-what do you mean?" Gabriel asked, gazing at Matthias.

"You do not belong here; your very presence has already altered this time period greatly." Matthias said, doubling over in a coughing fit once more. More blood spattered the walkway as he fell to his knees.

"Matthias!" Garren quickly approached him, but Ashylanya was already at her brother's side.

"But I thought we were headed out to find Jessica? At least, that's what she told us…" Sam blurted, pointing at Shelara.

"Naïve boy! Do you wish to alter this eras further?" Matthias spat.

Sam shut his mouth, his gaze still on Matthias.

"Now, you three; stand over there, with the others… Garren, step aside, please."

Garren quickly moved to stand next to Lehion and Shelara.

Joden stepped forward. "Now old friend, history has already suffered much alteration. Sending them back could be life threatening to them, not to mention you, in your current state!" Joden pleaded with the Anarian.

"It is a risk that must be taken," Matthias wheezed. "Now please, old friend, step aside."

Defeated, Joden stepped aside with the dwarf, as Alec, Ashylanya, and Makkari joined the remaining three.

Matthias stepped toward them. Raising his right hand toward the companions, he shut his eyes.

A golden ring of light snaked around the five. Ashylanya gripped tightly to Alec's hand. Lucy and Sam braced their arms with Gabriel's.

Makkari gazed down at his old friend, sorrow in his eyes as he put a firm hand on Ashylanya.

As the golden ring began to shine brightly around them, Matthias cried out, falling to his knees, the spell dissipating entirely.

Matthias fell limp to one side, losing consciousness.

"Matthias!" Ashylanya shouted, rushing to her fallen brother's side.

"I did not expect that he could… Seems that Xen'trath prevents you from leaving," Shelara said, approaching them.

"Stay back, Sulmothian!" Makkari boomed, barring the impostor's path.

The elf merely gazed up at him with half-lidded eyes. "My guise was not enough to fool you, it seems…" Shelara's voice had changed to a musical tone. "It cannot be helped, I suppose…" she sighed, stepping back.

The elf's impostor then began to transform, her face elongating to form a long snout. Scales began to appear in place of flesh. Her hair turned a dark violet, as her eyes gained a velvet coloration. A long, fluid tail emerged from her breeches, long spikes forming along its tip. The woman wore little to cover her form.

A sly smile formed on her reptilian face, with a seductive appearance. "I mean you no harm, at the present time," she cooed.

Alec stepped forward. "What do you want from us, Succubus!?" he shouted at her.

The others merely stood there, aghast.

The Sulmothian's eyes narrowed. "Naïve little pup, do not insult me by associating me with such filth," she hissed.

"Then what the hell are you?" Alec glared at the woman.

"Sulmothian…" Joden answered for her. "But not just any…" he breathed. "Azsheren, the shifter…" Joden gazed at the Sulmothian before them.

"What are Sulmothians?" Alec asked, still transfixed on the woman.

"They are draconic beings of unnatural power, shape shifting being their specialty," Joden answered. "But this one is not a demorae."

"What is your business with us, Sulmothian? Speak!" Makkari demanded.

"You would do well to show me respect, Makkari," she said, gazing at him with contempt.

"How do you know my name!?" Makkari asked, gripping the hilt of one of his axes.

"Matthias, of course… I owe him a favor; he did save my daughter's life, after all," Azsheren said, folding her arms.

"Matthias, help one such as you? Lies!" Makkari spat.

Azsheren chuckled. "You seem to know surprisingly little, to be as close to Matthias as you are," she said, with a smug look on her face.

Makkari pursed his lips, glaring darkly at her.

"So then," Lehion said, "what have you done with Shelara?"

"She's fine, should be back any minute now. I used your form to send her off to scout ahead."

Lehion stared blankly at the Sulmothian.

"You are saying that my own brother is associated with the demons?" Ashylanya asked, dumbfounded.

"Quite the oblivious bunch, aren't you?" Azsheri scoffed. "Demons, really? A label created by fearful idiots..." Azsheri chuckled. "No, I have not fallen to be risen again, so therefore, I am not a demorae, as they are properly called..."

Azsheri stepped forward. "Now listen carefully. I will tell you how you can save Matthias." Azsheren was now gazing at Alec.

"You must travel to the gate of twin passing... In seven days, a gateway will open which leads to my own homeland, the Nether," Azsheren explained.

"Are you mad?!" Garren barked. "You want us to enter the realm of Dragon-kind? Such a thing would be suicide!"

Azsheren sighed. "Once again, I am here to help you. I am not one of the mindless beasts controlled by the dark seven," Azsheri hissed. "As I was saying... Enter the Nether and travel to the dusk swamps; there you will find the one called Zarkov..."

"A pit whaler!?" Joden exclaimed. "Now I am almost certain you send us to die."

"Do you wish me to help you or not?" Azsheren barked, glaring at them.

Joden shut his mouth.

"Zarkov is a master alchemist of the high council, your only hope in saving your friend, as he is the only one who knows how to prepare a cure for the Time Fever he suffers," she continued, pacing in front of them, her tail flicking in agitation. "It is risky, and I will warn you that Zarkov does not much prefer company; he may just kill you all if he is irked in the slightest, but he is your only option," she finished.

Azsheren then approached Matthias, kneeling at his side. "You, Anari pup. Give me your hand," she directed.

Alec slowly stepped forward, extending his arm toward her, which she grabbed hold of, bringing Matthias' own limp hand to his.

Their markings touched, causing a blinding flash.

After the light had faded, Alec looked down at Matthias; he had stopped breathing.

"What did you do to him!?" Ashylanya breathed, kneeling by her brother with fear in her eyes.

"Fear not, I merely froze him in time, using the boy. To preserve him," Azsheren explained, as she hoisted his limp form from the earth.

Makkari snarled. "What are you going to do with him!?"

"Relax, I will take care of him while you seek out Zarkov," she explained. "I am off; may you be alive when next we meet."

Azsheren turned toward them a final time. "Also, Xen'trath is sure to be after the seed fragments, just so you are aware," she said as she seemed to fade, with Matthias, from existence.

"the gate closes three days after opening, and it only opens once every ten years, so I would make haste, if I were you." Azsheren's disembodied voice seemed to echo through their minds before fading.

The companions stood there for a moment, staring blankly at where Azsheri stood not a moment before.

Lehion turned to face them.

"It seems we have no choice; we must keep Matthias alive," Lehion said.

"But wha' abou' the artifact? Surely this is to buy Xen'trath time, lad." Garren said, folding his arms as he eyed Lehion.

"Even if that's true, if Matthias dies, this world will be destroyed upon the release of Xanadair," Joden interjected.

Lehion sighed, pacing now.

"Then we have no choice but to split into two groups," Lehion concluded. "We will have one group to go to the nether, the other to seek out the seed fragments," Lehion stated, eyeing the party.

"I'll go to the Nether," Alec volunteered.

"Don't be so bold, Alec; didn't you hear what she said? You could die!" Lucy chided.

"Well, someone has to go! I'm with Alec!" Sam said, moving to stand beside him.

"M-me too!" Gabriel said, joining Sam.

Ashylanya squeezed Alec's arm; looking at him, she smiled and nodded.

Shelara came running up to the party, breathing heavily. "I scouted the perimeter, just as you asked, Lehion," she stated. "It looks clear."

"A Sulmothian gave you that order, not I, but there is no time to explain; we are preparing to set out."

"To where exactly?" Shelara asked.

"To seek out the seed fragments before Xen'trath can get them," Lehion replied.

"I took an order from a Sulmothian… how bothersome."

"Like I said, there is no time to explain, but you will be coming with us."

Shelara nodded, still looking confused, turning to Lucy.

"Lucy, you come with us," Shelara directed. "I have heard you wanted to learn to use a bow. I will teach you."

Lucy gazed at Shelara. "You would do that?"

"Shouldn't be too bothersome, I suppose," she replied, with a smile and a wink.

"I will go with Alec," Joden stated. Makkari also went to Alec's side, not willing to depart from Ashylanya.

"Gabriel, come with us, I will train ye to figh'," Garren said, pointing to him.

"M-me?" Gabriel was dumbstruck.

"No, that oak behind ye…" Garren scoffed. "Looks like it's got more fight in it any'ow," Garren said, eyeing him. "Course I'm talkin to ye, ye nitwit."

Gabriel glanced back at Alec, apologetically, before joining Garren's side.

"It would seem we've decided then. Joden, I trust you know the way to the gates of twin passing?" Lehion asked.

"I dare say I know it better than I should," Joden mused, eyeing the elf.

"Then I leave them to you," Lehion replied.

"Do we even know where the crystals are?" Lucy chimed.

"Aye, I know where th'first is," Garren stated. "Within Hymorgahn, the city beneath the waves, lost home to my ancestors."

Gabriel eyed the dwarf nervously. "And what exactly do you mean by waves?"

"Beneath the ocean o'course!" Garren chided. "Maybe I should take the tree…" he grumbled.

"Alec, Sam… All of you, please come back safe for me," Lucy said, tears welling in her eyes.

"Don't you worry, sis, nothin's gonna happen to them with me here, promise!" Sam said, sticking a thumb to his chest.

"Rather high and mighty for a pup," Makkari said, with his arms crossed.

Sam glared back at him. "I know how to fight; you saying I don't?" Sam retorted.

Makkari shrugged his shoulders, grinning with one bottom fang over his upper lip.

"The journey will take six days; we should leave now, while the Edelion are still asleep," Joden stated.

"Good plan. Shelara, Garren, and you two, let's go," Lehion directed, turning.

Gabriel took one last look at his brother; worry etched his features as he began to walk.

"Be safe…" he whispered as they departed.

Chapter Thirty-Three

X en'trath… you failed me…" a dark voice hissed into Xen'trath's mind. "It does not surprise me, however."

"And what do you mean by that, my lord?" Xen'trath quaked before the crushing presence, somewhere in a dark cavern before a dark wellspring; the waters distorted Xen'trath's reflection, making him appear more hideous than he had before.

"To think the boy would be able to call forth the Time Reaver—that blade was my very bane, so long ago…"

"Forgive me, master," Xen'trath said, kneeling before the wellspring.

"No matter… the artifact, and the time warden, will be mine…" As the voice spoke, a dark aura enveloped Xen'trath. "I will grant you my touch of power, the dark fragment of the void…" The voice now sounded even more menacing as it spoke.

"The void fragment… one of the four…?" Xen'trath spoke in an fearful voice as pain seared and twisted his limbs. "You… Had it all along…? Agh!" Xen'trath doubled over as his body began to twist.

"This power I never granted to you, even in your future, is now necessary with the blade brought back from the depths of the sands of time…" the dark one hissed.

Xen'trath cried out in sheer torment as he fell to his knees; his torso began to twist violently, the shape mocking that of a serpent, his legs twisted around each other, elongating and ending in sharp black talons, as a second pair of legs grew from his hips.

One half of Xen'trath's body was covered in dark fur, the other bare flesh as pale as moonlight that grew taut over his muscles as a large pair of black wings erupted from his back. A long mangled antler began to grow from the left side of his skull above the only remaining Anarian ear he had left. The other seemed to rot and fall off, the hole quickly covered by a tangle of black phantom like hair.

His arms were now four instead of two; the two extra arms mocked those of a mantis. Xen'trath's right eye sunk back into his skull; a gaping hole filled with a dark penetrating evil was all that remained.

The left half of his form resembled the Anarian from which he originated, the right was a monster. Xen'trath's tail receded into his body, as two more barbed tails erupted from his lower spinal column.

Xen'trath clutched himself, writhing, as a dark crystal suddenly erupted from his chest, emanating a presence of deep corruption.

Xen'trath slowly opened his one remaining eye, gazing into the well; a dark blade slowly rose to the surface.

The hilt of the blade was engraved with a singular gaping mouth, that of a monstrous Demorae, twisted in eternal agony. The blade itself was shrouded in black mist, which caressed its sharp edge. A singular rune was embedded just before the blade's hilt.

"Now, Xen'trath... Take up my own mighty blade, the Demon's tear, render of souls... and strike fear into the hearts of all those who would oppose me!" the dark voice boomed. "They shall all weep, and despair..."

Xen'trath's grin was horrifying as he gazed at the blade.

"Go forth, reborn... feast upon their souls, my little voidling..."

Xen'trath laughed, a terrible darkened laugh that shook the foundations of the well.

"Yes... master Xek'roshule..." His voice sounded as though two voices spoke simultaneously.

Chapter Thirty-Four

"The journey to the gate of twin passing will be a treacherous one," Joden said as they walked through the dimly lit forest. "We will only have one stop for supplies, within the city of Evanshire; after that there are no other villages, so I hope all of you are prepared."

The group had come to the edge of the Edelion forest, gazing across the plain in the distance.

"Are we going to have to go back through that canyon again?" Gabriel asked, looking to the Arcaneight.

"Thankfully, the barrier will let you leave through a shorter route; its matrix is only designed to keep those out, not to keep those in."

"Joden? I didn't notice earlier, but where is Alavanda?" Sam asked.

"Ah, in my pocket, to keep her safe," the Arcaneight chuckled.

"I-in your pocket?" Sam asked, eyeing the man as if he were insane.

"Indeed…" Joden withdrew a small stone figure from his cloak pocket. "Alavanda is a familiar. I may summon and dismiss her as I see fit."

"How strange…" Sam replied, eyeing Joden blankly.

"Oh, not the strangest thing you'll see, I'm sure," Joden said, with a note of bemusement.

"So then, where are we going?" Alec asked, eyeing Joden.

"We will be taking, unfortunately, a more dangerous route… through the Agolian passage…"

Makkari noticeably tensed.

"The Agolian pass... I feared ever having to venture to such a place again..." he said, continuing on through to the plain.

"What's so bad about it?" Alec asked

"It crawls with dark and unspeakable horrors, lost souls, twisted and corrupt," Ashylanya answered in his stead.

"There is no other way, unfortunately. It is the sole passageway to reach the gates of twin passing."

"The city we rest at is a day's walk from here. We must make haste; if we miss the small window of time the gates open, we doom ourselves along with this world, with the death of Matthias."

"Then I shall call my remaining leophan..." Makkari said, drawing two fingers to his lips.

"That will not be necessary, it would seem." Joden halted him as he watched twin shadows descend upon them from the skies above. "It appears Azsheri has sent us aid."

The shadows drew closer; the figures of mid-sized dragons came into view, gracefully landing before them.

The dragons themselves were coated in azure scales, large leathery wings folded back against their lithe reptilian forms. Elongated necks craned as they lifted large horned heads.

Razor sharp teeth were visible in their maws, as eyes of glowing crimson gazed patiently at the group before them, while their razor sharp claws padded the earth.

Sam and Alec gazed at the drakes in awe.

Ashylanya giggled. "Never seen dragons before?" she teased. "Though these are a bit different; the ones I've seen don't have horns like this," Ashylanya said, eyeing the pair.

"It would seem our journey's success rate has increased," Joden calculated, approaching the drakes.

"You two, what are your names?" Joden asked them.

"Names?" Sam blurted. "They can speak?" he asked, still gazing at the intimidating creatures.

"Sarsssurusss..." spoke the hissing voice of one, answering Sam's question. "Melvessenussss..." spoke the other.

"Azsheri sends her own favored, rather peculiar of her..." Joden Muttered.

"Can we eat that one?" Sarsurus hissed, looking at Alec.

"Lady Azsheri forbidsss it," Came Malvessensus' reply.

Makkari eyed the pair of dragons, growing tense with the idea of having to go the route of flying.

Ashylanya gripped his arm reassuringly. "Are you still afraid of heights, Makkari?" she asked.

"Giant winged lizards—I must be going mad," Sam stated, gazing at them.

Sarsurus's eyes narrowed. "Sssurely one wouldn't hurt..." he hissed.

"No..." Malvessensus snapped his jaws at his sibling.

"Enough chatter, we will be taking you to the Agolian passage, from here..."

Alec and Sam hesitantly approached the dragons, as Ashylanya skillfully leapt onto the back of Sarsurus.

"C'mon you two!" she said with a giggle. "Flying is fun, though it does take getting used to!" she said, grabbing Alec by the arm and hoisting him up behind her.

Alec's tail had retreated between his legs, his ears folded back as his eye color shifted to a pale peach.

Makkari hesitantly mounted in front of Ashylanya, while Joden and Gabriel mounted Malvessensus.

Ashylanya reached back with one hand, to hold Alec's in an attempt to calm his nerves. "Just lean on me, okay?" she told him, gently squeezing his hand.

"Oh, don't mind me, I guess," Sam called to Alec. "You got a girl and I got an old man—seems rather backwards to me, don't you think?" he teased.

Alec grinned at Sam. "Jealous?" he called back to Sam.

Ashylanya giggled, squeezing Alec's hand tightly before relaxing.

Makkari rolled his eyes, as Joden seemed bemused.

"Hold tightly, mortals..." Malvessensus said, readying for a lunge into the skies above, as Sarsurus did the same.

Makkari seemed to lower his head, gripping tight to Malvessensus's scaled back.

Ashylanya leaned against Makkari's back in an attempt to calm his nerves, but her effort was fruitless.

The two drakes leapt forward, extending their wings and taking flight.

Sam cringed, huddling against Joden's back at first, before opening one eye to see that the trees below now looked like mere children's toys.

Sam extended his arms into the air. "Woohoo! This ain't so bad!" he called to the others over the rush of wind which buffeted against them.

Ashylanya seemed to be enjoying herself as well, as they ascended above the clouds.

Alec squeezed her hand tightly, frightened by the overpowering sound of the wind on his unfamiliar increase in hearing.

He was then awed, however, by the majestic view before him.

Large mountains were visible in the distance, a gentle mist shrouding them, with a speckling of trees. The sun shone down upon them, lighting the darkened nimbus all around them.

Makkari merely gazed down at the drake's back, unwilling to look anywhere else.

"I've always loved to fly!" Ashylanya shouted to Alec. "The clouds always felt like home to me!"

Alec gazed longingly at Ashylanya; the sun bathing her face complemented her beauty to him.

For the first time since parting from home, he felt happy, as if the rushing wind and the sunlight had kissed away his sorrows.

The wind billowed Alec's new length of azure hair back as his ears perked in excitement, his tail coiling itself around Ashylanya's.

"I never thought I'd ever experience anything like this!" Alec called over her shoulder.

Ashylanya smiled at him. A light blush tinged her cheeks as her own tail wrapped around his own.

"Enjoy it while it lasts!" Joden called. "I see something dark approaching!"

Makkari took a deep breath in, as Alec's eyes shifted.

"Black magic…" Makkari breathed.

Alec saw a wave of dark energy quickly approaching them, as the wind seemed to increase heavily.

"Hold on tightly!" Sarsurus shouted, as the twin dragons veered to the left in an attempt to avoid the maelstrom of dark energy.

Anxiety slowly began to build within Alec as they drew closer to the black cloud, its energy overpowering his senses.

"It's drawing us in!" Malvessensus boomed. "Brace yourselves!"

Not far off, Lucy and Gabriel trudged behind Shelara, Garren, and Lehion. Having come to a marsh-like area of the forest, thick mud caked their shoes as they slowly continued.

"Do you sense it too, Lehion?" Shelara asked.

"Indeed, it seems that there is black magic at work somewhere in the distance…"

"Are we almost out of here?" Gabriel asked, panting heavily from the effort of wading through the thick muck.

"Still got a ways te go," Garren replied, looking back at Gabriel.

"Just how far away is this place?" Lucy asked, exhausted as well.

"Abou' six days on foot; there's a passage tha' leads beneath the seas," Garren replied.

"Complaining won't get us there any faster… All it is, is bothersome…" Shelara interjected.

The five traveled for what felt like hours, until they reached solid ground, to the relief of the two youth.

Exiting the dusky swamp they came upon a vast desert. The skies had now completely clouded over. The sound of thunder rolled on the distant horizon.

"How does land go from forest, to swamp, to desert just like that?" Lucy asked, gazing at the vast expanses before them.

"The desert you see before us is known as Balgavian's Scar," Lehion explained. "Countless centuries ago, a great battle was waged here; no life has graced the earth since…"

"But what about the huge skeletal wing in the distance?" Lucy asked, eyeing Lehion.

"That would be the key reason why life no longer grows here. The wing you see is only a small part of a foul dragon known as Galakrond," He answered.

"On th' other side o' this desert is th entrance to the passageway to me 'omeland…" Garren stated, taking a step onto the dry earth. "This journey won' be easy on me, one of the sea."

"Let's get this over with then. I've packed us plenty of water skins, as well as rations Nadrek was kind enough to supply us with," Shelara stated, taking a step onto the parched earth.

Before taking another step, Shelara suddenly plunged beneath the ground.

"Shelara!" Lehion shouted, hurrying to where she had vanished, only to fall through the earth as well.

The earth was suddenly turned into churning liquid as it pulled Garren and the two frightened youth down below.

Gabriel grabbed Lucy's arm, clinging to a tree root with his other hand.

"Hold on, Lucy!" Gabriel shouted, trying to pull her up, but the suddenly living earth beneath them seemed to be sucking them in violently.

Gabriel lost his grip on the root, sending the two cascading down beneath the earth, which returned to normal upon consuming the party.

Chapter Thirty-Five

"Hold on tightly, children!" Joden called over the roar of the wind, as it buffeted them from all sides.

The clouds had now darkened to near pitch black, ominously rumbling all around them.

Alec gazed quickly at the blackening clouds, catching a glimpse of a dark figure in the distance with his enhanced vision.

"There's someone there!" Alec pointed in the direction of the figure.

"We must descend now!" Joden shouted to the dragons.

"What's going on!?" Sam shouted.

"There is foul magic afoot! We must leave the skies immediately!" Joden shouted again, as the drakes tried their hardest to descend.

Alec's ears perked as the fur on his tail stood on end; the same had happened with Ashylanya and Makkari.

As they left the clouds it had begun to rain violently and lightning streaked the skies.

"Hold on!" Joden's shouts were muffled by the powerful winds, which battered them, causing the dragons to spiral out of control.

Ashylanya slipped from her place behind Makkari. Alec caught her hand quickly.

"Ashylanya!" Makkari shouted, trying to reach her.

"I won't let you go!" Alec cried, pulling her in slowly, despite the dragon's violent movements.

Sarsurus had now broken one of his wings, plummeting toward the earth below.

Alec pulled Ashylanya to himself as Malvessensus righted himself, now diving toward his sibling, who had begun to quickly fall from the skies.

Sam and Joden clung tightly as the ground below drew nearer; Joden was muttering an incantation under his breath as the ground quickly approached.

Makkari clung tightly as Malvessensus gained speed in pursuit of Sarsurus.

Alec held Ashylanya tightly, his tail wrapped around the dragon's own lithe tail, holding on with his legs.

Ashylanya's heart beat fast against his own.

Before striking the ground Joden finished his spell, as a large water-like substance cushioned their fall.

"I cannot ssslow down!" Malvessensus roared.

Makkari and Alec braced themselves, and Alec continued to hold Ashylanya tightly to himself, as the drake struck the earth hard, with a sickening crack.

The three were thrown from the dragon's back, rolling onto the earth with a hard impact.

Joden hurried toward the three, having leapt from his dragon's back, Sam close behind.

"Can you stand, boy?" Joden asked Alec, but Alec's consciousness faded before hearing anything else.

"Why do you continue on, boy? Your efforts are futile..." a dark voice echoed through Alec's mind, as his mind faded as he lost consciousness.

"Lucy..."

Lucy had begun to stir, slowly opening her eyes, to be greeted by dim torchlight.

Slowly rising, her body ached from striking the ground below hard.

"Where am I?" Lucy breathed, taking in her surroundings.

A narrow corridor was before her. The chipped stone walls were adorned with ancient symbols and claw markings. The symbols were familiar to Lucy's brain as she inspected them.

Rows of torches hung evenly along the walls that appeared to be dripping with crimson fluid. The dim lighting cast an eerie contrast to the ancient hallway.

"Hello? Sam...? Shelara...?" she called, only hearing her own faint echo.

Lucy began to walk down the corridor slowly. Her footsteps echoed off the hard surface of the marble flooring, which seemed to be caked with moss from small cracks in its otherwise pristine surface.

"Lucy?" a voice echoed back at her.

"Gabriel?" she called back, only receiving her own voice in return.

"Dear sweet Lucy...!" a musical voice cooed back.

Lucy froze in fear.

"W-who's there?" she stuttered.

"You don't remember me?" the voice echoed back in a haunting tone. "That hurts, Lucy!"

Lucy began to run; the marble floor began to pulse, a dark liquid oozing from the surface as she ran.

"IT HURTS!" the voice wailed as a grotesque figure lunged at her from the shadowy wall.

Lucy screamed.

"Xen'trath!?" Lucy wailed.

She was being shaken hard by a rough hand.

"Get ahold of yourself, lass!" Garren was shaking her in an effort to awaken her.

Lucy's eyes flew open. She looked deathly pale, as her eyes bulged out of her head in fear.

"W-what happened!?" she cried, shaking violently.

"You were havin' a nighmare swah 'appened," Garren reassured her.

"B-but it felt so real!" Lucy now had tears in her eyes.

Garren patted her on the shoulder reassuringly. "We seem to 'av fallen into a sort o' cavern," he explained, stepping aside to give her a better view.

They were indeed in a cavern; large arching walls of stone joined to form a rough looking vault, and a shallow lake seemed to encompass the area.

They sat on a small patch of dry land in the cavern's center. A dim light from a small hole in the chasms roof served as the only light source, casting an eerie glow over the lake which encompassed them.

Glancing to her left, she saw Lehion leaning over Shelara's unconscious form. Gabriel was to the right, gazing at her.

"You all right, Lucy?" Gabriel asked with concern.

"I-I'm fine..." Lucy stammered, her heart still racing.

Shelara had begun to stir, slowly sitting up. "What the hell happened?" she groaned.

"I have no idea, though judging the distance from where we fell..." Lehion glanced up at the barely visible peak of the cavern. "We shouldn't have survived a fall like that."

"Then how?" Shelara said, standing.

"Someone must've inervened," Garren stated, gazing upward.

"That... would be me..." spoke a female voice which seemed to fill the cavern.

A figure emerged from the shadows, coming into view. The stranger was that of a haggard Anarian woman, though different from what any of them had seen before.

This Anarian had a large pair of wings; the feathers were a stained white with faded azure, folded back against her shoulders.

The Anarian was fully matured, with an elongated snout and sharp looking fangs. Faded rust-colored eyes gazed at them through an untidy mane of hair which extended far past her thighs.

A long bushy tail hung limp behind her, the color matching the dirt-caked snow-colored fur, giving the appearance she had been down here for weeks, even months.

Her wolfish ears rested within her mane, barely visible through the tangled coat. One of her clawed hands was severely mangled, indicating that she too had fallen into this pit.

She wore dark colored robes, which masked the unhealthy thin state of her body.

"Who are you?" Lehion asked, facing her.

"I am Anessa..." She spoke in a soft voice, belying her wolfish appearance. "Mate to SoluVerik, leader of the Anarian tribes."

Chapter Thirty-Six

Alec slowly opened his eyes, darkness greeting him once more. Trying to move his body, Alec felt as if he were carved of stone.

His frame seemed to be hovering in the darkness, which drew on as far as the eye could see.

"Alec…" the voice of Ashylanya called to him.

"Ashy…Lanya…?" Alec attempted to speak, but his tongue felt heavy.

A strange glowing light appeared before him, illuminating a dark crystal.

Alec gazed at the gemstone as Ashylanya's form came into view, though her form was much different than Alec had ever seen.

This version of the girl he knew sustained a fully matured Lycan form; an elongated snout extended from her soft fur-coated visage, the color of a soft midnight blue.

Her ember colored eyes gazed gently into his own; as she drew closer to him, a large pair of wings slowly became visible behind her, and the smooth feathers were a deep violet.

Ashylanya extended one pawlike hand toward him, gently caressing his face.

"Alec, come back to me…" she softly whispered.

Another figure emerged from behind her. This one looked like a much younger version of the Dawn Strider, her large innocent eyes gazing at him, almost in fear.

As she approached, Alec felt warmth on his flesh, as he slowly started to grow fur where the light of the crystal the little girl carried touched.

As the young strider drew closer Alec felt his face change, resembling Ashylanya's.

Soft black fur coated his form, leaving a gentle white on the tip of his newly formed snout.

"Wolfy…" the girl whispered, with a wide smile; her voice echoed through the darkness as both she and Ashylanya faded.

What is this…? Alec thought to himself, before fading out as his own wings, a solid black, formed.

Alec slowly opened his eyes, awakening from the dream to see Ashylanya sitting next to him, her arm in a sling.

"Ashylanya… Your arm…!" Alec was lying in a bed with grey linen sheets. Gentle rays of the setting sun lit the small humble room through a small window with opened shutters.

Alec… I'm so happy you're okay!" Ashylanya knelt next to him, holding his hand gently in her own. "My arm will be okay; it's broken though."

Alec gently touched the wound and a glowing light filled her arm, as she looked on in amazement.

"What did you do?" she breathed.

"I'm not sure; something just told me to place my hand on your arm…"

Ashylanya removed the sling, clenching and unclenching her hand. "How did you-"

"I dreamt of you," Alec interjected. "You had taken on a full form of Lycan…"

"M-me?" she gasped, blushing lightly.

"You had beautiful wings, the color of violet, with black…" Alec replied softly.

"Fully transformed…?" she breathed.

"There was someone else there too, a little girl who resembled my mother… She had a necklace, just like you… and when she came close, the light of the necklace transformed me too…"

Ashylanya looked awed. "Another pendant…?"

They were interrupted by the light creaking of a light wooden door, as Joden entered.

"Joden... How are they...?" Ashylanya asked.

"The two are badly injured, with broken limbs, but they will live," Joden stated. "It would seem, however, that you have recovered fully, thanks to Alec," Joden noted, eyeing Ashylanya's arm. "Makkari has already awoken and will return shortly."

"What about Sam?" Alec asked.

"Oh, alive and well," came Sam from a chair to Alec's right. "Sure... guess I don't exist when your ogling yer girlfriend," Sam teased. "Glad you're all right, you took the hardest of the fall with Ashylanya in yer arms."

Alec looked over at Sam, blinking. "I didn't even see you there... when did you...?"

"'Bout the same time you were undressin' her in yer head," Sam mused. "Am I right? I was layin' in the bed next to you."

Alec and Ashylanya turned beet red. His eyes shifted to a light magenta, but before he could say anything, Joden interrupted.

"We cut down our travel time by a few days. You should rest, Alec" he said, eyeing Sam.

"I suppose..." Alec said, turning his head toward Ashylanya, who was still blushing.

Later that evening Alec lay awake, mulling over everything in his dreams in an attempt to make sense of it all. Ashylanya had dozed off, her head resting on her arms over Alec's leg. Sam had since left to see the city for himself.

Makkari, feeling relieved to be on solid ground again, sat idly in a chair close by, nodding off, his arms folded in front of his chest.

Alec gazed at Ashylanya's sleeping form, feeling curious as to why they had grown so attached at such a fast pace, though he truly did not mind.

Alec listened to the gentle sound of rain, drumming on the rooftop of the small room they had rented. Joden informed him that they had the room for the night.

Alec's moment of peace was interrupted by loud footsteps coming toward the room and the door flying open as Sam rushed inside.

"Alec!" Sam panted.

Ashylanya and Makkari awoke, groggily eyeing Sam.

"What is it, Sam…?" Alec asked, sounding annoyed.

"I-it's Jessica! Come quick!" Sam blurted.

Ashylanya lifted her head just in time to avoid being toppled over as Alec leapt from his bed, bolting for the door, leaving Ashylanya gazing after him in muddled confusion.

"Where did you see her!?" Alec demanded, following Sam.

Makkari sighed, staring after the two. "So it's come to this… hope he's ready for disappointment," Makkari muttered as he stood up and stretched. "We should go too, Lady Ashylanya."

Ashylanya nodded, still half asleep, before drifting off again, her head lolling to where Alec had lain not a moment before.

Makkari smiled with a light chuckle.

"Guess she really was exhausted," he muttered as he walked out the door, gently shutting it behind him.

Chapter Thirty-Seven

"Is there no way out of here, Anessa?" Shelara asked, standing before the shallow lake's surface.

"I have only seen one way," Anessa replied. "At the edge of this lake, there is an orifice, though not even I can hold my breath long enough to reach the other side."

Shelara was now eyeing Garren.

"Wha' you lookin' at me fer?" he said, taking a step back.

Not a half an hour later, the dwarf found himself tied to a long rope Shelara had taken from her pack.

The dwarf grumbled to himself as he stood near the edge of the hole Anessa had described.

"You're our only shot, Garren. Let us know what you find," Shelara directed.

"Bloody elves, usin' me like some kind o'errand boy..." Garren muttered to himself.

"What was that, Garren? I couldn't hear you; you really should speak up!"

"I'm goin', I'm goin'..." the dwarf shot before diving below the water's surface.

"Sure this will work?" Lehion asked, walking to her side.

"It's our only chance," she replied. "Bothersome, really..."

Anessa now sat next to Gabriel and Lucy, cringing in pain from her mangled paw.

"How long has your arm been that way, Anessa?" Lucy asked, eyeing the mangled limb.

"Two days since falling down here. I think it might be infected," she replied.

"Here, I know how to set it for you at least; let me help," Lucy offered.

"You know how to do that, Lucy?" Gabriel asked, eyeing her.

"I learned a while back how to do first aid," she replied. "Honestly, I'm quite surprised you've only been here two days, the shape you're in, looks like a much longer time…"

"I was lost within the desert before this… I came in search of a rare stone used in tribal rituals," she explained. "I did not expect to fall into such a trap."

"I see," Lucy said. "Now, this is going to hurt a lot," Lucy warned, gripping her arm firmly.

Anessa howled in pain as Lucy applied pressure, forcing the bone back into place. "Gabriel, there is a bandage in my pack; could you grab it? It should be by the water's edge.

"Sure," Gabriel replied, walking over toward the now strangely resonating pool.

Gabriel froze, seeing a pair of eyes gazing at him beneath the water's surface. "Uh… Lucy!" Gabriel hurried back to her with the bandage. "T-there's something in the water!" Gabriel stammered shakily.

"What is it, Gabriel?" she said. Taking the bandage from him, she began wrapping the Anarian's arm.

"L-lucy…!" Gabriel now shook as he watched something emerge from the water's surface.

"What is it, Gabriel!?" Lucy asked. Noticing Anessa gazed at it as well, Lucy turned.

To her horror, twisted looking beings made purely of water had begun to rise from all around.

Shelara and Lehion rushed to their sides, weapons drawn.

"Did Garren trigger a trap?" Lehion questioned, eyeing the figures that slowly edged toward them.

"That blundering fool…" Shelara replied, readying an arrow.

"Weapons won't harm these; our only chance is to run," Anessa stated.

"And where exactly do we run to?" Shelara shot back at her.

Her question was answered by a low rumbling coming from the far end of the cavern, as an ancient passage slowly opened, with Garren standing on the other side. "I found the way ou'!" the dwarf shouted, keeled over from the pace he had traveled. "Stepped on a few faulty stones ere and there, but I don't think…" Garren looked up at the group. "Oh bloody 'ell…"

"Everyone follow close!" Lehion shouted, charging forward, cutting into one of the creatures, stunning it for only a moment before the blade wound closed and reshaped the watery being.

Charging past, evading the creatures closing in, the group barreled past Garren, nearly toppling him over.

Garren turned and ran with the others as the watery beings charged through after them.

"Wha' the 'ell are those things!?" Garren huffed as he ran behind them.

"They are Tomb Guardians! Just run!" Anessa shouted.

The group picked up speed as the twisted guardians closed in on them. A narrow doorway visible ahead seemed to be slowly closing.

"Hurry!" Shelara shouted, throwing herself under the door's threshold, the others following suit as the door rumbled shut behind them.

Garren seemed to be caught in the door.

Lehion sprinted up to him, cutting him free.

"Not me pack!" Garren shouted. "Me lucky pipe was in 'ere!"

"Better than a limb, dwarf," Lehion spat.

"Let's move, no telling what else could be lying in wait for us," Lehion said, turning.

"Me pipe…" Garren huffed, reluctantly leaving the tightly shut passage.

———————————————

Alec and Sam made their way through the large city of Evanshire. Walking down the marble pathway they halted at the entrance to a pub.

"She's in here?" Alec asked, casting a sidelong glance at Sam. "Are you sure?"

"Yes, Alec! I saw her at the bar, mumblin' to herself about losing some fight, as she drowned herself in ale," Sam replied, approaching the door to the pub.

A large sign above the door read "The Golden Horn."

Sam pushed open the door. A large cloud of smoke greeted the pair, causing Alec to cough as they entered the pub.

Glancing inside, the pub was packed full; grubby looking men huddled around tables playing cards, laughter and jeering could be heard all around as waitresses milled about serving food and drink.

Alec then saw her, noticing her only by her long fiery mane of braided hair.

A large bearded man had sat down next to her.

"Hey, sweet thing… Lemme buy you a drink," spoke the man with a gruff sounding voice.

"Piss off…" the drunken voice of Jessica spoke.

"Now tha's no way fer a lady to talk," the man said, placing an arm around her shoulder.

Jessica grabbed the man's arm not a moment later, twisting it.

"I said… piss off!" she growled, throwing his arm back at him.

The man got up, lumbering away. "Harlot," he spat.

Jessica was on him in an instant, her fist striking him hard in his jaw.

The man fell backwards, overturning the table where a rowdy looking bunch played cards.

The pub was now in an uproar as a brawl broke out, the waitresses fleeing.

One raggedly dressed woman grabbed Jessica by her braid, resulting in getting the wind knocked out of her by a decisive kick to the stomach by the disgruntled Jessica, sending her flying as she caught a burly commoner's fist with one hand, throwing him over her head into another table.

Alec and Sam merely watched agape, as Jessica singlehandedly brought down one after another without so much as blinking.

"I don't think trying to talk to her now would be a good idea…" Sam said, grabbing Alec by his tunic and forcing him to duck as one short man went soaring over their heads out the door.

"Anyone else!?" Jessica bellowed, eyeing the remaining bunch that averted their gazes. A low groan came from one of the beaten brawlers.

"Didn't think so," she said, returning to her seat as if she hadn't just beaten down twelve men twice her size.

"I'll have another, bartender," she slurred, eyeing the short man, who was huddled against the back of the bar.

"Don't make me beat the stuffin' out of you too!" she said, glaring at him.

"R-right away missus!" the bartender squeaked, hurrying to pour her another mug of ale.

"You… sure that's her…?" Alec whispered, eyeing Sam.

"You two… what're you gawkin' at?" Jessica said, turning her head. "Bit young to be visiting pubs."

Jessica turned toward them; seeing Alec, her eyes narrowed.

"An Anari pup? Crawl back to yer mother's teat. I don't wish to be disturbed by the likes of you."

Alec gazed at her, ignoring the irony in her statement.

"But you are his mum." Sam said something he should not have.

Jessica stopped, mid-pull from her mug, eyeing Sam with malice. She shattered the mug with one hand.

"What was that you just said, boy?" she hissed. "That thing's mum!?" she scoffed.

Alec gained a wounded appearance from her response.

"I-it's true! I mean, in the future, I suppose," Sam stated, eyeing her nervously.

Jessica began to laugh, bringing her fist down on the table.

"What is this nonsense you're spouting, child?" she said through tears of mirth.

"What? You're from the future, or somethin'? You're killin' me; you're quite the comedian!" she gasped through a fit of laughter.

Alec slowly walked toward her.

"Alec! What, are you mad?!" Sam blurted.

But Alec did not hear him; he seemed fixated on the laughing woman before him.

"You took me in and raised me…" Alec breathed.

Jessica backhanded him, sending him falling backwards.

"Don't speak of such nonsense, little pup," she spat, now looking serious.

Alec rose again, moving closer. "You raised me and Gabriel…" he persisted.

"What is wrong with you!? You like being hit or somethin'?" Jessica glared at Alec, slapping him again, but he held his ground.

Alec withdrew something from his pocket, placing it on the bar. "Your mother would have been proud of what you did for us…" Alec breathed.

"You dare-"

Jessica looked down at what Alec placed before her, causing her to freeze, her face contorted in a mix of anger and sorrow.

She turned away from him.

"Leave me… alone," she breathed.

Alec gazed at her for a long moment before turning. "Let's go, Sam," Alec said, defeated.

Slowly the two left the pub, Alec giving the woman he knew to be loving and kind at one point a final glance.

A single tear rolled down Jessica's face as she grasped a small coin within her palm. Engraved within were two words, one on either side: 'Hope' and 'Devotion'.

"Mother… what do I do…?" She tucked away the small coin, which had been her mother's last treasured gift.

Jessica cried silently, seeing that same coin upon the cold surface of the bar.

Chapter Thirty-Eight

Lehion was tense as he walked through the dimly lit corridors of what appeared to be a long abandoned tomb. The others, feeling the same, followed closely behind him.

"I don't like the feel of this place," Shelara said, eyeing the walls, which were lit with eerie blue flamed torches. "It feels like something dark dwells here..."

Garren was looking glum, having to leave behind his bag which carried his favored pipe. He followed behind, his head lowered.

"What was so important about that pipe, Garren?" Lucy asked, keeping close to him.

"Was me father's..." Garren replied, sulking. "Gave it to me before he died, he did."

"I see... I'm sorry..." Lucy said, with sympathy in her voice.

Garren shrugged, continuing on behind Shelara and Lehion.

Gabriel jumped as he felt something brush past his feet. "What was that?!" he breathed, looking frantically at the aged marble flooring.

A large rat had skittered by him, turning back to look at him before running off.

"You're too jumpy, lad," Garren scolded.

Anessa paused, sniffing at something she sensed in the air.

"What is it Anessa?" Lehion asked, as he gazed at her back.

"Banterlecht..." she breathed.

"Banterlecht?" Lucy asked, eyeing her.

Lehion appeared to be alarmed at those words. "We must move, now!" he shouted.

The party broke into a run.

"What is a Banterlecht!?" Lucy shouted, trying to keep up her pace.

Her question was answered by a low, guttural cry from behind them.

Glancing back, Lucy experienced pure terror as she saw the large beast which now pursued them.

The creature was covered in eyes, along his mangled and twisted arms and legs, some half opened, others fully opened, glaring at the party, with bloodlust. Long snake-like tendrils flailed wildly from its arched twisted back; its jaw parted in six ways; three reptilian tongues flailed about as if longing to consume their flesh, and a long spiked tail flailed wildly as it chased them at alarming speed.

The party was met with a path that split two ways, turning a sharp corner.

"This way!" Anessa shouted.

Shelara readied an arrow, turning as she ran, firing off an arrow which pierced one of the beast's eyes, causing it to flail in agony as it writhed about, knocking against the walls.

The party continued to run, as the narrow passage began to shake violently with the beast's throes of agony.

Regaining its composure it continued its pursuit, all of its eyes wide open now as black blood oozed from the ruined eye, gazing at Shelara in fury.

Anessa withdrew something from her robe, tossing it behind her at the creature's clawed feet.

The small stone she tossed emanated a blinding light, incapacitating the beast, as it was blinded by the light.

Coming to a bend in the path as the passage began to collapse, the party turned; running down the corridor's winding curves, a doorway came into sight just ahead of them.

"Get inside, quickly!" Anessa shouted.

The party crossed the threshold of the doorway as the passage collapsed behind them moments later.

Garren panted heavily, falling to one knee as his heart raced in his chest. "Of all th' places to run into one o' them!" he wheezed.

Garren glanced up at Lehion and Shelara, whose gazes were fixed on something before them.

"Wha' is it?" Garren asked through his heavy breathing. Getting to his feet, he walked up to them, peering beyond the two elves.

A large altar lay before them. A large stone statue of a seven-headed dragon was just beyond the altar, gemstones in each of the carving's eyes.

A tablet rested at its base, which read "The final resting place of Thron'shagar."

"Thron'shagar..." Anessa breathed. "We are exactly where I need to be..."

Lehion looked toward Anessa. "Thron'shagar, such a beast has only been told of in folklore... What is so important that you needed to be here?"

"The last breath of Thron'shagar is the true reason there is a vast desert above. The latter tale of Galakrond is merely a myth. Formidable as he may have been, Thron'shagar is far more powerful," Anessa explained. "I lived to see this beast's breath create the marred earth above... his altar is what keeps life vacant above..."

Gabriel cast Anessa a sidelong glance. "Just how old are you?" he asked.

Anessa ignored the question, approaching the altar.

"So... you used us to bring you to this altar...?" Lehion held a note of accusation in his tone.

"Forgive me, but I needed to end this curse, and only a Velenar dwarf was able to open the doorway for me, to reach this particular altar..."

"And just what will happen when you end this curse?" Shelara asked, seeming disgruntled at having being used.

"The desolation above will be undone..." Anessa said, approaching the statue.

The statue itself was ancient. Moss grew over the cracked stone of its carved talons, and chips along the dragon's form were visible over its entirety. The gemstones in each of the eyes were of various colors, matching that of a particular element.

"The blight crystals—to think they were hidden here all along..." Anessa breathed, lightly touching the rough stone of the statue.

"What is it then, Anessa?" Shelara asked, approaching her.

But Anessa did not respond.

Reaching slowly for one of the embedded crystals she touched it, causing it to faintly glow.

"The very crystals prevent all life from thriving, but only above," she stated, turning toward them.

A low rumbling came from the statue at that moment, as all fourteen crystals began to glow brightly; the statue suddenly began to move, shaking off an eon of caked dust and moss.

The dragon statue returned to life, with an ear-splitting roar.

As a battle was about to take place somewhere far off, Alec seemed to sense that his close friends were in danger. Having met Makkari outside of the pub with Sam, the big Anarian rested against its outer wall.

"Alec..." Makkari said, walking up to him.

"What?" Alec shot, his head lowered, as to not show the tinge of dark orange that clouded his eyes.

"You have to have known how she would react to you." Makkari stated. "The event that makes her an ally has not happened yet, or rather, it may not happen at all, this time."

Alec looked up at him. "What do you mean?"

Makkari sighed. "When she changed last time, it was due to an act by Matthias; as he is not here for the moment he needed to be, she may never change..."

"Then I'll be the one to change her, no matter what," Alec said, gazing into Makkari's eyes.

"I think you have already..." Sam said, eyeing the weeping form of Jessica within the now darkened pub.

"What did you do?" Makkari asked, watching Jessica.

"Before she died, last time… she gave me a coin that was given to her by her mother. She told me to give it to her past self in order to spark an alliance… It's strange; it's almost like she knew Matthias would not be able to help her this time…" Alec explained.

"I hope whatever was done worked; she was stubborn even then," Makkari replied. "For now, we should head back to the inn."

"I sensed something earlier," Alec stated, eyeing Makkari. "Lucy and Gabriel—they are all in danger; somehow I feel it in my gut."

"Shelara and Lehion, as well as the dwarf, will not let them come to harm, fear not…" Makkari whispered.

A few minutes later, the three had returned to the inn. Alec found Ashylanya to be fast asleep, curled up in his bed. Joden had not moved from his chair by the room's small fireplace, seeming to gaze idly into the dancing flames.

"I trust things went well?" Joden asked, as they entered.

"Hardly…" Alec said, approaching his bed. He looked down at Ashylanya's sleeping form and could not help but smile.

Makkari approached, gently lifting her and carrying her to her own bed, as Alec plopped down onto the mattress. Sam lay in his own bed, turning his head toward Alec.

"Bet you're let down that he didn't leave her there, eh?" Sam teased.

Alec did not reply as he gazed up at the ceiling.

"Cheer up Alec; we'll get to her, don't worry." He said, eyeing Alec.

"I hope you're right," Alec sighed.

Makkari had sat down in his chair, casting a glance at Alec, before shutting his eyes and drifting off.

"You have a bed too, ya know," Sam commented to Makkari.

But Makkari did not reply.

A vision of Alec flashed through Lucy's mind as they faced the now living dragon in all its horror. *Alec, I hope you're okay!* she thought to herself, as she watched the dragon slowly shake off the dust of age.

"Jus one thing after another…" Garren muttered, withdrawing his axe from the harness on his back, now eyeing the very alive effigy before him.

The two elves readied their bows as well, though Anessa seemed to just stand there, gazing at the colossal stone beast.

"Why did it suddenly come to life!?" Lucy shouted, slowly backing away from the monstrosity before them.

"I-I dunno…!" Gabriel replied shakily.

As the dragon statue gained full motion, it let out an ear-shattering roar, bringing a large clawed foot down on Lehion, who jumped away in time to avoid being flattened.

He let fly an arrow, but it merely ricocheted from the statue's stone flesh, narrowly missing striking Shelara.

"Watch it!" Shelara shouted at him, rolling away from a buffet of the statues powerful wings.

"'Ow do we fight such a beast!?" Garren shouted, as his blow was repelled; not even a scratch could be seen on the menacing leviathan.

Anessa still had not moved, still gazing at their attacker.

"You'll be killed! Move!" Lehion bellowed, too late as the statue's tail came down on the Anarian, seeming to crush her.

To the surprise of Lehion and Shelara, the Anarian was intact as the beast raised its tail, revealing Anessa, who did not even waver.

"How's that even possible?" Shelara gazed at Anessa in amazement.

Slowly the Anarian withdrew something from her robe as one of the dragon's large heads lashed at her but did nothing, as it passed right through her.

Anessa held up a small vial, with runes engraved in its glass, and opened it, causing the dragon to freeze right before another of its heads could crush Lucy.

Lucy had her hands over her head, her eyes tightly shut.

When nothing had happened, she slowly opened her eyes, looking up at the gaping maw inches from her face.

"W-what-"

Before she could say another word, the gemstones in each eye flashed, before they seemed to be drained of their light, as the multicolored energy was drawn into the small vial Anessa held.

As the last of the crystals' energy drained into the vial, she put a small cork over the opening.

Bringing the small object to her face she gazed momentarily at the glowing substance within, before shattering it upon the surface of the altar.

The tomb began to shake violently as a result.

"Wha did you jus' do!?" Garren shouted, as he watched the large statue crumble, while the others distanced themselves.

When the dust cleared, Lehion gazed at the Anarian.

"Forgive me for deceiving you…" she said, looking toward them.

"You—you're an Edelion!" Lucy gasped. "But how, then, did I touch you!?"

Anessa merely smiled. "You have a gift, young Lucy…" she said. "I have been in this tomb for over ten thousand years, awaiting the arrival of one who could open the way for me." Anessa spoke, over the crumbling of the vault all around them. "I am among one of the first Anarians to grace this world…"

"So now what happens!?" Shelara bellowed. "Are we to be sacrificed for the greater good of restoring life to the deserts above!?"

Anessa chuckled. "No… I will protect you and grant you safe passage from this place…"

The ceiling had begun to cave in; Garren rolled to the side, evading a large slab of stone from crushing him. "Then wha' is 'appening now!?"

"Life… is returning to the marred land above… The curse has been lifted." Anessa spoke as she seemed to slowly fade away. "What bound me here, so long ago after my demise, has been undone; farewell, mortals…" She spoke softly as her form unraveled, dissipating.

The group felt a warm light caress them, as the ground below heaved, large vines breaking through, bringing them slowly upward.

"Hang on, everyone!" Lehion called.

"Obviously!" Shelara shouted in reply, digging a small blade into the colossal vine she knelt upon.

Gabriel and Lucy hugged the vine that carried them upward, their eyes tightly shut.

Garren seemed to be caught hanging upside down upon a large thorn from his vine, grumbling to himself as the blood rushed to his head.

A dim light became visible in their ascent, welcome fresh air entering their lungs. As the last of the tomb's ceiling collapsed they found themselves returned to the desert above.

Shelara and Lehion leapt gracefully from their vines, as Gabriel and Lucy slowly edged down theirs.

They then stood in awe as they watched the dry desert become lush with thick grass and large trees with bright new blue leaves erupted all around them.

"I dare say we've altered time even further…" Shelara breathed, moving her foot as a bush began to sprout.

"'ey! Quit yer gawkin n' cut me down!" Garren shouted, wriggling on his vine, trying to free himself.

"Quit fussing, you look better at this angle in my opinion!" Shelara called up to him.

"Oh har, har! Jus' get me down!" he retorted, as he heard a tearing from his leggings. "Oh no…" Garren muttered. "No-no-no!" Garren blurted, as his leggings tore, sending him tumbling down, with a loud thud as he hit the ground.

Shelara's lip quivered, trying to hold back a fit of laughter.

"Get it together, you two… we have to move," Lehion stated, turning toward them.

"Can't we rest just a little?" Lucy asked, looking up at the elf.

Lehion sighed. "I suppose we should."

Gabriel let out a sigh of relief, plopping himself down on the newly lush earth.

The sun had already fully set by the time they finished setting up their small camp. The moonlight cast its first gentle glow upon the newly born jungle. The clouds in the sky had parted since their arrival, the storm having ended.

Lehion rested against a large tree, facing the fire they had made. Gabriel and Lucy had drifted to sleep by the fireside as Garren stood, his back facing them, mumbling to himself as he whittled a piece of wood, forming a new pipe for himself.

Shelara sat upon the limb of a large tree, one knee up to her chest. She gazed off at the vast expanse of jungle which never should have existed.

Chapter Thirty-Nine

Alec had awoken the next morning to find that Ashylanya now lay next to him. Alec gazed at her, his mind drifting back to his growing attachment to her.

He was also surprised that he had not dreamt last night, which was unheard of for him, as every night he dreamt, without fail.

Alec jumped as Makkari grunted as he stirred, quickly leaving his bed, not wanting the intimidating Anarian to see them lying together.

His sudden movement also awoke Ashylanya. She gazed about for a moment; noticing where she was, she too quickly got out of bed, casting a shy glance at Alec, her face flushing pink.

"I didn't realize I had slept in your bed, Alec, I'm sorry!" She spoke softly.

Alec looked confused. "But Makkari moved you to your bed last night," he said, gazing at her.

"I don't remember moving," she replied, looking confused.

"Oh admit it, you just wanted to lay with yer man…" spoke Sam groggily, followed with a yawn.

Ashylanya blushed madly. "I truly don't remember," she said.

Makkari had awoken, gazing at her knowingly.

"Fine! Don't believe me," she shot, suddenly looking disgruntled.

"Ash, it's okay…" Alec said, looking at her with concern.

But she did not hear him. Turning, she left the room without another word.

Sam blinked at where she had stood. "That was sudden."

Joden entered the room not a moment later.

"What is the matter with the lady?" Joden glanced around at them blankly. "She looked rather upset."

Alec cast an angry look at Sam, before brushing past Joden and following after Ashylanya.

Joden cocked one bushy eyebrow. "Well, no matter. We depart shortly now. Sarsurus and Malvessensus seem to have healed rather quickly. Though because of yesterday, we will be avoiding the skies."

Makkari looked relieved at those words, though still looking concerned at Ashylanya's sudden change in mood.

"Ash?" Alec called out after her, following her scent. Continuing through the city streets, his concern for her grew.

The city itself was vast. Tall spires that resembled elfish make towered around the city, large descending bridges connecting each one.

The ground level of the city was packed tightly with stone cottages. The city itself was peacefully quiet at this early hour, though looming clouds hung overhead; the scent of coming rain permeated the air.

"Ash?" Alec called again, suddenly catching sight of her by a tall singular tree in the city square.

Alec approached her, placing a gentle hand on her shoulder.

He was caught off guard when she swiftly turned, their lips meeting in a deep and passionate kiss.

Alec was startled at first, but slowly he closed his eyes, which had shifted to a shade of deep velvet, embracing her, as the rain gently began to fall upon them.

A single tear rolled down Ashylanya's cheek as she embraced him in return, their kiss deepening as their tails slowly entwined.

Makkari having followed Alec outside, stood nearby, watching the two. His arms crossed in front of his chest, as they usually were, he leaned back against a small cottage, a smile crossing his lips.

As Ashylanya slowly pulled out of the kiss, she gazed longingly into Alec's eyes.

"Ash…" Alec breathed, gazing back into her eyes.

"I'm sorry, Alec," she said with a smile. "It's just that... I've felt so alone... even with Makkari by my side."

"Ash... It's okay..." Alec replied, gently holding her hands in his own.

Ashylanya shook her head. "Throughout my long and tedious existence... the only thing that kept me going is this feeling I had that one day this curse of loneliness would end..." Ashylanya continued to gaze into Alec's eyes, squeezing his hand gently. "I found the end to this curse... when I first saw you... I just had this feeling that my pain was at an end," she said softly, as she took both his hands tightly into her own.

Alec had never felt this way before. His heart felt warm, as though somewhere deep down, he had always known it was because of her.

Prying eyes that went unseen watched the two young lovers with a malformed grin. The shadowy figure of Xen'trath then slipped away into the shadows.

"Touching..." came a sudden bone-chilling voice that echoed throughout the square.

Before the pair appeared a tall, heavily cloaked figure. Its robe was seemingly formed of cloudy smoke, and two vast blackened wings crested the man's back. A hood was drawn low over his face, revealing only an owl-like beak beneath.

"Who are you?" Alec asked, stepping in front of Ashylanya in a protective manner.

"A humble servant of the dark lady..." the man replied, with a bow. "I come bearing a warning..."

"And what would that warning be, fallen one?" spoke the sudden voice of Makkari, pressing the blade of his axe to the man's throat.

Makkari was halted, however, by a firm hand on his shoulder, that of Sarsurus.

"Let him sspeak," he hissed.

The shadowy man nodded in thanks to the dragon.

"You are being watched very closely..." the man began to speak. "The eyes of the endless void remain unblinking..."

"Melravehn…" came the voice of Joden from behind. "To see you here again, after such a long while…" He spoke, walking toward the owl-like man.

Melravehn withdrew his hood. "And I could say the same to you, Joden the tome keeper."

"My, what the demorae corruption curse has done to you… I am deeply sorry…"

"I do not need your pity, old one," the owl like man snapped, fixing a large blackened pupil on Joden. "All I need is your ears."

Joden's expression hardened at those words. "Then speak."

"Xen'trath attempts to gather the crystal seeds as we speak. Matthias, being weakened, gives the voidling the advantage…" Melravehn said, eyeing Joden. "The forest of lost time has been re-awakened, giving him access to yet another fragment of the abyssal seed."

Joden paled noticeably. "The forest of lost time… How is it possible?" he breathed.

"What exactly are you talking about?" Makkari interjected.

"The home of the Dawn Strider, bearer of one of the four crystals… it seems Lehion and the others have fallen into Xen'trath's plan perfectly…"

"The flows of time must be corrected. If Xen'trath merges the Dawn and the Dusk striders into one, all life will end." The fallen one spoke quickly.

"The dusk strider, meaning my true mother's twin?" Alec asked, eyeing the corrupted looking man.

"Indeed… the ones whose blood flows through your veins…" Joden spoke gravely.

Lehion and Gabriel practiced fencing one another as the sun rose upon the horizon.

"Hold your blade steady, boy; do not leave yourself open!" Lehion instructed, swinging the pole he had fashioned from a fallen tree branch to Gabriel's left.

"Stay on your guard!" he barked as he struck Gabriel's side, bringing a gasp of pain from the youth.

Lucy and Shelara practiced as well, Shelara instructing Lucy in the proper method of holding a bow.

"Keep steady posture; do not let your aim fall unsteady!"

Lucy let fly her third arrow, not far off the mark.

"Not bad Lucy, with more practice, you'll become a fine marksman!"

By midday Gabriel and Lucy rested, breathing heavily after hours of vigorous training.

Garren, having returned from scouting the area ahead, looked paler than usual.

"You all right, Garren?" Lucy asked the dwarf.

"Bloody fine, save for th' haunting chuckles I 'erd scoutin' th'forest," Garren muttered. "The voice of a little girl, whispering through the forest about something she called the hourglass wolfy."

"Could she mean Matthias, you think?" Lucy interjected.

"Dunno, only thing I know 's I couldn't find the lass, though each time I got close, th' roots of th' trees themselves lifted to bar me way!"

"What's in that pipe you're smoking, dwarf?" Shelara piped in. "There's a ghostly voice of a girl and shifting plant life?" she chided. "It's unheard of, ever since the Dawn strider was sealed away."

"I'm tellin' ye, it's true!" Garren blurted, his face crumpling into a look of agitation.

"And I'm telling you it's a crock of bull!" Shelara shot.

"Not entirely…" Lehion interjected. "Remember, the time line is being altered as we dawdle here; we're bound to see rifts and tears in reality."

Shelara gave Lehion a look of disbelief. "Seems I'm the only one sane around here; bothersome, really…"

The group packed up their camp less than half an hour later, making their way through the thick jungle. Plant life, surprisingly could still be seen growing at a rapid rate.

Even the plants they cut away healed and reformed after this passing.

"Many strange flowers over that way..." Lucy pointed to the left, as they continued. "Almost like starlight..." she breathed.

Lehion suddenly halted, turning toward the shining orchard.

"It can't be..." Shelara breathed.

The group changed course, wading through thick grass which seemingly gripped at their feet as they drew closer to the orchard.

"Step no farther, mortals," spoke a deep rumbling voice from one of the trees.

The party froze as a large tree root unearthed before them, barring them passage.

"The lady of the Dawn shall not be disturbed during meditation."

"So my theory was correct." Lehion breathed, gazing upward at the face of a gnarled ent.

"This matter is urgent, ent, please allow us through."

"No," the large tree rumbled. "Not without the permission of our mistress..."

"I can hack 'im into pieces if ye'd like," Garren mumbled, withdrawing his axe.

"No!" cried the voice of a young girl. "Please don't hurt Elmy!"

Not a moment later, a child rushed into their path, her arms outstretched defensively.

"Inconceivable..." Shelara gasped. "The Dawn strider, in child form?"

"We won't harm the ent, girl, but please, grant us passage." Lehion knelt before the girl now, dropping his weapons as the others did the same.

"Who is this girl?" Lucy asked, gazing intently at her. "She's so beautiful."

"Ceri, strider of the dawn," Lehion replied. "She is Alec's true mother."

Chapter Forty

"We have less time than we originally thought," Joden said with a grim expression. "We leave immediately; there is no more time to dally here."

"Where do we go from here?" Alec asked.

"The Agolian pass," Joden said over his shoulder.

Makkari seemed to tense at the idea of the long forgotten Valley between the mountains.

"I dread ever returning to such a place," Makkari muttered.

Ashylanya looked up to Makkari. "We don't have any choice, Makkari; you heard Joden. The light of my pendant should help us through."

"What's so terrible about this place?" Alec asked, looking at Ashylanya curiously.

"It is a long forgotten kingdom, once inhabited by the Sulmothian race, but now only Shade and Skythe beings inhabit such a place," Melravehn interjected.

"I've seen shades, but what are skythes?" Alec asked.

"Long dead demorae beings, of dark arcane; they can manipulate the minds of their victims to draw them in to their clutches."

"It sounds like a place I would avoid at all costs," Alec said, eyeing Makkari.

"And if there were any other option, we would take it, but even the skies are unsafe currently, so we will have to go through the passage," Joden said, turning on his heel. He began to walk back to the inn. "We have no time to waste; follow me, everyone."

"Then our business here is done. Sarsurus, Malvessensus, the dark lady requires you; you are to return with me immediately," Melravehn directed.

The twin dragons nodded in acknowledgement before the trio merely vanished into naught more than a cloud of smoke.

Half an hour later Joden had congregated everyone into the small room of the inn, having etched the exact symbols of Alec's markings onto the floor of the room.

"What I am about to do is a last resort," Joden explained. "It is very risky, as we have to tap into the Time Ward's power to activate it, which can cause instability within the marking's binding properties."

"Then wouldn't it be safer to walk?" Sam asked, eyeing Joden.

"It would take us five days on foot to reach the passage, and another three after reaching the other side. We will not have time. Knowing that Xen'trath plans to gather the fragments, we must make haste."

Sam nodded, staring blankly at the Arcaneight.

"We will be delivered, hopefully, within the heart of the Agolian pass, if I have the coordinates right; if not, we could end up somewhere less suitable."

Alec looked uneasy about the idea but continued to listen.

"We must all be on our guard. The moment we arrive, we will likely be assailed by skythes and shades, but hear me, if we encounter an abyssal, run away—do not attempt to fight it; it will consume you whole." Joden explained.

"The skythes are adept at auditory and physical illusions to lure their prey, which is why I have these…"

Joden held out his palm; several pairs of ear plugs were in his hand. "We will rely on sight alone; a skythe's voice alone is enough to place you into a permanent trance, as long as it lives."

"Even sight is against us though, old one," Makkari interjected.

"That is where Ashylanya's pendant will come into play," Joden explained. "We must all stay within the light of her pendant. Do not stray, no matter what you see in the shadows."

The companions gathered closely in the circle of the ley lines. Alec's heart pounded in his chest with anticipation.

"Ashylanya knows the way through, just keep your eyes on her and do not let your vision stray," Joden said. "Everyone put your earplugs in."

Joden waited for everyone in the circle to insert the noise canceling plugs to their ears before he reached for Alec's hand.

Alec stretched his hand out instinctively, displaying his fading runes.

Joden seemed perturbed upon seeing how much the runes had faded. "Nearly four gone..." he muttered, though unheard.

Joden gave the signal but was interrupted by a sudden burst through their door.

"Ah, Jessica, I was expecting you!" Joden said.

Everyone's attention was focused on the fiery haired woman standing at the threshold of their door.

"Jessica!" Alec breathed, removing the plugs.

"I don't know who you people are, but if all this time travel nonsense is true, I guess I really have nothing to lose," she said flatly. "I'm coming too; you could use someone who can fight."

Jessica had now joined them in the circle, inserting her own ear plugs; they sat within the now resonating lines.

Joden touched one long finger to the hourglass symbol on Alec's palm; the next thing Alec remembered was his body being tugged violently through what appeared to be a long, brightly lit tunnel.

The others had their eyes tightly shut, the sensation of being stretched filled Alec as they traveled.

The sensation then came to a sudden halt, as the light of Ashylanya's pendant shone brightly within a large pitch black valley with many pillars.

Joden directed through gestures, as the shadows all around them writhed with twisted faces, leering at their prey.

The group followed Ashylanya closely as thousands of shadows moved along the towering beams which once supported something vast. All of the shadows swarmed toward the light but were unable to touch the party, the light of Ashylanya's pendant shone so brightly.

The group moved with haste through the passage. A narrow looking corridor was dimly visible in the distance.

Alec's gaze shifted, enabling him to now see in the dark, as his eye color shifted to a bright teal. He watched in horror as all of the grotesque and twisted figures climbed down the walls after them, attempting to look away, but he found himself transfixed by their numbers.

Alec felt a sharp jab in his ribs as Makkari snapped him out of it, pointing at Ashylanya. Alec quickly hurried to her side, grasping her hand, which only increased the light's radiance, as Alec's mark burned brightly.

A deep rumble could be heard as Joden halted momentarily, before quickly waving his hand for them to move faster, as a roar pierced through their ear plugs. The chasm shook with the footsteps of a colossal beast.

Alec glanced back, seeing nothing, but he felt an overwhelming presence crushing down on him as they hurried for the narrow corridor.

Alec suddenly witnessed a sharp blade pierce Ashylanya's abdomen, causing her to fall to one knee.

"Ashylanya!" Alec cried.

But again, he was knocked from his illusion as Makkari struck his side.

Ashylanya gripped Alec's hand as they hurried on. The intricately carved pillars had begun to glow a bright red in color, as lines of light streamed down them. Joden seemed more urgent with his gestures as the pillars began to pulsate with energy.

The party entered the corridor, but Ashylanya halted them, as she pressed herself close to the wall, edging her way around a darkened pit, which now flared a bright blue. Alec caught Sam by his tunic, as he almost fell into the sudden shaft directly in their path.

The party followed along the walls to another doorway, which they entered quickly; Jessica was the last to enter the threshold, casting a glance back at the brightly glowing light below.

The companions had entered a vast room with many stone bridges. Staircases leading to lower floors snaked every which way, but Ashylanya continued down the path ahead, as a deep rumble shook the vault they had just entered with heavy footsteps.

The party was then caught off guard when the bridge began to crumble, hurrying to the other side. The bridge had cracked in two as Jessica leapt to the other side, being caught by the arm by Alec, who held a firm grip on her, pulling her up. She gave him a nod of thanks.

The shadows continued to writhe all around them as they persisted; visions of long dead beings flashed in Alec's vision, their flesh rotting or having rotted away completely, as their blank eyes stared hungrily at the group.

Sam kept his sights focused on Ashylanya the entire time, not willing to look away, as he heard a foreboding rumbling drawing ever closer.

The party then found their path blocked by an enormous beast, seemingly tethered together from the remains of many other living creatures; a lipless maw revealed razor sharp teeth as it took another step forward, the runes along the walls pulsating with each step it took.

Hollow blue light radiated within the creature's eyes as it raised a blade made of pure shadow.

Alec stood in front of the group now, something within him instinctively causing him to move against his own will. Slowly the same familiar blade with which he had defeated Xen'trath materialized on his arm, as his eyes glowed a bright blue with the return of the hourglass pupils.

"You will take no more loved ones from me!" A deep voice came from Alec that he was unfamiliar with, which could only be the wardens, as Alec's hair now resonated a bright azure, mixed with starlight.

The entire party was in awe at Alec's transformation, as Alec lashed the blade at the beast, who took a step back.

Long horns bent back into the beast's ragged mane, the tips flaring red, as it began to charge toward Alec.

Alec let out a cry as he charged the beast. Blocking its blade with ease with the large shield attached to his blade, he cleaved upward, splitting its head in two, causing it to fall into the chasm below, striking each wall on its way down, as it's body crumbled into no more than dust, causing the chasm to rumble violently.

The group stood in awe as they watched Alec momentarily before the blade itself shone brightly on its own.

"Follow me." The voice of the Warden echoed in the minds of the party. Alec began to hurry down yet another narrow corridor, slashing through everything that was unfortunate enough to stumble into his path, their bodies disintegrating into sand as the blade grazed their flesh.

The party followed Alec quickly through the tomb as they themselves now fought the beasts around them, Joden burning several of them away with soul flames as Makkari and Jessica hacked their way through the crowds of shadowy figures, seemingly blinded by the light of Alec's blade in combination with Ashylanya's pendant.

Alec and Sam noticeably aged as they continued on, their forms growing taller, as their muscles grew toned; the mane of azure hair fell mid-back on Alec now, as they pressed on, Sam growing a noticeable beard.

A light source was then visible at the end of a long tunnel the next turn they took. Running down the tunnel, they slew everything that barred their path, the welcome light of the sun greeted them upon exiting the cavern.

Alec halted, as the blade withdrew back into his palm. His eyes and hair color returned to normal, but the changes to his body were permanent. Alec and Sam had aged four years with the energy he exerted, making him nineteen years old, Sam twenty years.

He fell to his knees as the sun grazed him, losing consciousness.

"Alec!" Ashylanya cried, running to his side. Removing their ear plugs, the party surrounded the young man.

"What in god's name was that?" Jessica asked, gazing down at Alec.

"The Time Reaver, in combination with the strider's blood..." Joden said, eyeing Alec's limp form. "Xanadair must have taken control of him." Joden himself had aged somewhat, though there was not much of a difference in his appearance.

"We should rest here for a while…" Makkari grunted, slumping against the stone wall of the old kingdom.

"I agree…" Jessica said, joining his side, taking a deep pull from a water skin, scarce streams of grey now flowed through her long mane of braided hair as the Warden's presence had aged her as well.

Later that evening, the party had set up camp, having put a good distance between themselves and the Agolian pass. The party had found themselves in a long undisturbed forest, leading into the valley where the gate was to open two days from then. A waterfall could be seen in the distance, indicating a nearby river.

Alec, not recalling his acts of bravery, spent the evening asking questions on how they had gotten to where they were.

Ashylanya filled him in on the details, which stunned Alec, who was now five feet eight inches in height, much to his surprise upon awakening.

"I really did all that?" Alec said, eyeing Ashylanya.

"Even I was surprised," Sam interjected. "Didn't think you had that kinda fighter in you," he teased, with a punch to Alec's arm.

"I think, Sam and I will need new clothes." Alec said, noticing that his tunic now exposed his middle, his breeches exposing his calves."

Ashylanya giggled, looking at the pair.

"We still have a long journey ahead of us; we set out at dawn to the valley of the Nether's pass," Joden announced from where he was perched upon a flat stony surface of a broken pillar. "The hard part is done, but there is still quite a ways to the gateway."

Ceri felt a prickle of energy run up her spine later that evening, a powerful force barreled down upon her. *There is someone using my own power,* she thought to herself, gazing at Lehion, as the sensation passed.

"So you're saying I have a son?" Ceri said, seeming pensive. "I don't really ever recall giving birth to anyone…"

"You have one; he is the current bearer of the Time Warden," Lehion explained.

"That can't be; Matthias is the current bearer..." the little girl mused. "Are you sure you didn't inhale too much of my pollen?" she asked. "It has quite the potent effect on the mind!"

"I am certain..." Lehion replied, eyeing Shelara, who seemed half asleep from the pollen's effects. "And you're certain the pollen isn't harmful?"

Mhmm!" the girl nodded her head. "It's kind of impressive that you're not in the same state; most would be out cold by now!"

"I can see that..." Lehion stated, eyeing Garren and the two youth, who were sprawled out on the jungle's lush earth, fast asleep.

"Where is it that you came from again? The elfish sky city, you said, right?" Ceri asked, eyeing Lehion.

Lehion nodded. "It's the sky city of Vel'naras."

"Ohhh..." Ceri said, as if trying to imagine a city that could be suspended in the sky.

Ceri looked up into the night sky with a wide smile. "The skies' children are out tonight; they are always so beautiful," she said, lying back in the grass, merely gazing through her trim of azure starlit hair, up at the stars themselves. Her long unkempt mane laid spread out along the grass, though surprisingly it remained untangled. The girl wore little more than a stitched dress, with leather boots, as well as leather gloves, both pairs of which had metal forged into them, as a precaution to keep her from exerting too much energy.

"So Alec is his name, hmm?" she said, still gazing at the stars. "I felt him; he used my energy."

"When?" Lehion asked, yawning.

"It's starting to get to you too, elf." She giggled. "About three hours ago. It was quite a lot of energy!"

"I see..." Lehion said, gazing up into the night sky.

"So you told me that you were seeking a fragment of the abyssal seed?" Ceri asked, still gazing up at the stars. "And that you think it's in the dwarfish kingdom beneath the waves?"

"I think it is," Lehion glanced at Garren. "Garren was quite confident that it was…"

Ceri gently shook her head, pulling down the front of her dress; she revealed a small glowing gemstone. "You found what you seek."

Lehion gasped. "Is that truly a fragment?"

"Yes it is, Mr. Elf," she said with a chuckle. "One of the fragments of light…" she said, her gaze shifting to Lehion. "Going to the passage to the sea kingdom would be a waste of time; its gates crumbled long ago, barring any access to the kingdom."

"Well, this shortens our journey…" Lehion breathed a sigh of relief, falling back to the base of the tree.

"I'd be willing to accompany you, to meet this so called son of mine," Ceri offered.

"You would leave this place and come with us?" Lehion seemed shocked.

"I have some ents who are very good protectors; they will watch over this forest while I'm gone." She chuckled.

"I will tone down the pollen's effects, so that you all may wake up the next morning, and we can head out!" she said, moving her arms animatedly.

Lehion spent a moment observing the girl. She was so innocent in this form. It was almost frightening knowing that she, combined with her twin, could cause mass destruction.

"I had a dream once…" Ceri began. "It involved a wolf-like boy, whose eyes shined with hourglasses. If this is the one you are talking about, I'd love to meet him!"

"Then we will head out at first light," Lehion stated, as he too began to doze off, succumbing to the pollens effects.

Ceri chuckled."Such lightweights, I don't even-"

Before Ceri could even speak another word, she too had fallen asleep. Drifting off, she chuckled. "Apparently in this form… I am too…" She breathed as she lost consciousness.

Chapter Forty-One

"Alec…"

Alec slowly awoke to see the same little girl standing before him as he had before, in his previous dream.

"So you are my son?" she giggled.

"W-who… Ceri?" Alec asked, his vision coming into focus.

"Yes silly wolf, it's Ceri!" She mused.

"But how…" Alec asked.

"I can travel through anyone's mind; it's a gift—what can I say?" Ceri interjected. "Don't let the dark one get to you; he's just a big meanie."

Alec merely gazed at the small child before him. "Oh, you aren't familiar with my childlike form?" She chuckled as a light engulfed her. "Is this better?"

Ceri now stood before Alec, a fully grown woman. Her long azure hair fell now to her thighs, as she gazed at Alec through her trim with glowing sapphire eyes.

Alec quickly averted his gaze, blushing, as she was unclothed.

"Oh you are so modest, dear…" Ceri chuckled. "Here, is that better?"

Alec turned his head, seeing her now with a tight black leather suit on; leather gloves and steel boots covered her hands and feet.

"So it was you who used the power from before…" Ceri said, gazing at Alec.

"I think so… I sort of blacked out," Alec said, eyeing the now fully grown woman before him.

"I was acquainted with your friends, the elves, the dwarf, and the two children; they all fell asleep from the pollen of my plants, but rest assured they are okay," Ceri said, her gaze unwavering. "We will be with you in the morning."

"But how is that possible? You're all on the other side of the continent," Alec asked.

Ceri chuckled. "You're forgetting who I am. I can transport anywhere I please. I rather didn't care for the dwarfish city beneath the waves, so I left, and it was so cold and lonely down there."

"So that means..." Alec gasped.

"Yes, I carry a fragment of the abyssal seed with me, though awakening me may not have been the best choice, as now all four fragments exist in one era, and this can cause a lot of problems, depending on who gets them all..." Ceri explained.

Ceri revealed the small pendant she carried, its light once more transforming Alec into a fully matured Anarian.

"It has the ability to reveal all the true forms of those the light touches," she explained, glancing down at her pendant.

"It's time to wake up, Alec!"

Alec suddenly awoke from the strange dream. The azure haired woman stood over him, a gentle smile on her elegant features.

Alec looked to his left to find Garren, the two elves, Gabriel and Lucy, sprawled out on the earth next to where Makkari lay, still asleep.

Jessica herself had just begun to stir; seeing the others suddenly appear before her, she jumped to her feet.

"Relax, Jessica," Joden said. "Ceri has brought them here."

"You mean the Dawn Strider... I can't believe she's more than folk lore..."

Joden chuckled. "Most can't, but here she is, standing just a few yards away."

"So you are my son..." Ceri breathed. "I can feel my energy coursing through your veins..."

Alec sat up, gazing at Ceri.

"You weren't kidding when you said you'd see me in the morning..." Alec breathed.

Ceri chuckled. "If I say something, I usually mean it!" she chided, with a light chuckle.

Alec looked to his left, just now noticing that Ashylanya slept next to him soundly, undisturbed by the sudden arrival of the others.

Sam had begun to stir, he himself leaping to his feet upon seeing Lucy lying next to him.

"What the bloody hell?" Sam blurted, gazing around at all the others who had just appeared, seemingly out of nowhere.

"What did I miss?" he said, groggily, eyeing his sister and Gabriel.

Lucy was the next to stir, sitting upright, peering around. "Weren't we in a jungle before?" Her head turned toward Sam, who embraced her in a long hug.

"Sam!" Lucy breathed. "How the hell did we end up here?"

"I dunno, ask the lady with the blue hair, think she knows." Sam gestured.

Gabriel then awoke, peering around; befuddled by their new location, he decided once more he must be dreaming, shutting his eyes and opening them again.

"Alec?" Gabriel asked. "Weren't we...?"

"There are obviously a lot of questions all of you have. I will fill you in," Ceri stated, as Makkari and the others awoke, peering at each other, confused as to why they were now all at the same location.

"I transported you all here, to your friends. The travel to the Dwarf city would have been meaningless, as its gates crumbled long ago. I have the seed fragment you sought," she explained, revealing the fragment momentarily, though it lacked the bright glow Alec had seen it with previously. "And you..." Ceri turned to Ashylanya, "bear yet another fragment, if I'm correct."

Ashylanya nodded, revealing her own, causing Alec's mark to pulse again, his sight shifting back to a dull peach color, as he saw the massive energy which Ceri gave off.

Ceri corrected it, with a simple touch. "You still haven't fully grasped my pendulum, it seems... My energy within you also seems to be unraveling your marking," she said, noting Alec's palm; the fourth mark had now completely faded. "I will teach you how to curb your energy, to stabilize your flow."

Alec merely nodded, gazing up at the woman that was his true mother, before his gaze shifted to Jessica.

Alec felt Ashylanya's hand on his own as she noticed Alec's gaze; she squeezed his hand. Alec turned toward her with a smile, a warm velvet returning to his eyes.

"Ah, young love…" Ceri said, with a chuckle, "you can see it in your eye color…"

Alec blushed deeply, as did Ashylanya.

"So then, where do we head from here?" Lehion asked, eyeing Ceri.

"We travel to the gates of twin passing, to locate Zarkov, the only one who can cure Matthias of his illness," Joden interjected.

They were suddenly interrupted by a low, bone chilling chortle.

"So the bunch has come together, and with two of the four crystals…" spoke the all too familiar voice of Xen'trath, as the party suddenly found themselves ambushed by twisted beasts.

Ceri's eyes narrowed as she gazed at the one who stepped from a rift in reality from directly behind Ashylanya. "I will at least have the two fragments…" he hissed.

"Ashylanya!" Alec shouted, gripping her hand as she was ripped away from him, taken through the rift with Xen'trath. "She will be the first of my corrupted…" Xen'trath mused, as his voice seemed to fade away, along with Ashylanya's presence.

"Ashylanya!" Makkari cried out, as Alec sat stunned by what had just occurred.

As the rift reopened, and Xen'trath's claws outstretched for Ceri, time seemed to slow to a halt, as the ambushers closing in froze mid-step.

"You cannot face him now, Alec…" Ceri said grimly.

Alec gazed around at everyone else, who seemed to be frozen in time as well; only Ceri and Alec stood untouched.

"Take my hand, Alec... I will train you to use my pendulum to its prime, in unison with the Warden's energy," Ceri said, holding out her hand. "You are not strong enough yet, to face Xen'trath. It will take three years, but time will not have moved more than a day by the time I am done with you."

Alec clasped Ceri's hand, as the world seemed to fade away around them. Leaving behind the scene of battle, as if leaving behind the stone effigies of the past, he cast one final glance at his friends, as they too faded away.

T his story was brought to you by the memory of my family and childhood friends, who I owe a special thanks to. The characters in the book were greatly inspired by my little brother Michael who played the part of Gabriel and my two best friends from my youth, Marina and Shawn, who played Lucinda and Samuel, may Shawn rest peacefully. To my Mother, Tammie Wilson, who played the part of Jessica, to my wonderful life partner Allison Rohlff, who played the part of Ashylanya. Also, another thank you to Ashley Renteria who inspired many of the races within this book. Many more books are to come to this series; I hope you are prepared for the journey to come.

This book was edited by Firstediting.com

Printed in the United States
By Bookmasters